THE HIDDEN SPHINX:

I0675429

World War II Egypt

The Hidden Sphinx: A Tale of World War II Egypt
Zita Steele

Fletcher & Co. Publishers
© October 2019, Fletcher & Co. Publishers LLC.

Author: Zita Steele
Cover Design & Photos: Illustrated photo of Egyptian statue created by Zita Steele, 2019. Tank photograph by Field Marshal Erwin Rommel, c. 1941-1942.

Interior design: Noël-Marie Fletcher
Photo of Zita Steele: Noël-Marie Fletcher

Cataloging-in-Publication data for this book is available from the Library of Congress.

Library of Congress Control Number: 2019950089

Cataloging information
ISBN-10 1-941184-29-4
ISBN-13 978-1-941184-29-5

First Edition
Published in the United States of America

THE HIDDEN SPHINX:

Egypt

by Zita Steele

Fletcher & Co. Publishers
www.fletcherpublishers.com

CONTENTS

NOTES FROM THE AUTHOR

This book marks a milestone in my life as a writer. I first began this project at age 15. My interests in military history, World War II, and ancient Egypt inspired me to create a written universe combining those elements.

My quest for this book led me to do huge amounts of research about World War II in North Africa. It also led me to discover the personal photography collection of Field Marshal Erwin Rommel in the National Archives and Records Administration in Washington, D.C.—thanks to the generosity of late archivist and scholar John Taylor, who was kind and enthusiastic in his efforts to assist the research of an aspiring 15-year-old girl novelist. My subsequent research on Rommel, his life, and his photo collection opened new chapters in my life and led me to create the *"Erwin Rommel: Photographer"* book series, a landmark achievement in military history of which I am proud.

This book, my long-dreamed-of novel, sat on the proverbial back burner for some years as I worked on other projects, and led a busy life working and traveling as a young journalist. I am very happy to have brought it to life and published it according to my original vision.

It is an amalgamation of stories and anecdotes woven together into one narrative—many tiny universes from across the years are contained within this work of fiction. This book was a joy to write, and I hope people enjoy reading it.

I also wish to express my thanks to all those who contributed to this project in some way, however large or small. I learned early in life that my interests did not always receive encouragement. I extend warm appreciation to those individuals who shared their suggestions and insights with me, and especially those who spurred me onwards in my military-history research while others were skeptical about a young woman's enthusiasm for soldiers' stories and matters of war.

This Book

This book is a work of fiction. Although it is rooted in historical research, it is a creation of my storytelling imagination. All characters are fictitious. I also have taken what may be called "artistic license" with regard to names, locations, mythology and certain military groups.

My interest in military history is centered on the human person. That said, anyone interested in reading up on the mechanisms of rifle models, identifying serial numbers on obscure vehicles, or counting grooves on the bottom of tank shells will be very disappointed. Those details do not hold relevance to me as they do to some others. You will not find them in this book.

I wish to note that the fictitious military force "Commando Group Sphinx" was inspired by two real British military forces, namely: the Long Range Desert Group (LRDG) and special forces Special Air Service (SAS) commandos. The LRDG conducted deep-desert scouting expeditions in North Africa; the SAS committed acts of sabotage behind enemy lines. Both often worked together. Their many adventures are well worth reading. Since these two historical British forces served gallantly during the war, I invented a fictitious commando group for my story so as not to impugn their honor. Other fictitious military groups in this story include: the Royal Army Investigative Corps and its subunit, the Counter-Insurgency Group, and the Royal Wensingham Rifle Regiment.

I also wish to draw attention to my descriptions of ancient Egyptian animal embalming. Most of the animals I define as having been embalmed by ancient Egyptians historically are correct. The ancient practices indeed were very similar to what is described.

There is a supernatural element in this book. If you are a hardnosed-reality purist and disdain spiritualism, it can't be helped. It is a real part of the story.

Also appearing in the book are some situations that occurred in real-life war experiences. These have been integrated into the novel and adapted to my fictional narrative.

Last but not least, this book is meant to spark your imagination and create an informative and, above all, entertaining experience. I would not recommend it as course material to teach a history class. I would recommend it to anyone who likes reading about soldiers, World War II, Egypt, and adventures.

Poetic Quotations

You will notice quotations from different works of poetry and literature introduce the chapters in this book. These quotations are there to provoke thought and fire the imagination. All passages have some relevance to the chapter they precede.

They have been selected from works of English, Middle Eastern, and German poetry and literature—which are all cultures represented in this book.

A special mention goes to the book *"Poems from the Desert: Verses by Members of the Eighth Army, with a foreword by General Sir Bernard Montgomery"* (1944), from which many of the quotes are drawn. These poems were written by soldiers of the British 8th Army and published in book form during World War II. The poems originated from a literary contest held by the 8th Army. All poems actually were penned in the North African desert.

Artwork

All illustrations contained in this book are original works created by me. All are my hand-drawn sketches.

I also designed and created the cover art. The tank and sandstorm photos on the front and back covers were rare colors snapshot taken by Rommel in North Africa. The other photographs and artwork were created by me.

"Here are sands, ignoble things,
dropt from the ruined sides of kings."
—Francis Beaumont, from "On the
Tombs in Westminster Abbey"

PROLOGUE: THE SHADOW OF DEATH

"Everywhere radios blare,
Sordid street and city square,
Wailing music thin and high,
Jungle rhythm from the sky."
—"M.E. Medley" from
"Poems from the Desert" by Pvt. J. Broome

—1942: Cairo, Egypt

The crescent moon rose high over the narrow, crowded streets of nighttime Cairo. It was a sultry summer evening. The yelling gaggle of merchants that usually packed the alley-like boulevards were gone with the moonrise. Instead the streets bustled with crowds of people in search of a decadent good time. Most of these thrillseekers were British citizens—expatriates, residents, workers, and, especially, soldiers. The Kingdom of Egypt, theoretically neutral, was occupied by a British force now embroiled in war. The armies of England and its worldwide empire battled fiercely against the armies of Nazi Germany and fascist Italy in the sandy abyss of the Western Desert. Nothing definite was known about the war's progress within the borders of modern Egyptian civilization. The desert, as always, kept its secrets. In Cairo, rumors flowed as freely as the glimmering waters of the Nile.

Soldiers destined for desert combat enjoyed brief periods of lavish leave in Egypt's delirious big city. They buzzed like gnats into the bars, nightclubs, theatres and cabarets. The most popular form of entertainment was the local specialty—belly dancing. The men of cold Northern Europe salivated at the sight of curvy, kohl-eyed beauties twisting and bouncing around in sparkling less-than-garments. Egyptian cabaret owners welcomed the business, and there was no shortage of women willing to take the stage. The girls shimmied and the local economy boomed.

Tonight was the big draw. The performance of the century was about to happen. As British soldiers withered and died in a night bombing attack on the Western desert frontlines, their comrades in Cairo drank themselves silly waiting for an Egyptian dancer to flash her curves on stage. Azira Lashny, the so-called "Emerald of the Nile," was scheduled to perform for two whole hours at the Forty Thieves Cabaret, a huge nightclub venue near Giza.

Most men who frequented the Forty Thieves behaved like thieves when they were in the cabaret. It was an opulent establishment, staffed by neatly uniformed waiters, filled with white-clad tables and lit with candles in ornate silver lanterns. On an average evening, the clientele tended to be high-mannered gentlemen with low-level interests.

Tonight the place was packed practically floor to ceiling with all manner of males who wished to see Azira shake her hips, and maybe sing a few tunes while she was at it. They represented a wide berth of Cairo's population: British officers, ordinary soldiers, businessmen, government officials, taxi-cab drivers, librarians, and anyone else who had blown away their money on the expensive tickets.

One young woman stood alone on a small balcony overlooking the main stage. She was neither a waitress nor a cigarette girl. She was not wearing anything bright, suggestive or sparkly. She was an ordinary girl—white and lean, with coppery red hair. Her round, pale face, arched eyebrows and delicate features were a marvel of prettiness. She had a shapely figure and would have looked impressive in an evening gown. But she had no style tonight. Her expression was deliberate and she looked as if she were undercover in a dark blouse and plain skirt.

Nobody noticed her.

A look of cold determination gripped her as loud Middle Eastern instruments jangled and Azira the famous belly dancer writhed onto the stage. The roar from the men was deafening. It was inhuman and wild. Such a shout probably hadn't been heard in civilized society since the Romans had watched prisoners eaten alive by lions in the Coliseum.

Her calm green eyes focused on the whirling belly dancer, memorizing her moves. Her pale hand clenched on the balcony with firm resolve.

"Mind if I smoke?"

She was startled. A man in a suit had materialized next to her. He was so familiar and so ordinary that she had no idea what he even looked like after turning away from him.

"Good viewing spot here," remarked the man in a plain British way.

She didn't hear. She was too busy concentrating on the shimmering belly dancer—studying her art, trying to learn something.

She did hear the gunshot a minute later. It was a noise she wouldn't forget. An ear-shattering bang next to her head, followed by a strong smell of smoke. The faint flavor of lead hung in the air like deathly perfume.

Blood was all over her clothes, and a jagged white piece of shattered skull. Not hers. His. The man next to her, now missing part of his forehead and falling towards her like an evil dark curtain. She screamed, pushed him away. He disappeared over the balcony.

Pandemonium struck the concert hall below. Men shouted, a woman shrieked, and the jangling Arabic instruments screeched to a halt.

Whirling to flee, she glimpsed the dealer of death only for a moment. A black shape in the dark. The figure looked like a man, but was impossible to distinguish. He hovered in the shadows briefly behind the balcony. The shape of his head looked square, and he had no face. Only a single burning gold spot where his eyes should have been. This apparition only lasted for a wink in time. The next second, the phantom was gone.

CHAPTER 1: THE SWORD AND THE TORCH

"I love a game. I love a fight.
I hate the dark; I love the light...
I am no coward. I love Life."
　　　—"A Soldier—His Prayer" from
　　"Poems from the Desert" by anonymous

The sunlit rooftop terrace overlooking the Nile was beautiful and lonely. Shepheard's Hotel was a magnificent building. A Swiss-owned hostel, the place was British social headquarters in Cairo—at least when British gentlemen wanted to be seen behaving respectably. Cocktails trickled like fountains among tiled pavilions and colonnades; the plush indoor parlor was a backdrop for polite dinner-dances. It usually brimmed with chattering busybodies. Today, the sunlit terrace on the waterfront was empty. It had been requisitioned by a pair of grim-looking military officers—it would remain in their clutches as a no-go zone for at least an hour. Murder was a secretive business. So were British Army investigations.

"Is he really as obnoxious as all that, sir?"

"I can't say for certain. I've only heard rumors," answered the other officer, a stout older man who ranked as a Major, according to his stripes and badges. "There are lots of rumors."

They were talking about *him*—the man who was expected to appear and take the case from them. He was something of a legend in his own right. A mystery. A maniac. The only one their superiors in London believed capable of cracking the disaster with his bare hands and without needing oversight. The man was an independent attack hound—the perfect type to turn loose in a festering hot city full of spies and enemy sympathizers. He was ruthless. He'd get results.

However, his fierce reputation didn't inspire confidence in some people, including the two tired and sunburnt gentlemen now surrendering their case files and leadership to him.

"Never mind his personality. What is important in this situation is his expertise," the older officer chided. "Major Frost has an outstanding service record. He's served with distinction in India, Suez and Aden. Look at his personnel file if you doubt me. Rest assured that if any minor war broke out or political assassins struck, Frost was in the thick of it, squashing the fire before it got out of hand. He's a sterling career soldier—practically brought up in boots since his nursery days. He is rather new to the Investigative Corps, but—"

"I heard he only got this position because of connections in London," remarked the other soldier, an Australian sergeant. "He parachuted into our group from the frontlines after a little scrape in France two years ago. I wish a bullet bruise and a medal would get me a fancy promotion."

"Don't be petty, Bob. It wasn't just some medal—it was the Military Cross. He nearly died trying to save fellow officers in France. Good, strong-minded officers with tropical service experience are not easy to find. We can always use fresh new minds in our line."

The sergeant sneered. "We'll see how Frosty does with this case."

"Don't call him that to his face! He'll probably throw you over the balcony," his superior remarked, nodding towards the Nile beyond the terrace ledge.

"Yeah. Don't want to end up like our friend Oliver, do I?"

It was supposed to be a joke. But it was not funny. The mood soured with foreboding as the pair recalled the bloody dead man who had been peeled off the floor of the Forty Thieves Cabaret. A gunshot to the head at close range was ugly; a straight drop from a high balcony afterwards made it even uglier.

An ancient Egyptian dagger with a bronze hilt and flint blade was recovered from the corpse. It had been sheathed on the man's belt under his tuxedo jacket. Somehow, the sharp flint knife had managed to stab its owner when he hit the floor. It was an evil death.

The case had been assigned to the Royal Army Investigative Corps. The Corps cooperated with the Army Intelligence Corps, but was under an independent command. While the Intelligence Corps focused on gathering information from the enemy and disseminating it for military use, the Investigative Corps analyzed and solved complex cases behind British battlefronts. The Counter-Insurgency Group, or CIG, was a subunit comprised of field officers charged with ferreting out enemy agents and bringing down saboteurs.

The current case officer, Maj. Ronald Hathaway, belonged to the Investigative Corps, but merely the leader of an analyst unit. His replacement, Major Frost, was a battle-hardened, active CIG man.

"Whoever murdered our brave Special Forces officer in that sordid nightclub deserves to be burnt alive," muttered Hathaway.

The sergeant smirked. "Well, sir, if the rumors are true, Frosty is just the man to do it."

He arrived a few minutes later. Not with a boom or commotion, but with a very neat, light-footed march that resulted from decades of darting across obstacles and combat zones.

He was slightly below average height, with square shoulders and a slender, muscular build. He was tough and hardened by his fanatical devotion to physical training and exercise; his movements and mannerisms were quick and controlled. He was in his early 40s and looked years younger. His complexion was naturally a pale, light tan. The Egyptian sun had bronzed him further. It left a telltale white ring around his neck near the collar of his khaki uniform. He wore shorts instead of the usual brown dress trousers—favoring practicality over decorum.

Impolite efficiency was very much the style of Maj. Desmond Lockley Frost, known throughout the rank and file as "Frosty."

He had refined, sharp features. He had short, straight chestnut-brown hair with tinges of dark blond and deep auburn in it. He had thin lips, high cheekbones, a strong jaw and a neat, short mustache. His eyes were an extremely striking shade of cool sky blue. They brimmed with intellect and forcefulness of character. His gaze pierced.

On the left side of his neck was a large white scar. It was a jagged, X-shaped blemish that resembled a melted St. Andrew's Cross. It creased at its edges, especially when he turned his head. Obviously it was the effect of some surgery or injury, or both. It was impossible not to notice when looking at him.

He usually sported the standard military beret worn by Army Investigative Corps officers of his rank. The beret was midnight blue. Its cap badge represented his subunit, the Counter-Insurgency Group. The silver badge was a circular insignia depicting a sword chopping off a serpent's head. The sword was crossed in the center by a flaming torch representing the Investigative Corps. The outer ring of the badge was shaped like a chain, symbolizing the unbreakable unity of Great Britain's military forces. The badge was topped with a crown signifying the throne of England. Like all Army cap pins, it was worn above the left eye. The ornate insignia flickered in the sunlight.

Frost shook hands with the senior officer. "So glad to finally meet you in person, Major Hathaway. After our last telephone conversation..."

He continued speaking, expressing his eagerness to take on the case. He had a crisp, strong voice. It wasn't booming or loud. Yet it commanded attention. He spoke with an upper-middle class English accent. It gave a polished edge to his blunt speaking style.

After the two Majors were done greeting each other, the sergeant introduced himself. The gossipy one who was suspicious of the intruding Frosty. The Australian was called Bob "Brick" Wilmore. He was proud of his brief stint fighting Rommel's Afrika Korps in the Western Desert. His combat days ended abruptly when he snagged a coveted position among Cairo bureaucrats. He was a burly, dark-haired man who stood at a height of over six feet tall. He cast a disdainful beady eye upon Frost, who was much shorter and slimmer, as they shook hands.

To his surprise, Frost stared disdainfully back at him. Wilmore had gorged himself on Egyptian kebabs and stuffed pita dumplings since returning from desert service. It showed around his waistline. His paunch earned Frost's instant disapproval. "When was the last time you ran the Olympics, soldier?"

The "Olympics" was British Army slang for the standard physical fitness course in regional commands. The circuit in Egypt was a miserable sandy abyss in the wilderness outside Giza. Within sight of the pyramids, British soldiers died "Seven Deaths"—a series of hurdle jumps, a Great Wall of bayonet bags, a rope climbing course, a half-mile wire crawl, a dash over two hills of gravel, and a timed trench digging exercise. There was one final sadistic test—a fake minefield. Everyone hated it. The "mines" were deep, concealed holes in the ground, just small enough to catch the toe of one boot and big enough to net five men at once. Men desperate to reach the finish line got their boots stuck and tumbled flat on their faces into pits of limestone, rocks and scorpions. The sun sautéed them alive in their own sweat during these ordeals. Thus the horrid place was known among soldiers as "Dante's Inferno." Most men failed the fitness course at least 10 times before passing with satisfactory marks. Men who completed it usually felt very angry and ready to kill people afterwards, which was arguably the main point of the exercise.

All soldiers in Egypt were supposed to go through the Inferno regularly to ensure fitness for tropical service. Everyone avoided it like the plague and hoped Army headquarters wouldn't notice. Wilmore was among the slackers.

"Report to the Giza Army Training Facility tomorrow morning, 4 a.m.," ordered Major Frost pitilessly. "Be punctual. I'll be waiting for you, and if you're a minute late, I will have you posted to custodial duties. You know. Lavatories and waste bins. Better wake up early. Dismissed."

The senior officer surrendering his command to Major Frost made a plea for mercy. "Sergeant Wilmore is my adjutant. I agreed to hand over all case files and authority to you, but I didn't expect you to requisition my staff..."

"I'm taking over this operation as of right now," stated Frost bluntly. "That includes the use of your staff. Wilmore will be useful since he's already familiar with the case. I take an active approach to investigations—I like to work in the field. Wilmore won't be able to keep up if he doesn't pull his act together fast. Meaning no more cocktails."

He smiled icily. His eyes were amused. He had a dark and wry sense of humor—sometimes it provoked him to acts of teasing wickedness. "Go on, Sergeant. Off."

Wilmore decided that he hated Major Frost. He managed a wooden salute and went off seething.

Frost was blasé. He could slap the pride out of a subordinate officer in one blow and feel neither regret nor satisfaction. He was a hard man, and a very focused one. All he cared about was his job.

His counterpart, the soon-to-be-replaced Major Hathaway, was irritated. He wasted no time in getting straight to the point.

"Our prime suspect in the Forty Thieves Cabaret murder," said Hathaway, and gestured to a photograph on a nearby table.

It was a color photo. A young woman posed next to a ship's anti-aircraft gun. She was tall and pale with a round, pretty face and fearless green eyes. Her shoulder-length wavy hair was bright coppery red. She wasn't smiling. It was more like a reserved smirk. Her pose was bold—almost masculine. She looked ready to either fire the gun or blow it to smithereens. Either way, she appeared as if she would enjoy danger and action.

Frost's eyes widened at the sight. Usually he paid no attention to women. They bored him to tears. Most of them were silly with frivolous interests and sensitive dispositions. Frost, a hardened military man, had little patience for such women and couldn't relate to most of them. This woman was different. She was not only beautiful, but aggressive. Frost was aggressive. He appreciated that trait in people. He studied the picture. He found himself attracted to her.

"Her name is Eve Weathers. An American journalist, with *The Chicago Standard*. A suspected Nazi spy."

Frost stared intently at the girl's picture. He pointed to another picture on the table—an ugly black-and-white one this time. "And this?"

"A ceremonial dagger, found on the body. Seems to be an artifact of some kind. It may have significance—or not."

The two men sat down in rattan chairs as Egyptian waiter in a long white tunic and tall red fez came skittering across the tiled patio with a cocktail tray.

"What about the dead man? Have you unearthed anything dastardly about him?" asked Frost in a cavalier way.

"He was an undercover Sphinx commando. You know. The Commando Group Sphinx—desert Special Forces troopers. He should have been worlds away from here, sabotaging German supply and communications far behind enemy lines in the Western Desert."

Frost was puzzled. "What was he doing in Cairo?"

"We have no idea. That's the whole problem."

The breakdown of the case unfolded like a Chinese puzzle. Everything seemed simple, but too many edges and intersecting lines hinted at something extraordinarily complicated.

The facts were these. A man was shot in the head at point-blank range at the Forty Thieves Cabaret during a performance by Azira Lashny, a famous belly dancer. Everyone saw him drop from the sky and spatter against the floor near the stage, but nobody witnessed his deathblow. The lone person standing a hairsbreadth away from him when it happened claimed to be an innocent witness who had not witnessed anything.

Suspicious? Certainly. She was that American woman, the journalist named Eve. She was neither attending the performance for work nor entertainment, and could give no satisfactory explanation about why she was there. Neither could she explain why she was in that balcony standing next to the victim. Nor could she explain how the revolver that killed the man was found near her escape route—with all fingerprints wiped off it.

Did she know the victim? Actually, yes. The connection was rather distant, but it existed. She had interviewed him for an article she wrote several months ago. A story about Egyptian antiques.

The man's name was Ted Harper. He was a British expatriate who was heavily involved in art restoration in his job at a local museum. The nature of their personal relationship, if one existed, was unknown.

All of this might have been routine police work if not for a few complex details.

For example, the man's name was not Ted Harper. His name was actually Oliver Bryon, and he was a member of Commando Group Sphinx—a famed Special Forces sabotage unit charged with Saharan desert exploration and secret missions against the Germans.

This was discovered on a tiny Army identity disk found in the dead man's pocket. The metal disc was stamped with the bizarre symbol of a marching Egyptian sphinx—a lion with an Egyptian head prancing forward with its claws out and its tail in the air. Below the sphinx symbol was a coded serial number. Staff recognized it as a British Army ID number. They checked resources. The ID number identified the deceased as Oliver Bryon of Commando Group Sphinx.

Commando Group Sphinx refused to provide information about its dead soldier. It was a secretive group. Also, they did not keep in regular contact with their roving desert warriors.

A shadowy spokesman would neither confirm nor deny that Oliver Bryon was in Cairo; however, the mouthpiece did admit that a Sphinx commando was expected to be deep in the Egyptian desert instead of Cairo. The man's presence in the city was seemingly unauthorized.

The other interesting and complex detail was that the American girl standing close enough to murder him had connections to Germany. She spoke German fluently and was a foreign correspondent in Munich for *The Chicago Standard* until war broke out in 1939. Then, she left Germany for whatever reason and arrived in Cairo, where she worked for the same paper writing fluffy feature articles.

To thicken the intrigue, the belly dancer performing on the night of the murder, Azira Lashny, was a well-known Axis sympathizer said to worship Mussolini. The nightclub owner was from Switzerland—from Zürich, a German-speaking area that clearly seemed to be the wrong neighborhood of Switzerland to reside in.

Then there was that flint dagger. It was a hideously attractive thing—its bronze hilt was shaped like a winged Egyptian cobra with a human face. The hilt was inlaid with green turquoise and amethyst stones. The blade itself, extremely sharp, was pale violet flint and crudely carved. This strange dagger seemed to be old and valuable. An Egyptian military attaché took a perusing glance at it and declared, with anxiety and loathing, that the dagger was wicked and cursed. Afterwards it was locked up in an empty Army office since few wanted to go near it. Now it would be given to Frost to study or dispose of as he wished. Nobody had investigated it.

Major Hathaway, for his part, was convinced that the entire armies of Germany and Italy had personally plotted to slay Sphinx commando Oliver Bryon in cold blood—due to some secret mission, he supposed, of importance to the war effort. He looked for spies everywhere in the nightclub. He found so many people with possible motives and hazy connections to dark forces that he exhausted all his available resources.

No real evidence existed against anybody.

Meanwhile, the dead man was buried with honors and salutes thanks to Hathaway's personal sympathy in a British military cemetery outside Cairo. He was a brave desert raider, claimed Hathaway, who deserved better "than to die shot by a goose-stepping Yank tart at a gyppo striptease spectacle." Whether he left behind a family was unknown. The phantom mouthpiece of Commando Group Sphinx would give no comment.

Hathaway finished by saying he was glad to be relieved of the case and intended to enjoy his immediate transfer to Palestine. He gave no reason about why he was being transferred.

Frost believed the man was careless—Hathaway had bandied enough spy accusations to wake the dead. Likely British political forces wishing to curry favor with restless natives wanted to quietly brush a scandal out of "neutral" Egypt.

Frost was confident he could get to the root of the mystery without much trouble. He had already started to form his own lines of inquiry—completely different from his predecessor.

He didn't need to investigate spies lurking under every market tent in Cairo, nor twist the long ghostly arms of secret military groups for answers. He only needed to twist one arm. Probably a very pretty arm—but that didn't matter. Maj. Desmond L. Frost was merciless.

His piercing blue eyes were still focused on her picture, even as he stood to bid his predecessor goodbye. "Tell me one last thing," he said coolly. "Where does she live?"

In France 1940, he had experienced one of the worst ordeals of his life. Then Capt. Desmond Frost of the Royal Wensingham Rifle Regiment was gunned down by Germans outside a city called Lille.

The invasion of France happened so fast that it was quickly becoming a mere footnote in the unfurling history of the Second World War. For Frost, it was of pivotal importance. The invasion brought him face to face with certain death. That was something a man could never forget.

He was dashing around some freshly shelled ruins, leading a motley band of snipers against the steamrolling German invasion. Most of the men he commanded were fellow British soldiers. However, a few French civilians dragged old rifles out of their houses and tried to resist the onslaught. The Germans were an inexorable force—their tanks and motorcycles swarmed over fields and hills like mechanized ants, accompanied by hails of withering gunfire. Houses crumbled like broken matchboxes. Furniture blasted into the street. Many people fled for their lives. Those who fought faced shell bursts that rocketed in all directions.

Frost knew he was outnumbered and would soon be overrun. But he did not believe in surrender. He was a warrior in spirit and had made up his mind to die fighting—to protect a country that was not his because his own country demanded it. He did believe in retreat; he ordered a withdrawal as his men began to run out of ammunition. He gave them orders to clear out while he personally held up the Germans with a volley of fierce and skillfully executed sniper fire. His shots left many a shattered German helmet and wrecked several armored vehicles. He believed he was under solid cover and had no reason to think anyone could see him.

The bullet came at a moment he didn't expect it. Suddenly he fell. He experienced a dull, faint feeling like getting lightly hit with a ball. Then came the pain. It was horrific. He writhed on the ground and noticed he was choking. He could not breathe. He had been shot through the side of the neck. Blood filled his mouth. He panicked as he struggled for air.

Something gray moved in the ruins. A German. His steel helmet poked up sinisterly from behind a broken wall. The German wasn't content to leave this British captain, clearly fatally wounded, to die alone in a miserable pile of rocks. He wanted to be efficient—or perhaps cruel. He raised his rifle for another shot.

The German got his comeuppance quickly. There was a loud crack and then he fell dead. A disheveled Frenchman—a civilian—was Frost's unlikely rescuer. He was a very old man and his weapon, an ancient pistol, looked even older than he was. He dragged Frost to safety. Frost never found out who his French savior was; he went into shock and blacked out moments afterward.

He existed in a delirious, feverish state for what he later learned was over a week. His world was a blurred series of basements, attics, wine cellars, and other strange places where anonymous French people made it possible to hide him. Eventually he was rolled up in a blanket and dumped off among some British trucks near the northern beaches of France. He was identified and evacuated to England with some of his men. He should have died. There was no real explanation why he survived. Somehow the bullet that struck his neck passed through cleanly without causing permanent damage.

He lived to put on his uniform and cap again, and marched in the ranks after a very long, lonely stay in a military hospital. Frost had no family to write to him or visit him. He had hated his parents, who disliked each other. They'd packed him off to various boarding schools as a boy; there he first practiced the arts of war upon bullies who tormented him. Frost always had a sense of mischief and was restless. He enjoyed playing pranks on people and became a bully himself for a short time until he decided it was unfulfilling. He was naturally energetic, athletic, and strong-minded. He possessed keen intelligence and an instinct for strategy. A military career allowed him to develop his gifts and soar with them. Fighting and winning were the only things he enjoyed.

He tried to love once. A young Englishwoman he met while serving in India. Her name was Lydia, and she was the only woman that Frost, heartless since childhood, ever attempted loving. He tried not to think about her. Many years had passed. At times, her ghost visited him in the form of bad memories.

The impetuous young Frost was unbearably lonely during his military service in India. He made up his mind one day that he wanted to marry—someone. Who or what the lady should be like he couldn't imagine. He lacked social skills and superficial manners. He was, however, an expert hunter. He decided to snare himself a wife by inviting adventuresome British ladies visiting his Indian outpost to join him on hunting trips. Some of these lady visitors were scouting for respectable military husbands. Frost proposed to three women in short succession. None of them were very pretty or very intelligent. He tried to overlook it because there was a shortage of options and he felt desperate.

Lydia was the one who accepted. Like the two previous women he had proposed to, she was not pretty; however, she was talkative and outgoing. In fact, Lydia was a gadfly with a reputation for socializing and flirting. Her relatives were pressuring her to settle down. Frost knew nothing about women—he assumed Lydia's personality was typical of the female species and such things could not be helped. At any rate, they both needed to get married, and she made herself seem easy to get along with.

Frost had come of age in a cold prison of rules, school, and classist obligations. He was brought up in several wolf packs, beginning with his own family, continuing into his schoolrooms, and finishing at the military institutions he attended. Every man fended for himself in these arenas. Disputes were settled with punishments and violence. Frost had endured acts of cruelty and committed them against others. He grew up disbelieving in love. Yet he was independent-minded and trusted his own intellect. He studied people and read books. Over time, he developed faith in humanity and romantic ideals. He wanted more than anything to love and be loved by somebody. Lydia was his great effort.

Their marriage was a quiet disaster and lasted for a grand total of three years. A short span in time—but enough to cure Frost of any interest in women, marriage or family for the rest of his life. Frost and Lydia had completely different personalities. He naively believed that such differences would make their marriage harmonious. It didn't. Neither of them cared about each other's interests. They lived in two separate universes. He tried to bridge the gap. She was less enthusiastic. Lydia had a very weak constitution and was constantly catching illnesses— the harsh climate in India and local sanitation standards made risks worse. She became pregnant not very long after their marriage—however, she miscarried after five months due to physical frailty. Their sexual intimacy deteriorated afterwards and quickly became nonexistent.

Lydia often complained about Frost's rigid, militaristic personality to her friends. Gossip circled around like a boomerang and hit Frost from some of the officers he knew. It upset him. He was intensely annoyed by Lydia's airy socializing and habitual flirting with other British soldiers. However, the pair never had open arguments. Instead the atmosphere between them roiled with tension and antipathy. Frost avoided being home and worked more maniacally than usual. She occupied herself with her own fluttering and tried to pretend he wasn't there.

India eventually claimed her life. Frost wasn't surprised. There was a particularly bad mosquito crop after the rainy season that year. He predicted coldly that any mosquitos desiring to plague humanity would swarm Lydia and bring more disruptions into his life. He was right. She went strolling around some ruined temple with her friends and came down with malaria. He didn't care. He imagined the malaria would go away—she had caught it before and should have been immune.

He was supervising a military-training exercise with a group of Indian colonial soldiers when he heard the news. Frost, a skilled horseman, was drilling a local cavalry troop. He sailed over five hard jumps and had just wheeled his steed around with a smile on his face when a messenger ran over and told him, sincerely and tactlessly, that his wife was dead. It was a surreal moment.

He gave her a pauper's burial and spent the rest of his life trying to forget the whole thing happened. He was filled afterwards with even stronger negative opinions about society and humanity than before. He scorned British social hypocrisy. He despised weak, giddy women and wrote females off as foolish. He swore off romance. He vowed never to marry again. He determined that his soldierly career was his true love in life.

He reverted to his coldblooded ways after his brief attempt at love. He became more hardnosed and severe than before. He had deep inner convictions about morality, goodness, and world order. He made sacrifices for these things. But he had no patience for imperfect humanity—the weak, the stupid, the inefficient. Frost's only passions in life were for what he admired—war (which fascinated him) and soldierly perfection, which he endlessly pursued. The present Second World War gave him opportunities to excel at everything he was good at.

The ghostly rifleman of death that stalked France's battlefields had nearly taken his life, but he had survived for some purpose. Sometimes he believed he had a destiny. Other times his life just seemed like organized confusion.

He would need every ounce of his courage and discipline now. The case he had undertaken in Cairo would threaten to break him.

CHAPTER 2: DESIRE

"With one flicker of her eyelashes,
she could have slain a whole world."
— "Layla and Majnun" by Nizami Ganjavi

The girl was wearing nothing but glittering underwear when the two men broke into her hotel suite. Actually, it was supposed to be a belly-dancing outfit. It consisted of a neon violet-blue bra with sparkling sequins on it, and a scintillating fuchsia hip wrap that barely covered her thighs. Other than that, she was practically naked. Her body was white, slender and curvaceous. The sight of her crushed into exotic Egyptian dancewear was something to look at.

Major Frost froze inside the doorway. His blue eyes drew very wide, and for all his self-control, he couldn't tear them away from the sight. His mouth drew upwards in a bewildered smirk.

Behind him Sgt. "Brick" Wilmore, recalled from banishment for security purposes, blushed and turned away with a ridiculous grin.

The young woman was horrified by their sudden appearance. She screamed and ran away into the bedroom. A record playing saucy Middle Eastern music played faintly in her absence.

Frost tried not to laugh. "Miss Eve Weathers?" he asked dryly.

"Who are you? What do you think you're doing?" came her indignant squeal in reply. She was American; her accent was broad, but not nasal. It had a somewhat refined ring to it. "How dare you break into my home!"

"Come out here, please, where we can see you," demanded Frost.

"You wish!" she barked. "Not on your life!"

He did laugh this time. So did Wilmore. She shrieked angrily back at them, but that only made the situation more amusing.

The humid suite in the Isis Star Hotel wasn't exactly what a person could call a home. It was the closest thing a roving foreign journalist of her caliber could get that was decent and reliable living in Cairo. It wasn't a bad hotel, but it wasn't a stellar one either. It was run by a family of enterprising Greeks and naturally overpriced. The building was large, the rooms were small, and the suites were modest but inhabitable. The wooden floors were very old and creaky. The furnishings looked like British relics from the early 1920s—back when Egypt was still something of a marvel, when people thought winged horses and Eyes of Horuses actually made appealing decorations. Frost studied the place. He tried not to pay attention to the rakish brown pharaoh peeking one elongated white eyeball at him from a strip of wallpaper. A whirring ceiling fan swung back and forth, hard and fast enough to cool the room while guillotining intruding mosquitoes in midflight.

Frost stepped further inside. Light and agile, he glided across the old wooden floorboards with only minimal squeaking. Wilmore followed dutifully. His racket of heavy footfalls sounded like a maharaja's elephant.

"I am Maj. Desmond Frost of the Royal Army Investigative Corps Counter-Insurgency Group," he announced, recovering his composure.

Her voice peaked in confusion. "The what?"

"You could shorten it by saying the CIG of AIC," he added with a faint ironic smirk, "but it makes no difference. You're quite familiar with our people—you've already been interviewed a few times by Major Hathaway. He's with AIC. I'm from a different subunit."

"What?" It was an angry shout that time. "I'm done answering questions for you jokers! I have nothing to say to any of you!"

Frost was unfazed by her defiance. "I am here to take a statement from you. You will then accompany me to Giza Army Facility A, Subdivision II," he said inexorably. "Come quietly or else I will restrain you."

Silence crept into the room. She emerged from the bedroom in a loose blouse and khaki trousers. Her face was indignant. Her copper red hair was she tousled. She walked up to Frost and sized him up. He was shorter than she was. She was intimidated by the gallery of medals and insignias on his uniform. Nevertheless, she confronted him boldly.

"I'm a journalist and an American," she argued. "You have no right to—"

Frost stared back defiantly. "You're under arrest."

She put her hands on her hips. "On what grounds? You have no evidence against me."

"Sit down."

"I don't take orders from you."

Frost glared slightly. He was irritated. "See how far disobedience gets you—I've got all the patience in the world, but you don't have much time," he said with steel in his voice. "Within the hour, local Egyptian police will come for you. Unless you would enjoy rotting in a filthy Cairo prison, you will follow my orders."

She started to worry. "Why would the Egyptian police arrest me? I haven't done anything—"

Frost smiled. "You've broken the law."

"What?"

"I examined an article you wrote about Egyptian antiques several months ago. The one for which you interviewed a certain Mr. 'Ted Harper'—you know. That poor fellow in the cabaret you didn't murder," said Frost with chilling charm. "It turns out artifacts described in your article were stolen Egyptian antiques."

She protested that she didn't know the artifacts were stolen. He interrupted.

"I reported you and your newspaper to the Egyptian government for profiting from stolen cultural goods. The Egyptian government has already lodged a complaint with your superiors at *The Chicago Standard* newspaper," he said, brimming with poise and confidence. "You will be arrested and charged by the Egyptians—unless I intervene."

She sat then. It was a despairing collapse into a wicker chair.

"Just imagine. An attractive young lady like you alone with strange Egyptians. They have distinct views about how women should behave," said Frost, twisting psychological pressure into his words. "I needn't describe the hygiene in their prisons. You're a journalist—I imagine you have an idea of what the 'local' judicial system is like."

The girl called Eve looked up at him with a fiery glare. "This is a trap. You're doing this because you want to frame me for killing that man at the cabaret," she snapped. "You've harassed me so many times. Old questions, new faces. You have not a single piece of evidence against me. But you still won't leave me alone. You're worse than gangsters!"

He started to make a sarcastic reply, but she interrupted him.

"You must be the ones hiding something!" she accused. "What are you trying to cover up here? Explain why the British military is so obsessed with a cheap nightclub shooting."

"We can discuss that at my headquarters," replied Frost icily, angry at having been interrupted. "Are you coming along?"

"Let me guess—the murder victim was a Nazi. I just happen to speak German and lived in Munich, so you guys are putting the pieces together the wrong way," she theorized. "Is that what's going on?"

Frost's eyes lit up. He scanned her face, trying to read her thoughts. He was good at that. Based on his intuition, her words seemed like a clumsy guess. Or perhaps she was an artful liar.

"You underestimate our professional abilities, Miss Weathers," he replied. "British soldiers do not waste time putting 'pieces' together, as you say. We work thoroughly. I hope you'll be so kind as to help us. Your country is supposed to be our ally in this war, after all."

Eve bristled. "This is hardly friendly treatment."

"I think it's friendly to offer you a stay in our clean command post instead of an rat-infested Egyptian prison," he retorted, not losing an inch of his authority. "I don't have to be so generous, you know."

"This is blackmail..."

He interrupted. "Would you like to commit yourself voluntarily to British military custody?" he asked. "Choose. Legal immunity with us, or trial by fire under the Egyptians."

She covered her face with her hands.

"I didn't hear your answer, Miss Weathers."

"If I go with you, then—"

He motioned to Wilmore, who quickly produced a folded sheet of paper and pen. "Sign here," he ordered, interrupting her again. Both officers watched with hawkish scrutiny as the woman obediently scribbled a jittery signature on the page. They nodded at each other. The paper disappeared quickly into Wilmore's uniform pocket again.

Suddenly the atmosphere changed, and the two men became

more self-assured. Wilmore looked smug and condescending. Frost's sharp face glowed with lordly satisfaction.

Eve stared at them. She was overcome by the feeling she had made a mistake.

"Are these your suitcases?" Frost drifted across the room and nudged one of two large trunks with the toe of his short brown boot. "They look nice and big. Good. You'll need to pack them up right away."

"No way. Now you're kicking me out of this hotel? No. You can't do this. I refuse to allow it!" Overcome with newfound indignation, she jumped up from her flimsy wicker chair and rushed at the Major. She looked ready to punch him.

Wilmore tensed. His hand, trained by combat, subconsciously dropped toward the pistol holstered on his belt.

Frost neither budged nor flinched. "Pack up your things and get ready to leave," he ordered her again. "Or you can leave your belongings behind to be scavenged by the proprietors. It makes no difference to me."

"Exactly long to do you intend to hold me in custody?"

"For as long as I see fit," he replied. "That paper you signed gives me legal permission."

She would have protested, had he not interrupted her in a very calm and hard-edged way.

"Don't complicate matters further. There is a war going on. You must answer to military authority. You are not an American citizen here—you are a guest of Britain. You will not be given a solicitor, nor will you be able to contact your embassy or your employer. Do not expect to solve any of your problems by throwing tantrums. I am in charge here, and I am the only person you can negotiate with. Is that understood?"

Eve stared at the British officer and thought he was the worst person on earth. He was arrogant, exacting, and clearly in charge. She was a proud woman and allergic to obeying authority.

She made assumptions about him in that moment—that he was an egotist and a posturer. Irrational hatred filled her. She made up her mind to beat Frost somehow. He had overpowered her this time, but she had the will to fight him.

Frost saw the fight in her eyes. It energized him. He liked fighting. He was always confident he could win. He usually did.

Yet he also detected malice in her stare—personal loathing. It made him uncomfortable. Normally he did not care who liked him and who did not. This time it was different. The woman troubled him for some reason he could not explain.

He watched patiently as Wilmore helped the young woman pack her belongings. Curious, Frost strolled over to her writing table and glanced at materials around her messy typewriter. A pile of disorganized books caught Frost's eye. One of them in particular drew his attention—a book about weapons, with a picture of a gigantic medieval sword on it, saying, "*The Evolution of Knightly Combat.*" Frost loved military history, weapons, combat and things war-related in general. He picked it up.

This chance discovery led him to unearth a pile of buried literary treasures underneath, including such sparkling warlike gems as: "*Firearms of the West,*" "*A Definitive Guide to Ninjutsu,*" "*Rome's Finest Gladiators,*" "*Caesar and His Greatest Campaigns,*" "*A Bugler's Memoirs of Gettysburg,*" and "*The Battle of Salamis: Why the Persians Lost.*" Reeling in amazement, Frost also noticed a personal favorite of his: the famed analysis, "*On War,*" authored by Prussian General Carl von Clausewitz. Frost had enjoyed studying it in cadet school. The young woman owned a German-language edition.

The British officer was speechless. In his view, this was most astonishing find made in Egypt since Lord Carnarvon's expedition opened Tutankhamun's tomb in 1915. He looked at Eve in bewilderment. "Are these your books?"

"Yes," the young lady answered defensively. She rushed over to the desk and started snatching them to pack up. "This is my collection. Leave it alone."

He was shocked and intrigued. "You like...war?"

"Yes. Obviously."

"But I didn't think women liked war and fighting," Frost stammered in surprise. "I mean..."

"Well, I do," retorted Eve defensively. "It's the way I am. And I'm not sorry!"

"There's no reason to be sorry!" reassured Frost, observing her with great curiosity. "I own some of those books myself!"

She made no reply.

Half an hour later, they were in a brown military jeep jolting to the boondocks of Giza. The officers were silent. Wilmore the Australian, being of lesser rank, naturally was the driver. Frost sat in the back seat beside his unlikely American captive. Both of them studied each other in tense silence but pretended not to.

It was a noisy ride through Cairo made exasperating by prehistoric and modern traffic smashed into paper-thin streets. It was hot and dusty. Flocks of gabbling Egyptians darted in front of cars. Multiple men balanced on crooked bicycles. People dragged donkeys and balanced pots on their heads. Occasionally luxury cars packed with cackling Europeans cruised into the fray—those were the worst because they felt entitled to run over everybody. The locals had no problem swearing at rude foreigners. Naturally the visitors were insulted and swore back. This sparked unintelligible yelling matches rivaling the din at the Tower of Babel.

A Fellahin peasant suddenly thrust his dirty hands into the jeep, waving a mud-covered packet of hashish and a bundle of pornographic postcards at Frost and Wilmore. The peasant was one of many who tried to make a living by selling vice to foreign military officers. He yelled loudly and swatted the soldiers brashly, trying to hawk the goods.

Frost smacked the man's groping arms away and shouted something in Arabic. The peasant attempted to make a hard sale by throwing a pack of cannabis cigarettes into the jeep and demanding money; Frost threw the cigarettes out and barked a rebuke in Arabic, making an emphatic gesture with one hand. The peasant understood that well enough. He cursed and went off grumbling. Frost settled back into the seat, calm and nonchalant. He had seen many similar and worse scenes during a long career of Army service in Britain's colonies.

Eve was surprised by his ease handling the situation—and his convincing language skills. "You speak Arabic?"

Frost shot her a sheepish glance. "I don't know if 'speak' is the right word," he said frankly, with wry amusement. "I mean, I can get myself understood well enough, but it's hardly material for a polite dinner conversation."

His ironic humor caught her off guard. She accidentally smiled. "Is this your first posting in Egypt?"

"No. I'm quite familiar with the Near East," replied Frost. "I've done Egypt and several other oriental countries before."

"So, how long have you been serving here this time?" the

journalist asked.

He was evasive. "Long enough to know never to go to cabarets," he quipped sarcastically. "Nothing but trouble comes out of those places. What were you doing at the Forty Thieves?" He recalled the image of her in belly-dancing dainties and tried not to smirk. "You have an interest in...local arts?"

Eve looked drolly at him. "Don't you?"

"Beg your pardon?"

"It's all right. You don't have to pretend to be 'proper' in front of me," she dismissed. "It's a known fact that all the Englishmen here are crazy to watch belly dancing. They drool over it. They don't invite girls for coffee or tea, or a nice civilized drink at the bar. They just want to go to smutty hookah bars and leer at belly dancers." She sighed and looked embarrassed. "So, I thought—'Why not?' There must be something to it. Maybe I could learn to do it. The only trouble is the Egyptians won't teach me. I offered to pay Azira Lashny for private lessons, but she refused. Those crooks see it as business! They want a monopoly..."

Frost was awkwardly speechless. "You...mean...that's why you went there? You're trying to learn how to..." He let the words trail off.

She laughed, shameless and daring.

"Did you explain this when you were interviewed?" asked Frost, inclined to believe her.

"Yes. Multiple times. But that roaring old fogey refused to believe me."

He grinned with raffish delight. He was unfamiliar with the slang term "fogey" and thought it sounded horribly apropos. "You mean Major Hathaway?"

"Yes. Him. He is disrespectful and condescending," she complained. "The last time I met him, he had the nerve to insult me. I refuse to be interviewed by him again."

Frost gloated at the thought of sticking the unflattering Army nickname of 'Fogey' to his predecessor. He enjoyed ragging other officers.

"He can swan around all he wants, but he's not a real soldier in my opinion," declared Eve. "He couldn't fight anybody if his life depended on it. He's too fat—spends too much time swilling booze at Shepheard's. He's nothing but a tin star."

The Major beamed at her in approval. Her words sounded

exactly like something he would say. His eyes shone with cheer.

Eve was perplexed by his wicked grin. "You're not offended by what I said?"

"No. I agree with you!" answered Frost with a merry laugh. "I think I ought to let 'Fogey' know, the next time I see him. He has completely failed to impress you." He chuckled. "Hopefully the locals will chase him about in Palestine. That's where he's going—I've taken over."

"So, I won't see him again."

"You will not," he answered. "Relieved, aren't you?"

She fixed him with a mistrustful stare. "Somewhat."

He glanced at her skeptically. A very unusual young lady. Well over 10 years his junior—he couldn't remember her exact age from the file, but she was somewhere in her late 20s. Frost viewed her as a fledgling in comparison to himself. He wondered why a young woman of her beauty and apparent intelligence would choose to live alone in a hard place like Egypt. There were many things about her that intrigued him.

His mind returned to that treasure trove of military books again. He scrutinized her. "I saw you own a book by Clausewitz," he remarked. "You enjoy reading military books?"

"Yes," she answered coolly. "Why do you ask?"

"Because it's uncommon," stated Frost. "Most women have little interest in military science. They dislike war."

"That's true, by and large," she admitted. "But I'm different."

He smirked. "I noticed."

Eve folded her arms tightly and turned away. She didn't feel like talking anymore. Not to him. She was deeply upset about her arrest and powerless situation. She held Major Frost solely responsible. She nursed a grudge against him.

Frost didn't quite know what to make of her. She was clever, which he respected. She was also quite a spirited lass—a rare specimen. He was a dominating personality and admired other dominating people. He remained in awe of her interest in military history—a beloved subject to him, as fighting and soldiering were his life's passions. He was inclined to like this young woman...but she was a suspected assassin. He remained suspicious.

The fact that she worked a journalist also was unusual. Journalism was predominantly a man's profession—cut and dried. "Why journalism?" he asked out of curiosity.

Eve was guarded. "It's a long story. I'm sure it would bore you."

"You were a political reporter in Munich," he persisted. "How was it?"

"Good food, bad weather, grumpy Bavarians."

He broke into a bright smile again. Straight to the point. The words pleased him. They sounded like something he might have said.

The pyramids materialized on the pastel horizon. They were very impressive until one actually arrived at them. Then suddenly a visitor came to the rude realization of being dead tired, dripping in perspiration and staring at an enormous pile of blistering rocks. The sun was sinking steadily. The heat crushed. Oppressive humidity rose from the waters of the Nile that crept under bridges throughout the city. Mosquitoes were already coming out.

"Sir," Wilmore said suddenly from the driver's seat. "Are we still keeping our appointment at Dante's—I mean, the tropical-exercise circuit—tomorrow?"

"Yes. Bright and early." Frost was pleased by the idea. He was determined to keep in top shape himself and hammer the laziness out of Wilmore on the desert anvil. He glanced at the girl. She had physically melted—slumped over in the seat in the withering heat.

He smirked. He scorned such weakness. He decided he would need no interrogation rooms or holding cells to question this suspect. Egypt would be his instrument of cross-examination. The desert would draw forth her secrets.

The desert, however, had many secrets of its own. They lurked just below its treacherously calm surface like monsters of an ancient sea. They would break waves during this trip to Giza. The fortunes of the three people in that jeep would change forever.

When Major Frost arrived at his headquarters outside Giza, he was swiftly informed of two terrible incidents.

His predecessor, Major Hathaway, had died that same afternoon. A heart attack—not very long after surrendering his case files to Frost at Shepheard's Hotel. This news hit Frost with an incredible shock. He was shaken by it. So was everyone else who heard about it.

Secondly, the ancient Egyptian dagger recovered from the dead body of the murdered man at the Forty Thieves nightclub had been stolen. The dagger, which a local military attaché had instantly deemed "cursed," was locked up in an empty evidence office at an Army facility in Cairo. When an orderly went to collect it for transfer to Frost's custody in Giza, it had vanished.

Several British staff officers at the scene—very unimaginative and reliable types—swore a "ghost" had taken the dagger. Supposedly an assortment of peculiar and spooky incidents had plagued the building while the dagger was housed there. Glass shattered for no reason, a man's disembodied voice was frequently heard, and an overpowering aroma of perfume filled the air in different strange places.

Frost was skeptical of these reports. However, the dagger was undeniably stolen. He believed a soldier in the building must have hawked it to a local antiquities dealer for money.

The Major ordered descriptions of the dagger to be circulated to known dealers, and a reward offered for information about it. His inner intuition hinted that the dagger was an important clue to his investigation somehow. He would not give it up easily.

Frost, however, was disturbed by the news of his predecessor's death. He postponed continuing his investigation until the next day. He spent the rest of the evening alone in his private rooms in the garrison, collecting his thoughts and recovering his bearings. Dinner from the Mess Hall was inedible and sleep was impossible. Whenever he closed his eyes to rest, he was quickly jarred awake by jumbled images of dead men, daggers shaped like winged human cobras, German snipers, and Eve Weathers whirling salaciously in sparkling underwear.

CHAPTER 3: THE JACKALS AND THE HUNTER

"But glory is a kind o' thing I shan't pursue no furder,
Cos' that's the officers' perquisite—mine's only just
the murder."
—"The Biglow Papers" by James Russell Lowell

—Somewhere in the Great Desert, west of Alexandria

A desolate ruin stood in the wastelands of the Western Desert. Once it had been a temple. Broken pillars covered in hieroglyphics and unearthly symbols were everywhere—casting long dark shadows across what remained of stone floors. What were once mirrored pools were now the nests of serpents, jerboas and scorpions. Outside rose crests of enormous sand dunes, some as high as three-storied buildings. The heads of proud Egyptian kings jutted from the earth, bleaching white in the sun as their faces stared across the same desert they had stared blindly at for centuries.

A machine gun poked its glittering black nose out from beside one of those great statues. Flat helmets bobbed around the ruin. Exhausted men of the British Army baked in the sun. Flies buzzed ferociously around them, trying to bite moisture from their bodies. Many soldiers wore thin veils over their faces. Their clothes were stiff with dust and sweat. Their arms and legs were plastered with white bandages to protect wounds and scrapes from infectious, disease-carrying dust that was everywhere. There were about 15 men. They were nervous, tired, and edgy.

In their midst was a lone prisoner. A German. His face was invisible, covered with a dark mesh veil attached to his steel helmet. The mask gave him a ghastly appearance. His brown Afrika Korps uniform was stained completely with dried maroon blood. His hands and arms were tied behind his back with an elaborate twist of knotted rope. This rope was tied around one of the old Egyptian pillars—a drastic measure to ensure he could not escape. He knelt in the sun. Powerless. His shoulders sagged with fatigue. Yet silent, quick motions of his head showed he was alert. Patient. Listening sharply to every noise.

The soldiers avoided him. Some cast suspicious looks in his direction. Nobody offered him water or shade. Nobody wanted to touch him. They were afraid of him.

Clouds of dust appeared on the horizon. The soldiers' eyes were trained for months to notice the tiniest movements in fields of emptiness. They gripped their rifles. Some of them peered through binoculars. They were not sure whether to expect an enemy or a friend.

Eventually a small fleet of jeeps materialized—wide, low vehicles with large, sand-plow tires and submachine guns mounted on turrets above their doors. Men stood jauntily in the vehicles, like pirates hanging from the masts of ships. They were bronze-skinned and remorseless in the sun. They emerged closer into view in the shimmering heat like phantoms from another world stepping through a desert mirage.

"It's the Bedouins," a soldier sardonically announced in Army slang as he peered through his binoculars.

"Commando Group Sphinx is here!" shouted someone else.

They rushed to greet their fellow soldiers, abandoning their weapons in relief.

Meanwhile, the German in the dark veil picked up his head and stared straight in the direction from which the jeeps were coming. His masked black gaze focused eerily in exactly the right spot.

One British soldier, a commanding officer, cast a wary eye at the prisoner. "Make sure that demon can't move," he told one of his men.

The soldier strutted over and aimed a rifle at the German, clicking ammunition loudly in place. "Keep still if you want to keep alive," he ordered the prisoner. "Hands behind your head!"

The German, keeping his masked face turned towards the newcomers, slowly obeyed. His fingers were covered in dust and dried bloodstains.

The apparitions of the Commando Group Sphinx rushed toward the ruins. Sand billowed from beneath them like flying magic carpets.

The Sphinx commandos were wandering desert wizards. They were a corps of aggressive British soldiers living in the wastelands who spent all their time sabotaging enemy operations and hiding in oases. Like camels, they could go for miles without water. They could scale rocky cliffs, outfox sandstorms, dance over dangerously steep sand billows like Arabian genies, and create optical illusions. They knew everything there was to know about the wilds of Egypt and the Sahara. They had explored all kinds of unseen and unknown haunts. They navigated by the stars and tracked enemy movements without need of technology. They had adapted so much to the terrain that they seemed like desert natives. Thus, they had acquired the nickname "Bedouins."

One man stood out from the rest of the group. Their captain. He stood irreverently with one tall boot propped up near the windscreen, balancing perfectly as his jeep raced over sand at breakneck speed. His clothing and gear was a motley assemblage of a British uniform and desert dress. His light brown Royal Army jacket was emblazoned with a garish Union Jack patch he'd sown on the breast. His tall knee-high boots were the black-and-tan leather, lace-up moccasins of the German Afrika Korps—he had stolen them from a dead enemy soldier because they were soft and perfect for desert trekking. Bandoliers and gun belts crisscrossed his chest. His head and face were shaved clean to guard against fleas and lice. The most flamboyant thing about him was his bright emerald green turban. It was tied around his head in an elaborate ring and formed two long tails draping past his shoulders. It ripped behind him in the wind like the flying plumes of an Arabian horse's mane.

This daredevil raider captain belonged to a caste of British military lowlifes euphemistically dubbed the "Lower Ranks." They were rough vagabonds suited to gritty commando tasks—hunting, killing, foraging. Most were scallywags of low birth who served in grueling outposts in the far corners of the world. They came from the gutters of Britain. They had no family, titles or education. They spoke strange dialects of guttural English and smatterings of vulgar slang from frontiers where they served. They were transients. They were notorious for rapacious sex with foreign women, fathering sickly mixed-race children on every continent and transmitting diseases. They were coarse and brutal. They had no concept of honor or personal loyalty. They used the Army for survival and gain. They could kill without batting an eyelash. Not all Sphinx commandos belonged to this element of the British Army. But some did. The "Lower Ranks" tended to excel in horrible environments where life was cheap and violence was easy. This man had used his unorthodox talents to join Special Forces and become a Sphinx commando.

Details became clearer. The man was flamboyant. He had glimmering golden rings on all his fingers. Silver bracelet cuffs. He wore small, jeweled hoop earrings in the cartilage of one ear. His uniform was torn. Chinese characters were tattooed across his hands.

The British soldiers at the ruin frowned. They were used to seeing Commando Group Sphinx soldiers wearing kerchiefs and turbans, but something was seriously amiss here.

The men packed into the jeeps were of similar ilk. They wore motley assortments of clothing and gear. Most of them were British and wore torn British khaki uniforms. A few were not; there were a couple of Libyans and Italians. One of them sported an Italian Bersaglieri helmet—a large, gaudy tropical topi with huge black feathers springing out of it. All of them looked like ruthless castaways.

The soldiers realized at the last second that the visitors were not coming to help them. These were marauders.

A blast of gunfire ripped the air. Bullets tore viciously into the stony faces of the ancient Egyptian kings jutting from the sands. A pillar cracked and tumbled down. The bandits mowed down the unarmed soldiers using the small turrets mounted on their jeeps. Nearly all 15 soldiers fell dead in a few seconds— slaughtered in cold blood.

One remained alive. He groped in the sand helplessly, shot in the thigh and unable to move, as the bandit captain's fancy-laced boots alighted on the ground and pranced ominously toward him.

The captain had a small badger-like face and a wide, stocky build. His skin was heavily bronzed by the sun. He was in his 30s, but debauchery and the harsh desert sun had prematurely aged him. He looked 20 years older. What was visible of his shaved hair was a murky dark gray—another stroke of odd premature aging. His weathered face and arms were scarred. His features were cunning. His mannerisms dripped with scorn.

He walked up to the wounded survivor and kicked him viciously in the chest. His crews disembarked from their vehicles and began scavenging the dead for valuables.

"Who are you?" choked the survivor.

The captain grinned maleficently. His eyes were an atrocity to behold. One of them was pale green like a cat. The other was not an eye—it was a large solid gold marble with Egyptian hieratic script and a small carnelian in the center. He had lost an eye once in combat and replaced it with a golden Egyptian compass ball he'd ransacked from a tomb.

"Who am I?" mused the captain. He had a sharp cockney accent forged in the bowels of crime-ridden East London. He spoke with a singsong of slang and sarcasm. "What's it look like I am, Lance-Corporal? A Sunday visitor?" he taunted, reading the man's rank badges. "Tell you what, blighter. Just think of me like an old mate come back to fetch his laundry. And maybe some pretty trinkets while I'm at it," he said, gesturing flippantly at the Egyptian ruin. "Any nice-looking bobs in there, mate? Anything old and sparkly?" Not seeing a reaction, he pressed further for information. "What about dead blokes in bandages? Seen any of those in there?"

"You're with the Army?" The soldier glared. He still had enough fight in him to be morally outraged. "What do you call yourself, soldier?"

"You can call me Jumpin' Jehosephat if you like, mug. Don't make no blind bit of difference," sniped the captain. He leaned down and stared into the wounded man's eyes. His gaze was empty and hard as ice. Looking into it was taking like a punch to the face. "This is my backyard, muggins," he said. "What you lot doing out here where you got no business?" He pressed the muzzle of a revolver against the soldier's face. "Cough up or I'll give you a sip of hot lead."

The fallen soldier closed his eyes and gambled. He plotted to survive. "We got separated from our division during a sandstorm. We were lost," he admitted. "We managed to make contact with our group again and radioed for reinforcements."

"Reinforcements?"

"That's right." He lied. He tried not to think of his comrades who had been gunned down moments before. "We mistook you for them. They're supposed to arrive any minute."

The bandit captain seethed. "You're a lyin' weasel," he spat, pressing the gun harder against the man's jaw. "We didn't pick up on no radio traffic. Not a trace of livin' souls in this area—

except for you stupid nanas."

"Take a risk and stay here if you don't believe me," challenged the fallen officer, summoning his courage. "You're a disgrace to our country. I'd love to see you court-martialed and hanged—you dirty, illiterate toad."

The raider's face flushed. He took a lurching step back and blasted the man's arm with a bullet from his revolver. Blood sprayed into the air.

"That's for the jackals. They'll eat you up before dark." He turned to his comrades. "Lads. Let's take this one for a joyride later."

They dragged the injured soldier into one of the jeeps.

The German prisoner with the steel helmet and dark veil had risen again. He had cleverly flattened himself on his belly during the affray. All bullets missed him. As the silence of death fell, he slithered up again like a cobra. He glanced around dully through his black veil. Faceless.

The captain sauntered over to him. "Hello, bright-eyes!" he mocked, poking the German's black fabric mask with the muzzle of his gun barrel. "Look, lads, the clot's wearin' a veil. Veils is a bit old-fashioned in these them days, ain't it? Is it your wedding day, Brunhilda?"

His pack of followers laughed like hyenas. Their captain was the strongest and most cunning of them all. They esteemed him for his ruthlessness and ability to provide spoils. They lauded everything he said.

"Come on, lads. Let's have a look at the blushin' bride!"

The bandit ripped off the veil and sent the attached steel helmet flying off through the air. The German was a plain, homely looking man with dark hair and a severe countenance. He was young—probably in his mid-20s. Blood was smeared on one side of his face. He wore small round glasses. He looked about as fierce as a bank teller.

"*Guten Day!* Speakin' Zee English?" mocked the captain, unimpressed with the prisoner.

"Yes. I can speak English," replied the German fluently, with a slight accent. "I have studied in America before the war."

"Well, how about that? Bright little spark, ain't you?" The bandit freed the German from his bonds. He was astonished by the knotted ropes that restrained the German's arms and fastened him to the pillar. "What's all this spiderwebs for,

Hansel? You got pox or something?"

A moment of awkward silence fell. "I don't know why they tied me up like this. They were angry with me because I shot up some of their tanks. They were torturing me!" claimed the German. "They wanted me to die of suffocation."

It was a lie. He had asked for a fly mask; the British kindly tried to make him one. In response, he attempted to knife one of his helpers with a razor hidden in his boot. He was tackled and placed under restraints.

"Tell me, Jerry boy, is you a clever sort? Do you like money and girls and travel and all the other refined things in life?" questioned the captain, freeing the German. "Now's your chance to grab it all. Leave your cock-eyed Fatherland and the blinkin' war where it is and join up with my lot. Be a soldier of fortune."

The German rubbed his sore wrists and considered the offer.

"I'm the most fairest man you ever met. Won't touch a hair on you," proclaimed the captain, standing amid a scattered pile of bloody dead bodies. "You don't have to worry about no prejudices neither."

He pointed out the fact that Italians, Englishmen, and Scotsmen were among his crew, and claimed Germans as past members.

"I like Germans. They come in handy." He twirled the pistol in his grip for show. "Crackerjacks with spanners. Can do all sorts of fancy magic with wheels and motors and all them sorta things," he continued. "Can always use that round here. How about it, Jerry boy?"

"Yes. I will join," agreed the German. "Thank you for giving me this offer."

He stood quickly, casting aside his bonds. He politely offered to shake hands with the captain and the other bandits. They laughed at his decorum, but accepted his grip. "Nice to meet you. My name is...Siegwulf," he said, politely bobbing his head. "Siegwulf Eislinger."

"Right. Sigfried Icefingers. Got it," said the cockney captain with ignorant approval.

"And what is your name, please, sir?"

The captain's golden eye glinted in the sunlight. "Call me Ollie," he said. "Or Flag. Whichever suits your fancy."

"Flag?" the German repeated in confusion.

He jiggled one strip of his green turban. "Lads say the kerchief looks like a flag sailin' in the wind when we're out drivin'," he said, gesturing with one arm at the open desert. "Can't waste time. Let's get started!"

They scoured the ruin. All bodies were stripped to their underwear. Weapons, ammunition, clothing were loaded into the back of the jeeps. Gasoline was siphoned. The bandits mercilessly took postcards and pictures of girlfriends and family from the dead men's pockets. Some they kept as trophies. Others were scattered to the winds. Wedding rings and gold teeth were taken. Anything gold would be melted down and sold to dealers in Cairo.

Next came the search for artifacts. The captain called Ollie—or Flag—had a nose for ancient things. Almost like a sixth sense. He walked around the ruins of the old temple, back and forth, staring at things that weren't really there. He discovered a few hidden vaults. The robbers used grenades to blast holes in the walls. They discovered some temple artifacts, including some gold mirrors, tiny carved statues, and small bowls made of precious stones.

The German called Eislinger, following and studying his new master, noticed an old flint dagger on the captain's hip. It looked ancient. The blade was made of pale violet flint stone. The stone-inlaid bronze handle was eerie-looking—it was shaped like a human-faced Egyptian cobra with wings. It looked sinister.

The captain walked out of the temple—and, in his absence, Eislinger heard something like a man whisper in the thin air. The spooky noise made him shiver. He dismissed it.

Ollie identified a few other places that needed to be excavated. The men produced detonation and digging devices from their vehicles. They intended to blast open areas identified as possible treasure troves.

They did not get the chance.

Dust rose on the horizon. A large wall of it, enough to seem like a small army. They were about to be attacked.

The captain shouted. The bandits, despite having guns and ammunition, fled with their spoils, taking their new German comrade, Eislinger, and their wounded British prisoner with them. It seemed like a large force was making its way towards them. They were cowards and avoided pitched fights. Easy plunder was the only thing that mattered to them.

A few minutes later, a man arrived. He was alone and driving in an Italian armored vehicle. He had fooled everyone into thinking that he was a large force of vehicles by driving zigzagged across the sand and raising hellish dust clouds with maniacal glee. As the hatch popped open, he stuck out his head. He was a German. He had light blond hair, lively medium blue eyes, and a rugged square-shaped face. He was slim and somewhat short, with a strong build. He wore a tan brown Afrika Korps cloth cap, tilted at a jaunty angle. He was completely covered in dust.

A German voice garbled on the radio in the vehicle. Usually it wasn't safe to communicate by radio in this patch of desert—the British were awfully close and often intercepted signals.

However, this clever German officer was a mechanical genius. An engineer in peacetime, he had rewired everything so that his radio broadcasted signals at such a strange frequency that only one other German radio, located a vast distance away, could communicate with him.

"*Hallo? Sag mal was!*" hissed a comrade's voice from the radio, demanding that he say something. "*Hauptmann Von Rindl!*"

"He is gone," replied Capt. Elrich von Rindl, with a sigh of irritation. "They are taking him away. They're heading east again in the direction of Alexandria. What now?"

He slid out of the vehicle hatch and stretched his cramped legs, still wearing the communications headphones clapped onto his ears. He wore a khaki Afrika Korps tunic, brown officer's trousers, and black leather boots. The dressy uniform was ridiculous for desert war, but expected of German officers for the sake of protocol. And his medals, of course. He had acquired many medals from dashing deeds and naturally was proud of them. He did not have to wear his medals into battle—but he wanted to in case he died so that he would look his finest.

Von Rindl was an intrepid German Army desert ranger, also known as a "*Wüstenjäger.*" He was known for his buoyant, mischievous demeanor and his constant singing of the tune, *"The Yellow Rose of Texas"*—a peppy marching song he fell in love with after seeing an American cowboy film in the early 1930s. The song was obscure in Germany. His comrades had no idea what it was; it sounded like a German melody, but Von Rindl would never reveal its origin when asked. Soldiers consequently associated the song with him and dubbed it the *"Von Rindl Lied."* Von Rindl improvised lyrics in German with rhymes and humor. The song was his personal joke and battle hymn.

This unusual desert trooper was the son of hardy colonial pioneers. His wealthy family hailed from Southwest Germany. They owned farms in a German colony in West Africa where he was raised. He returned to his native Germany as a teenager. As a "colonial" German, he experienced difficulty adjusting to the rigors and orderliness of life in the home country.

He was not a career soldier; his passions were mechanics and science. He attended Heidelberg University, where he studied aeronautics. He was passionately curious about airships. He worked on various Zeppelin-style engineering projects in Germany's burgeoning airship industry. He developed expertise applicable to all manner of machines. As a graduate student, he gave teaching lectures on aeronautic gears. He wished to become a professor.

He met a girl during his stint as a graduate student lecturer at Heidelberg. She was 18 when they met; he was 25. Her name was Carla. She hailed from Spain, but was half-German on her father's side and was studying there on a foreign exchange program. Carla was a theology student. Their friendship blossomed into love over four years.

They met when Von Rindl was fined and jailed in the so-called "student prison" on campus. The jail existed to punish delinquents with university ties who broke the law on campus. Von Rindl belonged to a sword-fighting fraternity. Caught in an illegal fencing duel with a fraternity rival, he was incarcerated as punishment. Carla was an idealist who protested the existence of the student jail. Von Rindl's imprisonment became her cause. Nobody else cared about him, and frankly most students thought he deserved it. Carla, who had never previously met Von Rindl, ascertained the facts of the duel and was strongly convinced of his good character. She successfully campaigned for Von Rindl's release. He saw Carla only a few times during his incarceration; she was a beautiful, heroic slip of a girl, and he appreciated her kindness beyond words. After his release, the two spent more time together. They were both very interested in each other and quickly became inseparable. At first it was only a strong friendship. She was young and impressionable; he was older and shy. They shared many things together. Often they spent time together in the beauty of nature or quiet spots on campus. They talked about everything and nothing—theories about why people did things, or why the world turned the way it did sometimes. Reason. Purpose. Existence. It was an innocent and pure love, and went completely unconsummated until after two whole years of understated devotion, Von Rindl lost control of himself and kissed her.

Their happiness was whisked away by Carla's forced return to Spain due to political unrest followed by the outbreak of war. They both wept when they were separated, although Von Rindl controlled his sadness. Viewing himself as a mentor, Von Rindl tried to teach her not to cry. He told her it was useless, bad for the eyes, and a waste of time. It didn't stop her. Neither did it bridle the flood of emotional letters she wrote him. Von Rindl was a poetic soul and wrote equally emotional letters— huge piles of them, in fact, enough to fill closets. He gave her sweet nicknames. They decided they could not live without each other.

Like most loyal Germans, Von Rindl volunteered for military service when the Second World War broke out. He enlisted in the Army. Due to his interest in aircraft, he considered enlisting in the Luftwaffe—however, he discerned his chances of survival in the air were not good compared to those fighting on earth. A soldier on the ground had the advantage of his own arms, legs, and independent wits in the contest with mortal danger. A soldier in the air was bound to the fate of his aircraft—a single shot to the wingtip, a malfunctioning parachute or stray fog could spell doom for an otherwise agile man.

Due to his athletic achievements and experiences growing up in West Africa, Von Rindl was designated for service in special combat troops.

They put him in an elite motorcycle battalion first—the Motorcycle *Jägers*. These so-called "Motorcycle Hunters" wielded rifles and grenades while speeding on all-terrain bikes. A significant amount of mechanical skill was required. Von Rindl qualified with flying colors. He was assigned to invade Poland, but fate prevented him from leaving Germany. His motorcycle shorted out during the advance. An inquisitive engineer, Von Rindl decided to try to fix it himself instead of signaling others about his predicament. He was leaning over backwards in the road curiously plucking at wires when another German motorcycle sped around a hill and ran over him. Both motorcycles wrecked. The offending driver careened into the hill in a dust cloud. Von Rindl suffered a broken ankle. It was embarrassing. To cover up the blunder, the Army awarded him the wound badge. He recovered in time to participate in the invasion of France.

In France, Von Rindl won several Army decorations for his bravery. He credited these to his skill at "reverse engineering"— basically, breaking things. He figured out ways to make enemy equipment work backwards and German machines work better. His impudent sense of humor inspired him to experiment.

Stranded in France, he rescued a fellow wounded soldier by rigging a broken engine onto a bicycle and driving cross-country with it. He made a footbridge collapse under enemy soldiers by removing axle pins from its support beams; men and rifles toppled into a river and were fished out as prisoners. His true moment of glory came when he rigged trees to collapse on advancing British tanks. Setting a system of traps, he hid in the bushes and yanked a wire as the tanks rolled along a woodland path. Logs and branches fell from all directions. The tanks were buried immovably in leafy woodpiles. The crews surrendered with sour expressions. Von Rindl won many decorations for his antics.

Promoted, he was handpicked to serve as a special desert ranger in the Afrika Korps—his experiences in West Africa earned him special assignments.

However, Von Rindl's soul was not in the war. He was just getting by. His real goal was to survive so that he could marry Carla at the soonest opportunity.

There was grumbling and shuffling of paper on the other end of the radio. Two men's voices debated an issue in emotional, singsong tunes.

"Continue with your mission," came the order. "Follow Siegwulf Eislinger as far as you are able and execute him in whatever manner possible. His body is to be returned to headquarters for identity verification, per your original instructions."

"And the mercenaries?" Von Rindl, seated on the vehicle roof, peered through binoculars at the fleeing dust clouds in the distance.

"British commandos must be killed at once because they are not operating according to the rules of war and are in violation of international conventions," replied the signals officer with efficiency.

"But these are not real soldiers. They are dirty men in dirty, torn clothes—not even regular uniforms. They have shot all the British. They killed them all and even robbed them of their clothing!" He stared through the binoculars at the bodies in the ruin, and was overcome with disgust and indignation. "They left them in nothing but underwear. It's unbelievable!"

More silence. Chattering. "This has happened before to our own comrades. Possibly these are the same culprits. They are bandits!" the operator said eventually. "Eliminate all bandits. They are war criminals. Shoot them with Eislinger. All criminals must be punished."

Von Rindl, a German Army scout, was a resourceful and brave man. He had a zest for danger. However, he was skeptical of his ability to single-handedly kill a fleet of British commandos—or bandits, or whatever they were—armed with turrets on their jeeps.

"You promised to send me two armored vehicles and crews as reinforcements on this mission," stated Von Rindl. "When will you send these reinforcements?"

"As soon we can spare them. The supplies, as you know, are very short right now..."

His expression soured. His mouth pressed itself into a thin angry line.

"Perhaps we can send one vehicle. In the next several days...possibly."

"Perhaps I can kill the commandos by sneezing at them," quipped Von Rindl with dry sarcasm.

"*Das reicht schon, Herr Hauptmann!*" snapped the signals officer, offended by the sarcastic remark and trying to bark some discipline into the cocky captain. "You must understand that stopping Eislinger from committing more crimes is of utmost importance to the Panzerarmee Afrika. You must complete your mission even if it takes your very last breath. Then, when you are finished, you are ordered to—"

Von Rindl rolled his eyes, shrugged out of the headphones and jumped from the vehicle, leaving the chattering radio behind him. He strode lightly across the sand with confidence.

To amuse himself, he hummed his favorite tune and made up new absurd lyrics. "*Du kannst trink 'nen Schluck von Rotobstwein und sink im Wörthersee!* But the Yellow Rose of Texas *ist die* only one for me!" he improvised jauntily.

He took the opportunity to quickly explore the ruin. He was deeply disturbed by the sight of the dead men blistering in the sun. He had witnessed, from a distance, their murder at the hands of the bandits. It was senseless and cruel. Until this point, he had never seen anything like it during the Desert War, which was carried out with humane respect from both sides.

He picked up the ropes that had held the young spectacled man called Siegwulf Eislinger. The cords were thick—tied in complex knots. Evidently the British had somehow realized that Eislinger was dangerous.

They should have just shot him, thought Von Rindl in vexation and worry.

He looked into the bleached horizon with a tired face and sharp blue eyes. His mission was to track down and kill the young man with the boring stare and round glasses.

Von Rindl was an angel of death sent from the Afrika Korps to deliver justice to a criminal who had become a menace to his German comrades and to many others. The war—and the world—was much more dangerous while Eislinger, the lunatic, walked free.

Eislinger needed to die. Otherwise, that ordinary-looking criminal would surely become the Eleventh Plague of Egypt.

CHAPTER 4: WAR DREAMS

"Ich ging im Walde
So für mich hin
Und nichts zu suchen,
Das war mein Sinn."
—"Gefunden" [Found] by Johann Wolfgang von Goethe

Maj. Desmond Frost was still suffering from lurid flashbacks as a side effect of his prime suspect's belly dancing. He rose extra early in the morning and thoroughly read through case documents. Including and especially her file.

What he found there increased his admiration for the fiery American journalist. The girl was a real fighter. So was he. He liked her.

Her name was Eve Jocelyn Weathers and she was 28, born and bred in cloudy San Francisco. On her father's side, she was of English and Scottish descent. Her mother sprung from a long vine of Germans.

That, apparently, was the reason for her interest in Germany. It had been a few centuries since her mother's German ancestors abandoned their Fatherland for America, but the blood stayed strong. Probably because after the Germans emigrated, they spent the next several decades marrying other Germans.

One of her dominant German family names was Hecking. The Hecking family was a tangled tree of frowning mustachioed men from Hamburg, who spent their working lives designing porcelain crockery and their recreation time dueling with cutlasses. Their fighting spirit was strong. One of her great-great-great-grandfathers, a certain Otto von Hecking, was a German composer who sailed in the Dutch Navy, invented the first mechanical pressure cooker, married an American female boxing champion, then got bored in retirement and spent his golden old age killing alligators for leather in the wilds of south Florida. His descendants tired of the alligator-killing business, so they tried shark poaching off the coast of Northern California. Thus they ended up in San Francisco, where they branched into leather tanning and other violent means of earning a living. One Hecking forefather became a millionaire after specializing in terminating voles that invaded the lawns and gardens of the rich. He proudly claimed the lives of over 100,000 voles across the palisaded communities of Northern California.

Her mother, in youth, was a world-famous fencing champion during an era when women were supposed to mend socks to seem ladylike. Many old photos existed of a voluptuous blonde woman with a cold gleam in her eye, sitting open-legged on a stool like a samurai lord with a metal helmet on her lap and a huge sabre in her fist.

Her Scottish forefathers were no less militaristic. They had been warriors, hell-raisers, and rebels against every kind of authority before and after they arrived in America. One person in every generation was a notable firebrand; some of the most notable included "Tobacco Sam" (a notorious hijacker of British tobacco ships during the Revolutionary War); Habakkuk MacTavish (a famed abolitionist who led high-speed wagon chases across the Mason-Dixon line to free slaves); and Elsbeth Fitzmarion (the first woman in history to be arrested for bar brawling in Indiana).

The English line was surprisingly ordinary. One day an English botanist named Antony Weathers married a wild Fitzmarion girl. That union resulted in her father and her surname. Eve was the youngest of four children, and the only one to be cursed—or perhaps gifted—with the wild warrior spirit of her ancestors.

Eve had long been estranged from her wealthy and insulated relatives. She didn't get along with any of them and had "quit membership" of her family in righteous disgust. She had a strong social conscience, an interest in war, and a deep curiosity about Germany and international affairs. She also was a sensible and gifted writer. All these factors led her into journalism at a time when intrepid German-speaking reporters were in great demand across the world.

She was completely fluent in German—a result of self-study—and spent a year in Munich writing about feuding German politicians. Then Nazi Germany declared war and decided to banish American journalists. *The Chicago Standard* ordered her back to the United States to write agony-aunt columns, since they could no longer use her in Germany. She refused. She requested to be a war reporter on the frontlines. That was her ambition. Absolutely not, was the answer—the front was "no place for women." She fought tooth and nail for her interests. She threatened to follow Hitler's army into Poland to write war reports. A compromise was reached.

Her editors sent her to Cairo. Eve expected to write about the war in the desert. However, the Chicago editor who supervised her—an armchair journalist named Milo—played a devious trick. Milo was a timid, insecure man who liked to bark at people in his office and was scared of people who barked at him. He disliked Eve; she was too independent, too saucy. He had tried to crush her under his thumb many times and had gotten his thumb nearly bitten off many times in response. He decided to clip her wings when she arrived in Cairo. He refused to publish any war-related articles and assigned Eve to writing "women's interest" type stories—the kind that timid girls and old ladies liked to read. Eve's life became an Egyptian Purgatory as the excitement of war whirled around her while she was constrained to writing about British ladies' clubs and art exhibits.

She forayed into Egyptian history writing to save herself from dying of boredom. This led her to interview Ted Harper—the man who turned out to be undercover Commando Group Sphinx ranger Oliver Bryon. Harper was masquerading as an art-restoration expert working at the Nile Delta Antiquities Museum, a private institution dedicated to preserving the history of Nile marshlands.

Eve went to the museum one day to entertain herself. She found a flyer in the gift shop advertising "new and rare" antiquities available for private viewing. Harper was the only contact listed on the flyer. She rang him and arranged the interview.

Eve described Harper as an uptight Englishman who agreed to the interview but was terrible at answering questions. He was unfriendly. He allowed her to see some of the "rare antiquities." The small collection consisted of a gold ibis-shaped pendant, a pair of carnelian earrings shaped like sunbeams, an ivory jar, and a silver-coated cylinder with winged lions on it, described by Harper as a "wine horn." There was also a stone pipe with strange numeric symbols etched on it; this, Harper stated, was a "mummy pipe"—an object he claimed Egyptians used to "give the dead one last cigar" before burial.

He was reluctant to describe these artifacts and did so only under pressure. He could not date them. He was very controlling about which objects he wanted Eve to write about. He asked lots of nosy questions about *The Chicago Standard* newspaper, which irritated her. He could not explain where the antiquities came from—he claimed they had been found by a "team of researchers" employed by the museum. What were the researchers' names? Could Eve contact them? No—they worked only on a freelance basis and spent most of their time in the desert. He denied knowing their names or how to contact them. What was the restoration process like? He gave a few murky descriptions of how a person generally removes dust from an object. When would these objects be displayed at the museum? He didn't know.

Eve endeavored to save the article from being dull by asking Harper about himself. Usually interviewees liked to prattle about their life stories; many people she talked to in Cairo jumped at the chance to become "famous" in American newspapers. Harper reacted badly. He said he was English—which was very obvious—that he had worked at the museum for about five years or perhaps three—he couldn't remember—and in his spare time, he enjoyed playing cricket. He could not name any local cricket fields where he played.

In an endeavor to add human interest to the story, Eve politely asked Harper if he was married. He sneered and made a rude remark suggesting perhaps Eve was sexually interested in him. Eve made an equally rude remark suggesting she would rather date a camel herder, at which Harper flinched and apologized for his faux pas.

She left in a huff and scraped together a lackluster article based on the interview, which she promptly forgot. Her editors in Chicago thought the story was fantastic and mysterious. Eve thought the editors were idiotic.

How did she end up crossing paths with Harper at the ill-fated Forty Thieves Cabaret? Eve had no intention of seeing Harper again if he was the last man in Egypt. She went to the cabaret as part of a covert quest to learn how to belly dance. Apparently, many white females in Cairo were plagued with a huge crisis of jealousy caused by white men's single-minded fascination with Egyptian belly dancers. It was an epidemic. Perfectly respectable and pretty British ladies were ignored by husbands, fiancées, and potential male companions who swarmed like bees to the honey of so-called "gyppo panty-dancing" skits.

Eve, the bold American, decided to equip herself with knowledge of belly dancing. Clearly it was a feminine wile worth learning. She suggested it to a few British ladies she knew socially; they were scandalized to the point of shunning her. One plucky English girl accompanied Eve to a belly-dance shop out of curiosity—only to break down weeping in shame at the sight of herself perusing "heathen" sequined bras. She ran off in humiliation, and Eve realized that belly dancing was not for the faint-hearted. It made her more determined to master it.

She asked for lessons from locals. The Egyptian entrepreneurs were too wily to agree since it might spark foreign competition and deprive them of income. Thus, the feisty American journalist spied on local belly dancers to learn their art by imitation.

She learned a few tricks. Eventually she experimented on an unsuspecting Englishman seated at the long bar in Shepheard's Hotel. She was a bit drunk, she admitted—one too many Brandy Alexanders. She wrapped a long white napkin around her hips and shook her assets at a dignified British Army Signal Corps officer reading a newspaper. The man's eyes almost popped out of his head; he blushed as red as a beet and looked ready to faint of embarrassment and delight. Later that evening, he cornered her in a hallway and tried to assault her, which was a rather frightening experience. She escaped unharmed, while recognizing that random bursts of belly dancing could have strong effects on male targets.

Much of this information was included in statements she gave to exonerate herself from the suspicion of murdering Harper. She claimed complete innocence.

Details on her ancestry and family had been accumulated by a bored British Army Investigative staff officer who was a frustrated genealogist in his spare time.

Major Frost was engrossed in the woman's written life. He thought Eve Weathers was an extraordinary woman—a tough woman of wit and bravery, with audacity and humor to boot. All qualities he appreciated, especially since these traits also characterized his own personality.

He admired her.

Meanwhile, Eve had been swept into a grim room located near the officers' barracks in the wilderness of unincorporated Giza. A security detail was posted in the hall outside her door to "keep away the flies," as one soldier joked. Eve spent the night in a dank room with bare walls and a metal military cot that seemed like more of a booby trap than a bed. Jackals yowled outside. Dust filtered in through a large crack in the floor; she imagined cobras slithering into her chamber and was anxious. She had nothing but her two large suitcases. Her passport had been confiscated. She was not allowed to use the telephone. She was homeless. Her job had been jeopardized. Her future was uncertain.

One person was responsible for this persecution. A lean jackknife of a man with a brown mustache and cutting blue eyes. That marching automaton with the beret and the confident smile. Who cornered and arrested her! Who defeated her and forced her to surrender—for the first and only time in her life, ever! What was his name again? Major...Sir...

She sulked and brooded, staying up all night thinking of that man and how much she totally despised him.

"I'm surprised you weren't cleared of suspicion sooner by Major Hathaway," Frost told his pouting female prisoner the next morning. "I read your statements from various interviews. You built a strong case for your innocence."

"Major Hathaway was a nasty, old-fashioned jerk who didn't want to see anything except Nazis and spies. He didn't care about my statements. All he cared about was grilling me about my life in Germany," replied Eve. "He was a bad investigator and not very bright."

"Easy does it," Frost chided. "The man is dead, after all."

"That's his problem!" she retorted, already aware of the man's death due to the murmurs about it. "Will you release me now?"

"No. There are other details I need to clear up."

They stood outside as the sun rose over the pyramids in the distance. The sky was light reddish purple, and the air was somewhat cold. The empty landscape was an open canvas for the sun—it retained neither warmth nor coolness. Light was the only thing that gave it life. The sands absorbed dazzling sunbeams and burned like a grill.

The colorful, dreamy haze in the morning air was beautiful. So were the distant stretches of green palm trees along the Nile belt on the horizon. In a few hours, the sun would be aloft and its scourge would oppress the land like the whip of an ancient Egyptian slave master.

Frost stood with his boot propped jauntily on a rock overlooking a low, sandy valley that contained an obstacle course. Hundreds of British soldiers performed drills in the distance.

Across from him, Eve sat on a foldable wooden chair, looking formidably unhappy. She'd been rattled out of bed at an ungodly hour by knocks on the door. She was summoned into the Major's presence for questioning.

She was surprised to see her trim British overlord so disheveled. His appearance was an absolute mess. His brown hair was full of sand and sticking up in all directions; his shorts and shirt were covered in white limestone powder. He had a small, bloody bruise on one side of his face. He seemed physically tired, yet energetic and pleased with himself.

Frost had enjoyed a busy morning. In the blue dark before sunrise, he played football in the barren fields of sand with a tank crew on combat leave. It was a tough game. The men were so violent that they punctured the leather ball and gave each other many bruises. Frost relished it.

Then came his appointment at the "Dante's Inferno" circuit with his assistant, Sgt. Bob "Brick" Wilmore. The Australian was a sad sight as he faced the grim reality of working off the extra pounds he'd accumulated by eating too many pita dumplings.

A war ensued. Frost challenged Wilmore to a race. The Australian, proud of his past battle service, was determined to win. So was Frost. What followed was a vicious and disgraceful duel between the officers. Frost, of course, took the lead. He elastically defied the laws of physics. He sailed over hurdles, wrestled up ropes, and easily cut bayonet bags to ribbons. Wilmore, sweating, thundered along behind. At one point, Frost experienced a moment of insecurity in the fake minefield. The concealed-trap pits were changed regularly and required some examination. He was peering at a suspicious-looking rock when Wilmore, fueled by manly jealousy, careened blindly over an obstacle and skidded into him. They stumbled.

The ground exploded in a huge puff of chalky white dust. Both men collapsed unceremoniously into a deep hole. Frost cut the side of his face on a small piece of limestone. Wilmore landed on a beetle and crushed it to death. They both found the situation funny. Previously on bad terms, they established a sense of comradeship.

Frost was in a frisky mood afterwards. He was invigorated by a hard morning's worth of scrambling around in the sand and competing with people.

"Please pardon my appearance," he said rakishly to the woman across from him. "I was blown up this morning."

Eve was bewildered.

"Landmine trap," he explained with a macabre laugh, gesturing at the obstacle course in the distance. "If it had been a real war, you'd be talking with a ghost right now."

A wind blew slightly, sending a delicate veil of sand dancing around the pair.

"You'd better stop lying to me if you want to get out of here faster," Frost said suddenly.

"Lying about what?" She glared incredulously. "Oh, please. What nonsense is it this time?"

"Something about your story is not truthful," stated Frost in his blunt and assertive style. "I've thought it over and I'm sure of it. It's not your reason for being at the cabaret or how you came to 'know' Harper—or not know him. It's something about the actual shooting. Something doesn't make sense about the flurry you describe after someone else pulled the trigger." He walked closer, staring probingly into her eyes. "Who did it?"

"I don't know. I didn't see anybody."

"You're lying," he said carefully, scanning the depths of her eyeballs. "Why?"

She fidgeted.

"If you're as innocent as you say you are, then why won't

you describe the real murderer?" he questioned.

"Because you won't believe me," she admitted after a minute of interior struggle. "You'll made a snide remark and say I'm crazy or 'imaginative.'"

"Try me," he challenged.

"OK. Fine. I did see the person—or thing—that killed him," she said, looking very apprehensive. "It was horrible. I thought it was a monster."

"A monster?" He was surprised and intrigued. "That sounds very interesting. What happened?"

She reluctantly proceeded to describe how, turning to flee the scene, she witnessed a dark figure with a yellow Cyclops eye lurking behind the balcony. She got the distinct impression the lurker was male. Maybe because it looked large and bulky, she guessed. There was no face. Just a dark, square-shaped head and a glinting gold dot, right in the middle. It vanished quickly—seemingly into thin air. She was so confused she did not witness the actual moment of vanishing. One second it was there. The next, gone.

Frost said nothing. He was mulling over several fragments of information that seemed connected. Like haunted daggers, for example. He leaned against a broken limestone boulder and wiped dust from his jaw.

"When you were interviewing Harper...did you notice a dagger anywhere about him?" he asked after a long silence.

"No. Why?"

"He was stabbed after he dropped off the balcony. Right in the entrails by a strange old Egyptian dagger he was wearing. Some Army staff believe that dagger to be 'haunted.' Apparently the ghostly genius likes to smash glass and scorch people's nostrils with perfume," he said satirically. "If so, maybe your 'monster' is related to that dagger...unless you shot Harper, gutted him ruthlessly and chucked him over the balustrade. But I don't think that's likely."

She was outraged by the suggestion.

"I don't believe you could stab anybody," assessed Frost, studying her with intuition. "It takes nerve to stick a knife in. You've got spirit, but you don't have the stomach for it."

"I'm not a reporter who skewers people for giving bad interviews."

He broke into a wry smile. He liked the rough way she spoke.

Eve went on the offensive. She felt threatened by these interrogations and wanted to restore the balance of power. Now it was her turn to ask questions.

"Did that dagger get stolen yesterday?" she demanded.

Frost was surprised. "Goodness, you are sharp indeed! Got quite a pair of ears, haven't you?" He had not told her anything about the theft. "Why do you ask?"

"Tell me why you're investigating Harper's death. It's unusual for British military intelligence to take such an interest in an art restorer," said Eve. "What's really going on?"

"I don't see what good it would do to tell you."

"Why the interest in him?" she pressed, in true journalistic fashion. "Was he a thief? Is that why you accused me of writing about stolen antiques? He advertised those antiques in his museum. You can't deny he acted suspiciously when I interviewed him—he avoided all my questions. He probably just agreed to be interviewed to seem normal and keep other reporters off him. Clearly he was a fraud. But your role still doesn't add up. Why not turn this over to the police? Why does the Royal Army care about antique thieves?"

Frost eyed her with grudging esteem. She was very clever and evidently frustrated about being kept in the dark. He decided to take a small risk.

"His name wasn't Harper. He was a Special Forces ranger. He didn't belong here—should've been in the desert, climbing sand dunes and poaching Germans," he said concisely. "His bloody nosedive in the cabaret seems to have been the first time military authorities became aware he was in Cairo."

Eve analyzed the information quickly. "I guess if he was in Cairo on official business, you would know it already," she surmised. "And he wouldn't have been fencing stolen goods in a shady museum."

Frost smirked enigmatically.

"Well, I'm sure he's not the only crooked British soldier who ever set foot in Cairo."

"No. But the fact that he was in Special Forces is troubling, to say the least." He brushed limestone chalk from his uniform. The sun was coming up, and it was getting hot. He had places to go. "There. You have your answers," he said, with a sideways look at her. "Satisfied?"

"You still won't let me go?"

"No. When I am ready to let you go, you will be let go," he said tersely. "And right away, too. No reason to pester."

Eve studied the man and considered him an annoying ruffian. "Your wife must be a martyr."

A mild flash of emotion lit Frost's blue eyes. It only lasted a second, but that was just long enough for the journalist to perceive his distress.

"Ah. No marital bliss," deduced Eve. "What's the trouble, Major? Divorced or wishing you'd never said 'I do?'"

He glared at her. His piercing stare blistered with fury. The suddenness and intensity of his anger frightened her. "She's dead," he said firmly after a moment of icy silence. "You could call her a martyr, though—I suppose you could say my career martyred her. She died of malaria while I was serving in India."

She felt chastised. "I'm sorry..."

"No need to be sorry," said Frost tersely. "I'm not."

Eve stared in horror.

"That is to say, I don't miss her," he explained with a frown. "We were a bad match. Wanted nothing more than to get away from each other. Her death was a mercy to us both."

Eve struggled to recover from her surprise. "How long ago...?"

"Quite long," he answered in his clipped manner. "Don't be so surprised. I'm not the only Army officer packing an Indian misadventure in my kit. Quite a lot of colonial marriages fail. It's easy to become lonely in India and make seemingly good decisions for the wrong reasons—especially when you're young and faced with certain social pressures." He gave a cold, morbid smirk. "Thankfully it's over."

Eve didn't know what to reply.

"I'm now happily married to my career," he declared, self-conscious and wishing to reassert himself. "I find that I do much better looking after my military interests without being slowed down by foolish and irritating people."

The woman journalist smiled. She identified with his viewpoint. "I know exactly what you mean."

Frost was still irritated by her prying. "What's your sad tale?" he challenged sarcastically. "Lonely hearts, is it? Hoping to snag some clod with your cabaret dancing?"

The young woman was offended. "No! I'm not desperate,"

she said. "I haven't found anyone who's my type."

"Oh?" He leered. "What's that?"

"None of your business!" She was annoyed to be put on the defensive again. "I'll know the right type whenever I do meet him. Whenever that happens, he won't get away from me."

"May God have mercy on his soul," said Frost.

Eve was startled. His quip was completely ironic and delivered with such calmness that she was knocked off guard. The comment was insulting, yet his dry wit almost made her laugh.

Frost reflected on what she said. He admired her careful approach to relationship choices. There was something familiar about it.

"That's a good strategy. Have standards and don't plunge headlong into anything," he agreed with approval. "That's the proper way to go about things."

Eve felt awkward discussing her personal life. She changed the subject. "How did you know the antiques Harper showed me at the museum were stolen?" she asked. "You realized it when reading my old article? Then used that as a ploy to arrest me?"

"The items matched a tip we'd already received from a certain colorful gentleman who knows a lot about old and stolen things," he answered, with no comment on her accusation. "An Irish explorer. He's been sharing information with the Army. As a matter of fact, I'm leaving today to go and meet him. He's in Khafra. Ever heard of it?"

"No."

"An archaeological hole in the desert somewhere in the dunes between here and Alexandria. A bit hot and dusty, some flies. The usual sort of thing," he said coolly. A slight wicked smile slanted one corner of his mouth. "I'm sure your knowledge would come in very handy to us there. With your journalism background, you might notice details we could miss—it might even jog your memory about Harper, or that 'monster' of yours. You ought to come along."

Eve knew very well it was an order the British officer expected her to resist. He was testing her somehow. She rose to the challenge. "OK, Frosty," she said.

Now it was Frost's turn to be startled. His Army nickname had stuck with him across a lifetime and more than three continents. Like most British military nicknames, it was a sardonic derivation of his surname. Rumors were that he disliked the moniker, but that wasn't exactly true. It had a cartoonish ring that irritated him sometimes. However, it was a decent and unexciting moniker he accepted with grace. Hearing it from the woman shocked him. The shock soon faded. He didn't bother to admonish her.

Eve expected a reprimand. Instead the Major smiled faintly at her. It seemed he had no objection to her addressing him that way.

"You're a sly character," he said with cold admiration. "You know it, too. That's your problem. One of these days, young lady, you may be surprised to find out that the world is not your oyster."

She stood up and squinted at pyramids under the rising sun. It was a breathtaking sight. Scores of men, finishing their drill exercises, darted over the obstacles in Dante's Inferno like jumping brown ants in the valley. The ancient and the modern blended together in haunting harmony. The war looked like a dream here; a fantasy dwarfed by the sands of time. She walked past Frost to get a better look. "Wow, they're training!" she murmured.

Frost noticed a bright smile on her face as she went past. It bewildered and excited him. "You...enjoy watching battle drills?"

"Sure, I love it," replied Eve, looking eagerly into the ghostly sunlit valley. "But I've never had a chance to see like this."

A light of admiration shone from Frost's face as he watched her. Her figure cut a gorgeous, clean silhouette against the pyramids and the light. He noticed her copper hair, her pale complexion, and the commanding way she stood surveying everything—with poise, aggression, and intelligence. He thought she was beautiful.

Eve, squinting to see the soldiers in the distance, edged closer to the precipice.

"Not too close!" cautioned the Major. "The dirt will collapse beneath you."

She corrected her step, casting a hostile glance at him. "I'm sure you'd be glad to see me fall," Eve muttered as she pondered her uncertain fate. "You'd probably play a pipe and drum march over my tombstone."

Frost continued gazing at the warlike young woman. He decided she was wonderful.

"You're wrong about that," he replied, in a softer tone than usual. "I think I'd miss you if you were gone."

She barely heard him. She was used to hearing him speak in his projected "command" voice—it wasn't necessarily loud, but very sharp and forceful. His smoother, normal tone of voice slipped below her range of perception.

The pyramids held her under their spell. A few minutes later she woke from bedazzlement and realized he was nowhere. Instead, she was alarmed to behold Wilmore the Australian stomping towards her through the dirt and beckoning her to a waiting jeep.

"Hey, you. I forgot to ask—are you guys investigating that museum?" she questioned Wilmore as she accompanied him. "The one where Harper was working. Maybe they helped him sell the stolen antiques. You should look into it."

"Let the Egyptians investigate their own museums," came Wilmore's stony reply. "We're the Army Investigative Corps. We have other priorities."

CHAPTER 5: THE WISE MAN

"What did I see in the desert to-day
Beside the sand and rocks,
Where the distance fades into misty grey
And the shimmering mirage mocks?"
—"In the Desert To-day" from
"Poems from the Desert" by Bombardier L. Challoner

The journey to the place called Khafra was long and arduous. Human civilization withered into nothingness west of Giza. For centuries, the land in the west had been too hot and arid to settle. As a result, infrastructure was scare. Towns became smaller and scarcer. Roads were very narrow and tended to be jammed with traffic. A long dusty boulevard stretched on towards Alexandria with occasional intersections. Lush date palm trees appeared in lines and patchworks. Most of the traffic were Arab merchants on donkeys or horses, travelers to and from Cairo, and British military personnel going to and from battlefronts in the Western Desert. Security checkpoints dotted the roads in certain strategic areas.

Major Frost and his group had no trouble sailing past checkpoints in their jeep. Occasionally, he ordered Sergeant Wilmore, his driver, to go off road to cut ahead of traffic, but many obstacles and uneven ground made that difficult.

The group totaled four in number: Frost, Wilmore, Eve, and an Australian Second Lieutenant called Nye who was brought along for extra security. Nye was a tall, lanky man with a slouch hat who had been raised in the boondocks of his country wrestling cows and slaying crocodiles; he had nothing in common with Wilmore, a privileged "city boy." However, Nye had achieved a higher military rank than Wilmore. As a result, the two Australians disliked each other.

Frost had cleaned himself up from the morning's athletic revelry, and looked neat and tidy in his tropical uniform as usual. He wore his midnight blue Investigative Corps beret and was clean of all dust aside from what blew onto him from outside the car. He wore a small white bandage over the tiny cut on his face.

Sitting next to him in the rear of the jeep was Eve. She was outfitted in a loose white blouse and an ill-fitting pair of men's brown Army trousers in addition to a clunky pair of men's desert boots. She was told her own garments were "unsuitable" for a venture into desert terrain.

"What's with the mummy bandage?" asked Eve, quizzing him about the bandage on his face. "Don't tell me a tough guy like you minds a little scratch like that."

Eve expected him to bristle at the gibe. Instead the Major sneered. As a soldier, he was used to banter and rough talk. He enjoyed it.

"Of course not," he retorted. "But I do mind the sand. I suppose you've never heard of 'Egyptian death dust'.'" He grinned with morbid amusement. "I once knew a chap stationed in Luxor who cut his fingers open during a military exercise. He didn't bother to put a plaster on. Didn't want to make a fuss. The poor lad actually caused a worse fuss by what he did—or didn't do," Frost elucidated. "His fingers all turned green, one right after the other, and they ended up amputating his hand.

It was the sand, you see."

"The sand spreads disease?"

"Yes, the desert's like a wash basin that never gets rinsed or emptied," explained Frost. "Bacteria churns and boils across hundreds of miles. Open wounds must be bandaged in the desert. Otherwise they won't heal and things could get worse."

He smirked wryly at the fiery young woman. "Keep that in mind the next time you feel like attacking someone. If they fight back, you could end up wearing your own 'mummy bandages.'"

Eve threw him an annoyed look. "Stop making insinuations, Major," she replied with resentment. "I have no plans to attack anyone."

Frost glanced back at her with an amused twinkle in his eyes. "Really?" he asked, his mouth twisting into an irreverent smile. "Not even me?"

Eve was taken aback by his remark. He stared knowingly, his light blue eyes gleaming with humor. A look of mutual recognition passed between them. Eve melted into a smile. Frost's deadpan expression cracked. They both laughed. The tension in the atmosphere broke.

"You're spoiling for a fight with me," he accused, grinning raffishly. "You have been since the moment I crossed your doorstep. Don't bother denying it. I can tell."

She gave a guilty smile and glanced away.

"You like fighting," ventured Frost, sparkling at her. "That's why you're totally obsessed with war."

Eve shot him a warning look. "Don't bother poking fun of me," she menaced. "If you're the type who believes women should bake cakes and little girls should play dolls, don't try to impose your views on me. It won't work," she said. "Ask my parents if I used to play dolls. They'll tell you I played with toy soldiers and beat up my brothers in broomstick sword fights."

Frost laughed approvingly. "I'd never 'poke fun' of anybody with interests in war or fighting," he retorted, gazing admiringly at the young woman. "That's what I'm interested in!" He gave her another roguish smile. "I had similar experiences as a youngster—I liked toy soldiers and playing at battles, too. Why do you think I ended up joining the Army?"

His logic surprised Eve. The Major saw her bewildered look and burst into dry laughter again. His ironic humor was contagious. Eve couldn't help but share it.

She laughed. "Well, I guess that makes sense, doesn't it?"

"Certainly it does! You ought to have deduced it sooner, you remorseless news hound," ribbed Frost merrily. "You're supposed to be top notch, aren't you, you American reporters? Darting about the streets in a mob, chasing after gangsters and starlets with notebooks and cameras. You can write about international politics, but you failed to reason that a soldier likes fighting. You'd better work harder if you want to beat Fleet Street."

Eve exchanged a grin with him this time. He was teasing her—but she didn't mind. "In my own defense, I've met plenty of British soldiers in Cairo who believe women should have nothing to do with war," she explained. "A lot of men back in the States feel the same way. That's why my colleagues have tried to stop me from war reporting."

"Nonsense," rebuffed Frost, eyeing her with growing esteem. "Women like you are rare birds. There ought to be more of you. The world would be so much more interesting."

The young woman was astonished to receive compliments from the hardnosed Major. She scanned his face for any signs of flattery—and realized he was practically incapable of it. Frivolity was not his style. Clearly, he meant what he said.

She noticed an approving glow in Frost's eyes as he looked at her. It made her feel awkward. Nevertheless, the atmosphere between them warmed up.

Frost spent the rest of the journey engaging her in conversation. He was restlessly energetic. He loved "Army talk" and razzing fellow soldiers, provoking people, talking about war, and getting in minor fights. He joked about weapons, military leaders, and dissipated soldiers in Cairo. He constantly roasted Sergeant Wilmore about the latter's clumsiness on the obstacle course, much to the delight of Lieutenant Nye.

His dark and irreverent sense of humor raised eyebrows and laughs. He made horribly comical remarks about how much he fun he had shooting Germans in France. He satirized the exploits of an army unit he belonged to in India. He described grim battles in an ironic, incongruous way. His pithy yet elegant style of speaking made his anecdotes funnier. The soldiers—and Eve—enjoyed it. The young woman's interest encouraged Frost. He was spurred on by her enthusiasm.

Eve was entertained by his talk and interested in his stories, although she still resented him for arresting her and removing her from her hotel. Her present ordeal, entirely of his making, was not easy to forget. However, she quickly developed a basic understanding of his personality. She identified with Frost somehow—although she failed to understand this connection. The Major possessed some mysterious charisma she respected and liked. She could not withhold her interest in Frost's exploits or her laughter at his flippant remarks.

Eve shared her own stories amidst the soldiers' banter. Misadventures in Hitler's Germany, bureaucracy, bickering Nazi officials. The two Australian officers asked the journalist lots of questions.

She caught Frost stealing sly glances at her constantly during the journey. His piercing blue eyes came vibrantly alive with a strange light whenever he looked at her. He analyzed her, as usual—but Eve saw something had changed. She could not guess what. Her feelings of awkwardness around him increased.

In late afternoon, they came to a horrific traffic jam. Cars, military vehicles, and wagons were clogged in a huge knot that snaked far into the horizon. The vehicle inched forward for over an hour. The sun grew hotter. Everyone was drenched in perspiration and felt the life being sucked out of them by the withering rays. Frost became intensely aggravated. He rebuked Wilmore, the driver, in scathing language that shocked Eve and reduced the other two military men to a pair of saluting marionettes. Abuse, apparently, was the prerogative of commanders.

He ordered Wilmore to drive off-road to reach their destination faster. The jeep pealed into the desert with a huge explosion of flying sand. Eve bounced dangerously in the seat as the tires left concrete and civilization behind.

She hung onto the side of the door to steady herself. Frost reached over assertively. He grabbed her hand and placed it on a leather strap attached to the seat. His touch was brief and strangely gentle—and lasted a second longer than necessary. Eve wondered if he had tried to make a physical advance towards her. It's not true, she thought in disbelief. The Major's an arrogant loner. There's no chance he would flirt with me.

She looked at the man suspiciously. Frost regarded her with serene calm. He almost appeared innocent—except for that strange admiring stare that grew brighter whenever their eyes met. It wasn't lust. It was a deliberate emotion more intense than that.

Eve turned away quickly. She felt as though she were suffering from desert mirages. Until now, he had been only a cap and uniform in her eyes. She had been too busy resisting his authority to consider him as a human being—much less as a man. The Major seemed cold and ruthless. Now suddenly he was warmly animated, like a bitter stone statue that breathed to life in front of her. His attitude was friendly—and the look in his eyes seemed more than friendly. She did not understand how this had happened or why. She did not resent his attention. Oddly enough, she liked him and enjoyed his company despite her former prejudice. Confusion was the main source of her discomfort.

The jeep sped into a field of flat, rippling dunes. The sands were a strange blend of white and pale orange powder. Dust spooled into the air. The tall windscreen protected the occupants from the buffeting air and the dust around them. Wilmore enjoyed off-road driving and hurtled on at breakneck speed. He ran over a pale sidewinder. The whirling tires spit a dead, flying snake up into the air. The Australians laughed. Eve ducked in terror and bumped into Frost; she bounced into his shoulder and her head almost knocked into his. Her billowing red hair blew into his face briefly. Frost became flustered. Eve recoiled in embarrassment.

"Look! A gazelle!" exclaimed Eve, pointing at an animal in the distance and marveling at its charming appearance.

"Good!" approved Frost. "We can shoot it later if we get hungry."

He didn't notice the dismayed look that passed over her face.

Eventually they came to a place that looked exactly like the middle of nowhere. Not a single trace of human civilization was visible in any direction. Neither were there any trees nor vegetation. The desert had become an endless mathematical plane. Wilmore and Nye fumbled with a map and argued with each other. Frost drummed his fingers on the jeep door.

They agreed on something. Suddenly, the jeep lurched forward and took a circular route towards an uneven looking swathe of sandbars in the distance. As they approached the sandbars, the ground faded. Blended layers of sand and rock separated and became three-dimensional. The very earth seemed to unfold and, as if by magic, a lush green oasis materialized in front of them. It was a large oasis, about the size of a small city. Camels, tribesmen and military jeeps skirted back and forth in the greenery. Huts appeared. A small complex of military outbuildings stood on the fringes of green. A command post.

At the heart of the oasis was an enormous ancient ruin. It was a huge compound of square limestone buildings. Pillars carved from the very roots of desert bedrock reached up to the scorching heavens like pleas from mankind. A giant stone statue of an ancient cat goddess was the most conspicuous landmark. The cat's eyes were enormous. Her carved mouth was serene. Her monstrous ears and large paws were adorned in savage beauty with rings and bracelets. She had a short mane and the tail of a lioness.

The oasis of Khafra was one of several desert oases called the Isles of the Blest. Ancient Egyptians revered these sites as sacred wellsprings. They consecrated large temple cults to the worship of deities who were supposed to live in the oases. These temples had formed local hubs of industry. Legions of ancient merchants, builders, artisans, chefs, butchers, and craftsmen—to say nothing of priests and temple servants— devoted all their labor to the worship of the temple's stone god and any animals that resembled it. The temples became treasure troves; the gods were heaped with homages of gold from kings. Priests, rich with tribute, were entombed with their spoils.

This particular oasis was the site of the Temple of Yebes, a shrine dedicated to the twin essences of ancient Egypt's feline deity: Bast-Sekhmet. The whiskered goddess had two natures; as Sekhmet the lioness, she was a mighty queen of sun-fire and war, and a harbinger of raw spiritual powers. As Bast the cat, she was the gentle bringer of love and domestic joy. Hundreds of cats once lived here among the palm trees and colonnades—not as pets, but as divinities. They wore jewelry and were worshiped in the temple. Servants attended dutifully to their needs. But no more could the sounds of their meowing be heard in the oasis. The age of steel and war transformed the desert spring into a backwater military command outpost for the British Army.

The goddess Bast-Sekhmet, had she been able to see through her weary stone eyes, might have been surprised to witness Frost in his beret and khakis approaching her temple alongside a ginger-haired woman and two gun-toting military roughs. Egypt was no longer the garden of desert gods—it was an empire of warring foreigners.

They approached the temple on foot. A few Bedouins jockeying past on camels cast curious glances at them. They gawked mostly at Eve because foreign women were a very rare sight in this area. Military men in jeeps were common.

A large tent was stretched out at the base of the temple compound. Inside it, a dusty, robed man wearing a long white Bedouin head kerchief huddled on a pile of carpets over a pot of fresh Arabic coffee. He had dirty brown hands and dirty brown boots. He was armed with a formidable array of belts, knives, hand tools, and a large pistol that looked big enough to fell a water buffalo in one shot.

Frost peered into the tent and noticed a man's tan leather jacket, some books, notepads, and other items that looked distinctively European.

Wilmore turned haughtily to the Arabic coffee wallah. "Hey you, Ahmed, or whatever your name is," he called out to the man in the kerchief. "Where is Dr. Sullivan?"

The man poured himself a silver cup of coffee and sighed decadently.

"Hey, Sheikah man," he prodded again, more harshly. "Can you speak?"

"Hey mister. Would you mind wiping your boots off and closing the tent behind you?" said the kerchiefed man suddenly, in a melodious Irish brogue. "It's getting awful hot outside."

The soldiers jumped in surprise as the robed figure turned his head and revealed himself as Dr. Benen Sullivan, commonly known as "Ben," the shorter version of his Gaelic name.

Sullivan was named Benen after one of St. Patrick's closest companions and, true to his name, he was a companion to most people he met. He had dancing blue eyes, freckles, curly reddish golden hair, and a strong build. He was a renowned Egyptologist and archaeologist. He was a dashing, wandering scholar. He had made history by becoming the only Irish faculty board member of the English-dominated Royal Academy of Egyptology based in Cairo. It was an achievement he was very proud of. He was known for his strong and insightful criticisms of British tomb excavations and existing archaeological standards.

He was an expert on Egyptian spiritualism. He had many strange and unusual theories about hidden meanings behind objects and symbolism, which were usually proved right.

"Egypt is more than hieroglyphics. You need to read the land, the minerals, and the natural aesthetics of objects to understand Egyptian temple artifacts," Sullivan had once declared during a well-received speech at a U.S. academic institution.

He spent most of his time at Egyptian shrine sites doing research and analysis during excavations. He was usually accompanied by his beautiful wife, Rita—a famed explorer before her marriage—and their three sons, aged 6, 9, and 10, who Sullivan trained as his successors since their earliest years.

Sullivan first met Rita one day in a remote village on the French side of Switzerland. He was standing on a tall shelving ladder in a small mountain library reading rare research books. Being at such a great height surrounded by so many books, Sullivan the scholar felt like he was in heaven. Rita had just climbed the wrong way around a mountain and descended in search of a hotel. The library was one of the only large buildings in the area. After months of being lost and lugging hiking equipment, she felt like she was in the lowest circle of Purgatory. Dragging her suitcases into the library seeking refuge from snow, she struck Sullivan's ladder by accident and knocked him clean off his perch. He landed at her feet in an avalanche of books. Rita fell in love with him at first sight and decided to keep him. Sullivan gladly surrendered without protest. They were married three days later and had been inseparable ever since. Their family lived a literary, tribal existence. The couple and their children spent most of their time climbing walls, digging, dusting, reading, writing, drawing, and hiking, whenever they weren't lugging their worldly belongings back and forth on camels or in trucks.

Sullivan and Major Frost had known each other for about a year after meeting by accident in London. Both had returned to Britain from Egypt on brief professional trips, incidentally at the same time. Both were also due to catch the same London train to begin their journey back to Egypt when a German air raid struck. The two men were imprisoned in a muffled air-raid shelter for several hours with a host of other sundry people from various walks of life. Everybody was terrified. Sullivan, ever the buoyant Irishman, decided to lighten the mood by cracking impertinent jokes. Frost, with his roguish sense of humor, was also an incorrigible joker. The two of them struck up a repartee and kept the dense crowd amused with sarcastic comedic exchanges. It was the most enjoyable air raid anyone could have experienced. Sullivan had previously disliked British soldiers, and Frost had low esteem for archaeology. However, they became good friends afterwards. After returning to Egypt, Sullivan occasionally volunteered information to Frost's office that he thought would help the Major in the war effort.

At present, the Irish scholar was gathering archaeological data for a British-sponsored research project exploring the temple cult of Bast-Sekmet at Khafra, particularly the typical lifestyles of the cats who lived on the temple grounds. Sullivan had already made some landmark discoveries about the spiritual meaning of symbols engraved on ancient cat jewelry. He was working on a book about his findings.

Sullivan greeted Frost with a surprised smile. "Oh. It's you, Major!" he exclaimed. "What are you doing here? I thought you'd be in Cairo."

"We received the information you sent about the stolen artifacts trafficked to Cairo recently," said Frost, getting straight to business. "Those artifacts have become a central piece of evidence in an investigation I'm leading."

"And you galloped all the way over here just to talk about that?" Sullivan retorted impudently. "I've got a phone, you know."

Frost pulled a folded paper from his trouser pocket and threw it at him with an assertive flick of one hand.

Sullivan scooped it up. It was a large black-and-white photograph. The image showed a large dagger. The curved blade was made of jagged gray stone. The handle was metal. It was fashioned in the image of a winged cobra with a human face that looked distinctly ancient Egyptian. Square inlaid stones lined the cobra's serpentine body and wings.

Sullivan was fascinated. He examined the picture from five different angles and in three different areas of light inside the tent. He scribbled in a notebook and flung papers everywhere, opened and slammed books with enthusiasm. He forgot to say anything to anybody for a long time.

One by one, the others sat on cushions and drifted into fatigued boredom. Frost remained alert and standing at attention, watching every flicker of thought that crossed Sullivan's face.

"You could've done better than bringing me this flimsy piece of paper!" complained Sullivan, shaking the photo accusingly at the British officer. "How am I supposed to examine the thing?"

"It's been stolen," said Frost. "That's the reason why I'm interested in it. I would like to learn about any significance it has to my investigation. I want facts. I don't care about spiritualism. But in case it's helpful for you, this dagger is supposedly 'haunted'—"

"Really?" interjected a boisterous Sullivan, thrilled. He was absolutely delighted by the idea of a haunted dagger, to the point of startling everybody. He became friendlier due to scholarly joy. Then he realized his guests looked tired and half-starved. "Come on, sit down. Have some coffee. Want something to eat?" He shoved a tray of candied dates at Eve, who nearly dropped them. "Who's the lovely lady here?"

She brightened at the chance to speak. "I'm—"

"She's in my custody," interrupted Frost. "Army business."

Eve glowered at the British officer. He met her stare with cool confidence.

"What have you been up to, Miss, that you've gotten yourself taken captive by the Sheriff of Nottingham over here?" asked Sullivan, jerking his head sarcastically towards the Major. He shook his head in sarcastic pity. "God help you, poor woman."

Eve stifled a giggle.

Frost's eyes shifted down in discomfort. The proud career soldier felt somewhat stung by the remark. He did not want Eve to laugh at him.

Sullivan winked; the gibe was meant as a harmless joke.

"At peremptory glance, I can tell you a few facts about this interesting piece here," announced the Irishman, gesturing at the picture of the dagger. "I can tell just by looking at it that it is definitely ancient Egyptian—not Greek or Roman, and not a forgery. There's a tiny cartouche in the blade located barely below the crosspiece. Don't know if you can see it..."

Frost blinked, uninterested in details.

"Anyway, no forger would have put that there," Sullivan continued. "That," he said with excitement, "is what you call a 'spirit seal.' You see them sometimes on funerary artifacts, especially on mummified animals—the whole idea of a 'spirit seal' is to keep a ghost contained in something. Think of it like a cork in a bottle. The Egyptians used these seals to decorate animal mummies, to make sure the little critters followed their masters to the afterlife and didn't escape somewhere in the underworld—you wouldn't want the pharaoh's pet cat running away, would you?" He paused pensively. "I've never seen one on a weapon before. Very unusual." He shot Frost a dark glance. "Rather ominous, if you asked me."

"I suppose that's why people think it's haunted," remarked Frost, unfazed.

"Probably. They have good reason to think so," replied Sullivan with concern. "The only reasons I can think of offhand for a 'spirit seal' to be on a weapon like this would be either to capture the soul of somebody who wielded it—who knows why—or perhaps to capture the soul of someone who died by it." He reflected. "This could be a weapon used for an execution." He frowned, mulling his theory over. "But that's unlikely. The Egyptians were practical people—they didn't waste time bothering about the afterlife of every common criminal they punished. If it's true this blade was used to execute someone, it would have been a high-profile case, and the target of this 'spirit seal' would have been a pretty rotten apple."

"It sounds fascinating. Rather gruesome. Of course, there must be a market for this sort of thing," said Frost, impressed by the other's knowledge.

"Well, I could be mistaken. Sometimes the Egyptians used objects for ritualistic purposes that are uncommon. Magic wands, you name it. And the hieroglyphics are a bit hard to make out from this picture," admitted Sullivan, ever the critical scholar.

He lifted the photo again. "What type of metal is the handle made out of?"

"Bronze, allegedly," stated Frost. "I haven't seen it myself."

"Interesting. That shows that the dagger was intended to be used," Sullivan illuminated. "It wasn't just for decoration." He paced. "The ancient Egyptians used bronze to forge some of their strongest metal work. Like statues, for example. That's because bronze holds its liquid form longer when it's poured into a mold. When it comes out, it's harder and stronger than other metals, like copper for example. So, we know now that this piece here was made for some hard work."

"A sidearm, perhaps?" suggested Frost.

"Hmm. No." Sullivan squinted at the picture again. "The blade is made of flint. Correct?"

"Yes, as far as I know," answered Frost.

"Well, I can tell you that flint blades were often used by embalmers to remove organs from humans and animals during mummification," said Sullivan. "Flint weapons largely went out of vogue during the Bronze Age, but the ancient Egyptians still kept them around for certain 'uses,'" he said, rolling his eyes grimly, "the main reason being the sharpness. You can't get much sharper than the edge of a flint knife. And when you're an embalmer in a hurry to send the dead packing to the afterlife, it gets the job done."

"I don't mean to sound...macabre," said Frost, with a laugh and an uneasy smirk, "but I fail to see why one would need such a strong knife for mortuary purposes. It's the bronze handle that raises my doubts. A crosspiece, as you know, is normally used to strengthen the grip and protect the hand during battle." He smirked bewilderedly again. "I don't see why they'd have needed the bronze handle. Unless the dead weren't quite dead when they were being embalmed—" He broke into an impudent laugh.

To his surprised, the Irishman agreed with him. "You're right. I don't pretend to know as much about weapons as you do, Major—that's your line of expertise," he replied evenly. "But you have raised a valid point. Never before have I seen a hilt with a crosspiece on an embalming knife. Yet that is what this knife appears to be."

He frowned in confusion. "The key is this goddess right here," he said, pointing at the winged cobra's human face. "If I can figure out who she is, maybe I can figure out the historical purpose of this interesting piece."

"Goddess?" Frost exclaimed dubiously. He peeked at the

picture again with irreverent humor. "Do you mean to say that goggle-eyed centipede is supposed to be female?"

Everyone in the tent laughed—Eve especially.

"Remind me never to ask you to identify ancient symbols," quipped Sullivan, shaking his head. "This, Major, is a cobra—not a centipede! It's likely a deity of some kind. The Egyptians had several winged serpent deities that they worshiped for different purposes. But this gal doesn't look familiar…"

"How do you know it's not a man centipede?" chuckled Frost, beaming with mischief. "I mean, 'serpent?'"

"The two stones on either side of the face resemble ornaments commonly seen in female headdresses," the scholar answered, not skipping a beat. "A man wouldn't have worn ribbons on his wig—at least, not that we would know of."

The Major glanced at the others and made a wry face.

Everyone laughed again. Frost and Eve locked eyes and smiled at each other.

"Any chance I could examine the knife myself?" asked Sullivan. "There may be some details about the goddess that don't show up in the picture."

"No! I'm afraid not. I told you, it's been stolen. We don't know where it is," Frost negated. "It's probably just as well that way—I'm not sure if you believe in 'curses,' but this object does have an ominous track record. Two people associated with it have recently died."

Sullivan's round blue eyes got rounder with alarm.

"Its 'original' owner was murdered. Another person who handled the knife—Major Hathaway—passed away unexpectedly of a heart attack en route to Palestine," said Frost, matter-of-fact and nonchalant. "Naturally everyone's talking."

Sullivan held the paper gingerly, looking somewhat pale. His enthusiasm for the artifact seemed to drain away in unison with his complexion. "Well, I'm glad it went missing then," he said sardonically, recovering his sense of humor. "In fact, if you ever do find it, just leave it where it is. I'll work with secondhand sources…"

Frost grinned in amusement at the other man's unease. "Oh, but I almost forgot to tell you about the ghost!" he exclaimed buoyantly. "The knife is said to possess an evil genius that allegedly smashes things and puffs perfume at people."

The Irishman arched his brows in sarcasm. "Is that so?"

The Major snickered in disdain. "I can't attest to the validity of these stories, but I do know several usually 'normal' people who'd swear before a judge they saw it happen." He sneered, halfway disbelieving. "I have my doubts, Sullivan, but the witnesses in question are such steady chaps. Army staff, you know. They can't all simply have lost their marbles at once!"

"Perfume, you said?" Sullivan's blond brows furrowed pensively. "Hmm...that does sound funerary. If only..." He let his words trail away. "I'm starting to get a vague idea about the historical purpose of this knife," he announced after a moment. "Very vague. I'll have to check some literature before I can give you a definite answer."

The intrepid Irish archaeologist set the picture down on a small wooden desk, then turned to his guests cheerfully. "We're having fresh gazelle for dinner tonight," he said. "Stay and have some. It'll take me a while to pull my research together about this knife, and I suspect there's more about your investigation you want to discuss," he said to Frost. "Meanwhile, you've had a long journey. Might as well eat and rest up."

"Gazelle?" Eve was disgusted. She imagined antlers and hooves on a platter. "No, thank you—"

"Sounds wonderful. We'll take you up on it," announced Frost. "I had planned to quarter temporarily in the Army outbuilding just west of here. There should be some available barracks and a canteen. We will stay overnight—however long it takes for you to provide the information I need. I will not go back to Cairo until I have what I want."

It was a declaration. It was clear he would not budge an inch from Khafra—or probably from the tent—until he achieved his goal. The Australians didn't mind the stay. They were enjoying the outdoors and were pleased by the prospect of an Army canteen in the area. That meant free liquor.

Sullivan glanced at Eve.

"Where's the lady staying?"

"With us," came Frost's icy answer.

The Irishman arched his blond eyebrows. "In the barracks? With poor, starved, lonely soldiers?" He glanced at Frost. "You sure know how to raise hell, Major. I'll give you that."

"Better indoors with us than out here with the Bedouins," retorted Frost. "Besides, you underestimate this young lady.

She's quite a ferocious specimen. I'm confident she could box the ears of any soldier who dared to be impertinent." He grinned approvingly at Eve. "You'd likely enjoy that, too. Wouldn't you?"

The young woman was silent in surprise. Major Frost seemed to have completed his transformation from an adversary to an admirer. His metamorphosis continued to baffle her.

Sullivan glanced wryly at the British officer. "I suppose that's why you're handling her case," he said. "You're a fire-starter yourself."

Frost broke into a roguish grin. He gave Sullivan an appreciative slap on the shoulder. "It's true," he said. "Miss Weathers and I understand each other."

He fixed Eve with another piercing blue stare. She stared back, mystified. Frost took a hard look at her. Eve saw it again—a bright glimmer of appreciation.

"Clear out," he ordered his men, and gave them instructions to make arrangements at local military quarters for their brief stay there. They were told to unload and refuel the jeep, clean guns, organize equipment and other sundry duties. Eve remained in the tent, tired and oppressed. Major Frost would not allow her out of his sight.

"So, you wanted to ask me about the stolen artifacts I reported," Sullivan said. "Why the sudden interest now? What exactly has happened?"

Frost produced a squashed envelope containing a photo of the murdered man Ted Harper along with some photos of artifacts, including an ancient gold pendant, earrings, a wooden pipe and an ivory jar.

"I'll tell you," Frost said tersely. "I hope you have time to spare. This discussion will take a long while."

The story unfolded like a tale from the Arabian Nights in the tent at the ruins of the old stone temple. The air cooled and turned blue with the light of the rising stars. Wisps of sand skirted along the edges of the tent like tiny, whirling spirits. The air in the tent was rich with the strong fragrance of Arabic coffee and fresh dates.

Sullivan brewed date wine. It was an ancient Egyptian recipe he had learned from his research and perfected with practice. He added wild honey to it. He offered it to everyone with dinner, which consisted of gazelle meat cooked in spiced kebabs and various Arabic side dishes. The men gladly stuffed themselves; all of them relished the strong alcohol except Frost, who declined the liquor. The Major usually avoided alcohol, with rare exceptions.

Eve astonished everyone by savagely eating gazelle meat. At first, she hesitated to accept it—then noticed Frost studying her with his careful blue eyes. Eve realized the hardboiled soldier would judge her toughness depending on whether she took the food. She took it just to defy him, and the results amazed her. She actually liked the meat and wanted more.

Frost regarded her afterwards with approval. Eve was surprised to see him smiling at her. She was no less astonished when he courteously poured her a refill of drink and served her more food. Sullivan joked about the rough Major's sudden etiquette. Frost, with his rascally humor, took it in stride.

Sullivan kept his family in a nearby tent. He didn't want them hearing anything about a confidential British Army investigation. He went back and forth a few times, then reclined with the others and discussed dark matters in hushed tones long into the night.

The spirited Irishman maintained good relationships with several Bedouin tribes. These nomadic tribesmen noticed almost everything in their remote desert territories. They described things to Sullivan.

Sullivan had received information from the Bedouins months ago about an English soldier in the desert desperately trying to exchange stolen antiques for a camel. He had been walking for days in the wilderness. The Bedouins were surprised he had made it so far, but the man was unnaturally tough. He was familiar with the desert and its ways. He seemed to be fleeing something. He insisted that he needed to get to Cairo in a hurry.

The Bedouins recognized the objects as tomb plunder. They refused to buy. They did not describe this English soldier; many Englishmen looked the same to them. They did say he wore a brown kerchief on his head and mixed Arab desert garb with his uniform; that surprised them. The Bedouins described the objects in detail to Sullivan—an old necklace, orange stone earrings shaped like sunbeams, a carved jar, and a tarnished metal cylinder with lions on it, among other things.

Sullivan kept in touch with the British Army Investigative Corps occasionally due to his friendship with Major Frost. The Irishman morally objected to tomb robbing; he viewed it as a blight on humanity and an affront to ancient Egyptian civilization. The fact that British soldiers were involved in plundering land entrusted to them to defend was an outrage. He reported the incident.

Nobody, however, had noticed the report. It had been forwarded to some of Major Frost's colleagues who dismissed it as unimportant. It sat buried under pile of papers at a military office in Cairo—until Major Frost took over the Ted Harper case and ordered that recent report files be meticulously examined. A staff investigator noticed it and flagged it for Frost's review.

The stolen antiquities identically matched those described in an article Eve Weathers wrote about Harper. Harper's real name was supposedly Oliver Bryon—he was a member of Commando Group Sphinx, trained by the Army for desert missions behind enemy lines. He carried an antique flint knife with him that was obviously rare. He was in possession of valuable antiquities likely stolen by tomb raiders. Harper recently worked in Cairo as a "part-time art restorer" for the Nile Delta Antiquities Museum. He held that job using an assumed name and apparently without military oversight.

While in Cairo, Harper tried to advertise his stolen goods for sale by displaying self-made flyers at the museum—an act unauthorized by his employers, who were unaware of his doings. His scheme was interrupted when Eve stumbled across him and mistook him for an honest person perfect for a very public newspaper story. Harper was too afraid to arouse suspicion by declining the interview. Instead he lied and obfuscated facts to Eve to prevent her from writing an accurate article. And then...

Then he quite simply died. A gunshot blasted him off the face of the earth at a belly-dancing performance. His antique dagger had gored him in some sort of twisted stroke of justice. Or was it really justice?

Sullivan informed Major Frost that tomb robbing was on the rise in the Western Desert. He constantly heard strange and gruesome stories from his Bedouin acquaintances. Strange men roved the desert, armed for war, hunting the dead instead of the living. Tombs were broken and plundered. The earth was torn up and scarred by violent explosives and wild digging. The greed of these robbers turned them into murderers. Bodies of soldiers of various fighting armies—British, German, Italian— were scattered in the desert and stripped of all belongings. Various armies falsely assumed that Arabs were responsible. This resulted in military squads seeking unjust vengeance on the Bedouins and forcing them to flee their lands.

Grave robbers had long preyed upon entombed wealth in the Land of the Pharaohs, but the advent of modern international warfare in Egypt brought their return on a rampant scale. It was an epidemic, according to Sullivan. The tomb robbers themselves remained shrouded in darkness and mystery. Who were they? Where were they coming from? Were they on a particular side of the war? Nobody knew.

The dagger carried by Harper was still missing. Sullivan said the weapon was a rare piece. He estimated that a greedy soldier had stolen it from Army custody to sell it. However, the dagger's ominous spirituality was a matter of concern to him.

"You said two people connected to the dagger have died so far—to your knowledge," Sullivan asked. "What exactly was the nature of their association with it?" He was strangely somber. "Did they own it—or attempt to use it?"

"They merely handled it, as far as I know," Frost replied, looking very raffish as he reclined sloppily on a pile of cushions next to Eve. "Harper was obviously wearing it when it backfired. But I can't imagine Major Hathaway doing that." He shot a sideways glance at Eve and smirked irreverently. "He'd have looked a sight, cutting about with a scimitar on him. Rather ridiculous. He'd have known it, too."

The young woman broke into a grin.

It was contagious. Frost flashed a sharp smile and ribbed further. "Anyway, the poor old warhorse was felled by a heart attack en route to Palestine, not by a dagger," he remarked. "I very much doubt if the dagger had anything to do with it. Unless he suddenly became terrified of its ominous memory." He glanced roguishly at Eve. "More likely he was terrified of Palestine. It's not a nice place to transfer. A lot of soldiers in his position would've had heart attacks, too."

She stifled a giggle. He broke into a laugh, pleased with himself.

"You said people at Army headquarters are talking seriously about the possibility of a curse on that dagger," Sullivan said, objecting to the levity.

"Yes. They'd talk about anything," rejoined Frost flippantly. "You could probably convince them that a bucket was cursed if you tried hard enough..."

Eve laughed loudly at that one. Frost was surprised by her boisterous reaction. He grinned and became more animated.

Sullivan sighed in exasperation. He was trying to have a serious discussion about important spiritual matters, but his listeners were chattering like frisky chipmunks. "Listen up, the pair of you!" he said, snapping at Frost and Eve. "It sometimes happens that Egyptian artifacts have effects on people that don't seem to be directly related. Just because you can't see something doesn't mean it's not there. It sounds like this dagger is a very poisonous specimen. My advice is, if you do come across it, don't touch it. Do you understand? Hands off!"

Frost looked rebelliously up at him from the cushions. "If there really are 'will-o-the-wisps' amid the ruins, how do you manage, then?" he demanded with dry sarcasm. "Do you have some sort of 'shield' that keeps it all away, or—"

"Yes, actually." Sullivan pulled out a medal on a strand around his neck and showed it to them. It was a silver pendant with an image of St. Patrick's staff and several Irish religious symbols on it. "Best sorcerer bane, ever," he quipped as he put it away. "I got no reason to worry. But as for you people..." He sighed and shook his head reproachfully at them. "I'll do more research about the thing. In the meantime, keep well away from it."

Major Frost was annoyed by the end of the evening. His investigation brought him to the very edge of proving at least one Sphinx commando was a desert smuggler. But that man was dead. The trail to the other thieves—if there were actually any—was lost. He was unsure what to do next.

CHAPTER 6: ESMERALDA

"Huntress, beautiful one, whose victim I am—
limping, a willing target for your arrows.
I follow obediently my beloved,
Who owns my soul."

    —"Layla and Majnun" by Nizami Ganjavi

The discussion ended on a lighthearted note when Sullivan changed the subject to the history of brewed date wine. The Australians showed great interest. Chatter filled the tent. Major Frost had no interest in frivolity. He was preoccupied with weighty matters. He exited the tent by slipping out a back flap facing the ruins of the temple.

Eve watched him disappear. She had been unable to tear her eyes off him all evening. She was interested in Frost. She did not understand the reason. Maybe because he was sharp-minded and made her laugh with his sarcasm. Or maybe because she admired his toughness. She esteemed capable fighters. She had come to respect Frost and was curious about him.

Nevertheless she was intimidated by the man's sharp change in attitude towards her. He practically glowed whenever he looked at her. She didn't understand it. If she hadn't known better, she'd have thought the Major was strongly attracted to her.

But Eve was convinced she did know better. Frost was a self-professed loner. Proudly career-focused, he had sworn off "foolish" relationships. Any romantic interest from him was impossible—a breach against untold laws like astronomy or physics.

Yet natural laws seemed turned upside down since they had embarked into the untamed seas of the desert. She, too, had experienced a strange reversal of fate. She now liked and respected the man she had sworn was her personal enemy. How had this happened?

A few tortured minutes later, she took the risk of following him. She wanted to speak to him again. The Major was a decent guy, she thought. Cold, clear-headed, professional.

Clever. Funny. Older and wiser. He had interesting things to say, and she had questions. Talking with him was always a pleasant experience. Eve hesitated. But what if there was something more than casual friendship behind the Major's sparkling stare? She wasn't ready to face that possibility—it was too mind-boggling. Was being alone with him really a good idea? Of course it's fine, she thought, chastising herself for imagining ridiculous things. Frost was a military monk, and she was a hermit writer; that's the way the world made them, and it was impossible for either of them to deviate from their predestined planetary courses. There was no reason to avoid speaking with Frosty.

The young woman stumbled in search of him and was glad. Oddly enough, she wanted to be around Frosty. The world was strangely dimmer when he was out of her sight.

She blundered outside and found him quickly. He was pacing at the base of the ruined cat temple. Hands in his pockets, shuffling, fidgeting, staring into the great dark beyond as if trying to chart the stars. He was always alert and constantly restless. Spools of blue sand whirled past his boots in the moonlight. It was bright outside—almost as bright as daytime, only the light was clear, pale silver. The moon was a huge white disc in the limitless sky. The night's mirror of the sun. The desert ancients had worshiped it for its illuminating splendor.

Frost turned sharply and saw her. His expression brightened instantly. He looked glad to see her.

"Wow. This looks magnificent!" Eve remarked, gazing at the ruined temple. Its limestone vaults, pillars and hieroglyph-carved roofs looked fantastic in the brilliant moonlight. "I've never seen anything like this before."

He was surprised. "Never seen what?" he interrogated, glancing around. "A ruin?"

"Not like this one," she admitted. She felt embarrassed. For all her panache, Eve spent a lot of time running late to various city appointments and hunkered over a messy typewriter. "I don't get out of Cairo much..."

He smiled, animated by a sudden frisk of energy. "Well, come on then!" he beckoned her. "Let's see it!"

"What?"

"You want to explore an old ruin and you've got one right

here staring at you. No reason why you shouldn't have a look at it now," he exclaimed. "I'll come with you."

Eve approached him and was encouraged by his lively enthusiasm. But perhaps he was only offering to accompany her out of courtesy; she was reluctant to inconvenience him. "But you've been here before, haven't you?"

"Yes, but that's no reason why I shouldn't see things again if I want to," retorted the Major. "The world doesn't always look the same, you know."

The remark silenced her. Moments later, she was on the brink of entering a wild silver-blue wonderland of ancient pillars and scarab-winged arches. The ground was uneven. The temple base was higher than earth level. Frost scaled it in a few nimble steps and offered her a hand up.

She hesitated. The energetic young woman was used to taking care of herself and disdaining help from others. She had half a mind to tackle the jagged wall head-on, but the climb looked somewhat difficult.

"Take my hand," urged Frost, flapping his arm impatiently. "Come on! I won't bite you."

She accepted his grip. He pulled her up in a very brisk, businesslike fashion. The strength of his arm surprised her; the Major looked slender but was evidently made of iron. He hoisted her over the wall in seconds without trouble.

An awkward moment came afterwards. Frost did not immediately release her hand. They stood on top of the wall facing each other. He relaxed his grip, yet his hand stayed frozen around hers. Eve was startled by this. His touch became surprisingly gentle—soft, even. Then he dropped her hand. He looked intently at her as if he wanted to say something. Eve became bewildered. She didn't know what it was about, but this behavior didn't make sense to her. She thanked him for his help and walked off among the pillars.

Frost spryly kept up with her. He was very cheerful and courteous. He helped her ascend broken steps and bypass toppled walls with poise and gallantry. He also pointed out hazards to avoid such as potential snake dens.

This led them to have a stimulating discussion about how to kill cobras—a fierce and gory topic they greatly enjoyed. On an artistic note, Frost showed her a few temple carvings he found worthy of speculation.

Eventually, they came to a lone standing wall. Traces of blue, red, and white paint were still barely visible on its surface in the unearthly glow. The wall showed several scenes from an ancient Egyptian marriage ceremony. The Temple of Bast-Sekhmet was, after all, partially dedicated to the values of love and domestic happiness.

Eve didn't pay much attention to the mural; it seemed odd-looking to her. Instead she considered the man's sharp profile in the moonlight. She had not paid much attention to his appearance until now. She eyed his features and found them attractive. She thought he wasn't bad-looking.

Frost stared at the wall paintings and fidgeted restlessly. "I guess it's about love," he remarked, nodding at the wall. "I don't know much about ancient Egypt, but I suppose love occupied a lot of people's minds, too, back then. I suppose all people focus on it at some point or another. The Greeks invaded Troy because of it, Shakespeare wrote sonnets, and the Egyptians... drew pictures, it seems."

Typical flippant comment. Typical of Frost. He cracked an irreverent smile and so did she. But underneath the surface, he didn't feel like joking.

"It's a beautiful thing—love," he said. Some invisible screen behind his eyes broke and he looked down. "At least it ought to be. Those of us who've attempted it know it does not always exist where we want it to," he added somberly, staring at the empty sand. The atmosphere clouded with gloom. He broke it with a ray of hope. "One's heart can break. Yet even that doesn't stop us from wanting to love again."

Eve became suddenly aware that Frost was staring deliberately at her.

As a journalist, she was slightly desensitized to other people's feelings after having lived in Germany. She got used to dealing with a rigid mix of hard facts and abstract ideas. She could be literal to a fault or theoretical to an extreme. Sometimes complex logic outweighed common sense. Hints bypassed her. Now, for example, she was oblivious to the notion that Major Frost was thinking about her when he spoke of love. The idea sneaked across her mind, briefly—but drowned in her brain as nonsense. She guessed Frost was talking philosophy—using his personal experiences to make theories. Rhetoric.

She could not have been more wrong.

Frost steadied his resolve. He felt sick with love. The affliction had been steadily coming over him ever since he first met her. He surrendered to it after they left civilization behind and got lost in each other's company in the desert. He was smitten with Eve. He hadn't expected it to happen, but he wasn't trying to fight it. Eve was the embodiment of everything he admired, and it was impossible for him not to be in love with her. His heart melted whenever he saw her. Passions of admiration and desire were consuming him, driving him out of his mind. Eve had a grip on him—she moved his very soul. He made up his mind Eve was the one for him. He wanted her.

The question was how to achieve this. There were so many obstacles in the way—not the least of which was her naiveté, which alternately charmed and frustrated him. He was going to have to say something, at some point. He would have to bare his emotions somehow. It wasn't easy for the British officer. He was wounded by the very idea of rejection. He had been rejected several times in his youth, but those humiliations were nothing compared to the shattering heartbreak he would sustain if Eve turned him away. In any case, the Major had no Plan B. His mind was made up.

Now seemed like a good opportunity to say something. She was no good with hints and neither was he. They were like-minded in everything. What was needed, then, was a clear, forceful statement...

"I heard that you got the Military Cross for valor in France," said Eve suddenly. "Is that true?"

He was derailed from his purpose by shock and indignation. "Who told you that?" he demanded, startled by the question. "Has someone been...*gossiping*?" He imagined his two Australian subordinates whispering behind his back and was morally outraged. Oddly, though, neither they nor Eve had been much out of his masterful sight during the journey. Frost was puzzled by that. "Exactly when did any of you have *time* to gossip?"

"I wasn't gossiping!" snapped Eve, offended by the accusation. "I heard someone mention it when I was staying at the facility in Giza."

He felt chastised. "Oh."

His secretive reaction surprised her. Eve expected him to

be ready to boast or show off—most men would have. Instead Frost seemed strangely self-conscious.

"I just asked because I was curious. You know things about me, but I don't know very much about you," Eve explained. "If you don't want to talk about it—"

He jumped at the chance for some level of intimacy. "I did win it. The Military Cross," he disclosed tersely. "I was shot while defending France from the German invasion two years ago. It should have been a fatal wound. But I survived." He steadied his nerves and made a confession of weakness. "I was hurt badly and it was...a frightening experience."

She was surprised by his candor.

"But it didn't stop me from getting right back into the fray afterwards," he was quick to add, reasserting his strength. "As you can see, I'm quite well. Never better!"

"And afterwards you joined Army Intelligence?"

"It's the Army Investigative Corps. It's different from Intelligence, although our departments cooperate. Intelligence focuses on gathering information from the enemy; we focus on making sense of complicated information in our own backyard. I'm with the CIG—Counter-Insurgency subunit. But yes, I did transfer jobs after my escapade in France," he admitted. "I had done a bit of work previously as a military analyst. I was brought up in a rifle regiment, and as you know, I enjoy fighting. But I wanted to put my skills to better use."

He smiled again. His mood brightened up whenever he looked into her eyes. "Anyway, there's not much to know about me. I'm not an interesting person. I'm very ordinary. I work—and that's it," he declared with wry humor and pride. "I don't go to casinos or nightclubs or soirees. I hate parties. I don't dance the jitterbug or play the guitar—"

She laughed.

He flashed a crooked grin. "I'm just a soldier, that's all," he said, shuffling in the sand with his hands in his pockets. "What you see is what you get."

"Well, I think it's very impressive that you earned the Military Cross," said Eve with quiet sincerity. "That's a great achievement. You're a very brave man."

He was overcome by happiness to hear she esteemed him as brave. It was one of the greatest compliments he had ever received.

"Well, I'm impressed by your battles, too—like your struggle to do war reporting," he said, quick to return her approbations. Perceiving an opportunity to speak his mind, he ventured further. "You're a remarkable person. You've lived quite a full life, for someone so young—"

The words irked her. So many times people drew attention to her age. She was always too old or too young according to someone's estimation. It irritated her. "Please don't say things like that," Eve interrupted. "I believe a person is as young as they feel. And I don't feel very young at all."

"I didn't mean it to sound diminishing," protested Frost, regarding her warmly. "I was only trying to say that I...I hold you in high regard."

Eve felt flustered. "Well, that's a very nice compliment. I think you overestimate me. Anyway, it's a kind thought," she acknowledged. "Thank you..."

"I'm not being kind!" he argued, vexed. "I'm being honest. There's a difference."

She smiled and decided to evacuate the vicinity out of sheer awkwardness. "I think I'd better find my room now," she said, drifting away.

"So soon?" He seemed disappointed. "All right. I'll take you there. You don't know where the building is..."

He escorted Eve to the Army outpost on the outskirts of the oasis. It was very small outpost, jam-packed with military transport trucks. There were barely three dirty rooms left available for traveling soldiers to stay in; he obtained a key for one of them and gave it to Eve outside the building. Men wandered around restlessly. The half-lit ruins of the old cat temple loomed nearby like a ghostly castle.

"Well, there it is!" said Frost, nodding towards the barracks. He shuffled his boots in the sand and looked wistfully at her. "Sorry I can't do any better." He hesitated with unusual indecision. "Unless you'd like to stay with Sullivan," he suggested reluctantly. "You'd probably be more comfortable. But I'd rather you stay here." He fidgeted with his hands in his pockets. "This place is more secure, you know—"

Eve was surprised by his empathy. "It's fine. Thanks."

He stared intensely at her. A heavy silence fell.

"I guess I'll see you tomorrow," said Eve in an attempt to bid him *adieu*. She thanked him for his impromptu tour and an overall pleasant evening. "I'm going in now. Good night."

Frost reacted with dismay. "Wait just a moment," he insisted. "Just hear me out. This may seem hypocritical, but I believe...I owe you an apology," he said with sincerity and shame. "It's become very clear to me over these past few hours that your presence at the nightclub was a mere coincidence. I know now that you were not involved in the shooting. I ask for your pardon if I behaved unnecessarily harsh towards you."

The woman blinked in astonishment. Witnessing the Major apologize was like witnessing a lunar eclipse. "You don't have to apologize. You were just doing your job," she said sincerely. "You've been very professional. I appreciate that."

Frost was somewhat heartened by her encouraging words. However, her verbiage seemed cold and dispassionate. This lack of warmth dampened his spirits.

He was very attracted to the woman in a profound way. He admired everything about her character. She was also beautiful. As a result, he had developed deep feelings of affection for her—very strong feelings in a very short time because he was a decisive person.

However, he was aware Eve had a history of disliking him. At least, she had seemed to in the beginning. He wasn't sure how she felt now. She seemed to enjoy talking to him, yet she remained distant. Why? He didn't understand. Maybe it was because of his behavior earlier. He was trying to overcome any remaining resentment.

"Good night," said Eve again, after another minute of mutual nervousness and staring.

Frost endeavored to save the conversation. "You don't have to turn in now, if you don't want to. It's perfectly safe out here," he suggested. "There's a canteen nearby." He waved his arm in the general direction. "I'd go with you, if you wanted. I could... buy you a drink, if you like."

"No, thanks. I'm tired," declined Eve, unsure why he was suddenly so sociable. "I want to get some rest."

His eyes fell. He fidgeted again—spurned. He masked his crestfallen feelings with blasé cheer. "Ah yes. Of course," he acknowledged, trying to smile. "Well..."

"Good night," said Eve courteously for the third time.

The phrase fell heavily like the knoll of a bell. Frost glanced down, then took one last look at her before conceding to a withdrawal. It was a burning stare, very deliberate and brimming with a storm of hidden emotions. Eve saw it—it pierced her soul and made her freeze breathlessly for a second before she was overwhelmed with confusion and ran off.

Frost watched her leave and felt tormented. He wasn't sure if he was being overlooked, postponed or rejected. The situation burdened him. He decided to get drunk.

He went foraging for liquor in the Army canteen. He invited his men, Nye and Wilmore, to join him. They accompanied like loyal hounds ready for play. They wanted in on the fun.

Frost rarely broke from his self-disciplined lifestyle, but there were exceptions. Occasionally, he engaged in random acts of deliberate self-indulgence. He was a spirited man and could be rowdy. Once his inhibitions were gone, he became 10 times rowdier.

He found a case of white wine in the canteen storage room. Bottles fresh from Cairo. It was one of several such cases en route to troops fighting in the Western Desert, along with other foodstuffs. Frost and his men pooled some money together to pay for the case, then ripped into it like ravenous animals and started drinking. While they were doing this, they ran into some other soldiers—mostly military engineers and transport truck drivers—sojourning in the oasis as they traveled along various routes. Something like a party started.

Eve was awake in her room when she heard trouble coming her way. It was a dingy, miserable chamber. The bed was an iron military cot covered in a hanging mosquito net. A dim bronze lantern dripped from the ceiling. A dusty Arabic carpet was on the floor. Leftover trash and random objects from men who stayed there before littered the room, including some indecent picture postcards and a dirty Army hairbrush.

She wore a loose, knee-length cotton tunic with embroidery that Sullivan had given her as a courtesy. It came with a pair of ballooning Arabic trousers; the outfit was supposed to be for desert travel. Instead Eve used the tunic in lieu of a nightdress. It was cold—all heat evaporated from the desert at night, giving it a winter chill. No blanket had been provided for her.

She sat on the cot and sighed. She wondered what would happen next.

Soon she heard mayhem unfold. It came from somewhere outside the window. She heard Major Frost. He was shouting at the top of his voice and roaring with drunken laughter. Some kind of fight broke out. Men yelled. There was scuffling. Blows. More guffaws. Something broke with a loud crash. A motor roared and faded. More bellowing. Then his voice again—hysterical giggling, like a delirious teenage boy. This was accompanied by a chorus of raucous male laughter. An object struck the window with a dull thud and cracked the glass. She withdrew anxiously behind the mosquito net. She mistrusted the soldiers. The only one she trusted—in a strange way—was Frost, who seemed now to have gone crazy. There was mumbling outside.

Silence fell afterwards. It lasted a long time.

She reclined on the torturous cot and had just convinced herself she was comfortable when suddenly her bedroom door flew open with a thunderous crash and banged quickly shut. She shot up in bed.

There stood Frost. He drank her in with his eyes. His light blue gaze was clouded with rebellious intoxication. After several hardy doses of strong wine, he felt ready to burn down the Great Pyramid of Giza. His uniform was rumpled and dusty. His beret was crooked on his head; it had fallen off, and being drunk he put it back on sloppily. He sported a bleeding bruise on his fist—he'd been brawling. He stared at her with desire.

She extracted herself from the mosquito net and sat upright. "What are you doing here?"

Frost leered. He swung across the room and plopped down next to her on the iron mattress, which jolted beneath their weight. He looked at her with mischief. "Come on," he said, tugging at her makeshift nightdress. "Let's have it."

Eve was struck dumb with shock. "Frosty, what on earth—"

"That scandalous dance of yours. I have decided that I want to see it. Do it!" ordered Frost, blunt and matter-of-fact even in his drunkenness. "The whole thing. Top to bottom." He made a twirling motion with his fingers and indicated that she should undress. "Go on! Show me what the fuss is about."

She looked incredulously at him.

"What's wrong? No veils? Here's one!" He tore the mosquito

net from the ceiling in one clean, ferocious swipe. An explosion of plaster rained upon their heads. A metal hook fell skittering across the floor. Eve screamed and jumped off the cot. Frost thought it was hilarious and laughed hysterically.

"Dance for me, Esmeralda!" he shouted, and threw the net on her. He watched her struggle to pull it off and giggled even harder.

Eve threw the net on the floor. She was irritated and flustered. She saw the impish grin on his face and laughed with him. She covered her eyes in embarrassment.

He was excited that his unruly antics amused her. "Come here."

She noted his intense stare and realized its meaning. There was no escaping it now. She had prejudged the military officer as an emotionless loner. Evidently she had been wrong.

All those sparkling looks, compliments, and stealthy attempts at hand-touching suddenly made sense. Obvious, in the end. Eve felt like an idiot. She had failed to see the proverbial forest in front of her by abstracting every tree. Now the truth was staring her in the face, wearing a disheveled khaki uniform and a look of dreamy attraction on his face.

"What's the matter?" coaxed Frost impatiently. "Afraid of me?"

Eve hesitated. "A little."

She liked Frosty, yet had mixed thoughts. She didn't understand how she had unwittingly won his affections. Like him or not, she had no intention of tumbling into bed with him at a moment's notice—it seemed like that was what he expected.

Frost expected nothing one way or another. He was annoyed at Eve and grappling with a storm of pent-up love—the kind of love that could devastate a person's heart or delight them past the brink of immortality. He hoped to make it obvious, but she still didn't get it. For a fleeting moment, he wished she would alleviate his torment with a hug or a kiss. No such affections were forthcoming. Desperation made him more rambunctious.

He hurled his beret onto the floor and flopped flat on the bed, reclining on her pillow.

"What are you doing? Cut it out!" Eve protested loudly. "You cannot stay in here. Frosty, I don't know what's gotten into you. But please..." She marched over. "You need to leave. Now."

He relaxed rebelliously on the squeaky cot. "Chuck me out, then."

"I will!" she menaced, completely annoyed. "If you do not get out of here right now, I will physically drag you out!"

He closed his eyes and stifled a dangerous smile. "Very well," he sighed. "Have at it."

She was frustrated by his disobedience. She didn't particularly want to drag the British soldier from her room. Instead she hoped he would surrender to threats. "Get up. Now. Otherwise I will use force!"

Frost gave a permissive wave of his arm. "Bombs away!"

She glanced back and forth, wrung her hands, hesitated, then stepped forward with a determined glare. "Don't say I didn't warn you."

She leaned over the cot, grabbed Frost by both arms and attempted to drag him off. To her great fright, Frost's arms grabbed back. She shrieked as he reeled her into a clumsy embrace. She toppled over and landed in the cot with him. He laughed wildly. "Is that the best you can do?" he jeered. "Really? This is supposed to be 'force?'"

She twisted his arm. "I'm being merciful because you're drunk!"

Frost resisted her attempts to wrangle him. "Show no mercy!" he gibed. "Do your worst!"

It started off as a halfway earnest wrestling match, then quickly turned into frivolous horseplay. They both laughed. He tousled her hair. Eve struck him with the pillow. Frost, a rugby player, rolled on top of her. A heavy silence fell. Frost, transfixed with admiration, started stroking her face and gazing into her eyes. He glowed at her.

"May I kiss you?"

It seemed like a superfluous question, and Eve was surprised he asked it. She made no attempt to get away. Despite her qualms, she liked Major Frost.

He stared deeply into her eyes with fervent affection. Then he concentrated on her for a moment and kissed her mouth softly.

She had no will to resist. More than anything, she was confused.

She expected him to be forceful. He had a slim yet muscular build. He was naturally strong and rough. However, Frost had different intentions. He wanted to win Eve's heart. He hoped to achieve that by being gentle and seductive. He kissed her again. Not once, but more than a few times, stroking her face softly and pulling her tightly against his shoulders. However, the hardboiled military officer had lived in isolation and lack of intimacy for a long time. He was nervous, which caused his movements to be slightly awkward.

Eve didn't stop him. Neither did she return his affections immediately. Her heart pounded. She liked him. She enjoyed his kisses and embraces. Yet, she was mystified by his gentleness. Why was this icy and domineering man showering her with such tenderness? After a few seconds, she kissed him back. That pleased Frost. But only for a moment.

He was crestfallen that she did not return his passion in full measure. "What's the matter?" he guessed, his eyes misting. "You hate me, don't you? Please don't hate me."

"That's not true," she refuted. "I like you."

He lost his breath at the words. Feverish adoration engulfed him again. "Good. I was worried you didn't."

She stared into his face. His pale blue eyes burned with devotion. She recognized he was not acting out of mere lust. He was behaving too romantically; his eyes melted when they met hers, and his touches glowed with ardor. Evidently he had strong feelings for her.

"I think you're wonderful! Extraordinary. Perfect," swore Frost ardently, touching her face. "I love you, Eve," he said, losing his last inhibition. "I am completely in love with you."

This declaration stunned her. Especially because she knew he was sincere. Eve felt intense affection emanating from him. It wasn't just a fleeting crave or a drunken binge. He truly felt what he said. His confession was a turning point in their lives. Their relationship would never be the same. What it would become had yet to be determined.

Frost stared at her as if expecting a rebuff. "You don't mind?"

Another strange and ridiculously polite question. So very British. She found it endearing and smiled. "Of course, I don't mind..."

Frost squeezed her tightly in his arms. He was delighted that she was willing to accept his feelings. He closed his eyes and buried his face against her neck.

"Why?" she breathed in confusion. "All the sudden?"

"You're strong. The strongest woman I've ever seen," he said. "I told myself I didn't need any girl, anymore," he muttered. "Too complicated. Pressure. Pain. Better to just forget it. And I did—until you came along. I want you to belong to me," he declared. "You must be mine."

She smiled faintly. This commanding behavior was characteristic of him. "I only hope you remember all this in the morning."

The mention of morning jarred him into a panic. "Don't send me away!" he pleaded, mumbling in her ear. "I want to stay here. With you. I promise I won't try anything improper," he insisted. "Let me stay. Please."

Eve smirked at the word "improper." It sounded so typically British—so typically Frost. She didn't have the heart to protest his presence in the room anymore. She wanted him to stay.

He threw his arm across her and drifted off in a state of glowing, affectionate happiness. Eve studied him. He was a tired soul. He spent all his energy on his career, which he clearly loved. However, his single-minded focus on his job was not completely rewarding. Obviously, he had wounds behind his hard edges.

They both went to sleep together. Eve felt at peace with him beside her. It was the same for Frost. He wouldn't let go of her.

Judgment day came the next morning. Frost was dreaming about her. It was a sensual dream. He dreamed they were in bed together and he was touching her body. In contrast to all his previous dreams about Eve, this time Frost could actually feel Eve's physical form—as if she were truly there. His subconscious mind was pleased. This was certainly an improvement! No harm done, it was only a dream after all.

Frost, always energized in the morning, felt very amorous. It was time to show the phantom Eve what he was made of. He made a rough effort to straddle her. To his complete shock, the heavenly apparition shouted loudly. Something hit him like a punch to the stomach.

"All right, get out!" her voice clamored. "You broke the truce. Out!"

He came to and panicked. He found himself crammed in a cot next to her, tangled up in her arms and legs. She was wearing a tunic that looked like a nightgown; it was rumpled and pulled up above her knees, exposing her bare thighs. His uniform was a wrinkled mess. A broken mosquito net was flung nearby. Chips of plaster on the floor indicated the net had been forcefully ripped out of the ceiling. His beret peeked at him from the floor in silent mockery.

He noticed his abdomen was sore. Eve had struck him with a sharp blow of her knee, apparently in self-defense.

The British officer went limp and stared at the ceiling in embarrassed horror. He shut his eyes and prayed aloud. "Dear God!"

Eve peered at him and realized he was confused. She shook him by the shoulder. "Hey, Frosty," she said. "What's going on? Are you even awake?"

Frost, flushing with embarrassment, forced himself to open his eyes again. He clearly remembered confessing his love to her last night. However, the rest of the evening was a blur. It seemed he made some physical progress with her afterwards. Or had he? Her angry knee-strike to his stomach was not a good sign.

She looked at him affectionately, waiting for him to speak.

"Listen. I recall our conversation last night. But I can't remember what I did afterwards," he said, flushing red in the face with self-consciousness and struggling to regain his composure. "I sincerely hope I...didn't do anything you disapproved of," he said stiffly. "If so, I apologize. It wasn't my intention to offend you."

She laughed. "Great speech! Do you say that to every woman?"

He was mortified by the accusation. "No, certainly not!" he protested in dismay. "I've never said it to anybody!"

"Who is Esmeralda?"

"Who?" he exclaimed. He experienced an incoherent flashback. He remembered a mosquito net flying through the air. His face flushed. "Oh, heavens..."

She giggled harder.

Frost was humiliated. "I was talking about a character in a novel. By Victor Hugo." He fidgeted and looked at the floor, uncomfortable. "It was the girl in the 'The Hunchback of Notre Dame.' Esmeralda. The gypsy dancer." He tried to seem composed. His tan face was tinged red. "I intended to be a nuisance. But I really don't know what I was thinking..."

Eve squealed with mischievous laughter.

It didn't seem funny to Frost. He was unsure if Eve was mocking him. It was a destroying thought. He scrambled to evacuate the room in shame.

She saw his wounded expression and stopped him. "Do you remember what you told me last night?" she asked, grabbing his arm gently. "You said a lot of wonderful things. You said you're in love with me."

He sat on the edge of the cot and looked away awkwardly. "Yes. I remember that," he replied, glancing shyly at her. "I may have been drinking, but that's why. Because I wanted to tell you...and I wasn't sure if...." He let the sentence die. "Anyway, I did tell you. I truly mean it."

"Good," answered Eve. "Me, too."

She astonished the Major by leaning over and giving him a strong kiss on the mouth. Frost stared at her in glad surprise. The woman gazed back at him with brightness and warmth in her eyes. The British officer was completely disarmed. He melted into a boyish smile, then scrambled to organize himself. He made a trivial excuse and fled the scene.

A chorus of whooping Englishmen's voices assaulted him from all directions as he left her room.

"There he is! The man of the hour!"

"What was all that rumpus last night? I thought I heard a big 'crash and bang!'"

" 'Dance for me, Esmeralda!' " someone mimicked, hooting with delight. "Had a nice dance, did you, Major? Lucky sod!"

Frost grinned sheepishly at the other men and said nothing. His humiliation was only a trifle. His spirits soared and his heart was full of new confidence. Eve liked him. It was the best thing that had happened to him since he could remember, and he was ridiculously happy.

His happiness was dampened by Sergeant Wilmore, who dashed over with a desperate expression as Frost exited the building.

"Some news came in over the wireless from H.Q., sir," said Wilmore. "Something's happened. It's about tomb robbers."

CHAPTER 7: PHANTOMS

"A universe of space, infinite sands
Unbroken line to mark off cloudless blue...
The desert, mighty, void of hope, immense
Disturbed from tortured sleep by sounds of war."
—"Desert Warfare" from
"Poems from the Desert" by Signalman G. Harker

News was breaking across Army wires. It was still developing. Nobody was quite sure yet what was going on. However, it was very serious, and the truth seemed to be growing more sinister by the minute.

A man had been picked up in the desert to the west. A Lance-Corporal of the British Army. He had been located in a wide, wild stretch of volcanic bluffs and furiously hot sand dunes in the Saharan oblivion somewhere southwest of Alexandria. He was half-dead and surrounded by the remains of three jackals. The man was shot in the arm and thigh. He had been left to die outside a jackal lair. The soldier was sunburnt. He was beaten full of dark bruises. His wrists and knuckles had been violently broken. Despite these ordeals, he tenaciously survived. Through superhuman willpower or divine assistance, the soldier strangled all three jackals that attempted to devour him. He sustained injuries from these harrowing wrestling matches with the bloodthirsty beasts. He lost three fingers. One of his arms was bitten very badly—clean through to the bone. The gunshot wound to his leg nearly destroyed his thigh muscle and would likely leave him permanently crippled. His injuries were hopelessly infected.

The soldier was miraculously recovering despite his grave situation. He had been found by a Special Forces commando unit on its way back to Egypt from a mission behind German lines in Libya. Initially, the wounded soldier tried to fight his commando rescuers. He was under the impression they were trying to kill him.

The troopers treated his injuries, trussed him up in a blanket and dropped him off at a remote Army hospital. He received emergency aid. Then he was trucked to a backwater hole of a town called Tell el-Abir, located closer to Alexandria. The town was fully garrisoned and outfitted with better hospital facilities. He underwent surgery there. His name was Johnston.

British Army officials were keenly interested in Johnston's misfortune—it had all the earmarks of a war atrocity. The initial suspects were the usual ones—Germans or Bedouins. Grimacing Army Investigative Corps officers were ready to take statements from Johnston as soon as he recovered enough strength to describe what happened.

According to Johnston, the individuals who shot him, smashed his wrists and knuckles, beat him to a pulp and abandoned him to die outside a nest of jackals were not enemy soldiers or tribesmen—they were British marauders, driving in British Special Forces vehicles, under the command of a ruthless killer with a London accent who wore a Union Jack blazoned on his tan Royal Army jacket. Apparently, these raiders massacred all of Johnston's comrades, who had been isolated and lost during a sandstorm. The campsite was ransacked. The bodies were plundered, stripped nearly naked, and left to rot. This news caused shock and horror among the ranks. Army officials were thunderstruck and at a loss for an appropriate response.

The detail most worthy of attention was the fact that Johnston, the stouthearted victim of this monstrosity, overheard and memorized the robber captain's name: Ollie.

As yet, nobody could identify who this "Ollie" might be. The Commando Group Sphinx did not share information with nor answer to other Army departments due to the secret nature of their missions. Forcing their cooperation would be an administrative hassle. Meanwhile, murderers ran free.

Sergeant Wilmore, tuned in to the coded news broadcasts, picked up on this detail with alacrity. The Australian's memory was jogged.

The murdered man in Cairo was found carrying an ID disk marked with the symbol of a marching sphinx and an Army serial number.

This serial number identified a Sphinx commando named Oliver Bryon. The lead investigator at the time, Major Hathaway, assumed the murder victim was an undercover agent for Commando Group Sphinx. He assumed the identity disc proved the victim's identity. He assumed that Ted Harper and Oliver Bryon were the same person, and that Bryon was dead.

Wilmore had a terrible feeling that the late Major Hathaway had been wrong. Although it was possible that a stout English name like "Oliver" belonged to more than one Sphinx commando, it seemed unlikely.

It seemed more realistic that Oliver Bryon was still alive. That he was the murderous bandit captain called "Ollie" who had attacked Johnston's comrades and was using top-secret military privileges to slaughter and pillage. That the Sphinx commando ID disc found on the body indicated he had a role in the murder in Cairo.

One person could shed greater light on Oliver Bryon's identity—the mangled Lance-Corporal Johnston, his lone surviving victim and an eyewitness to his crimes. A few well-put questions to Johnston would finally reveal the truth of this hideous and shameful case staining the honor of the British Army.

And only one person could ask just the right questions and get needed results: Major Frost. Wilmore wasted no time in telling his commanding officer the details and urging him to go to Tell el-Abir to interview Johnston.

Frost snapped into action. He had no time to waste.

He barked orders at his soldiers, dashed back and forth and threw things into the jeep. The last person in their group to know where they were going was Eve. She had barely gotten dressed in her ill-matched blouse and military trousers when Frost invaded her bedroom again.

"I'm going west. There's been a new incident," he announced curtly. "You will stay here with Sullivan."

"What incident?" demanded the journalist. "What's happened?"

Frost was torn between love and efficiency. "I'll tell you that later," he said as an awkward compromise. "Whenever I do come back. I must drive to Tell el-Abir on the coast to interview a witness in hospital. It's a long way away, and I have no idea how long I am going to stay." He was very downhearted, but tried to seem in good spirits. "That's the Army for you. Nothing is predictable, but we get the job done."

Indignation seized her. "No, you won't!" she protested. "You're not just going to leave me here. I won't have it!"

"I am the one in charge of this operation. Not you," snapped Frost.

"Why are you doing this?" challenged Eve. "You must be trying to get rid of me because of last night. You're embarrassed and you don't want to show it in front of your men."

He was speechless with surprise. He looked away, feeling slightly wounded. "No. That's not true," he replied with affection. "There's nothing to be embarrassed of. I regret nothing. You shouldn't, either."

His sincerity surprised her.

"The fact is, I am required to go farther into the Western Desert. We will be much closer to the battlefront. Since you're well-informed about the war, I needn't tell you how fluid that battlefront is," he stated. "The desert is like the open sea, and Rommel's troops are like corsairs. They are sly ambushers and notorious for appearing in unexpected places." He paused. "Not to mention there are bandits—some of our own Special Forces navigators seem to be using their skills for dark purposes. Things will be much less safe."

Eve tried to interrupt him, but he spoke over her.

"The worst thing in the world that could happen to me would be to lose you in some senseless disaster," he said, his voice cracking suddenly with emotion.

"But—"

"If you stay here, at least I will know that you are safe. That will help me concentrate on doing my job," he said, matter-of-fact. "That is the whole reason why women should stay behind when men go to war."

"How can you say that? You sound just like all the others!" she accused in desperate disgust. Tears of sorrow threatened to overtake her. "I could understand this coming from a wimp like Milo, or my other editors, or any of those stupid saps in Cairo. But, you, Frosty...How could you treat me like I'm some kind of helpless idiot?"

"That's enough!" commanded Frost, annoyed and wishing to silence her outburst. "I know better than anybody that you're neither helpless nor an idiot. Otherwise I wouldn't like you."

Eve grabbed her few existing travel belongings and marched up to him. "I'm coming with you!" she announced, staring him resolutely in the eyes. "If you don't agree with it, try and throw me out of the jeep."

He broke into a mischievous smile. "That sounds like fun," he admitted wryly, despite his apprehensions. "But I don't think we have time for it this morning."

She kissed him and left the room.

Dr. Ben Sullivan had a pleasant morning with his wife Rita after a hard night's worth of scribbling in notebooks, scouring textbooks and scuffling through ancient scrolls. He was exhausted. Thankfully Rita had revived him. She spent the entire morning serving him herbal tea, sharing chocolates with him, and twirling his curly reddish-blond hair with enthusiasm. Rita cherished Sullivan and enjoyed pampering him. Sullivan loved Rita and enjoyed being her pet. Ready to face the day, he put on his tribal robes and head kerchief for another day of sunny archaeology research. He drifted out of his tent, just in time to see the Major's jeep careening past in a cloud of dust.

"Hey, you!" The Irishman panicked. He ran into the tent, ran out again carrying a large book in his hand, and hijacked a camel being led past by a Bedouin man. Sullivan snatched the reins from the Bedouin and scaled the animal in one fluid jump. "Sorry, I'll be right back!" he apologized to its bewildered owner. He wheeled the camel around and whacked it with the edge of his book. It bolted into a run and chased the jeep through the oasis.

"Sir," said Sergeant Wilmore after a few minutes of driving, "there's an Arab following us."

The occupants of the jeep turned around and saw a robed figure yelling something unintelligible, furiously spurring a camel and waving his arms angrily in the air. His performance could have fooled anybody into believing him to be a local tribesman. The giveaway was the large bound book he used instead of a camel rod.

"It's Sullivan," said Major Frost. He turned to the driver. "Stop!"

Wilmore hit the brakes sharply. Dirt and chalk pieces spit into the air. Everyone in the jeep rolled forward. Eve nearly banged her head on the seat in front of her, and Nye's

Australian slouch hat fell off.

Sullivan loped up to them, frowning indignantly. Further back down the road, a barefoot Bedouin man pelted towards them, clamoring for the return of his camel.

The Irishman leaned over the jeep door and lightly whacked Major Frost on top of the head with a sharp tap of the book. Frost jumped and tried to save his beret from being flattened.

"Where do you think you're going?" harangued Sullivan with typical impertinence. "I stayed up all night doing research about that dagger for you monkeys in uniforms! You're just going to disappear without even knowing what I found out?"

"I'm sorry, Ben. I would have liked to stay on, but I just heard this morning that I have to leave," replied Frost in his terse style.

"I found the answers to your questions," Sullivan continued obliviously. "It turns out that it is a dagger used for animal embalming. You know. Mummifying animals! That is the reason why it was made with such a strong handle. Sometimes they had to mummify big creatures, like hippopotami, for example, and the work wasn't so easy—"

"I can leave Lieutenant Nye here to be briefed by you and then rejoin me later," interrupted Frost. He turned to Nye and nodded. "Hear Sullivan out and meet me in Tell el-Abir in two days." The Australian obeyed and got out of the jeep.

Sullivan leaned cross-legged over the camel, peeking boyishly out from his kerchief like a jaunty Irish Aladdin. "May I ask what is the reason for this terrible hurry?"

"The usual thing. Army business," said Frost.

"Army business, my foot!" laughed Sullivan. "I know very well what you've been up to, you scoundrel," he said, pointing his robed arm accusingly at Frost. "Drinking, fighting, causing a ruckus! You were loud enough last night to wake up every mummy from here to the Suez Canal."

Frost smiled impishly and said nothing.

"It's all in this book. Not only did I find out what the knife was used for, but I think I've identified who may have owned it!" crowed Sullivan with zeal. "It's all in this book!" he said, and dropped the book unceremoniously into Frost's lap. "Read it when your head clears."

The Major looked at the book. It was a dusty, leather-bound thing with the title, *Notable Animal Embalmers of Ancient*

Egypt, embossed on it.

"I'll brief Lieutenant What's-his-Name well and fine, but you need to brush up on your literature to understand the dagger's evil history," continued Sullivan. "I'm sure it's haunted by a wicked phantom!"

Frost was sneering. He dismissed the talk as the ravings of a superstitious Irishman. "I assure you, I have no interest in ghosts or curses," he said with an air of finality. "Also, the dagger is no longer relevant."

The Irish scholar shook his finger at the Major. "Now listen here, Captain Blood—" He was cut short by a stupefying sight. He noticed Frost holding Eve's hand. "What's this? Do my eyes deceive me?" he wondered in astonishment. "I thought you were a righteous scorner of female company, Major. What did you do to him?" he asked the woman. "Did you bewitch him with potion?"

"Wouldn't you like to know," said Frost with a triumphant laugh, and kicked the back of the driver's seat. "Goodbye, Sullivan."

The jeep pealed off with a plume of dust.

Sullivan hopped down from the camel. He turned around and saw its barefoot Bedouin owner closing in on him. The Irishman promptly handed the reins to Lieutenant Nye and ran away.

In the jeep, Frost handed the book to Eve. He had no interest in myths or legends—he had other priorities in his investigation. She examined the book briefly, then set it down on the floor of the vehicle. She reached over and held Frost's hand again.

Frost, overcome with a romantic impulse, wrapped his arm around her shoulders and kissed her on the face. He held her tight as they glided past the enormous stone statue of the cat goddess, Bast-Sekhmet, and flew into the empty sea of the desert again. He held her in silent devotion for a few minutes. Eventually, he spoke. "This journey will be difficult," he said, "but I'm glad you came with me."

She leaned on his shoulder and felt the silent glow of his love. It was an unseen, yet tangible force. She did not understand how he could have such intense admiration and affection for her in such a short time.

She reached the conclusion that he was a decisive and

intellectual person with set values, who recognized her as his female ideal. He had studied her and read about her life in case files; she knew less about him. Yet she also felt admiration and attraction for him. She was willing to accept his heart.

Wilmore peered enviously through the rearview mirror at the pair. He was extremely jealous of Frost's luck with Eve. The Australian had been covertly interested in Eve since she first appeared in his midst. He was a self-important man who prided himself on his large physique. He believed himself to be God's gift to all women. Thinking himself naturally attractive to all females, he had tried, with so many clumsy jokes and show-off gestures, to garner Eve's attention.

But it hadn't worked. Instead, the woman gave herself to Frost—the most irritating commanding officer Wilmore had ever served under. Frost the arrogant. Frost the punctilious and the demanding. Frost the warlike—whose conceit, aggression and will to command rivaled Julius Caesar.

Another major sticking point was the fact that Frost won her without even trying. Eve ignored Wilmore's manly peacock swaggers, but she threw herself feverishly into Frost's undeserving arms when he invaded her bedroom. At least that was how Wilmore imagined it. Everyone in the barracks had heard the shouting and revelry coming from that room; the crash, the laughter, the huge jolting squeaks on the bed. Then Frost emerged the next morning with a sparkle in his eyes. It was infuriating.

Wilmore took special umbrage at it because he believed Eve's attraction to his commander was unjustified. Frost was older, thinner, and shorter than Wilmore. In the zoo of life, Eve was a glorious flamingo who had chosen a graying cheetah over a nubile rhinoceros. That wasn't supposed to happen, Wilmore thought—he was only a sergeant in rank, but physically he believed he should be considered king of the jungle.

All this might have just been typical male rivalry, but something dark grew from Wilmore's jealousy when he saw the couple embracing tenderly in the back of the jeep. In that moment, his envy turned into cold malice.

His ill will towards Major Frost would soon bear terrible consequences.

CHAPTER 8: DEATH STALKERS

*"The harsh round moon that menaced with its
coldness,
The bitter winds that flayed our tents to hell,
And laggard time that taints our minds with madness,
Confined unceasing in a boundless cell."*
— "There was the Richness" from
"Poems from the Desert" by Lt. E.Y. Barnard

They spent an entire day driving westward through a vast, lonely wilderness. The landscape became a shifting kaleidoscope of colored sands. Orange, red, yellow, and white powder melted together into crested dunes and rippling fields of nothing. The terrain was still relatively flat—however, farther to the west, a huge sea of dunes appeared in the distance.

They were huge monstrosities of dunes—literal mountains of sandy powder, scraped from every corner of the land. Tossed by the malicious impulses of skirling breezes and dancing winds, the dust heaped itself into towering piles. The dunes made pretty pictures. Sunlight cast long, slanted shadows down their crooked spines. However, they were very dangerous entities. Special skills were needed to climb them and especially drive over them. One false move could send a heavy human or motor vehicle plunging like Icarus from a sunny heaven down through clouds into a smothering abyss.

Frost had no intention of driving through the dune sea. He intended to chart course north and bypass it. It was impractical to assault the dunes head-on; it would be very tiresome. Also he had Eve to consider. He imagined her plummeting out of the jeep and disappearing into an avalanche of cascading sand. The thoughts greatly disturbed him, and he refused to take any unnecessary chances.

He ordered Wilmore to make towards the north and eventually get onto the coastal road. It would likely be jammed with military traffic going to and from the battlefront; however, it was a paved road, and there would be little risk of wild desert phenomena or accidents.

The Australian grudgingly obeyed him. He drove leadenly and slower than he should have due to spite. Frost threw him out of the driver's seat and took the wheel at intervals—he supposed that Wilmore needed periods of rest. Eve was very uncomfortable when the sergeant sat next to her or was not busy driving. He gave her strange and hostile glances. She had a feeling he hated her.

The hot, dry wind and the sun baked all of them. They were tired, perspiring, and horribly thirsty. The bright light reflecting upon the pale sand in every direction stung and wore out their eyes. All of them were relieved when day faded and turned to nightfall. The air cooled—the temperature would drop drastically and turn to ice as sunlight, the true life of Egypt, faded away like a dream.

As darkness fell and the land became a hasty mist of blue and gray, a ghostly scene drifted up to the roving jeep. It was a gruesome and haunting sight. It would forever be burned into their memories.

A small fire twinkled ahead. The soldiers assumed it was a campfire. They clutched their weapons and peered anxiously through their binoculars. Frost, peering sharply through the glasses, saw a burning Bedouin tent and dark human figures scattered in the dirt. Dead bodies.

"What is it?" asked Eve nervously.

Frost lowered the binoculars with a steely expression. He was not fazed by death or violence. He snapped an order to Wilmore, and they both disembarked from the jeep, carrying firearms. Wilmore clutched his semi-automatic pistol. Frost, a seasoned rifleman, took a rifle from the jeep and carried it expertly slung in his arms.

"Stay here," the Major ordered Eve.

Naturally she disobeyed. She followed the two men after a few minutes of curiosity and impatience. Walking towards the campsite, she tripped over something soft and looked down. It appeared to be a dark branch. She realized there were no trees in the area. Peering closer, she gasped in horror and sprung backwards with a jolt. It was the piece of a bloody human arm.

Frost was angry. He shoved her roughly back into the jeep without a word. He glared icily at her as he waited for Wilmore to return.

"You were right, sir. There's nothing," Wilmore said after he shuffled back.

"They're probably not far," muttered Frost, scanning the dimming horizon. "We can't stay here. We must head in a different direction—we need to clear out of this area at once."

"Headlamps in the dark might attract unwanted attention," countered Wilmore with concern. "We might make a fair distance before it goes completely dark. But even then, it's risky—the light from the headlamps could make us a target."

The two men continued to plot their course of action while Eve waited impatiently to be informed. They paid no attention to her. The woman became frustrated. Eventually she seized Frost's arm.

"Would you please tell me what is going on?"

He looked wearily at her. He was tired and worried. He muttered something to Wilmore, who piled into the driver's seat again. Frost hopped into the vehicle and sat next to Eve. He put his arm around her shoulders. His embrace was tender, but very tense. He squeezed her with anxiety.

The vehicle moved off very slowly, hardly making a noise or raising any dust. The deathly fire and the bodies disappeared into the gray like evaporating mist.

"It was a massacre. Bedouins," Frost said bluntly and without empathy. He recalled the destroyed campsite—Arab men, women, and children slaughtered and left to decay. The carnage was fresh. The blood hadn't been dry very long, and the fires of depredation were still burning. It appeared to be a war crime of some kind. This was due to the fact that several of the dead were found in odd positions that indicated military-style torture. One man was hanging from a tent pole with his arms tied neatly in a manner commonly used to restrain criminals in European countries. He had been stabbed to death.

"It was probably the Germans—although I have never seen anything like it here before," said Frost. "The Afrika Korps has been fighting a clean war so far. Most of the time, they utilize tribesmen as their agents, or as suppliers. I can't imagine the reason they would do this. It's impractical."

"Unless it's not Germans," Eve suggested, considering all possibilities.

Frost fell quiet. The other alternative was that the butchers were Italians or British soldiers. The first possibility seemed ridiculous to him; the second was horrifying and unbelievable. Once upon a time, he might have been furious that such a statement had impugned the honor of his precious Royal Army. Now, because of alleged tomb robbers and rogue Special Forces rangers, he could not exclude his own people from suspicion.

"Nothing was stolen," he said. "I don't believe tomb robbers did it."

The jeep drifted towards the dune sea—the very area Frost wished to avoid. He was forced to reconsider his route due to the threat of an armed force lurking nearby.

Eventually they came to a stop. It was too dark to go on— Wilmore was right, headlights from a vehicle might attract pursuers or even enemy fire.

They maneuvered into a small rocky gully and made camp. It was freezing. They drew some blanket rolls out of the jeep and piled them on the ground in places where they planned to sleep. Frost arranged his sleeping area a polite distance away from Eve's, but still close enough to watch over her and reach her if necessary. Wilmore noticed and was incurably envious.

Dinner was a horrible canned substance commonly consumed by desert military forces. It was supposed to be meat and potatoes, but it tasted vile. Eve almost gagged on it. Frost gave her such a disdainful look that she felt shamed into eating it. They drank water from canteens that tasted like sour metal. Their source of light was a tiny electric lamp that produced no heat.

The night brought pitch blackness. The desert suddenly became a jet black, terrifying void. When it was time for sleep, Wilmore took out a small jug from the jeep that reeked of abrasive chemicals. He threw it around in the dirt, making a perimeter around the vehicle and the blankets. Eve looked at him questioningly.

"Scorpion bane," explained the Australian. "Made it myself."

The woman scooted uncomfortably in the dirt. The idea of lurking crawlers made her nervous.

"They come out at night. Climb on you," Wilmore added with glee, sensing her fear. He hoped to spoil any romance for his rival by frightening the other man's female companion. "See, the little terrors have no blood in their veins. Sunlight cooks them, and at night they get really cold. They like hiding in nice, cozy warm places." He grinned wickedly. "Ever heard of the 'deathstalker' scorpion?"

He began to regale her with a grim description of the Saharan deathstalker scorpion, a common sight in the desert that often plagued British soldiers. The small insect was extremely poisonous and known to crawl into sleeping men's clothing for warmth. He described an occasion when once, fighting the Germans in Libya, he had awoken to find a deathstalker nestled in his arm. He was about describe how he had slain the scorpion when Frost, tiring of his antics, stopped him.

"Enough, Sergeant," he said curtly. He turned to Eve with mischief in his eyes and the slightest flicker of a smile. "That's enough about silly things like scorpions. What you really have to look out for is something far greater and more formidable." He paused for dramatic emphasis. "Have you ever heard of the Saharan vampire camel?"

She burst out laughing. Wilmore was shamed.

Frost described a fanged camel with monstrous bat wings. He tried to keep a straight face and inevitably lost his composure with amusement as she giggled hysterically.

"Go to bed!" he laughed wryly, swatting her. "And remember, if you do hear one coming, please alert Wilmore," he joked. "He is the best at killing vampire camels—and scorpions, too."

The moon rose high and brought some illumination to the dark night. The two men agreed to take turns keeping watch. Major Frost volunteered to go first. Wilmore announced he was going to sleep. Time passed in silence.

Frost reclined in his blankets and looked at the stars. Suddenly he heard scrambling noises in the gravelly dirt nearby. It was Eve. She was jerking and swatting at something under her blanket. The Major stared, bewildered.

"What on earth are you doing?" he whispered.

"I thought I felt something crawling around here!" she responded in a hushed tone. She poked her head out of the blankets and looked desperately at him. "Frosty! Are there really scorpions?"

He sighed. "Oh, for heaven's sake." He was moved to pity by her wretched expression. "Come here," he beckoned softly. "Come over here, you."

Eve gladly grabbed her blankets and dragged them right next to his. Frost was surprised. He expected her to come sit with him, not sleep with him. He welcomed this encouraging development.

They reclined side by side. Frost wrapped his arm around her tenderly. "Stop fussing now. I'm here," he consoled. "I've got you. No reason to be terrified of scorpions..."

He held her hand. She squeezed his grip nervously. "How do you know they won't come around here?"

"They won't," he murmured calmly. "Scorpions hate me. I'd swear. They can sense I'm a mean customer. They know they wouldn't stand a chance against me..."

She stifled a giggle.

He smiled and held her tighter. "Hush up now. It's all right."

To his surprise, she threw her blanket over him. She wrapped her arm around his waist and snuggled against his shoulder. She closed her eyes. Frost was overjoyed.

"Eve, I want to kiss you," announced Frost, holding her tightly under the blanket and barely restraining himself from carrying out his intentions. "May I?"

"Yes. For goodness sake, you don't have to ask me."

Wilmore cracked his eyes open into thin slivers; he was not asleep, but rabid with pent-up jealousy. He had been dreading this moment. He was furious at the idea that they would have sex in his presence during the night. The notion made him feel impotent and envious enough to die.

Eve and Frost started touching and kissing. Before very long they were entwined on the ground. Their feelings for each other had grown stronger. Eve was totally overwhelmed with affection and attraction for him. His kisses thrilled her. Every time he touched her, it made her blood rush. It wasn't mere passion. It was love.

Frost stopped himself from going too far. He didn't want to wake Wilmore up. The British officer was a disciplined man who lived a life of cold pragmatism. He respected Eve, and did not wish to make his chivalrous love into an undignified spectacle in front of his junior officer. He kept his affections within the bounds of kissing and caressing her.

"I love you. I can't live without you," he whispered. "You may think I'm crazy, but I'm not. I mean it."

Eve looked into his eyes and touched his face. She decided at that very moment that he had completely stolen her heart. "I love you, too."

"Do you?" he asked eagerly. "Really?"

They were interrupted by a strange, shrill noise in the night that sounded like some type of bird.

Eve was alarmed. "What was that?"

Frost was suspicious. He listened in silence for a minute. He settled down and wrapped both arms tightly around her. "Probably just an animal," he muttered. "Honestly, what I'm really worried about is Germans." He closed his eyes. "That massacre we saw today was awful. I should've gone back towards Cairo and taken a highway. It would have cost more time, but we'd have skipped this trouble. This is my fault."

She rubbed his chest.

"I expected it would be dangerous. I'm not entirely sure we're in the clear," he sighed in stress and exhaustion. "There's not much I can do except bear the headache. One reaps what one sows."

"Stop talking like that," she consoled. "We'll be fine."

He sighed heavily and looked agonized. He embraced her tightly. His arm muscles were tense as bowstrings. "I don't know. I feel something's wrong," he said. "I don't know what it is for certain. But I do know that I'm right about it. It's been creeping up on me all evening." His hand started trembling slightly as flashbacks returned to him. "I had this very same feeling the day before the Germans shot me in France."

Eve glanced at him with wide eyes. She had never heard the story.

"There weren't supposed to be any Germans at Lille. Suddenly, they appeared," he said tensely. "I tried to hold them off with a few men. This is what happened." He pointed at the large X-shaped scar on the side of his neck. "I should be dead—only God knows why I'm not." He grimaced. "That is what happened to me the last time I had this terrible feeling."

She kissed him gently. "Nothing terrible will happen," she said. "Everything will be all right. I promise."

"You promise. As if you can control anything," he said wryly, peering at her affectionately. "You certainly think you can." He stroked her face and looked at her. His eyes glowed with admiration. "Beautiful, brave girl."

She kissed his mouth again fervently. He relaxed and buried himself in her arms. Neither of them noticed the dark and malevolent presence looming nearby.

Wilmore was fit to commit murder. He turned pale from

envy and his fists were clenched in the dust beside him like a pair of covetous claws. He stole baleful glances at them. He had dark temptations about the deadly pistol at his side. Homicidal visions drifted up to him like mocking ghosts in the dark. Tiny mirages of hate spurred his mind to ugly places it had never gone before. He was painfully aware that he lacked female company—he had a wife, actually, in Australia, but that didn't count now.

Why couldn't he be like the tomb robbers, and take what he wanted? There was no law in the desert—nobody to arrest him, to court martial him, to see what dark deeds he stooped to. Images flashed in his brain. He could shoot the Major and drag the woman behind the jeep...

His conscience protested. He managed to bring his temptations to a grinding halt. He was ashamed of himself for entertaining those shadowy thoughts in his mind.

However, witnessing Frost's burgeoning romance took a toll on him. He was beside himself with dismay. His face was covered in sweat from the sheer tension of his inner struggle. By the time his turn came to keep watch, the Australian soldier was fatigued and edgy.

He failed to perceive the threat steadily crawling towards them.

A gunshot cracked, echoing in the arid emptiness as the sun climbed a blood red horizon. It was a flare pistol. It flew into the sky like a shimmering purple lark and dropped like a falling star. A signal.

Frost woke up with a jolt and a small gasp. He instinctively shielded Eve with his arm as he sprang into a crouch and seized his rifle. His eyes scanned everything in milliseconds.

Wilmore came to with a start. He had fallen asleep on his watch. He reached for his pistol in confusion.

"Take cover! Quick!" Frost kicked Eve desperately, trying to force her to hide under the jeep. She scrambled between the wheels and flattened herself under the undercarriage.

He braced the rifle easily in his arms and ensured it was ready to fire. He signaled to Wilmore. They both ducked and darted around cautiously with their guns ready, looking for something to kill. Nothing was there. At least nothing visible. Rapid scans through binoculars revealed nothing.

Frost was sweating bullets. He expected Panzers to appear any minute to blast them to smithereens. He snatched his belongings, pulling his Major's jacket and beret on in a hurry.

"Let's bolt," he murmured to Wilmore. "How fast can you drive?"

"Like a demon, sir."

"Do it!" He dragged Eve from under the jeep and pushed her into the passenger's seat next to Wilmore. "Keep your head down," he ordered her. He hopped lightly into the back of the jeep and spread himself as low as possible with the muzzle of his rifle pointing out from between the seats. "I'll shoot anything that follows us. Go!"

The jeep lurched forward. Suddenly there was a scream of fury—a man's voice, seemingly from nowhere. Wilmore skidded on the brakes as a hooded man wearing a torn green uniform literally jumped out of the sand nearby in a burst of flying dust and attacked with a knife. The ambusher had been concealed in the dirt the entire time. Now he attempted to stop the jeep from leaving by breaking his cover. He was on Eve's side of the front seat. He lunged toward her.

Frost spun around with the rifle and shot the attacker with a swift cracking shot. He had protected his beloved Eve. However, in doing so, the Major had also exposed himself to enemy fire. Frost was now standing upright in the vehicle—an open target.

He and Eve were looking straight at each other when the shot took him.

There was a loud crack from somewhere in the distance. A slight whirring noise that barely lasted a second. The bullet hit Frost in the front of his left shoulder. The shooter had been aiming for his heart—and missed. Instead it tore into his shoulder blade. Blood spurted out.

Frost was off balance in the jeep when the bullet struck him like a fist. He fell. He toppled backward from the vehicle. His rifle fired into the sky as he hit the earth.

Instead of trying to save his commander's life, Sergeant Wilmore stepped hard on the accelerator and left Frost to die as shouts and more gunshots rang into the air.

Eve's adrenaline rushed with panic. "Stop! Go back!" she

screamed in fury. "Go back and get him, you coward!"

Wilmore ignored her. This was his jealous revenge—the ambush would allow him to murder Frost without having to do it personally.

She tried to jump out of the speeding jeep. Wilmore yanked her violently by the hair on her scalp, holding her captive. He shook her. "Shut up and hold still!"

"No!" She punched him in the throat and kicked the steering wheel. The jeep swerved dangerously close to a sand dune.

Wilmore was forced to release her to control the speeding vehicle. "Stop it!" he yelled. "You'll kill us!"

"Fine! Then we'll die!" she screamed, and kicked the wheel again.

Wilmore lost his grip, and the jeep crashed. Eve was able to predict the crash as she felt the chassis start to spin sideways. She climbed onto the door and jumped from the vehicle as far as she could. Her legs hit the ground awkwardly, and she tumbled several times before her body rolled to a halt in an open dust field. She was bruised and dazed. She heard the jeep smash like a train wreck behind her. She stumbled to her feet and ran to Frost. She didn't bother to check what happened to Wilmore. She didn't care.

The jeep turned over. It slid on the sand. Wilmore hit the brakes too fast as it turned, and it spun out of control. The heavy metal vehicle flew head-on into a sand dune with a terrific explosion of dust, sending waves of sand bursting like fountains into the air. The weight of the falling sand created a vortex. The jeep rolled like a top as it buried itself in the dune. Wilmore got tangled up in the driver's seat and fell out, just in time for the jeep to land on top of him. He was pinned sideways under the vehicle and several hundred pounds of sand that avalanched on top of it. His body was crushed. He was still alive, but could not move.

Meanwhile, Major Frost had pulled himself to his feet again and readied his rifle, bracing himself for a one-man showdown. The heat of battle possessed him. It was a fever. He stopped feeling and noticing things. He was oblivious to the blood pouring out of his shoulder. Oblivious to the realization that his Sergeant had deserted him. He existed to fight and kill.

Figures appeared. Moving objects. They were not humans to Frost. They were shapes that needed to die. His rifle became like part of his body as he raised it expertly and fired, over and over again, with the mastery of a man who had devoted himself singly to the arts of fighting and soldiering for a lifetime. A shape rushed towards him. Pop. It dropped. Another flew by. Pop. It fell, with a big red puff that time. They fell like dominoes. One of them tried to throw something at him. Stupid little gnat, thought Frost with superiority, and cut it down with a blast of bullets. Frost, perspiring, started to smile with fierce enjoyment. He relished competition. This was turning into a game. A challenge. A sport, even. Like playing cricket or rugby, or hunting rabbits. How many of these idiots could he take out in the next few seconds? What tricks would they try and use to beat him? He couldn't wait to see because he couldn't wait to outwit and shoot them. It was fun.

He ran out of bullets. No more pops left. Still targets running around, though. Just waiting to die. He dashed around with gusto, ducking and diving with bullets flying everywhere around him. The noise spurred him on. He had thunder rushing in his veins. He noticed a nice big handgun on one of the dead dummies—a historical Italian-made monstrosity that seemed to predate the First World War. He snatched the pistol merrily. Not sure how it would fire. He'd find out. He waited until another dummy presented itself for shooting. Pulled the trigger. Boom. The gun fired like a cannon—sent the dummy flying back three feet. The recoil of the gun and the terrific boom it caused startled Frost. He laughed.

Suddenly, he lost his balance and collapsed. He was confused. His body felt like a dead weight. His arms and legs moved. But the rest of him was frozen. The past and present blurred together. He'd felt this way before. He gasped and reflexively reached towards his neck in a panic, expecting to feel blood. It wasn't 1940, but he didn't know that. His hand-eye coordination was gone; his fingers weren't working the way he wanted, and he couldn't reach anything. His heart pounded rapidly, and he felt clammy. Sick. He felt dull pain in his left shoulder, and something stinging his side. A sharp sting, like a wasp. His battle fever faded.

He stared at the sky and realized he was in Egypt and would probably die in a minute or less. Where was that stupid Sergeant of his? Who knew. He remembered someone. Someone he loved. Yes, her name was Eve. She said something that made him laugh. Something in Cairo. About a fog. No, it was the word 'fogey.' Some American nonsense. It was funny. He was sitting next to her in a jeep, and they were talking about something he couldn't remember. Her hair looked gorgeous in the sun—a nice bright copper color.

Sand crunched next to his ears as he faded between reality, memory, and fantasy. Someone leaned over him. The burning hot muzzle of a gun pressed against his cheek. Then it withdrew.

Frost hardly noticed. He was becoming delirious from blood loss. His mind was miles away.

"Well, well! It's a Major," said a sharp East London voice. "See them stripes and badges, lads? This bloke's worth something."

CHAPTER 9: THE TRAP

"There's a Devil in the dawn,
Horrific spawn of last night's hideous Moon,
That hung above the gun's inferno.
And smiled on men that died too soon."
—"Morning after the Barrage at El Alamein"
from "Poems from the Desert"
by Bombardier F.E. Hughes

"The injuries are not fatal," announced the German after more than a minute of meticulous scrutiny and examination. He knelt over Major Frost, whose khaki jacket and shirt he had unbuttoned. Blood poured everywhere. It stained the German's fingers as he pointed in demonstration. "Only two shots—the one here in the shoulder and then this one in the side. But since he is rather thin and this jacket is large, the bullet has aimed slightly over too far and only has made a sharp cut..."

"It's called a 'nick,' Sigfried."

The tomb robbers circled around the fallen British officer like vultures. Several of their jeeps had been completely shot up, and many men were dead. Frost had done it. He had shot them all, somehow. He would have continued to shoot them, had not the young bespectacled German with round glasses called Siegwulf Eislinger taken a calculating aim at him.

Arching around the windscreen of his jeep like a serpent, Eislinger focused a razor-sharp eye at Frost and estimated the precise location of his internal organs. He fired once, using a long-barreled pistol. A direct shot through the stomach would have killed Frost—but the Major, a moving target, was difficult to hit, and also very lean and wiry thanks to his fanatical physical exercising. The shooter had overestimated the mark. The bullet missed Frost's stomach and bored through the side of his jacket, ripping off a slice of skin on his side. The non-fatal wound was very bloody and caused Frost to collapse of faintness due to hemorrhaging.

Now Eislinger examined the man he had failed to kill. On all sides, the German was surrounded by dead fellow thieves. They were slumped over machine gun turrets, hanging upside down from their jeeps, sprawled across the sand with their legs twisted, bent over backwards with shattered skulls in the dirt.

Of the men who had set out in the raiding party, only half were left alive. There were more tomb-robbing crews in other locations so the full strength of their force was not yet depleted. However, it was a significant loss of manpower. The survivors reacted without remorse. They had no real emotions. They were sharks in the desert who existed to kill.

The raider captain—known as "Flag" or Ollie—stood jauntily over Frost with one laced black-and-tan moccasin propped on a dead robber's back. His shadow fell long and slanted in the light of the rising sun. His emerald-green turban glowed in the reddish haze. The ancient flint dagger he wore flashed like a curved crescent moon among the bandoliers, belts, and weapons strapped like ribbons around his body. His golden eye gleamed in the sunlight.

"Let's take him, then," Ollie said. "His rank will bag a pretty price from your old chums."

"I am sure they will pay a lot for him," agreed Eislinger, dressed in a ragged combination of his tropical German Army uniform with colorful Libyan militia trappings mangled into it. He wore a flat British helmet, complete with a bullet hole, on his head as a sadistic trophy. "I know that the Afrika Korps needs information to win, especially right now. You can name your price."

"Bright twinkly spark you are, Sigfried Icefingers. Sharp as glass. Glad I picked you up," said the captain with an approving sneer. He kicked Frost in his wounded side and smiled maliciously. The Major writhed in pain and passed out.

"Lads, haul this fine English gentleman into the fleet. And try not to break his neck, while you're at it."

They laughed. The captain ordered them to collect Frost's belongings, including his beret and his rifle; these would be sold with him as part of his "package." A motley group of British raiders lifted Frost like a rag and cast him roughly into one of the jeeps. Drops of blood spattered everywhere leaving a trail.

"The only problem that might be a concern is the bleeding," mentioned Eislinger, staring at the quickly drying red liquid in the sand. "If he bleeds to death or gets an infection, then we cannot sell him and our plan will be useless."

"Quite the scientist, ain't you, son?" snickered Ollie. "I'll worry about that. Meanwhile, I have a slight little chore for you—set these blokes alight. Let 'em barbecue awhile, then bury 'em. Make sure nobody don't find nothing too easy."

He gestured at the dead bodies of their former comrades, then wheeled on Eislinger with a knowing grin.

"You're perfectly suitable to doin' it, Sigfried. Lads tell me you've got a hankering for that sort of industrial labor. Went off on your ownsome last evening and 'played cards' with a crop of Bedouins. Ain't it?"

Eislinger smirked slightly. He indeed was responsible for the massacre of Bedouins that had taken place in the area. He admitted nothing.

"Nasty little creeper, ain't you, Jerry boy? A regular maniac," mused the captain, studying his new recruit. "I think I'm startin' to latch onto why them Royal Army noddies trussed you up like a holiday goose."

The German was slightly insulted by the comparison. "You told me I could do anything I liked," he protested with righteous indignation, looking bookish and yet menacing in his captured British pith helmet. "Anyway, what is the loss?"

"Listen, son. I like crazy little piranhas like you. But don't take too many liberties with them hopeless Bedouins," warned

Ollie, slinging his smoking revolver back into a holster on his hip. "Bad thing about Bedouins is, they got cousins. I mean lots. Last thing we need is the whole flippin' tribes of Saudi Arabia scunnin' round here lookin' to lop our heads off."

Eislinger was chagrined at the rebuke.

"You see, Bedouin gents are terrible clever at creepin' through the dust, and they like a good game of 'cards' just as much as you do." Ollie leered and tilted his head like a taunting Cheshire cat. "Mind that for the future."

The captain turned away and scanned the surroundings. "Where's the other one, then?" he asked his comrades. "You know. The boontrotter. The blinkin' Australian."

Suddenly a whisper swept past him. Like a low, mumbling voice of a phantom man. The captain bristled. That noise haunted his every footstep. The noise was always malicious. It always came to threaten him.

There was a very slight rustle in the sand nearby.

Ollie whirled. His revolver twirled into his hand faster than that of a Western gunfighter.

Eve shrieked as the bandit captain shot the pistol clean out of her hand with one bullet. She stumbled and fell out of her hiding place.

He grabbed her. Next thing she knew she was kneeling in the dust in front of him. He had a gun barrel aimed at her forehead, and his fist gripped her hair. Behind him, his underling Eislinger obediently dragged bodies into neat rows and splashed gasoline on them, while assisted by fellow raiders.

Eve faced her fate with furious tears burning in her eyes. She had initially assumed that the man she loved, Major Frost, was dead—so she recovered Wilmore's pistol, which had fallen out of the jeep, and crawled back to the campsite. She was hell-bent on slaying the murderers in a last battle of revenge. All the blood of her German warrior ancestors and Scottish rebel forefathers flared up in her veins. She intended to go down fighting her enemies. No regret, no surrender. She would die in a blaze of vengeance and glory, unconquered. Proudly she would pass into the afterlife and find Frosty waiting for her there. That was her determination. She hid, aimed at the canisters of gasoline in their leader's jeep and was prepared to begin a lethal rampage with a fiery explosion when she heard the raiders talking. She heard them say that Frosty was alive.

Her hands trembled with relief. Her goal changed. She became single-mindedly determined to rescue him.

Now, Eve's life and death hung in the balance. She needed to be careful if she wanted to stay alive. And she needed to stay alive for Frost's sake. His survival depended on hers.

She decided to take a risk. In order to hide her intentions, she would pretend to be the kind of woman she hated, the kind of woman these blustering roughs wanted to see—weak and helpless.

Eve started squealing and covering her face. "No! Please don't hurt me!" she wailed, pretending to cry. "Help! Somebody help me!"

The captain was fooled by the act. He sneered. He brutally kicked her. The heavy blow stung terribly. Eve fell to the ground and wanted to murder him, but masked her fury. Instead she rose with pitiful tears and a simpering expression. "Oh, don't hurt me, please!" she groveled. "Please. I'm worth more alive!"

The captain grabbed her chin and stared into her face with burning lust. "Yeah, I can already think of one reason why I might keep you breathin', gorgeous," he said, thumbing her lip. "I got a bit of fluff in Tripoli, but she's down sick havin' a kid last I saw. Not much fun. Want to take her place, is that it, Fluffy?"

"I'm a German spy," she blurted, inventing a story. "These men captured me and were taking me to Alexandria to question me."

"That why were you kippin' with our Major over there?" challenged the captain. "Don't think nobody saw you takin' a tumble with him last night. We was round here the whole time, just waitin' for the right time to introduce ourselves." He gestured sardonically with his hands, indicating that the robbers had been inching slowly up towards the campsite during the night. "We took a peeksy through the glass and saw the pair of you havin' a cozy little tussle." He chuckled. "Sort of friendly for a poor captured little spy, ain't it, Fluffy?"

Eve turned to Eislinger and addressed him in German. He jumped in alarm and stared at her. Eve spoke like a native; her accent was perfect. She used her family history and knowledge of Germany and journalism to invent a convincing and persuasive story. She claimed her name was Hannelore Hecking, alias "Nightingale," and that she was from Munich. She said she was given a secret identity and posted to Cairo undercover to spy on British officers. She claimed to work as a journalist and a cabaret dancer. She claimed to spy on the British Army by seducing officers with her exotic dancing. She said she had an affair with the Major, and he was trying to cover it up because he didn't want a stain on his proud Army service record. She said the Major and his associates in the Army Investigative Corps suspected her of various misdeeds, although they couldn't prove anything. The Major was forced to arrest her and take her to Alexandria. She claimed she had valuable information concerning the Afrika Korps and that the Oberkommando der Wehrmacht, German's central military command known as the OKW, would surely pay for her repatriation.

Eislinger was very excited. He believed all of it and told the captain a summarized version leaving out some details. "This means we can sell both of them, together or separate, and make a lot more profit!" the German robber declared.

During her narrative, Eve failed to realize that she had unwittingly compromised one very critical detail—the bandit captain, Ollie, zeroed in on it immediately.

"Oi. Did you say Army Investigative Corps?" prodded Ollie, with a look of anxiety on his face. He pointed demandingly at the unconscious Major Frost. "This berserker here. Did you say he's an Army flippin' investigator?"

Eve started trembling. Her fear in those seconds was indescribable; she did not know whether she had saved the man she loved or condemned him and did not know what words would seal his fate. Yet, she needed to give a reply.

She cautiously replied to Eislinger, in German, that she believed the Major was from the Army Investigative Corps but she did not know for certain.

A new flurry of activity started; Ollie, the leader, scrambled over to the jeep to examine Major Frost. He started tearing anxiously at the man's uniform looking for clues. He studied his badges and emblems of rank. He saw the Major's midnight blue beret nearby and swooped it up in a flurry. He scrutinized the insignia on the silver cap badge. The CIG unit symbol—of the sword decapitating the serpent—was unknown to him. However, he did recognize the Corps emblem of the flaming torch.

"Cripes! He is from blasted Army Investigations!" spat Ollie, crushing the beret in his hand and flinging it onto Frost's limp body. The tomb raider wheeled on Eve in a fluster. "And you're tryin' to guiver me into thinkin' that a Army Investigations officer would waste his time taxi drivin' a piece of Jerry fluff across the desert? That's peasant work! I'm in the Army meself, sweetheart. Special Forces commando. Know these things, I do." He pointed his finger accusingly in her face. "Cough it up! What's the real reason he's out here?"

He slammed her with his boot again. She toppled over with a gasp.

Eislinger was vexed by the outburst. "If you damage her too much, maybe the Afrika Korps will not pay ransom," he suggested.

Tears welled in Eve's eyes. This time they were genuine because she was in great physical pain from the last kick. Her ears rang as blood rushed to her head from the trauma. She addressed Eislinger in German again. She told him she had confessed to everything she knew; she could not comment on British Army infrastructure matters because they were not her business.

Eislinger nodded. From a German perspective, this unswerving and myopic attention to performing a single duty was believable.

"She is telling the truth. It is not her specification to know about the specific details of how the British do things in their Army administration duties," he said. "She only knows about what her own job is. She has told us everything."

The bandit captain was suspicious. "You sure about that? Because now you mention it, I think I done seen you before someplace, Fluffy," he uttered, jerking her face back and forth in his hand and examining her carefully. "I knowed I have. Somewhere. Ain't it?"

Eve informed Eislinger, in German, that it was possible the man could have seen her before, but she did not remember.

"And why does you talk English like a Yank, then, Fluffy?" demanded the captain, kicking her sharply with the heel of his boot.

She fell again. Again she was enraged enough to murder him. Again she rose and pretended to be helpless and sniveling. "Please don't hurt me anymore," she begged. "I learned to speak with an American accent to protect myself."

"That's right!" Eislinger agreed with a buoyant nod. "The German military would never send someone to make secret reports talking with a German accent. It's too obvious!"

The raider captain, Ollie, flushed in irritation. It all seemed perfect. Too perfect. His base instincts told him she was lying.

"Where's the other mug, then?" asked Ollie. "Thought I saw summat take a dive into the dunes out yonder. Some kinda dust puff. I'd have checked meself, but we was all too busy playin' croquet with Doc Holliday over here," he said sarcastically, jerking his head at Frost lying wounded in the back of the jeep. "Quite a savage customer, this one. Makes Tarzan look like a tea biscuit. I'd hate to play football with him—he'd probably rip me ears off!"

The men laughed.

"So what happened to Mr. Waltzing Matilda, then?"

Eve had to think fast. Her first instinct was to admit to wrecking Wilmore on purpose, but decided against it. She whimpered and said the Australian lost control of the jeep because he was so frightened of the raiders.

That sent them all laughing. Again, they believed her. They were flattered by fear—and she knew it.

"Icefingers, light them bonfires, would you? Meet me back at the Casbah—and remember, no more playin' billiards with the blinkin' Bedouins," ordered Ollie. "Let's shove off, lads."

The raider captain took a group of men with him in two jeeps; the others he left to "clean up" the site.

Ollie seized Eve roughly and dragged her along with them. "I'll find out why Army Investigations is muckin' about in my backyard," he menaced. "You'll come along nicely with me."

CHAPTER 10: FIRESTORM

"Parched earth, whose sterile dust the burning winds
In choking clouds with aimless fury, sweep
Across vast treeless plains without intent.
The yeastless flame of Death's bitter bread."
—"The Desert" from
"Poems from the Desert" by Lt. M. St. J. Wilmoth.

Siegwulf Eislinger set fire to the bodies of his former comrades with no emotion. There was no honor or fellowship among the thieves. Only the most bullish and ruthless of them survived the hazards of their violent lifestyle.

They knew no pity.

Eislinger watched the bodies smolder in the dust. He was perfectly suited to this type of environment. He was a quiet, merciless sadist. His random murder sprees behind desert frontlines had made him an enemy of his own German comrades—as the Afrika Korps and their Italian allies courted the favor of North Africans to support their war effort, Eislinger flouted military orders and soldierly honor in favor of covert butchery. He was single-handedly responsible for several gory massacres in the wild nowheres of the desert. His victims belonged to no particular race or people. They just happened to be in the wrong place at the wrong time. Usually they were unarmed and unprepared for an attack.

Like most psychologically motivated murderers, Eislinger was a coward and an opportunist. He had killed Libyans, Tunisians, Arabs, Berbers, Greeks, and Vichy French allies—he had even murdered Italian colonial settlers doing laundry outside their desert plantation homes. He had also targeted unarmed British and Indian POWS in the past.

In the confusion of war, Eislinger's murder sprees had been mistaken for partisan activity. Opposing sides blamed each other. The British thought he was the Germans or the Arabs. The Germans thought he was the British, or the Bedouins, or disgruntled local natives. The various local natives and tribespeople thought he was acting on behalf of one of the great opposing armies fighting on their lands—either the Axis or the Allies, they couldn't say which. Eislinger was very clever about concealing his intentions and covering up his murder frenzies; he felt a sense of power at the consternation felt by his Afrika Korps comrades due to his massacres. He did not believe his guilt had been discovered.

There was no real explanation for his madness. Who could explain how such an unassuming young man had become so wickedly perverse?

Eislinger had an uninteresting family background. The son of a Bavarian schoolteacher, he grew up in a small rural village known for chicken farming. He had three sisters and two half brothers; none of them were very bright, talented or hardworking. His mother was a strict woman known for her love of gardening and sweeping. His father, the teacher, was a local rake notorious for affairs and debauchery when he wasn't lecturing about literature in his schoolroom. Nothing related to the parents, however, explained the son's descent into deceit and psychopathy.

What nobody knew about Siegwulf Eislinger was the fact that he was raised from his earliest years by a murderess. His nursemaid, Magda, worked for the family as a so-called "Putzfrau" cleaning lady and was responsible for babysitting the children. Young Wulfi, as he was nicknamed, took a strong liking to his nanny, who had a very different personality whenever his parents were gone. Magda's name was actually Wartrud, and she was responsible for a notorious unsolved murder spree in a small Bavarian farming community called Hinterkaifeck. The name of Hinterkaifeck lived in infamy. The place became a byword for death when an entire family, including children, was massacred on a farm one cold winter day by a pickaxe-wielding maniac for no apparent reason. The massacre occurred in Germany's era of poverty and chaos following the First World War, and the local police—then ex-army officials—were incapable of solving it. Years melted by and the dead drifted into the limbo of old cold cases; the woman responsible for slaying mothers and infants with a pickaxe turned her hands to rocking cradles and sewing clothes for the children of the Eislinger family. She was never found out nor apprehended. Siegwulf liked Magda better than his own mother; she had a cruel, devious sense of humor he identified with. He discovered Magda's role in the Hinterkaifeck slayings; one day during his teenage years, he realized the truth when he saw her startled reaction to an anniversary article about the murders in a local paper. He found it amusing and was not bothered by it. He wrote her letters until the day she died peacefully of old age in their home.

Now, Magda's legacy lived on in Eislinger—he continued her established custom of slaying unarmed innocent people to amuse himself. Yet, the fact that Magda had existed in his life and played a role in his upbringing did not make him the murderer he had become. Something about that darkness appealed to him inside. He had freely chosen it.

He watched fire leap from the corpses of his former thieving companions and felt very privileged to be alive. He was glad the British had captured him after one of his desert massacres—his brief stint as a POW was awful, but becoming a tomb robber was the best thing that ever happened to him. It allowed him to freely indulge his violent whims.

A bullet whistled through the air like the scythe of avenging death.

Eislinger did not see or hear it. He turned his head to give orders to a fellow robber. That petty action saved him from a shot to the head. The speeding bullet caught Eislinger straight in the left ear and took most of his ear off in a red flash. He gasped and ducked to the ground in terror, clutching the wound as blood poured from it through his fingers. The other robbers continued organizing their jeeps, oblivious to what had happened. The shot had been silenced. They didn't hear it.

Less than half a mile away, Afrika Korps ranger Capt. Elrich Von Rindl stared attentively through the scope of a high-powered sniper rifle. He was positioned lying flat on top of his captured armored vehicle, which he had camouflaged using an elaborate barrier of brush, sand piles, and rocks. He had been there watching the tomb robbers since dawn. He regretted that he had not been able to intervene in their ambush against the British jeep; he considered breaking cover to help the British party, but did not want to compromise his position or his chance of completing his mission to kill Eislinger and recover his remains. Von Rindl had decided it would be simpler to kill Eislinger first, then search for and assist what remained of the British travelers in the jeep.

Cautious yet daring, he watched through the scope as Eislinger dropped. He could not see if he had scored a fatal hit. Eislinger did not appear to be convincingly dead enough. He focused his calm, medium-blue eyes and decided to take another shot. He was about to pull the trigger when suddenly Eislinger scurried across the ground and hid under one of the jeeps.

Von Rindl sat up with a jolt. Anger and frustration filled him. Somehow that spree killer who deserved death for his crimes kept evading execution. Filled with indignation, he decided to take a calculated risk and attack Eislinger's group head-on.

The robbers noticed something was wrong; their de-facto commander was shivering and hiding under a jeep. They did not see the wound to his ear, nor did they realize that the blood trail on the ground was left by him. They assumed it was from the previous shootings at the site. Neither did they hear any noise nor see any cause for alarm. Assuming that

Eislinger was having a nervous fit, they began to mock and laugh uproariously at him.

Suddenly, Eislinger bolted from his hiding place with blood dripping from his mangled ear and yelled for them to drive away. They panicked. Some of the men stood to fight; two others got into a jeep with Eislinger and drove off in confusion.

Eislinger huddled behind the windscreen and fought hysterical fear. He knew the shot was meant for him alone.

There was only one explanation. The Afrika Korps had sent someone to kill him. His comrades had been suspicious of him. Somebody must have gossiped, sneakily reported information about him to military authorities or spied on him. Now the German military was trying to execute him. Evidently they had reason to be convinced he was guilty of his crimes—maybe they had been secretly amassing files and data on him for some time before sending a hammer to fall on him. He had no idea.

He hadn't seen the blow coming, which convinced him that it came from his own people. Typically Germans did not announce actions beforehand; they simply took action. Germans who determined to take action against something usually never gave up, either. His compatriots were probably outraged by his excesses—which had jeopardized their Army's strategic goal of maintaining its stability in Africa—and certainly he would be given no second chances to redeem himself in the eyes of their Fatherland. A patriotic assassin stalked his footsteps; someone he didn't know. Someone who would not relent until Eislinger fell dead. The faceless assassin would probably be awarded a medal for killing him and given a military promotion. Eislinger felt personally threatened for the first time in his life. It was terrifying.

A bullet struck one of the jeep's tires with German precision; the vehicle spun out of control and veered sideways. Another single-minded bullet cut a taut, straight line into a gasoline canister in the rear of the jeep. The canister exploded. The jeep rocked forward and burst into flames.

The other tomb robbers bailed out of the jeep and took cover. Eislinger, fearing the next shot, tried to hide behind the windscreen rather than expose his body to the deadly sniper who had somehow caught up with him.

Hunter and hunted then saw each other. Through the shimmering hot air rising from the flaming jeep, the two Germans locked eyes.

Von Rindl, ever the expert wilderness ranger, had outmaneuvered the jeep by cutting ahead of it and positioning his vehicle on a rocky outcrop. He was hiding between two rocks with his rifle poking out like a branch. His cloth Afrika Korps cap was visible above those rocks, as was his rugged, dust-covered face. His astute blue eyes glared icily at his target.

Eislinger focused on the ranger in dread through his round glasses. There was the assassin. Indeed an Afrika Korps man. Probably one with sinister gifts for hunting and tracking—one of many wily German outdoorsmen employed in the upper echelons of desert service. Eislinger didn't recognize him.

Their exchanged glance only lasted for a moment before Von Rindl took another shot. Eislinger evaded it. He ducked for cover and scrambled out of the jeep a millisecond before the high-powered bullet shattered the windscreen to pieces. He hid behind the flaming body of the jeep, preferring fire to gunshot death.

Von Rindl was outraged. He was highly irritated that his target kept evading the deathblow at the last second. There was no reasonable explanation for it—he found Eislinger like a cockroach that kept dodging the final blow of a punishing shoe. A rat's instincts, thought Von Rindl in resentment, and reloaded his rifle. He was determined not to leave the scene until Eislinger the mad killer was dead and his mission was accomplished.

He did not get the chance.

The overpowering smell of moisture and dust filled the air. Von Rindl gagged on the scent of chalk and mud. He pulled away from his vantage point and glanced around. He noticed the air around him was a strange light blue. In the distance, a small veil of dust blurred the horizon. An innocent, gauzy-looking haze. Two seconds later it seemed to have grown larger and wasn't so distant anymore. His eyes widened in dread. Lowering his rifle, he dove into his armored vehicle and drove quickly to the base of the rocky outcrop. He parked the vehicle between a pair of boulders, bracing for the onslaught.

The sandstorm hit mere seconds later. Like all sandstorms, it was a stealthy assailant—virtually silent until it set upon its victims with a sudden loud roar. North African sandstorms were completely unpredictable. They could form in seconds, travel at lightning speed and last either minutes or days. They battered the landscape. They vacuumed piles of sand from one end of the desert to the other. Winds could travel well over 250 miles per hour; others were less severe. They tore aircraft to pieces, hurtled cars and heavy artillery into the air like cardboard toys, buried tents, and sent unsuspecting soldiers flying through the air. Many men of opposing desert armies had disappeared during sandstorms—fatally lost, or simply strangled and torn by the winds.

Wind squeezed the life out of the sand. Fine dust melted in the pressure like water. Scratchy sand granules forcefully permeated every tiny crack in sight. Cars were hardly safe from the smothering force of sandstorms. In fact, car interiors could be suffocating—sandstorms wedged dust into cars and covered entire vehicles in dirt. The atmosphere became completely sealed beneath pouring dirt. Air inside became unbearably hot and thick with dust.

Von Rindl took cover in his vehicle, which rattled wildly back and forth in the storm but remained stable due to its location. He covered his mouth and nose with his Afrika Korps jacket, trying to filter out the dust. Breathing was difficult and painful. The air visible outside the small vehicle windows was completely dark brown. A writhing Nubian cobra hit the window and flew past it, carried by the roaring winds. He sighed bitterly in the oppressive heat.

His mission was unfinished. The raiders had likely escaped, and Eislinger the murderer was still free.

CHAPTER 11: IN THE TOMB OF THE SUN

"Gone is the might of Rome—the fertile land
On which proud Antony and Caesar looked,
Has withered with the crumbling aqueduct
And all is sunken in the drifting sand."
—"Libya" from "Poems from the Desert"
by Bombardier L. Challoner

The dune sea loomed like a huge billowing ocean. The bandits headed straight for it. Eve, riding in the front of the captain's jeep, felt anxiety as she saw the rippling mountains of sand ahead. Some sand swells towered over four stories high; some even higher. These heavy mountains were made of nothing but translucent powder. They snaked for miles like huge gyrating crescents of pure light, dust, and air. They looked impossible to climb, much less drive over.

Ollie stood propped with one boot on the jeep console and the other balanced on small footrest between the seats. He hung jauntily onto the edge of the windscreen with one arm, much like a sailor hanging from a ship mast. Sometimes he switched his grip casually onto the front turret of the vehicle. At times, he pranced like a cat around the console and door tops as the vehicle rocketed over uneven surfaces at full speed. His skill at balancing was incredible. The tails of his emerald green turban whipped wildly in the wind.

The jeeps glided. They made almost no noise—their motors whirred silently and the dust clouds they raised were minimal. The tires were nearly flattened and the wheels were rigged with strange spur-like devices. The jeeps were like high-speed sand plows. Even so, Eve doubted their ability to scale the monstrous ocean of dunes ahead.

The captain sensed her dismay. He grinned fiercely. "Ain't never heard of Commando Group Sphinx. Have you, Fluffy?" he challenged. "If you had, you wouldn't look so bloomin' terrified. Fine 'Jerry spy' you are!"

Eve tried to show no emotion in response to his probe.

"I'm a Sphinx commando," vaunted the captain. "Regular genie, I am. Been all over this stinkin' desert—from here to the bonny banks of Algiers since the war first started in Africa. Army don't care where I am, long as I get dirty work done. I'm a real corker at knifin' Jerries in their sleep. I'm the terror of the flippin' Afrika Korps! Don't tell Sigfried, though—the lad might take it wrong." He laughed murderously. "Anyway, I don't kill much in the way of Jerries these them days. Fat lot of good it does killin' people when there's money to be made. Ain't it?"

Horror struck her at the sudden sight of Sergeant Wilmore and what had once been Major Frost's military jeep. It had flipped over on its side and pinned Wilmore crookedly to the ground beneath it. Both man and vehicle were half-buried by a vengeful sand dune, broken by an avalanche. The second jeep of tomb robbers stopped to scavenge the wreck. They disembarked and started plucking pieces from the engine and siphoning gasoline. Wilmore pleaded for them to release him from his deadly entrapment. The raiders were merciless brigands. They ignored him.

Eve turned away from the sight with glistening eyes. She resented Wilmore, but to see him meet such a pitiless end wrenched her soul. The coldness of the robbers was disgusting.

One reaps what one sows, Major Frost had told her the night before. That was certainly true in the case of Wilmore. He left his commander stranded to meet a cruel death and now he was being left to meet such an end. She abandoned her feelings of remorse to the justice of the desert.

Eve watched a sand dune growing closer and closer to the windscreen with dread. It was a huge tan wall about to crash into them. Ollie crouched like a spider on the console. He tied one his turban tails over his face like an Arabian veil and turned to Eve. Only his eyes were visible above his bandit's mask. His pale human eye, and his gold metal eye with the tiny carnelian in the center. He grinned and winked the metal eye at her. The gold sparkled in the light.

A little gold flash. A yellow dot. Eve remembered it suddenly. She had seen it before. In Cairo. In a cabaret. During a performance. Behind her in the dark...

This man shot Harper in Cairo, she realized, remembering the gun smoke and the blast. He was the real target of Major Frost's relentless investigation. Clearly, the British Army had been at a disadvantage when they started investigating. They confused the murderer with the victim and gotten names wrong. Meanwhile, the killer literally stared her in the face. She felt sickened.

They hit the first sand dune. Eve closed her eyes and hung onto the seat, expecting an explosion of dirt. No such thing happened.

She felt herself rising, as if in an elevator. High into the air. Flying. She opened her eyes and saw the jeep literally floating up the side of the dune as if riding a wave.

The captain stood at full height, defying gravity. He tapped her with his boot to get attention. He stepped halfway out of the soaring jeep and balanced on the side of the door. He walked back and forth on the thin edge of the door as the jeep sailed higher along the crest of the dune. Then he hopped onto the console again. He was showing off.

Eve looked over the side of vehicle and saw a sheer drop. She perspired. The jeep turned. It maneuvered like a seesaw over and around the dune crest. Then it slid down the dune on a rippling dust current. The vehicle angled sideways for balance during the descent.

The captain continued to stand, bracing himself against the windscreen as he calmly rode the waves. He leaned expertly in different directions as the jeep moved. Another dune came. This one was a behemoth. Probably about five stories high and half a mile wide. They drove straight for it.

The jeep soared again and curved during its ascent. The vehicle almost completely turned over sideways. Ollie, the captain, crawled to the other side of the console like an acrobat and propped his legs against the door and the windscreen, using his weight to balance the vehicle. Eve for several minutes was convinced she would fall out of the seat; she hung on tightly. The robbers made no efforts to help her; the cutthroats lived by their own wits and had no sympathy for anyone. She would survive or perish on her own merit.

The jeep balanced itself again and slithered like a snake across the top of the dune. Eve could see the entire horizon from here—even the very outer edges of the paved highway to Alexandria in the distance. It was a poignant moment. How she would have loved to glimpse the Great Desert in all its vast majesty with Frosty at her side. Now the British officer was badly wounded—possibly beyond help. Eve hoped he would survive long enough for her to somehow save him from these ruthless killers.

Crossing the swells was like traveling into another world. A world where nobody existed. The bandits and their jeeps seemed to be the only living creatures in this beautiful, eerie universe. No law. No order. No time or space. Danger was the desert's breath, and the landscape fickly changed with every wind. Everything was in flux.

A sandstorm struck the desert shortly after they emerged from the dune sea. Ollie noticed it first—a faint scent of dust and moisture in the air. The robbers glanced everywhere and noticed the miniscule signs of its approach.

The captain gave orders for the convoy to travel faster. The jeeps, already traveling at very high speed, doubled their pace. They moved like comets. The noise from the wind suction around them was deafening. Dust clouds ripped high into the air behind them like fiery tails.

Eve glanced at the captain, Ollie. He brimmed with arrogance, standing propped on the front of the jeep as if on the prow of a warship. She noticed the ancient, curved flint dagger glowing like a crescent moon in his belt.

She recognized the dagger. Major Frost gave a picture of it to Dr. Ben Sullivan, the archaeologist in Khafra. The bronze handle was shaped like a winged cobra with a human face—Frost had joked that the figure looked like a centipede. It had been found on Harper's body in Cairo and later stolen from an Army building where it was held as evidence.

A wise and warm Irish voice returned to her memories. *This dagger is a very poisonous specimen. My advice is, if you do come across it, don't touch it,* said Sullivan. *I'm sure it's haunted by a wicked phantom!*

"Well! We'll see how little old Sigfried holds up in a powder party," remarked Ollie, sarcastically referring to the sandstorm. He was delighted that his fellow thieves would get stuck in it. "Kid ain't been tested proper by the desert yet—let's see if he don't drown!"

An ancient Egyptian ruin speckled with palm trees appeared in a valley that seemed like a dent in of the center of the world. This was the hidden oasis of Wadi Asra—the bandit captain Ollie, with his East London knack for rhyming and slang, dubbed the place "the Casbah." The wadi was one of many lairs where the robbers roosted. It was surrounded on all sides by treacherous terrain that even native tribesmen found hazardous to cross.

Once the ruins had been the shrine of the ancient Egyptian god Ra-Horakhty, a deity personifying the combined spirits of the sun king, Amun Ra, and the falcon prince, Horus. The ancients were convinced that both Horus and Ra lived here due to the strange orange light the sun cast over the oasis at high noon and the many falcons in the area.

The temple ruins, full of undiscovered riches, had already been sacked and pillaged by Ollie and his crew. They sold the gold and artifacts to dealers in Cairo and Alexandria. Some of it was melted into bricks. A large percentage of the funds raised were used by North African merchants to finance Hitler's war effort, while the rest of the money was squandered by Ollie and his men on pleasure and dissolution.

They had raped Egypt. Cultural treasures that should have belonged to the Egyptians were hawked to foreign collectors. The proceeds were used to pay for military invasions, prostitutes, and drinks. What was once a sacred shrine was now a lonely, crime-infested skeleton.

Major Desmond Frost lay on the broken sandstone floor of a dark, hieroglyph-covered chamber that once housed an altar of worship to the god Ra-Horakhty. Carved images of a falcon with a crown of sunbeams coming out of its head were everywhere. An electric lantern glowed from a grand niche in the wall; the robbers had put it there. It cast long ghastly shadows in the vault.

Frost was barely awake. He was in terrible condition. He was faint from blood loss; his clothing was caked with dirt and dried blood. His untreated gunshot wounds were swollen. Riding strapped inside the robbers' jeep during the tumultuous voyage through the dune sea had done him no good. The sun had scorched him. He was gripped with a fever and cold chills.

Preparing for the sandstorm, the robbers had hauled the Major inside the ruin and literally tossed him facedown on the floor. In pain, he managed to roll over and remained frozen there drifting in and out of consciousness.

The first thing he became aware of was Eve. She was a dim and kind presence in the dark. At first he thought he was dreaming. He realized he wasn't when he felt sharp metal tweezers digging painfully at his injured shoulder.

He jolted. She touched his face, trying to calm him.

"Hold still," said Eve. "I'm going to take the bullet out."

She had already removed his shirt, and scrubbed sand and grime from his wounds using a cloth doused in water. Frost, an athlete, had a hard, wiry frame and muscles like rocks. His skin was marked with tan lines from the blazing desert sun—and also the many scars he'd accumulated during a lifetime of sports and violence. His neck bore a pale and misshapen white scar shaped like a St. Andrew's Cross—a fatal shot wound he had cheated two years ago in 1940.

His present-day injuries were much less severe. The gunshot wound to his shoulder was swollen and inflamed, but the bullet had struck hard cartilage and started to work itself out; its metal edge was visible. His side was bloody from where Eislinger's bullet gashed him; the wound was deep but clean. No vitals had been struck, and no bullet was embedded. He would need some strong bandaging and probably several stitches.

What surprised Eve somewhat were the tattoos on the Major's body. Tattoos were fairly uncommon among middle-class British officers like Frost—but he had always been a rebel. Eve now discovered the lasting symbols he kept hidden under his clothing. Two were visible. Both were large. The first was on his upper arm; it was a winged griffin with a crown on its head and crossed rifles behind it. It was the insignia of the Army's Royal Wensingham Rifle Regiment, in which Frost had proudly served for years. The second was a Hindu design on his left breast near his heart—it was the profile of an elephant head, filled with foreign script, and its outline was formed by tiny curved swords. Eve had no idea what the symbols meant. She only saw strange pictures of beasts and weapons.

Meanwhile, the soldier stared up at her in pain and confusion. Eve tried to calm him by stroking his forehead. "Those men gave me some medical supplies and told me to help you. The leader wants you to recover so he can ask you questions," she explained in the gloom. "They planned on selling you to the Germans. I don't know what they're thinking now—whatever it is, you need to get better. Just bear with me."

He winced and instinctively jerked his arm as she made a second attempt to remove the bullet in his shoulder. She was rough with the tweezers.

"Hold still!" ordered Eve. "I know it hurts—but if I don't do this, nobody else will." She pinned his arm down and steadied the tweezers again. "Don't move. It'll be over in a second, I promise."

"You and your promises," breathed Frost with dry sarcasm. He tried to ignore the stabbing of the tweezers. Blood trickled down his shoulder. He perspired with pain. "Why are you here?"

"I came back," said Eve, anxious to distract him with conversation. "Wilmore drove off and tried to abandon you. I stopped him."

"How?"

"I wrecked the jeep," she answered bluntly. "Then I convinced these demons to take me prisoner."

He saw the determined frown on her face and thought her reckless bravery was endearing and strangely funny. He melted into a crooked smile and would have laughed, had not the bullet emerged just then. There was a brief, excruciating sting. The sound of metal skittered across the stone floor.

She mopped blood from his shoulder. The wound burned, but Frost felt relieved. It was easier for him to relax now. Eve leaned over him and kissed his forehead.

"My beautiful girl," muttered Frost, experiencing gladness and regret at once. "You should have escaped when you had a chance."

"Impossible," refuted Eve, with a distant ring of Germanic resolve in her voice. "I had to stay with you. There was no other choice for me."

A thin blast of sand gushed past the doorway. The sandstorm had arrived. The robbers had constructed makeshift "drawbridges" to block floods of dust from the Wadi Asra temple passages in these instances. The barriers were mostly effective. Even so, sand got in. Thin veils of dust surged through crevices and snaked along the sandstone floors like willowy, ghostly arms.

"Death dust," Eve breathed in quiet panic. She recalled the words of warning that the Major had once spoken to her about the risk of sand-borne infection. *The desert's like a wash basin that never gets rinsed or emptied. Bacteria churns and boils across hundreds of miles. Open wounds must be bandaged in the desert, he had said. Otherwise they won't heal and things could get worse.*

"Sit up!" she urged, trying forcefully to lift him. "Please. I have to make sure sand doesn't get in your wounds." Frost raised himself partially from the floor in pain and struggled into a sitting position.

The robbers had given Eve a thin roll of bandages. The material was hardly sufficient to wrap severe injuries—a doctor would have scoffed—but Eve was determined to make full use of it to cover his wounds. She wrapped the bandages tightly around his waist, then bandaged his shoulder. During this time, they were nearly embracing. Eve barely finished tying the last bandage when Frost suddenly put his arms around her and gave her a hug.

"You're a good nurse," he muttered. "Best I've ever had. I ought to get hurt more often so you can look after me."

She almost told him to stop joking, but her heart changed when she saw a shadow of grim strain on his face. Despite obvious suffering, he acted calm and self-controlled. He even attempted to mask his hardship with humor—a uniquely British phenomenon. It was strange, she thought. Brave. She loved him more for it.

"Don't worry. I'll get us out of here," said Frost. "I don't know what you've told them. But from now on, keep quiet and let me handle things..."

Boot steps sounded in the passage outside. There was a strange whisper like a murmuring man's voice saying something indistinguishable. The sound of cracking glass accompanied it. The scent of the sandstorm mingled with the strong and unmistakable smell of perfume.

Frost sensed something very wicked and uncanny in the atmosphere. The hard-edged military officer experienced a tinge of apprehension. He felt the woman in his arms chill with fear.

A shadow appeared in the doorway. Not a ghost, but a living person—the raider captain who wore the emerald green turban. Frost stared at him. It was the first time the Major had a chance to behold the prime suspect of his investigation up-close. He noted the man's muscular frame, Chinese tattoos, mangled Army jacket, flashy gold jewelry, and Afrika Korps moccasins. Also he recognized the sinister-looking ancient Egyptian dagger glowing in the dark on the robber's belt.

"Well, well. If it isn't the hidden 'Sphinx,'" said Frost to the man as the winds of the sandstorm whistled eerily outside. "Nice to meet you, Ollie Bryon. I've been looking for you for quite some time."

The words visibly stung the robber captain. His shoulders tensed. He took a half-step back.

"Oliver Bryon of Commando Group Sphinx," Frost stated sharply. "That's you. Isn't it?"

"So...you digged it all up, did you?" the bandit retorted in his thick cockney accent. "I thought you lot mistooked me for Ted Harper. You know, the bloke who copped it in Cairo recently."

"Nearly. Your 'Sphinx' ID disc was on his body," answered Frost coldly. "I suppose you shot him and put it there. Are you very eager to hide?"

"Oh, is that what you think?" He stepped into the room. The glow of the lantern darkened the shadows on his cunning, badger-like face. "Who might you be then, Mr. Army Investigations? Was you the bright spark who peeped under the tombstone and realized the tosser weren't me?"

"Why bother killing him in Cairo?" questioned Frost coldly. "Harper was one of your accomplices. You could easily have killed him in the desert and nobody would've noticed. Unless you performed this elaborate drama just to dupe Army powers into writing you off as a dead man. You must've spent a long time plotting an identity swap. All this trouble, just to play dead? What really happened?"

The captain leered in amusement at the prospect of a dangerous conversation. He crouched on the floor in front of the Major and Eve, defiant and volatile. "Sure. I killed the blighter," he admitted with an insolent laugh. "I had my reasons."

At this point, Ollie looked closely at Frost and noticed the tattoos on the Major's arm and chest. The robber was surprised. He noted the griffin symbol, but keenly focused on the Hindu elephant with swords.

"Well, looksy that!" said the tomb raider with a sneer. "Spent time in Bengal, did you, mate?" He was pleased with the discovery. "There them ink sweeps looks a bit familiar," he said, pointing. "I knowed a bloke that used to serve in India. Got himself a nice bit of patchwork done on his arm in a dusty little hellhole outside Calcutta. Can't remember the name of the bloomin' place. Used to rave about it, he did." He grinned. "Same artist, I reckon. But you don't look like the type of 'officer gentleman sir' to go swannin' about them type of places. Bit of a rake, are you, Major Muggins?"

Frost glowered. "I'm a soldier," he retorted, "not a saint."

The bandit guffawed with scornful laughter. "Well spoke!" he crowed. "Yeah, I could tell you was a vicious sort. Real clever with cannons, ain't you?" He smiled sinisterly, looking either ready to shoot Frost or congratulate him. "Have yourself a good time in India?"

"It was dirty and miserable," replied Frost, staring at the criminal unflinchingly.

The bandit's eyes lit with approval. "Ain't it ever?"

"What about your 'service'? Did you enjoy...China?"

"Wrong guess! I grabbed these here beauties in Singapore," leered Ollie, flashing the Chinese character designs on his hands. "It says writings of love poetry. A local tart done it for me." He nodded demandingly at Frost. "What's yours mean?"

"Answer my questions about Harper's murder," Frost ordered coldly.

Ollie laughed mockingly again. "You want some hints?" He chuckled. "Right. You have the look of a decent sort of scrummer. I'll gab. Maybe we'll have ourselves a bit of understanding," he said sarcastically. He turned to the woman and snarled at her. "Clear out, skirt!"

Frost used one arm to push Eve gently towards a corner behind him. He motioned for her to stay there.

"Right. She's your 'skirt'," said the raider, arching his brows in mockery. "Fine. You manage Fluffy, then. Just make sure she don't bother me. I don't have no patience for women."

Frost's eyes glowed with hate. He kept his self-control in check—barely.

"First things first. My name, as you nosy parkers have guessed, is Ollie Bryon," admitted the robber, enjoying the attention he was getting. "That's how they used to call me when I first started runnin' with Commando Group Sphinx. These them days the lads call me 'Flag,' and I do like the soundin' of that much better."

He reclined and crossed his tall, laced boots jauntily across the floor. "Once upon a time, there was a nasty little blinker by name of Ted Harper." He paused for drama. "Actually his real name were Ted Bailey, and he used to flit about with us Sphinxes, too. But that were a long time back. We'll just call him Teddy," he said. "Teddy boy weren't so half as good a soldier as me. Used to drive me sometimes, he did. Stupid little donkey ran straight over a trip wire once with Jerry confetti attached to it—barbwire tips and screws. That's how I lost me eye." He pointed at the shining gold eye in his head and rolled it for show. "Teddy wanted a piece of the business. I let him in. Old times sake and all. Then the little mosquito decided to steal from me."

"Some gold jewelry, a pipe, and an ivory jar," interjected Frost, remembering the artifacts Harper had tried to hawk from the museum. He looked at the dagger gleaming in the shadows from the man's belt. "And perhaps something else more valuable."

The robber smirked in the dark. "Teddy never were too bright. Halfway to the Nile he ran out of petrol and hoofed it." He laughed in contempt. "Tracked Teddy down, I did. Little sand rat set himself up cozy in Cairo. Worked at his little museum. Thought he were safe from me. Waited long enough, I did. Then 'pop' went the weasel."

He looked up at Frost with a boyish expression. "So to answer your question, mate, I'd have loved to top him off in the desert. Have made for a fine jackal snack, Teddy would've," he said lightheartedly. "But I had to do it when I done it. Couldn't wait no more. Had to get my lucky charm back."

He ran his fingers lovingly across the flint dagger. The bronze handle shaped like a winged serpent glinted in the dark. The electric lamp flickered nearby for no reason. Footsteps shuffled outside the door—nobody was there. Frost noticed the strange noise and knew it was supernatural. The robber ignored it.

"That's the 'lucky charm' you mean?" questioned Frost, gesturing at the knife.

"That's right," Ollie retorted in stubborn, stone-faced defiance. "Dagger of kings, this. It's me royal septic."

Frost blinked drolly at the man's illiteracy. "Do you mean 'scepter?'"

Ollie scowled at him. He ignored the remark.

"Sorry to make a fuss. I'd hoped by throwin' me name chip on Teddy boy, the police'd get tangled up with you lot, then you lot'd get mixed up, ask the wrong pifflin' questions and stay out of my business. I'd play dead for awhile. No harm there, ain't it?" He smirked crookedly. "See, I don't got no blitherin' family so bein' officially dead don't matter. Bein' dead would do me a bit of good. Business model's more important than a war service record."

"Yes, you have made quite a 'business' of things. Haven't you?" remarked Frost, bridling his scorn. "It'll dry up when the war is over, though. What will you do then?"

The captain was irked by the notion of his escapades coming to a close. "Either the war won't end or I won't outlast it.

I'm a fightin' bloke. That's the only way I'll have it," he declared.

"Who are you fighting, exactly?" retorted Frost calmly, with a sardonic twist in one corner of his mouth. "I'm a fighting man, too, you see. Naturally I'm very interested to find out what you're up against. So far I haven't seen you doing much in the way of fighting aside from fighting to put money in your pockets and terrorize unarmed people. Is that what you mean?"

The robber captain, infuriated, exploded. He lunged across the floor and punched the wounded British officer in the waist with a hard slam of his fist. Frost anticipated the blow and managed to block it slightly with one hand. Nevertheless, it struck near one of his wounds. He fell over wincing. Despite the pain, the Major was defiantly cheerful. He laughed.

"Belt up, slime! I'm specialer than you!" menaced Ollie with illiterate conviction, looming over the Major and pointing a threatening finger at him. "You're nothin' compared to me. I'd like to see you snip a Jerry's gizzard when he's sleepin' without makin' no noise, eat sand rats and sidewinders for breakfast, or go hikin' past a week without no water. I'm the best!" he declared. "That's why I'm in Special Forces."

"Really? I don't see you with the rest of your unit—or whatever your lot calls a military formation," said Frost, struggling to regain his breath after the hard blow. "I don't see you pursuing the enemy. I see no discipline. Not even a decent uniform. Is that leaf-green head rag part of your kit?" He smiled mockingly as he saw a discomfited look pass over the robber's face. "You, Ollie, are a scavenger with military training. You're no soldier."

The other man's face flushed with rage. His jaw tightened. His hand fell to the knife on his belt. "Funny thing," he said in a trembling voice. "I done heard somethin' like that recent from another Army mug. He got ate alive by jackals."

"Actually, you're wrong," quipped Frost. "That man survived and told everyone about you. You're famous!"

Ollie was puzzled. He recoiled and waited for clarification.

"The whole British Army is after your hide," taunted Frost. "Everyone's talking about how you killed your comrades and left them to rot in the desert. The men in every rank and department would find it a joy to hang you. Even your superiors in Commando Group Sphinx know what you've done."

"No. I don't believe it," refuted the captain, trying to sound firm but clearly panicked. "My command don't care where I am, long as I croak Jerries. They ain't watchin' after me—never was. Asides, we Special Forces trackers are a close-knit bunch. Brothers, us lot. Fair number of my squaddies is in business with me. The rest would never cross me."

"Don't pretend to know loyalty, Ollie," dismissed Frost with indignation. "You use your 'skills' to rob dead men instead of fighting enemies of your country."

Ollie lost his temper. "What do you know about it?" He jumped to his feet and shouted. "What even is my country?"

"England, I assume. Unless you inherited that Bow Bells accent from some backwards side of the earth," quipped Frost.

"None of your filthy business!" roared the tomb raider. He hopped back and forth towards Frost, waffling on the brink of violence. He restrained himself and spat venomously on the floor. "You'd better hope you don't catch gangrene afore I can hawk you to the Jerries. Right now you got value. The minute you get sickness, you don't. That's when I'll tear you up!" he growled.

"So you're not going to kill us, then?" Frost was bewildered. "Why not? I should think you'd want to silence us after all the information you've passed along."

"I'm sellin' you to the Jerries, Major Muggins, because I need petrol and pennies. Whatever dirt you heard from me don't make no blinkin' difference to them—or you, where you'll end up," he replied. "Jerries pay money for brass like you. Harvest information from officers, they do. Pack you right up and ship you off to blitzin' Berlin, heck as like, with a great big bow sayin' 'Gestapo, please torture me,' wrote all over you." He grinned with malicious satisfaction. "Likely the fact you're an Army investigator will make your trip very excitin.' "

He turned to Eve with dull lust in his eyes. "Ain't quite decided about Fluffy over here," he mused. "I got uses for Fluffy—but I don't like sharin' skirts, and likely the other lads'll get terrible jealous if I'm the only one havin' fun. Not good for the camp. Asides, Fluffy annoys me. There's just somethin' about her I don't like."

He jumped towards Eve and jerked his boot as if to kick her. He saw her flinch and laughed with sadistic delight. "Then again, I ain't had no refreshin' company in awhile," he pondered spitefully, aware of Frost's anger and feeling empowered by it. "Maybe I can share with the lads, this time." He winked at Eve. "Or maybe I'll just knock her over when nobody's watchin.'"

Frost bristled. His blue eyes smoldered like embers in the dark. "This woman is mine," he stated. "Touch her and I'll rip your eyes out with my bare hands. Then you'll have to wear two marbles," he swore, with a sarcastic nod at Ollie's false metal eyeball. "How would you like that?"

The bandit was taken aback by the threat. His sense of fun withered. The cocky smile vanished from his face. He tried to laugh, but there was nothing remotely comical about the way Frost stared at him. The British officer glowered like a lion crouching in the bushes, about to shred a buffalo to pieces. He looked deadly.

The robber was sheepish. He wasn't used to being snarled at by others. He was a scavenger who had grown complacent attacking dead and defenseless targets. Like a vulture, he was leery of a struggle with a rabid enemy.

He studied his prisoner. The Major was obviously wounded, but the murderous look in his eyes and his forcefulness made his threat believable. Ollie weighed his options. Theoretically, he could kill or maim Frost with gunfire to take Eve—but that would spoil his plan to sell the officer for money and supplies. He decided to concede.

"Keep her, then," he said with a disdainful snort. He leveled another pretend kick at Eve, saw her jump, and laughed wickedly again. "I hate 'skirts,' anyway. All stupid cows, in my opinion."

Ollie turned to leave but halted at a jarring sight. For the first time, the bandit caught a glimpse of Eve's true nature. He saw the woman glare at him. Never had he seen such a look of seething aggression on a female face. It startled him. He glanced between her and Frost and perceived commonality.

"Fine pair of demons, the both of you," he remarked. "If you was to strike a nail in my coffin, she'd help you hammer it in. Ain't I right?"

At that moment, the glinting dagger in the bandit's belt suddenly detached itself from him and dropped onto the sandstone floor with a loud crash. The sound echoed in the dark vaults of the ancient temple.

The blade skidded across the floor and landed within Frost's reach. The eerie human face on its cobra-shaped hilt gleamed in the dimness as if trying to allure him with a wink.

It seemed almost as if the knife, possessed by a will of its own, was tempting Frost to snatch it and use it to kill its master.

Frost seriously considered grabbing it. The only thing that held him back was the memory of Ben Sullivan's voice talking about spirit seals, curses and evil ghosts.

It sometimes happens that Egyptian artifacts have effects on people that don't seem to be directly related, Sullivan's words returned to haunt him. *Just because you can't see something doesn't mean it's not there. It sounds like this dagger is a very poisonous specimen. My advice is, if you do come across it, don't touch it. Do you understand? Hands off!*

Although not inclined to believe in such things, Frost was inwardly repulsed by the dagger. He also had witnessed some strange phenomena in its presence that reminded him of the talk at Army headquarters in Cairo. Glass cracking, whispers, the sudden and suffocating odor of perfume. He didn't want to tempt fate. He had too much to lose.

This moment of decision passed by fleetingly before Ollie the robber captain snatched the dagger back with a rough swipe. Frost thought he saw the handle move itself away from Ollie's hand as he reached to reclaim it.

A strange whooping noise echoed through the passages. A trilling male yell that seemed made by a thousand voices. For a moment, the three stared at each other in nameless anxiety—all of them thought it was supernatural. Until one of the robbers, another Briton, came running down the corridor screaming for help.

"Flag! Come quick!" he shouted. "We're being attacked!"

CHAPTER 12: CROSSED SWORDS

"Think how many royal bones
Sleep within this heap of stones;
Here they lie, had realms and lands,
Who now want strength to stir their hands."
—"On the Tombs in Westminster Abbey"
by Francis Beaumont

Thundering hooves shook up dust among the ancient stone ruins as Bedouin tribesmen launched their surprise attack. More than 30 sword-wielding horsemen in flying colorful robes came swooping into the tomb robbers' stronghold at Wadi Asra to take revenge. The Bedouins slashed down and trampled tomb robbers emerging from temple buildings using slender cutlasses.

The tribesmen were skinny yet unusually strong. They had sharp, angular faces like desert falcons and burning dark eyes. Some wore boots made of soft hide; others were barefoot. These men who lacked shoes were prouder than the richest emperors. These warriors were monarchs of the wilderness.

They were relatives of the tribal group massacred the previous day by Siegwulf Eislinger. Hours after the massacre, three Bedouin camps knew about the killings and who was responsible. A war party set out the following day. Until now, the Bedouins had not interfered with the activities of the tomb raiders. Provoked, they sought reprisal. They had traveled during the sandstorm to surprise and kill their enemies.

The tomb robbers exited the temple building in confusion and either fled or fired side arms in vain when they saw the stampede of Bedouins. Two of the robbers made a daring escape in a jeep with one Bedouin warrior in hot pursuit. His fine robes and tassels identified him as a tribal dignitary. A sabre flickered in his thin hand like a whip of moonlight. His pearl white horse galloped faster than a stroke of lightning. Its airy, hopping little hooves and bouncing plume of a tail made it resemble a desert fairy. The delicate creature raced like a furious flame dashed from the wheels of Elijah's divine chariot. The jeep cleared the ruin and made straight for the open desert, spitting dust and gravel in its wake. The Bedouin warrior was determined to catch it. He sang something to his horse. His chant stirred the beast's spirit beyond known limits. Its heart was moved by its master. Defying all odds, the horse excelled itself. Its speed at a breakneck gallop increased by nearly three times faster.

One of the robbers tried to maneuver a machine-gun turret to bear on the Bedouin as he caught up with the jeep. The Bedouin zigzagged out of the way. Then the Arab stood by digging his heels into his horse's sides and straightening his legs. Floating there with acrobatic flair he stretched his arms out. His robes billowed like the rippling wings of a huge eagle diving for a kill. With a shrill war cry, he swung his arm. The flashing blade in his hand struck faster than the flickering tongue of a snake. The would-be gunner's head sailed off with one clean hit. The driver's head soon followed. The jeep careened into the emptiness, a carriage of death. The Bedouin gave a victory cry and waved his sword. The bloody blade shone in the sunlight. His head kerchief and tassels flounced magnificently as his horse pranced, raising tufts of triumphant dust.

The tribesmen took vengeance on the remains of the men who had murdered their relatives. The bodies of robbers in the temple complex area were posthumously decapitated. Their hands, also, were chopped off. The corpses were stabbed multiple times. All crew members who accompanied Ollie, the captain, to the hideout were killed.

The captain himself escaped almost certain death at the last minute. As his men cried for him to help save their lives, Ollie fled. The bandit leader raced deep inside the temple complex and made a hasty exit through a pitch-black limestone escape tunnel once used by the Egyptians as a passage to a yard of sacred animal tombs.

Ollie darted through several cracked-open tomb chambers, bypassing their ruined sealed doors. He disappeared through a labyrinth of tomb vaults that housed the remains of sacred Apis bulls. The bulls, perceived as divine by the ancients, had been elaborately mummified and adorned like four-legged horned kings. Seven bulls were entombed outside the temple; each had its own tomb. The bulls, in their original state, had been mummified in kneeling and standing positions on large platform altars. They wore golden death masks, and their horns were decked with jewels and rings. Their legs had been wrapped in the finest linen; their hooves were dipped in bronze alloy, and their entrails had been enshrined in canopic jars of the finest ivory under statues of the death god Anubis.

The tomb robbers had ransacked the bull tombs. Ollie and his bandits had thrown the bulls from their altars, pried the jewels from their horns, ripped their amulets and ceremonial dress off, and torn away their golden death masks. Even small gold rings in the bulls' mummified ears had been ripped away. The antiques had been hawked to underworld dealers and sold to high-ticket collectors in foreign lands. Some of the gold was melted. All the proceeds were wasted on cheap vice. Canopic jars lay smashed on the floors of the tombs next to the ravaged bodies of the beasts. One tomb's altar chamber was littered with cigarette butts, dusty erotic postcards, and boot-trampled entertainment magazines.

Ollie was oblivious to the destruction he caused. He escaped upwards through a ceiling vault breached by ancient tomb robbers long ago—they had left a rope ladder hanging from a ceiling duct which, due to the dank atmosphere in the tomb, was still flexible and preserved.

The bandit captain scaled it in a few instants and popped out into the bright light of the afternoon sun in an empty field of mausoleum mounds far behind the temple. Cries of the Bedouin warriors echoed in the distance as he made his escape on foot, heading towards a range of steep red-colored stone cliffs to the west. He was quick and silent. He disappeared into the abyss of the desert like a mirage.

Meanwhile, the Bedouins completed their revenge and took battle trophies. They plucked bright pins from the dead men's uniforms, took their guns, their ammunition and their leather belts. They stole the armed jeeps by climbing around the vehicles, and literally unwiring and rewiring circuits and gears in different directions.

They also found foodstuffs the robbers had stored in the temple. None of the food interested the Bedouins except for some British military-issued canned peaches, which seemed tasty. They also found a supply of water tanks. They carried away as much as they could and went off, rich with booty. The warriors sang songs of triumph. Arabic chanting soared across the dunes as they disappeared into the horizon.

Major Frost and Eve escaped the raid by concealing themselves behind a large stone statue in the temple's main worship room. The room was halfway filled with a stone carving of Ra-Horakhty, the falcon-sun deity, jutting out from the wall with immense unfurled wings and a crown of sunbeams. A large stone altar—large enough to sacrifice two bulls on top of—stood in front of the statue, separated from the stone god by a deep trench filled with dust and gravel. In former times, the trench had been used to kindle a wall of sacred smoke around the statue and also to catch blood runoff from animal sacrifices. The tomb robbers had vandalized the statue of Ra-Horakhty by scratching graffiti onto it; otherwise, they had left the room untouched because they had no use for the space.

Frost, wearing trousers and bandages, had no time to make a proper escape plan. Dragging Eve with him as the sounds of Arabic yelling and the screams of dying men filled the air, he swooped up a handgun from a scattered weapons cache and ran into the main worship room on accident. He threw Eve a pistol and told her to hide behind the stone wings of the massive god statue. He concealed himself behind the altar and planned to use it as cover for a shooting affray.

Nothing happened. Men ran back and forth shouting in the front of the temple. Shots burst in claps and rang down the halls like applause. Distant horses whinnied. One robber attempted to run into the room via a hallway; he was cut down by a tribal swordsman and mutilated before he crossed the doorstep. Afterwards, Bedouins ran in and out of the room with armloads of booty, sometimes dropping things as they made their way back and forth.

Then they were all gone. Vanished, like a brief desert thunderstorm. The silence of death fell upon the temple like a dark shroud.

Frost waited until he was certain no enemies were in the area. Then he emerged and took charge of the area by reconnoitering each room and the outside entrance to the temple. He assessed the dead men; all of them were Ollie Bryon's tomb robber crew. No dead tribesmen were to be found—and, unfortunately, no dead Bryon was found, either. Clearly the bandit captain had escaped or hidden himself somewhere. Frost's instincts told him that Bryon had left the area somehow and was no longer on the premises.

The Major then gathered his belongings, including his beret and his bloodstained uniform apparel. He attempted to clean these off using some stale water that the robbers had collected in an ancient rain cistern. Afterwards he was able to dress somewhat normally again. Soaking wet, he returned to the main worship room.

The supply situation was not good, he told Eve. The Bedouins took all of the jeeps and most of the water canisters.

There was probably a cistern outside; if one existed nearby, its location was unknown. Thankfully they had weapons left and some food. No radio or communication equipment was to be found anywhere. How they would return to civilization was a mystery that needed solving—especially since, to the best of their knowledge, there were more tomb robbers coming to Wadi Asra to regroup with Ollie.

They argued. Eve was in favor of leaving immediately and hiking on foot; Frost was opposed to it. He believed they needed to recoup and hold the temple as a position until help could be reached—possibly they could ambush the other tomb robbers and hijack a jeep with radio equipment. Eve had little faith in the plan. Despite her warrior spirit and admiration for Frost, she doubted their ability to successfully hijack a fully manned jeep outfitted with machine gun turrets.

The British Major was not used to having his authority disputed. The argument became heated and bitter. At one point, Eve tried to stomp angrily out of the room, but changed her mind when she nearly tripped over a bloody corpse in the hall. She returned to Frost with a pale countenance and was silent. Frost was irritated. They did not speak for several minutes. Sitting on the floor angrily reloading a pistol, he was overcome by an affectionate impulse and wanted to reconcile. He turned to her.

A strange noise pierced the air. They looked at each other in alarm.

Someone was whistling. It echoed through the empty halls. Eve immediately recognized the tune to the American folk song, "The Yellow Rose of Texas." At first, she thought the unseen whistler was an American or British person. Then the singing started.

> "Ich bin neulich hier in Nirgendwo,
> ich stürm' die ganze Nacht!
> Die Tanten nenn' es nicht genug,
> Sie fordern aller Macht!
>
> Die können wohl vom Bergle spring'n,
> Oder brech'n Sie die Knie,
> but the Yellow Rose of Texas ist die only one für me!"

The singer was unmistakably male and German.

Eve was caught off guard by the songster's sarcastic humor. Clearly he was a German soldier—but evidently not a loyal Nazi. Besides singing an American tune, he derisively referred to German army officials as his "aunts" and criticized them for being too demanding; his comic lyrics suggested they leap off a mountain or break their knees.

Frost didn't care what the man was singing. He was armed and ready to shoot.

He did not get the chance.

The crafty German slipped in through a side door. He materialized in a corner like a ghostly apparition. He was a dusty figure in a khaki uniform. He wore knee-high black jackboots and a cloth Afrika Korps cap, crowned with a white eagle insignia, tilted jauntily on his head. A pair of large, aviator-style goggles on his face caused him to resemble a praying mantis. He cradled a silenced sniper rifle in his arms. Medals glinted dully from his breast and waist. He was completely covered in sand powder.

The German leveled the rifle. He snapped in a crisp and strangely melodic voice, ordering Frost to lower his weapon. *"Die Waffe nieder!"*

Frost stared in surprise for a moment, then defiantly aimed at the enemy soldier.

Eve jumped up and threw herself between the two men to prevent disaster. Fluent in German, she quickly made herself an interpreter. A brief haggling match started. Eve tried to explain and bargain; the German asked abrupt and detailed questions. Eventually the atmosphere warmed over and the German regarded Eve with a friendly expression.

"He is not a tomb robber or a partisan," she explained on his behalf. "He is an officer of the Afrika Korps. He won't harm us."

"Tell him to put the gun down!" shouted Frost.

She interpreted. The German shook his head and barked back something in a clipped tone.

"He says no. He says for you to drop your weapon," she translated.

A standoff ensued. Both men, authoritative and used to having their orders obeyed, refused to submit. The impasse came to an end when the German, exasperated, made a proclamation.

"He says he will only agree to put down his weapon if you swear on your honor as a British officer that you will not try to shoot him afterwards," Eve interpreted, perspiring in apprehension. "If you do try any such thing, he says you will certainly fail and he will kill you as an enemy combatant."

Frost rattled off his version of an "honor oath" with typically rough irreverence. "I, Maj. Desmond L. Frost of the British Royal Army, solemnly swear that I will not shoot your sorry self unless you provoke me to do it," he declared boldly. "In which case, I will gladly shoot you and put this ridiculous bargaining to an end!"

Eve looked desperately at him. He was unrepentant.

The German peered curiously.

Trying to appear calm, Eve turned to the German and assured him politely that the Major swore vigorously to do him no harm. The German appeared satisfied with this explanation. He set his sniper rifle down on the floor. He did not, however, make any gesture of surrender.

Instead, he strolled over and pulled the goggles from his face. Rings of white skin like pale raccoon eyes were left on his face where the suction had sealed dust away. The German had a rugged face, a thin mouth, short light blond hair and clear, dancing blue eyes. His manner was wry and confident. He studied the Major with intellectual humor as if the other man were an amusing scorpion glaring at him from a bottle.

Frost didn't budge or flinch. The Major was naturally bold and aggressive. In the face of wartime opponents, he remained indomitable. He probed the German's eyes with hawkish acuity, trying to scan the enemy's thoughts. Usually Frost, with his talent at reading faces, gained insights into a person's disposition in moments. But this character was an enigma.

The German spoke again. A long blur of merry, singsong sentences.

"He says: 'It seems like you both need a ride. Would you like to come with me? I can gladly drive you,'" Eve interpreted. "'I have a truck just outside. I need some supplies from here. You need a lift. Let's make a deal.'"

Frost menaced him with the pistol. "This is what will happen. You will give us the vehicle and you will navigate us out of here. You will do exactly as I say without any protests," he commanded. "From now on, you are a prisoner of war."

Eve arched her brows in imploring disbelief. Again, Frost was unrepentant. She dutifully translated most of what he said, in slightly politer terms.

The German laughed. He folded his arms behind his back, nodded towards the exit and started gibbering again.

"'Please. There is no need to act gruesome or wave weapons around. We are not gangsters or cowboys,'" Eve translated, stifling a smile at the German's wry humor. "'I have nothing against you. I need supplies and I know that you need assistance. I saw that you have been ambushed recently outside the dune ocean. What happened to you was unfortunate.'"

Frost bristled. "He followed us?"

"No. Not us. Someone else," Eve translated in response to more German clucks and chitters. "He has some things to discuss that might interest you. Would you like to go somewhere more comfortable and talk, he asks?"

The Major agreed to the suggestion but refused to relinquish his weapon. He collected the German's sniper rifle. He allowed the German to collect gasoline canisters from the robbers' supply dumps. He ordered Eve to bring extra guns, food and ammunition. When addressing Major Frost, Eve made the mistake of calling the British officer by his Army nickname, "Frosty."

The German was delighted to hear it. Her American pronunciation made it sound like the German word for "rust." He found it comical. "*Rostig?*" he repeated gleefully, pointing at Frost.

Frost shot Eve an edged glance. "Not sure what it means, but it sounds like the name of a Swiss yodeler," he muttered sardonically to her.

Eve was at a loss for how to fix the blunder. She tried to tell him the proper name was "Frost," a word which had an identical counterpart in German. However, the Afrika Korps man, with his impertinent sense of humor, had already made up his mind to christen the Major "Rusty" instead. It was impossible to correct him.

"Von Rindl," announced the German, introducing himself. He stuck his arm out buoyantly to offer Frost a handshake.

Frost derided the gesture. He found it completely ridiculous in such circumstances to shake hands. Given the war hostilities between their two countries, he was inclined to refuse. But he saw Eve, his heart's desire, scowling desperately from a distance. Frost realized she would resent him if he did not make concessions. He accepted the handshake. The German grinned, wrung his arm with a quick jolt, and bustled off carrying a gasoline canister.

Eve marched over to Frost. Interpreting between two armed and stubborn men in opposing armies was wearing her nerves thin. The German was a marvel of cordiality. She blamed Frost for all difficulties.

"Thank you for being polite!" she snapped. "I was afraid you'd start a fight."

"And? What's wrong with that, I ask you?" retorted the British officer. "I am armed. He is not. If he tried to assault me, I'd blast him dead, and that'd be the end of it. We'd take his motor and be halfway to Alexandria in no time, and there'd be one less German in the Afrika Korps."

Eve regarded him with speechless disgust.

Frost's strong blue stare broke. He avoided eye contact and his jaw tensed. He gave her an injured glance. "Please don't look at me like that," he said quietly.

The woman's attitude softened slightly. "I'm trying my best to make everything go smoothly," she explained. "Please don't make things harder than they already are!"

"Your interpreting is not the problem here. It's him!" said Frost, nodding in the direction the German had gone. "He has little reason to be so friendly to us. Something seems wrong. I don't trust him."

"I don't trust him, either," she admitted in a half-whisper. "But he's treating us well—he thought I was from Germany and asked me. I told him I'm part German and that my German family name was Hecking. He warmed up. He considers me a comrade," she explained. "Let's try to get along with him for now. We can get out of here. Maybe he can even help you with your investigation. There won't be a need for violence."

Frost sighed tensely as the German marched back into view. "Let's hope you're right," he said. "If not, don't blame me for taking matters into my own hands."

CHAPTER 13: RITUALS OF EXECUTION

"Auf! Sattelt mir mein Pferd
Und legt darauf den Mantelsack
So reit' ich hin und her
Als Jäger vom Kürpfalz."

—"Ein Jäger aus Kürpfalz"
[A Hunter from Kürpfalz] German folk song

V on Rindl escorted them efficiently to his vehicle, parked on one side of the temple. It was an Italian armored vehicle that opened from a top hatch and could fit several people inside. He assured them that there would be no surprises. He was traveling alone, he admitted. However, he did have radio contact with the Afrika Korps who would look for him if contact ceased.

He stressed the fact that he was being monitored to the mistrustful Major Frost, who still looked capable of killing him, to discourage any assassination attempts. Eve insisted that neither she nor her British military comrade intended to do him any harm. Von Rindl, a canny observer, believed in Eve's goodwill—but remained on guard against Major Frost.

The two men watched each other tensely as Von Rindl refueled the vehicle and tossed supplies into the hatch. The German's attempts at sociable comments fell flat. Frost was no good at being superficially friendly in the best of times and among his own people. He was extra reticent due to caution.

Frost decided to pose a series of questions. "Tell me, Von Wrinkle, how much do you estimate a chap like me's worth in barrels of petrol?"

Von Rindl watched the British soldier's face astutely as Eve dutifully translated.

"These thieving monkeys wanted to sell me to your lads for petrol," he explained. "What do you think? Could they have made a deal?"

Von Rindl snorted in disdain. "I don't trade on the black market, but to me it sounds like crazy pipe dreams," he retorted saucily. "I'd be surprised if anyone in the Afrika Korps would even give me any petrol much less trade it with others. Not much petrol is left! Even this supply I found here is very short."

"Most of your spare tins getting blown up, eh? That's what I thought," replied Frost. He gave a sharp, mocking grin. "Italian supply ships explode in the news everyday. The blasts make such lovely pictures..."

Von Rindl interrupted. "Even hospital ships are getting sunk in the Mediterranean," he said. "Nobody in the Afrika Korps in their right mind would give away petrol. Unless they want to continue the war riding donkeys!"

Frost broke into laughter. "That would be a worthy sight!" he exclaimed. "Well, there are plenty around in case you ever need them. Camels, too."

The German did not find the Major's satirical style of humor very funny.

"So, you've no idea how these blokes came by the idea of snagging German petrol?"

"They probably use middlemen. Or maybe some Italians are trading our petrol for cigars. That wouldn't surprise me," Von Rindl answered dryly. "I admit, it does sometimes happen that we 'buy' kidnapped British officers for goods. High ranks tend to make desirable purchases."

"Not something you're considering, I hope," said Frost. "You'll find I'm very much not for sale."

"I have better things to do than go Easter-Egg-hunting for Tommies," retorted Von Rindl curtly, offended by the remark. "Ranks and badges make no difference. One Tommy to me is the same as another. None are worth selling."

"Did you hear that? The cheeky beggar called me a Tommy!" said Frost with a sharp grin, before Eve had a chance to scramble the translation.

Trying to pacify him, Eve suggested the remark wasn't meant as an insult.

"No, I understood that word!" Frost interjected, still grinning dangerously. "Heard it before. In France. A stout German officer tried to get us to surrender. He called out to us, in very bad English, 'Tommy Englishmans, you are conquered!'" said Frost, mimicking with cavalier humor. "His head blew off seconds later. One of our Matildas pitched him a beamer," he said, using cricket slang to describe the tank shot. "Bowled his block right off!" Frost recalled the scene with a morbid smile. "Everybody laughed for some reason," he admitted. "I think it was the timing."

Eve was horrified. "I refuse to translate that!"

"He's a soldier. He can stomach it," dismissed Frost. "Ask him if he served in France."

She saw Frost's finger lurking near the trigger of his gun and suspected the worst. "Frosty," she implored. "Please stop!"

"Stop what?" retorted Frost with outraged innocence. "I'm not doing anything!"

Von Rindl watched the conversation suspiciously. "What's with this guy?" he asked Eve. "Something is wrong here."

"Nothing's wrong," assured Eve, trying not to look nervous. "Frosty was wounded earlier, and I think he's a little jumpy. Please stay calm, and don't say anything sarcastic. We don't want a misunderstanding."

"Wounded, yes. Jumpy, maybe. But you don't trust him," assessed Von Rindl, his eyes narrowing in consideration. "Neither do I."

"I do trust him!" she protested.

"With your own safety, yes," said Von Rindl with a thin, wry smile. "But you're not wearing a German uniform."

"What's he saying?" demanded Frost.

Von Rindl interrupted to spare Eve from another awkward translating bout. "Come inside the truck. We can have a decent conversation," volunteered the German, much warmer and politer than usual. "Would you like some tea? I have some British rations."

Eve looked at her companion in exhaustion. "Do you want English tea?"

Frost was astonished. "Yes." He cracked an ironic half-smile. "But since it's already mine, I shouldn't have to ask for it," he joked. "Where did a German pinch our tea from?"

Von Rindl sensed the other man was attempting friendly banter, but the Afrika Korps ranger was too unnerved to respond. His mistrust of Major Frost had reached new heights.

Eve tried to compensate by being as warm and German as she could to Von Rindl. She quickly won his respect and the beginnings of his friendship. They shared a common language and culture, and understood each other.

She also understood "the German way"—a certain code of behavior shared by most Germans. This was nothing that could be taught from a textbook; it came naturally to her and fell over her like a spell whenever she was among other German people. The "German way" was almost indefinable yet distinct. It was present in the way one snippily moved one's hands when handling objects, in bobbing one's head during a conversation, in tiny understated glances, and in various lilts and crescendos of spoken German. Lacking were the unappreciated traits of clumsiness or carelessness. There was precision, alacrity, and hardy spirit in the "German way." It governed all aspects of German behavior ad infinitum. It was instantly recognizable to Germans, who often identified compatriots by noticing small mannerisms. Most of the time, Germans admired each other for these mannerisms—due to the fact that Germans were concerned with processes and perfection. It often happened that Germans could revel in odd things such as the neat way another German scribbled or organized objects.

Sometimes Germanic perfection could be so exciting that two Germans befriended each other while performing chores like dusting or folding. Teamwork forged bonds. Exactly such a thing happened to Eve and Von Rindl when they were loading the vehicle for departure. Already on good terms, they enjoyed snappily handing each other supplies and crisply stacking cans of food in the vehicle. The true moment of epiphany came when they shut a small window in the vehicle. They moved their arms in unison and flicked dust off the glass at almost exactly the same time. It was a heartwarming moment. They looked at each other with sparkling approval.

Frost felt alienated. He could neither speak German nor understand the apparent familial bliss that blossomed between the German soldier and Eve. It was upsetting. Eve, the woman he loved, suddenly transformed into a complete foreigner. Furthermore, he had negative impressions of Germans—he had been nearly killed by them and suffered many hardships at their hands on battle frontlines, not to mention cultural losses he felt due to the Germans' London Blitz bombings. An educated military man, Frost was not a bigot and found it possible to respect Germans for their history of military achievements. However, he had hard feelings towards Germany that were not lightly founded.

He did not trust Von Rindl and did not feel safe. He wanted Eve to be her old self again, to return to being someone he knew. He wanted her to go back to normal.

The interior of the vehicle was a clean, orderly space with folded maps, papers, and a garbling radio. There were several built-in seats inside the metal-reinforced vehicle walls. They lowered themselves inside using ladder of metal rungs descending from the hatch.

Explaining he needed to report his location to the radio, Von Rindl gained permission to use his communication equipment. Von Rindl uttered a few harmless words to his contacts—Eve couldn't make out everything he said, but it seemed innocent. Frost, still armed with the handgun, watched suspiciously.

"Drive," ordered Frost, motioning Von Rindl towards the driver's seat and sitting behind him with the pistol ready. "Make for Alexandria, and don't try anything stupid."

Von Rindl was intensely annoyed at Frost. He had done everything possible to facilitate peaceful relations. He did not like being threatened or treated like a hostage. He decided to take a small risk. As he took the wheel, Von Rindl pretended to get his boot stuck on a piece of communications wire; while stooping to "untangle" himself, he pressed a small signals switch hidden under the console without anyone noticing.

An emergency signal traveled to his command post instantly. The Germans received it and reacted in unison like a silent pack of sharks. Like most Germans, they took action with no sign or forewarning. The radio simply went quiet.

Eve noticed the sudden radio silence, but failed to realize what it meant.

Frost steadied himself. He was very uneasy because he and Eve were cornered with this strange enemy officer. It was anyone's guess what was really going on. Eve was too trusting and lacked desert warfare experience; Frost found it difficult to manage the German and keep track of their developing situation at the same time. At this point, he was not sure if Von Rindl would last the journey or if the German's blood would end up being spattered all over the console.

He tried to make the most of the opportunity to gain information. "You said you were following someone," he remarked. "Who is it?"

Von Rindl, driving, asked Eve to serve them cups of tea—there was a small brewed canister of stolen British black tea in the back, with some dirty porcelain cups. He offered some to Frost, who readily accepted.

The German took a sip and turned jauntily to glance at Eve as he was driving. "Come sit here in the front, so you can hear me better," he told her over the crushing roar of tires over sand and gravel. "This guy will keep us talking for the entire way, and there's no use shouting."

He introduced himself as Capt. Elrich von Rindl, a proud soldier in the Afrika Korps, originally from South Germany by way of West Africa. He informed them upfront that he was under orders to hunt and kill a dangerous German criminal traveling with the tomb robbers.

The hunted man's name was Siegwulf Eislinger. He was a young fellow with glasses—Von Rindl showed them a photo and asked if it looked familiar. Eve failed to recognize it.

Frost said it did look familiar—he said it looked like his grandmother's sister, minus a gray braid. Eve laughed at the joke. Frost grinned, pleased by her reaction. Eve was unable to translate the humor to Von Rindl. She could only say the Major found Eislinger odd-looking.

Von Rindl explained that his target, Eislinger, was a spree killer who brutalized and massacred unarmed civilians. This had been occurring for quite some time. Only recently had the Afrika Korps ascertained that Eislinger was responsible.

He was supposed to have been arrested—however, Eislinger disappeared during a sandstorm. An all-points-bulletin had been put out. Due to typical German secrecy and bureaucracy, most Afrika Korps soldiers were only told that Eislinger was "a suspicious person." Eislinger rematerialized in the company of a Panzer unit a great distance from where he was last seen. The Panzer unit commander covertly reported that "the suspicious person" was at hand. Army commanders sent Von Rindl, the chosen executioner, to squelch Eislinger.

It was supposed to be an official German military execution— very tidy and well-ordered and not to be seen coming. The plan was that Von Rindl would appear and pretend to be seconded to the Panzer unit. He would make the unit commander aware of his true purpose in private. They would arrange for Eislinger to be cornered in such a way that escape was impossible. Then Von Rindl would restrain Eislinger, shoot him neatly, and take the body back to headquarters in a sealed medical bag for identity verification.

However, this convoluted plan was doomed to fail. The

Panzer unit was destroyed before Von Rindl could arrive. It seemed that British soldiers attacked the Panzer unit and exterminated all soldiers in it—except for Eislinger, who was kept alive for some reason.

Von Rindl arrived at the Panzer unit's location and inspected the death scenes. He suspected Eislinger actually had killed the tank crewmen—who must have raised his suspicions somehow—and then manipulated British soldiers into taking him prisoner. Von Rindl found British tracks and, failing to locate Eislinger's body, correctly judged that the British had taken the murderer captive.

Afterwards, these British soldiers had all been killed by the tomb robbers. Yet again, Eislinger was spared and roamed free.

Von Rindl explained that he was thoroughly sick and tired of chasing this maniac across the desert—however, his mission was morally and strategically important, and he could not abandon it either as a soldier or as a man.

"The *Panzerarmee* cannot allow Eislinger to exist because he is causing a huge disruption behind our frontline," he said. "His actions stir up local unrest. You survived what happened with the Bedouins today. If Eislinger keeps up his madness, we will be forced to fight many armed uprisings instead of just one British Army. There is no way we can hold any territory if we are faced with so many partisans from different communities. We could lose Africa. Furthermore," he added, "it is not right that Eislinger is allowed to murder freely. He must be stopped. There is no reason for these people to die. It is wrong."

"Are you telling me because you're hoping I'll kill him?" demanded Frost, evaluating the story for veracity.

"No. I'm telling you because you asked me what I'm doing here," Von Rindl answered sharply. "But if—God forbid—I am prevented from fulfilling my mission, do the world a favor and get rid of him. He has destroyed enough lives. The last time I saw him, he was wearing a flat British Army helmet," he warned ominously. "His murder sprees could affect your side of the war, too."

Eve, thinking of the helmet, suddenly remembered Eislinger as the German person she spoke to when they were first captured by the tomb robbers. When informed Von Rindl, he did not seem surprised. He said he had been in a shootout with Eislinger earlier, but had lost his trail due to a sandstorm.

"Your story makes no sense, Captain Von Rindl," Frost announced suddenly. "Germans are notoriously good at killing people. I know that from experience. You're telling me the entire Afrika Korps was administratively incapable of killing a single man under its very own roof. I don't believe it!"

Von Rindl was chagrined by the accusation. "It's shameful, but true," he responded. "Sometimes, I wonder whether the Army should have ordered regular soldiers to shoot him earlier. But that would have been a disgrace and also very bad for morale..."

The vehicle braked suddenly and came to a halt. Von Rindl claimed he needed rest from driving; he opened the top hatch and hopped out into a beam of faded sunlight. Frost climbed in pursuit.

Eve noticed a large leather-bound book propped on the floor beneath the driver's seat. She recognized it. It looked like the large Egyptology book given to them by Dr. Ben Sullivan, who swore to its importance. It was presumably lost with the demise of Sergeant Wilmore and their jeep. She seized it. *Notable Animal Embalmers of Ancient Egypt*, read the embossed title.

"Frosty!" She grabbed Frost's ankle as he ascended the vehicle hatch. "Look what he has!"

He almost slipped and fell. "Oh, for heaven's sake!" he snapped, and kicked her hand away. "Stop it!"

The sun was sinking slowly towards the horizon. The heat was cooling, and the light was dimmer. Shades of orange and violet began to paint the sands. Red cliffs appeared in the far distance. Somewhere to the north was the sea. Frost, pulling himself lightly on the vehicle roof with both arms, looked anxiously for any sign of the coast or the highways that led to Alexandria. Nothing was apparent. He sighed wearily and stared into the beyond.

Von Rindl offered him a can of peaches. He accepted it. They sat next to each other on the roof of the vehicle and looked sullen. Frost reclined jauntily near the edge of the roof with a crooked beret. Von Rindl sat up straight and let his boots dangle over the edge.

"Have you got any medical supplies?" Frost gestured at the bandages on his shoulder. "No? Blast it. No speakee any

English?"

The German shook his head.

"Really? Not even the 'Yellow Nose of Texas?'" the Major prodded sarcastically.

Von Rindl smirked. The British soldier's sharp mind and strong powers of perception surprised him. *"Nein,"* he demurred. *"Leider nicht."*

The two men stared sharply at each other. It was a look of mutual awareness; each man knew the other one was a cunning rascal. It was not a reassuring experience.

Frost harpooned peaches with a small knife that the German had used to open the can. Eve emerged from the hatch onto the roof behind him. She was offended by Frost's snappish treatment of her earlier. Now she sulked.

"Would you like some peaches?" the British officer asked in a sarcastic tone, sweeping the can towards her in a welcoming manner. "I vouch that they're gruesome and taste like salt. One bite and you'll never be hungry again! It's magic." He set the can next to her with a metallic smack. "Come on, have some."

She ignored the offer. She curled on the roof nearby and stared into the Egyptology book with a remote expression. "Leave me alone," she rebuffed. "I'm trying to read Sullivan's mythology book. He said it would explain the dagger. Remember?"

The young woman asked Von Rindl where he had found the book. He replied it was lying in the desert near the remains of their wrecked jeep. He confirmed that Sergeant Wilmore was dead, but said it was impossible to bury his body because it was pinned beneath an immovable ton of sand and metal.

Eve informed Frost of his fellow soldier's death. The news passed over him like a brief chill. He glanced down, glanced up again and continued eating without emotion. A career of violence and war taught him to write death off.

The book was more complex than an encyclopedia. It was densely packed with information from translated ancient Egyptian, Greek, and Roman records. The passages were blended together and crosschecked with footnotes and endnotes. Eve had to thoroughly examine each passage.

She noticed Sullivan had bookmarked one page and penciled a large red circle around one chapter heading. He had pinned a handwritten document to the page. It was full of his explanatory scribbling.

"Look! Sullivan left you a note," she announced. "It says 'Rituals of Execution in Ancient Egypt.'"

Frost rolled his eyes.

"Most of the time, Egyptians withheld burial rites from condemned criminals to prevent their entry into the afterlife. But this was not always the case this," Eve read aloud from Sullivan's note. "Sometimes judges wanted to deal out spiritual punishments for dead criminals in the afterlife. Therefore, they needed to make sure criminals had an afterlife. Sometimes they tried to trap the criminal's life forces of *ka* and *ba* using a ceremonial object. This would put the brakes on a ghost before it could cross the finish line to divine judgment. The ghost would remain stuck in a state of torment, unable to return to its physical body or to be judged worthy of an *akh* soul by the goddess Ma'at in the afterlife—"

"And that is precisely why ancient Egyptian civilization collapsed!" Frost cut in irreverently. "They were more interested in being dead than being alive and productive. They got their wish. To this day, Egypt is most well-known for its dead people."

Eve shot him a reproachful glance and kept reading. "Cases of funerary punishments were very rare." The note was finished. "That's all he wrote," she said. She glanced at the page behind it. "Now, what does this say? The chapter he wants you to read is called, 'Ne'rah.'" She struggled to pronounce the strange ancient Egyptian name. "Lord High Animal Embalmer in the year of'—"

"Oh, throw that confounded nonsense away, will you?" exclaimed the Major in aversion. "I will tell Sullivan that it has been completely useless—if ever we do see him again."

"There must be some reason why that creepy Ollie guy is obsessed with the dagger," she theorized. "Maybe Sullivan's theories can help you understand his motives!"

He smirked in disdain. "What motivates Ollie, my dear girl, is money," he said sardonically. "We need understand nothing else." He paused. "The only questions worth pursuing now have to do with his 'racket'—who works with him, who's really in charge of the group and how deep this virus has spread into Army Special Forces. That's what I am interested in."

"Don't patronize me."

"You're mistaken, sweetest lady. I would never dream of

patronizing you!" said Frost.

Eve glanced at him and concluded he was being sincere and impudent at the same time. "Then stop treating me like a golf caddy."

"I don't play golf. It bores me."

"Oh, be quiet!"

Von Rindl observed them arguing, rolled his eyes and flopped down flat on his back with his cap pulled down over his face. He started humming "The Yellow Rose of Texas" to drown out the bickering.

"Why should I?" demanded Frost, insulted.

"Because I'm trying to concentrate on something very serious here," the woman retorted firmly, "and you are distracting me!"

Eve turned away. She fidgeted to arrange herself comfortably on the roof and focused on reading the book.

Frost sulked in silence for a few minutes. Seized by a fit of rebellion, he speared a peach on the end of his knife and flicked it at her. It landed with a gory splat on the page of her book. Eve jolted in fright and nearly fell off the vehicle roof. Frost laughed riotously as the woman shrieked in anger.

Von Rindl glanced at them from beneath the shadows of his cap and was bewildered by the spectacle. He thought the British Major was a barbarian unlike any English person he had ever witnessed. Obviously, this ruffian was tormenting the poor woman. Von Rindl pitied her—he considered intervening, but felt forced to wait.

Frost grinned wickedly and brandished another speared peach. "Got you, didn't I?" he taunted. "That's what you get for being so unkind to me."

She recoiled. "Do that again and I'll clout you. Seriously."

He hurled another peach and rejoiced as she lost her temper. "Go on. Try it!"

For a moment, Eve honestly wanted to hit him. She looked up at him in sheer exasperation. Then she saw the impish affection on his face and melted. He was a rogue and she liked it. Instead of hitting him, she yanked his beret down over his eyes. He snared her in his arms and tousled her hair. They both laughed. He kissed her face.

Von Rindl was baffled by the sight. He sat up suddenly and addressed Eve in panic. "This man is...your 'friend?'"

"Tell him to go away," muttered Frost.

She replied to the German in the affirmative.

"Oh well," said Von Rindl awkwardly. He looked conflicted, glancing back and forth between the vehicle hatch and the couple. "I suppose I should offer you both an apology. As long as you have his postal address, the situation should turn out fine."

Eve was confused. "What?"

"I am sorry," apologized Von Rindl sheepishly. "Please forgive me."

Something about the way he said the word "forgive" made the hair on the back of Eve's neck stand on end. She sat up straight and stared in shock at the German as a distant mechanical whirring sound rushed into the air.

"What's going on?" Frost asked in confusion.

"I don't know," she breathed in terror. "He did something!"

Frost seized his handgun and aimed it at the German. Von Rindl raised his arms over his head in surrender and looked to his left.

"*Sie sollen aber nicht schießen,*" cautioned Von Rindl. "*Dann bringen Sie sich richtig um.*"

"He said you might as well kill yourself if you shoot him," Eve interpreted numbly.

The mechanical whirring noise mutated into a grand, rolling crush. Frost recognized the sound of tank tread and looked up in ghastly dread. A German Panzer, complete with a bright black-and-white cross symbol, rocketed straight towards them with faster horsepower than multiple automobiles. The turret faced them. Frost found himself staring into the mouth of a long-range gun as it loomed closer into view.

"I didn't do this out of malice. I thought you were plotting to kill me," Von Rindl said to Frost with a resigned shrug. "I tried to end hostilities, but you were not cooperating. You refused to give up your weapon, and I cannot allow myself to be taken hostage. It was impossible to travel together with this situation. Please understand."

Eve was so upset that she did not bother to translate.

Frost's eyes flashed in fury. Von Rindl, anticipating a violent reaction, quickly ducked and kicked the British officer off the vehicle with a boot slam to his torso. The blow was not meant to be cruel; however, it stung Frost's gunshot injury and wracked him with pain. He landed in the dust next to the vehicle tires as the Panzer rolled up like a metal monster. The tank cast a long shadow over him. Its hatch opened.

"Drop the weapon. Raise your arms. The war is over for you!" a man announced in strained English on a loud microphone. "You are a prisoner of the German Army."

Eve shouted and tried to climb down the side of the vehicle to join Frost. Von Rindl, fearing she might jeopardize her own safety, shoved her roughly toward the vehicle hatch. She fell inside, struck her head on a metal ladder rung, and dropped unconsciously to the floor like a rag doll. Afterwards Von Rindl drove off in a spray of dirt, taking the woman with him.

The vehicle pealed off as Frost stood up. He turned in panic to see Eve being torn away from him. He was trapped by the enemy. The deadly Panzer stopped him from pursuit. It was a galling experience—one of the worst he had ever lived through.

A thousand thoughts flashed through his mind. He considered running, but that would do no good. One couldn't outrun a Panzer. He considered shooting, but that wasn't an option, either. Ordinary bullets were useless against tank armor. Perhaps he could get inside and throttle the crew, then commandeer the tank. Hope of that seemed dim—German soldiers were already crawling out of the tank hatch like ants and preparing restraints for him.

Despair and anger filled Major Frost with anguish. His piercing blue eyes misted with emotion as he tried in vain to think of a way out. He dropped his handgun in the dust and experienced the sting of defeat.

CHAPTER 14: SMOKE

"There spread a cloud of dust along a plain,
And underneath the cloud, or in it raged
A furious battle, and men yelled, and swords
Shocked upon swords and shields."
—"Opportunity" by Edward R. Sill

His hands were tied behind his back with a slip of strong black cord. He was marched into the tank; he had trouble climbing aboard with restrained hands, but the soldiers dragged him. The lone English interpreter—whose English was rather lacking—demanded to know his name and Army affiliation. Frost refused to speak.

He was stuffed into the tank with a crew of four. The interior of the metal war machine was roasting hot. It reeked of dust, gasoline and sweat. Frost was unable to see where he was going and lost his sense of direction. He tried to time their journey; this was more difficult than it seemed. He concluded based on faulty calculations that they went a relatively short distance from his capture site before coming to a stop.

This would mark the first time in his long military career that Frost had been made prisoner. He had overcome colonial rebellions and armed insurrections. He had defeated various nasty climates in the hot and horrible places of the world. He had mastered the art of his profession in mind, body, and spirit. He had even escaped death itself. And now he was being led like a sheared sheep to become a formal captive of his enemies, the Germans. The woman he loved was kidnapped from his very grasp, and he powerless to stop it. Desmond Frost had never felt so bitterly oppressed in his life.

Exiting the tank, he expected to find himself surrounded by a host of Germans and barbed wire fences. To his relief, no such things were apparent. Instead, he was dumped unceremoniously out of the Panzer and led to a small nest of foxhole trenches where a group of eight dusty, uniformed Germans were dug in behind two large gun batteries.

They jabbered to each other, pointed, and shoved him into a trench. He sat in the dust and roasted in misery. After a few minutes, the Panzer crew departed. There were no other Panzers in the area; Frost was pleased by that notion.

Called away to battle, the tank crewmen left the British Major in the custody of gunners who were supposed to watch him until a prisoner transport vehicle could retrieve him. All Afrika Korps vehicles were experiencing severe difficulties and shortages due to lack of gasoline. Therefore, the POW transport truck—or the "jail wagon," as the Germans called it— was not running regularly and could not be expected anytime soon. Frost gave the gunners baleful looks. They avoided him. Eventually, one man, a tall and trim older German with an ecclesiastical air, offered him water from a canteen. And that was when the trouble started.

A bickering festival resulted that gave Frost—although he did not understand their language—a clear picture of disharmony among the German gunners. He studied everything.

The discord among the German squad was rooted in the personal animosity of two warring men who were peacetime neighbors. One soldier hailed from the grand city of Nuremberg, the other from a small next-door town called Fürth. Nuremberg considered itself a "city of kings" due to its history in the Holy Roman Empire; it had housed an emperor and elite medieval merchant guilds. Fürth was an industrial city inhabited by laborers. Citizens of both municipalities hated each other since time immemorial for unknown reasons. In the Middle Ages, the cities had been far enough apart to prevent open war. Modernity brought roads, infrastructure, and growth. The two communities burgeoned and bumped into each other, and an age of bitter feuding began.

Each side blamed the other for starting the dispute. "It's those Nürnbergers who started it," according to the people of Fürth. "They're so proud because they had a Holy Roman Emperor there and because of the Reich Party Day rallies. They think they are so special because they invented those ridiculous small Nürnberger sausages. But they are really nothing!"

In contrast, the inhabitants of Nuremberg claimed the peasants next door were the real culprits. "It's all because of those people from Fürth. They are strange, mean rustics. Their accent is atrocious. They get along with nobody. Even their whole town is organized backwards. Fürth is an eyesore and should not be next to Nürnberg!"

The feuding neighbors often attacked each other during sporting events. Citizens of Fürth who attended Reich Party Day events were bowled out of stadium bleachers and pelted with mustard hurled by outraged Nurembergers in the rows. These brawls in the benches ruined several Nazi propaganda film reels. Military manpower needed for crowd control was excessive; as a result, German city officials in Nuremberg required an extra army of security guards. Tourists visiting the city for cultural events were shocked by the troops of boot-wearing, steel-helmeted enforcers toting heavy batons around every corner. They believed this to be a phenomenon of

Nazi militarism. Indeed that was partially true—but the other underlying reason was to stop neighbors from the twin rival cities from street fighting.

Fate placed two men from the warring cities in the same North African gun battery. To make matters worse, their respective roles in artillery duty forced them to work together during shooting barrages. Their mutual hatred fueled their energy. The pair could be seen grimacing and baring their teeth at each other as they fired shells and reloaded their heavy gun. They were one of the fastest gun teams in the Afrika Korps; their speed was due to the fact that they couldn't bear working with each other any longer than necessary.

The man from Fürth was called Wiesner; the man from Nuremberg was Krump. When not fighting the enemy, they fought each other—most of the time with snubbing battles and contests of pretending not to see or hear each other. Occasionally arguments exploded.

This strained the camaraderie of the others in the outfit and forced them to take sides. Only two refused to participate in the skirmishes—these conscientious objectors were the highest and lowest ranks in the group.

The first was Horstbach, the *"Hauptmann,"* or leader of the gunner group. Horstbach, a proud Bavarian, hailed from a tiny forest village where he drank dark beer, hunted boars, chopped trees, hummed romantic ballads, and admired small songbirds. He had no patience for the antics of these stupid foreigners from Franconia—they were Franks, and thus of a different regional ethnicity than he was. He constantly snapped at them to end their fussing. Sometimes, he wished for their deaths. "I hope you both are killed in battle so I don't have to hear your hen-squabbling anymore!" he would bellow, meaning it.

The other pacifist in the group was Richter, a pious and self-important Protestant organist. Richter had the odd distinction of being both the oldest soldier in the lot and the only one who failed to excel the rank of Private. His favorite pastimes were reading Scripture and giving sermons. He was mistaken for a pastor, yet had not achieved this goal. He'd flunked ecclesiastical school. That was a source of pain to Richter. He opted to stay close to the altar through music. He vented his anguish during church services by banging organ keys with wild passion. His arm-jerking, finger-crashing, and foot-kicking rivaled the performances of Beethoven and produced noises fit to soundtrack a silent monster film. His improvisations frightened old ladies and made small children cry. Local German churchgoers glared narrowly over their shoulders at the organ loft, grumbling about the crazy organist. Nobody, however, complained openly.

It was this Richter who offered the captive British Major some water from his canteen. His action sparked discussion. One of the men disagreed, saying it was useless to waste German supplies on a prisoner. Krump, the man from Nuremberg, came to Richter's defense. Naturally Wiesner, his neighborhood rival, disagreed vehemently. A drama of debate ensued, climaxing when Krump and Wiesner, mutually insulted, started a contest of kicking gravel at each other. Captain Horstbach ended the discussion by hurling an empty coffee tin at the pair. They both ducked. The others laughed and the arguers, humiliated, fell silent.

Frost watched the personalities with interest. The astute British officer hatched a plan to exploit the disunity.

He didn't take action until after nightfall. The moon rose high and bright, the sole source of light in the gloom of the desert. The gunners did not use any lanterns or light fires due to the risk of being strafed by enemy aircraft. Moonlight cast a blurry white veil over empty fields of sand and rock. The atmosphere was waxy and freezing cold. Disappearing light had taken away all heat. A wintry chill gripped the air and turned breath to small puffs of vapor.

Frost was given a pale gray blanket to tuck himself under—a task made difficult by the restraints on his wrists. After pleading with his captors through desperate looks and gestures, he successfully won the sympathy of the saintly Protestant, Richter. Frost's hands were untied. The Germans scrutinized him to see if he would make any escape attempt. Frost curled under his blanket in a trench and stayed motionless.

Dinner was a few cans of tinned blubbery meat shared behind the guns. The men gathered in a group to eat. Frost was invited to join them, although some of the Germans gave him resentful looks. He smiled and pretended to be at ease. The meat was disgusting, even worse than British rations; he forced himself to swallow as much as he could. He needed strength to succeed.

They smoked afterwards. The Germans were hungrier for cigarettes than food. Their hands trembled with eagerness as they passed the few packs they had around.

Frost asked for a cigarette. The British officer did not smoke—in fact, doing so made him ill due to the afterlife of critical wounds he had sustained in 1940. The shot that had passed through the side of his neck left a scar inside his throat that was practically allergic to cigarette smoke. Frost took a cigarette in order to study the Germans. Doing this, he noticed that one of them—Krump the Nuremberger—was in possession of a fancy engraved silver cigarette lighter. Krump lit his cigarette for him.

Frost forced himself to smoke. He gripped the inside of his blanket with a shaking clenched fist as he struggled to suppress the overwhelming come-on of a coughing fit. After a few smokes, he pretended to feel sick from his bandaged gunshot wounds. He lay down on the ground and feigned sleep. The Germans stayed up talking. Eventually, they also lay down and went to sleep.

One man kept watch. He sat a far distance away on a dusty outcrop of the gun embankment. His back was turned to Frost. He listened to jazz music playing quietly on a radio.

Frost noticed through stealthy slit eyes that Krump's fancy cigarette lighter was sitting in the open. He also noticed Krump sleeping nearby. A short distance from Krump and his cigarette lighter was his rival, Wiesner—the one who always fought and argued with him. It was time to take action. He would need to distract the night watchman; otherwise the watcher might hear the sound of his footsteps and stop him from escaping.

The British officer checked to ensure the others were asleep and the watchman was not looking in his direction. Then he quietly tucked his beret in his pocket and tied his gray blanket around his shoulders like a tartan. He intended to use the gray cloth as camouflage. He stealthily crept across the ground and grabbed the cigarette lighter. Then he turned to the sleeping Germans with a look of cold, calculating detachment. Wiesner was his target.

Putting himself in the mindset of a malicious prankster, he flicked the lighter flame on and calmly lit the seat of Wiesner's trousers on fire. Afterwards, he tossed the lighter next to the sleeping Krump and fled in silence.

He ran northeast at breakneck speed as screams exploded and shattered the night air. Frost was a fast runner. He had never run so fast in his life. He had spent the whole day plotting his course of escape—he was sure he could somehow reach British lines by pursuing this direction. He flew over the rugged terrain with swift, clipped steps.

It took the Germans several long minutes to realize what happened. True to Frost's predictions, the initial suspect for the torching was Krump, who was rudely awakened by the sound of Wiesner burning and howling abuse at him. Everyone jolted awake and rushed in panic to put Wiesner's fire out. The night watchman was distracted by the sight and sound of the flames and did not notice Frost's flight. Wiesner, screaming in agony, accused Krump of torching him. Krump vehemently denied it. Captain Horstbach threatened to shoot both of them, while Richter the pious deigned to unfasten Wiesner's trousers and inspect his burnt hindquarters. Wiesner was humiliated and tried to prevent his rear from being inspected by kicking and punching; Richter and a handful of other men forcefully subdued him. The man was pretty badly scorched—there were second and third-degree burns in awkward locations. Would-be investigators discovered the guilty lighter on the ground in Krump's sleeping area and accused him insistently. The soldiers hissed, flapped their arms, pointed fingers, and foot-stomped at each other in the throes of a strenuous German argument.

Someone ran to the radio and demanded a medical officer. The radio operator asked in a panic if the British were attacking. The gunner replied negative and was forced to report—in awkwardly polite language—that urgent medical aid was needed to treat a soldier's burnt rear end. The radio operator, astonished, asked meticulous German questions. How did it happen? When? Was it an artillery-related accident? The operator repeatedly asked if there were hostile British forces in the area. The caller, vexed, denied the enemy was involved. However, during the interrogation, he remembered they had a British prisoner with them—he glanced around to look for the prisoner. That was when he realized the prisoner was gone.

A few minutes later, a hunting party set out. An eagle-eyed German looked through night vision antitank binoculars in every direction and fastened onto the sight of Major Frost's shadowy figure disappearing into the moonlit distance. No troop transport trucks were in the immediate area; the Germans decided to pursue him on foot. With unanimous precision, a pack of them snatched rifles and flashlights. They ran after him with alarming speed and focus. Radio signals were sent out.

Frost was still running at top speed when, suddenly, he felt a tremor in the earth and heard distant thunder, followed by a dizzy whirring noise. He dove flat on the ground for cover. A shell sailed over his head and exploded at a distance in front of him. Captain Horstbach had done it—he desired to avenge the dishonorable trouser-burning incident by blowing the British escapee to smithereens.

The Major jumped up again and ran in a zigzagged pattern to avoid shellfire. Another shell whizzed and exploded far away to his right, spitting up a huge fountain of dust and rocks.

Frost skidded to a halt. A cliff yawned at his feet. It was a steep mountainous slope covered in sharp black lava gravel. In the distance, he could barely see twinkling lights. Were they British lights? He heard voices shouting and whirled around to see the shadowy figures of running Germans melting towards him with flashlights. They had him cornered.

He decided to dare the jump. He pulled the blanket off his shoulders, crouched and rolled over the edge of the steep cliff. He tried to use the blanket as a hold on the rocks to catch surfaces around him and slow his descent. It did stop him from hurtling down the cliff. However, it didn't work very well. Inevitably he slid and lost his balance on the way down. The blanket snagged some things and missed others. It pulled stones from the earth and sent gravelly dirt flying everywhere. He descended with a seismic crackling noise, leaving a trail of dust clouds behind him in the dark. One of the Germans took a shot at him. A bullet ricocheted past. He heard the echoes of arguments from the top of the cliff.

The Germans debated whether it was ethical to shoot him or not. The majority insisted the prisoner needed only to be recaptured since he was unarmed. One man, who was very angry, said the British officer had forfeited his right to fair treatment and deserved to die. Despite the objections of his comrades, this German continued shooting.

Shots pounded into the sand and sent gravel flying. Frost managed to get to the bottom of the hill safely. He scrambled behind a large boulder as shots whizzed past. He left the torn gray blanket protruding from behind the boulder to confuse his pursuers. Then he crawled off on his belly, keeping his head down and using his knees and elbows to move forward. After an eternity of inching through sand and slithering across the ground, he reached his goal: the lights. The first light he reached was a campfire.

The truth hit him with horror. The men occupying this area were not fellow British, but enemy Italians. The Italians were a lively bunch. They smoked, laughed, played cards, and loafed in their stocking feet while listening to loud American music on the radio. They didn't care about the brilliant gleam their campfires cast in the night or the risk of aircraft strafing—they figured life was short anyway, so they might as well enjoy it. One of them spotted Frost lurking in the sand—the creeping British officer, grim-faced and sandblasted, was an alarming sight. The Italian jumped up yelling. No weapons were drawn. Instead the group panicked and started to run away in a herd. They assumed the British Army was attacking.

Frost, desperate, had an idea. He chased them, waving for them to stop. "No! Wait!"

One of the Italian officers spoke English. He waited and heard what Frost had to say. Frost said he needed to escape—in exchange for safe passage, he offered them an unusual reward.

"I know where to find some Arabs who would buy me from you," he said, pointing in the direction he presumed the Bedouins who raided Wadi Asra earlier had gone. "What would you take in exchange for me? Coffee? Tea? Petrol? Name your price!" He made a case for his ransom.

The Italian officer's reply surprised him. "I have a different idea," he said. "Take me prisoner!"

Frost blinked. "What?"

"I don't want to fight this war anymore," the officer replied. "None of us here do. This war is for the Germans. Besides," he pulled a dirty envelope from his breast pocket, "my mother keeps writing me these terrible letters. I cannot bear it any longer." He showed Frost a tear-streaked scribbled letter with a religious picture of St. Lucy pasted to it. It was a strange old image showing a beautiful woman carrying a palm leaf and a pair of eyeballs on a platter—his patron saint. He put it away. "I want to be captured so I can go home."

His name was Luciano Attriali. He was from a noble family from Northern Italy disillusioned with the fascist regime. He was well-educated and had translated several ancient Roman novels into English; he desired to become a historical literature teacher in London. Nevertheless his father had been in the military, and he was expected to honor the tradition. However, his father had since died. Luciano, the only son, wanted to survive for the sake of his mother and young vulnerable sisters. He had considered deserting, but it was too shameful. However, he explained, there was no dishonor in being captured. He wanted Frost to pretend to "capture" him and escort him to British lines using an Italian truck. Daylight would bring scrutiny. Nighttime was beginning to fade. It was now or never.

Half an hour later they were speeding away like fiends across desert badlands in a large canvas-covered truck. Seven of Luciano's friends, also anxious to be "taken prisoner" and quit the war, piled into the back of the truck to join them. Men who couldn't fit in the back balanced on the sides of the truck, standing on the vehicle's tire hubs and running board whilst hanging onto the canvas shell for dear life. Fellow soldiers who stayed behind bid them teary goodbyes and resolved to flee combat at the soonest opportunity.

Meanwhile, the German gunners descended the hill and searched for Frost's body. They found nothing but the dirty blanket he left behind. They tried to ask the Italians in the area if they had seen anything. The Italians spoke little German, but guessed what the Germans wanted. They were extremely disillusioned and felt no loyalty towards their German allies. They also wished to protect their friends who had escaped to freedom. They pretended to know nothing.

British tents appeared in the distance as the jolting canvas-covered truck hurtled onward, heading east. Frost leaned out the truck window and waved his arms to indicate friendly intentions as flat British helmets darted and ducked behind fortifications. Several British soldiers approached to investigate.

Frost smiled wearily in the pink light of the rising sun. He was safe. Yet his wintry blue eyes glistened with grief. He had lost his Eve. He did not know if he would ever see her again.

CHAPTER 15: GHOSTS AND GAMES

"Nicht ist alles Gold, was gleisst,
Glück nicht alles, was so heisst;
Nicht alles Freude, was so scheint;
Damit hab ich gar manches gemeint."
—"Nicht is alles Gold" [Not all is Gold]
by Johann Wolfgang von Goethe

She awoke with splitting pain in her head and a minor concussion. The German scout, Elrich von Rindl, had arranged her in a reclining position on a blanket in the back of his stolen armored truck. He hovered over her, touching her face with a damp cloth. He was worried.

It took Eve several minutes to remember where she was and what had happened. Her mind froze between English and German. The first thing the American journalist said was: "Where is Frosty?"

Von Rindl understood the question. He looked guiltily at the floor and sighed. He gave no answer. He only stared at her expressively and hoped she would draw the obvious conclusions.

Grieved tears swelled in her eyes.

"The man was crazy. It was either him or me," asserted Von Rindl, defending his actions. "I could not have continued driving with him here, threatening me the way he was doing. It was impossible." He paused. "Anyway, he is alive and unharmed. There is no reason to be crying."

She covered her face in misery.

"Why this whining?" demanded Von Rindl in indignant confusion. He sat down on the floor of the armored truck in a huff. "He is only going to a prisoner-of-war camp in Europe. They have a temporary internment camp here, then they ship the prisoners over to Italy. I know which department to contact—I can tell you the address. You can write a letter and ask for him. When the war is over, he will be released, safe and sound."

His encouragements were useless. She forecasted an endless eternity of trying to find and contact Frosty without success. Eve plunged into despair.

"You don't know for sure!" she replied in German. "He could go missing—or sink on one of your transport ships crossing the Mediterranean. It happens all the time." She trembled, in shock at his capture and disappearance. "Besides," she added, "Frosty will try to escape. I know it. If they catch him escaping, won't they shoot him?"

Von Rindl quietly considered the scenario. "Probably they would just recapture him and send him off to Italy faster," he estimated. A faint, wry smile crossed his face. He corrected himself. "Unless he does something very stupid or barbaric. I suppose that's possible."

Eve stared blankly at the ceiling. The world looked like a dull paper bag now. Empty and superficial. She had fallen in love for the first time in her life and had lost. She no longer cared about anything.

Her feelings surprised her. She had despised Frost initially— at least, she had wanted to despise him. She viewed him merely as an instrument of injustice. She hadn't noticed much about him when they first met, other than that he was bossy and intelligent. In retrospect, perhaps she thought he was a little handsome—at least at first glance. She was too busy resisting him to pay attention.

Layers of prejudice peeled off during their trip to the desert. She got to know him pretty easily. Frost was a hard-edged man—battle-tested and cynical. He could be ruthless and calculating. She admired that about him. Yet, he had other sides to his personality. He was straightforward, sharp, forceful, and boisterous. He was a perfectionist with an absurd sense of humor. He was capable of warmth. He eroded her defenses with so many gleaming looks, wisecracks, and sly smiles. Even his voice changed when he spoke to her. It lowered from a snappish command tenor to a velvety British baritone. When he confessed his admiration for her, she knew it was genuine. He kissed her and caressed her with devotion rather than mere desire. She had never experienced that before. It melted the ice in her blood.

She realized that Major Frost somehow had managed to fall deeply in love with her. This shocking revelation forced her to reflect on her true opinions about him. She realized there was absolutely nothing about Frost she disapproved of. In fact, she liked everything about him. He was extremely strong, both

THE HIDDEN SPHINX: A TALE OF WORLD WAR II EGYPT

outwardly and interiorly. He was handsome, highly intelligent, educated, and articulate, in addition to being rough and rowdy. He was a natural leader and a fighter. And he had a good heart.

Eve, also, was a fighter and natural leader. She had no patience for dull or unintelligent people. Women were foolish and irritated her. Most men disappointed her—they were either stupid, controlling or viewed her as only a pretty face whose stubborn independence needed rubbing out. Some men were cowardly or unassertive. Other men suffered from the illusion of machismo; underneath their ballooning insecurity and façade of testosterone, they were weak. Eve had always wanted love, but she demanded greatness. She could only give her heart to a man she truly admired. Frost was that man.

Finally, she had found him. And lost him.

"I can't regret what I did. It was necessary," Von Rindl maintained stubbornly. "Better him a prisoner than me dead. If he does something stupid and gets killed, that's his fault. Not mine."

The woman fixed him with a withering glare. "I would rather have stayed," she said. "Why did you bring me here?"

"It would have been bad for you to stay. I could not hand you over in good conscience. It would have been dangerous for you on many levels," the ranger replied darkly. "I did not report that I was traveling with a woman. Surely the Panzer crew noticed you and will tell somebody. They'll suspect me of debauchery—I'll probably get a formal reprimand. But better that than the alternative. You would've been shipped to who-knows-where and probably treated worse than any regular POW."

"I suppose they would've assumed I was a spy and interrogate me," she grumbled. "Ugh. I'm so sick of that accusation. It gets so tiresome."

"Naturally it's very suspicious that you're wandering out here—especially as an American, who speaks perfect German. Of course, you seem like a spy!" he answered. "But you told me you're a civilian and a journalist. I believe you're a good person. I believe you're telling the truth. That's why I didn't turn you in."

"What are you going to do with me?" she wondered. "I can't accompany you on your mission. I wouldn't be any help in executing Eislinger."

"Not really. Also you would eat through my supplies faster," he agreed. "Also I don't know where Eislinger went. I must start tracking him again. It's long and difficult work. There's no reason for you to be subjected to it." He took off his cap and wearily brushed dust from his short blond hair. "I'll take you someplace where you can walk back to your side of civilization."

"Walk?" she snorted skeptically. "That sounds lovely!"

"I can't drive too close," he retorted. "The British would catch me."

It was pitch black outside. The night air was cold. Von Rindl bundled himself up in a brown overcoat and threw another blanket on her. They were both exhausted and hungry. Von Rindl rummaged through his restocked foodstuffs and tried to cobble together something hearty. It was an awkward dinner. A particularly poignant moment was when he offered her a can of peaches. Eve was reminded of Major Frost. Her eyes misted with sadness.

Von Rindl attempted to preserve the cordial atmosphere by starting a discussion. He was an intellectual and curious person who enjoyed learning. He was often deprived of intelligent company. Having an English-speaking guest gave him a chance to entertain his mind.

He decided to discuss the Egyptology book he'd found near the wrecked jeep. He had whisked it down the vehicle hatch during their flight from the Panzer. Now he picked the book up and examined it in front of her.

"I hope you don't mind that I kept this," he said with courtesy. "There isn't much of a chance to acquire interesting English books in Germany—so many things have been censored by the government." He gave a thin smile. He hoped she would reciprocate his attempts at friendliness. "I saw you reading it. What is it about? Would you tell me?"

The journalist glanced at him. She remained upset with him for arranging Frost's capture. However, she realized that the German was being sincere. Too proud to apologize, he had first tried to justify his actions. Since that had not availed him, his last options for maintaining a good relationship were to explain his point-of-view and focus on something mutually agreeable. Eve recognized what he was doing. She sensed no ulterior hostility from Von Rindl; he was a pragmatist and seemed genuinely good-natured. Enmity on her part was useless—and perhaps unjustified. She decided to forgive him.

"It's a book about famous Egyptians who mummified animals," she admitted. "Does that interest you?"

"More than sandstorms and mirages," replied Von Rindl wryly, glad that she was making polite conversation. He gestured at his pile of dirty maps near the driver's seat. "My reading options here, as you can see, are a bit lacking."

Eve flipped the book open at the part she left off. She saw Sullivan's note—and an unruly peach stain on the page. Sadness filled her as she was reminded of Major Frost.

"What does it say?" prodded Von Rindl, hoping to distract her.

"Looks like an old ghost story," she answered, scanning the pages and assessing her ability to summarize a complicated English text in colloquial German. "You'll have to be patient with me. I don't know how to translate all these words properly."

"That's fine. Give it a try!" he answered with cheer. "Maybe I can learn some English. Anyway, I'm too tired to drive anymore and we have a long night ahead."

She resumed reading from the chapter entitled, "Ne'rah, Lord High Animal Embalmer."

The unfortunate saga was the story of a rogue animal embalmer, who was spiritually punished in death to prevent the gods from forgiving him.

A man named Ne'rah was a lord embalmer of animals during the reign of an ordinary and uninteresting pharaoh. Ne'rah was one of a huge retinue of embalmers inhabiting a necropolis—a massive graveyard called a "city of the dead"—in a wilderness near the Upper Nile. Embalmers' lives revolved singly around performing mummifications and rituals for the dead. Human remains, of course, were important.

But in the religion of ancient Egypt, some things were even more important than people—namely, animals. Beasts were worshiped as gods. A wide variety of creatures were considered sacred. They required special funerary rites.

Ne'rah was an elder highly respected in his profession. He oversaw the embalming and mummification of many noteworthy animal-gods during his lifetime. For example, he mummified the Great Baboon that made its home near the pharaoh's residence—a rare striped specimen, thought to be an incarnation of the god Thoth. And he mummified the Holy

Toads, which mysteriously appeared one day in a temple pond. Not to mention the Divine Hedgehog—quite a remarkable case, requiring much skill. Other sacred animals he mummified included: shrews, vultures, falcons, cats, cows, lions, fish, lizards, hippopotami, fruit bats, snakes, waterfowl, gazelles, ostriches, foxes, and jerboas.

Animal embalming was a high-powered job. Practitioners were believed to be very holy because their work involved "godly" manifestations.

A leader in his profession, Ne'rah was accorded special privileges and honor. What nobody knew about Ne'rah was that he was a remorseless career tomb robber, who worked with a gang of thieves to plunder the remains he helped bury. Ne'rah feared neither god nor man—the horrifying inscriptions on tomb walls and seals menacing intruders with divine punishment did not faze him. Ne'rah did not actually believe in divinity—everything he did in public was hoax and hypocrisy. He did believe in enjoying himself. He cracked open sealed doors for robbers, squeaked open coffins and pilfered golden amulets from corpses with nobody the wiser. He used his ill-gotten gains to finance a lavish lifestyle. He prayed in public but was privately depraved. Nobody suspected him; he was too pious, too professional.

Until one day, they caught him.

Officials put him in charge of mummifying a Holy Crocodile. The enormous beast, thought to be divine, swam one day into a temple ritually flooded with waterfalls from the Nile. The giant crocodile settled in the temple pond. Its appearance impressed the Egyptians so much that they thought it was a deity. The crocodile was thought to be the very incarnation of the Nile god Sobek himself. Nobody could figure out why Sobek had ignored his existing temple on the river and instead chose to float down a canal to a more remote desert location. But they accepted his wishes.

They redecorated, remodeled, and re-consecrated the temple in the reptile's honor. It became the Holy Crocodile Temple. An enormous new waterfall system was added, with additional cavernous ponds. The imposing new structure was built halfway underwater. The crocodile spent three human lifetimes there being pampered and fed chickens, goats, hippopotami and eventually bulls. Occasionally, it grabbed some temple workers, too, but nobody minded. It grew to mammoth size. People prayed to it. They gathered in crowds, hoping to be splashed with water from one flick of its tail. They carved figurines and statues of it.

One day the monster died. The temple priests plunged into despair. They had made a booming business selling souvenirs and charging worshipers admission to see the beast. Disillusioned at losing their income, they tried to convince the Holy Crocodile to return by holding a resurrection ceremony. It didn't work. They opted to keep it alive through embalming and mummification.

The funerary rites for the Holy Crocodile were unquestionably the most lavish that Ne'rah was ever put in charge of. The beast was showered with more riches and perfume than any person in Egyptian history. Ne'rah was supposed to embalm it and prepare it for burial in one of the biggest sarcophagi the ancients ever built.

It took half a year to embalm the crocodile. Like mummified humans, it was gutted, salted, stuffed, oiled, perfumed, painted and primped before being padded with expensive ribbons. It was covered with precious metals and loaded with jewelry. More than three expert jeweler guilds made a lifetime's fortune designing the jewelry of a single dead crocodile. Its coffin was an expensive behemoth. The huge gold and lapis sarcophagus filled an entire vault hollowed into the bottom of the drained crocodile pond. The coffin was draped in luxurious silk on the inside. It would be sealed shut when the mummy was placed inside—layers of wax, resin, melted metals, wooden darts, and suppressed air-trigged booby traps would prevent the coffin from ever being opened again—at least not without significant harm to human life.

Ne'rah struck the night before the internment in the coffin. He and his friends made sure the guards were drunk on drugged date wine. He bypassed all the sealed doors and slithered through secret embalmers' passages. They arrived in the corpse's chamber. Ne'rah knew exactly where the amulets were hidden in the mummy bandages because he had put them there. Confident nobody would ever discover what happened, he and his helpers started unwrapping parts of the crocodile and pilfering amulets. They had brought buckets of rocks and quick-drying resin to help fill empty jewel pockets and reseal the bandages. They removed most of the beast's jewelry—Ne'rah even cracked out the crocodile's false alabaster, jewel-encrusted teeth using his embalming knife. He filled in the missing gaps with wood chips.

Afterwards, stones and other objects were stuffed into the mummy where its jewelry had been to disguise gaps. Bandages were rewrapped and coated with resin to glue them back into place. The men used fans to make the glue dry faster.

Doom came when they were nearly finished. The jewelry was gathered into sacks and ready to be hauled off. Ne'rah moved the bags of jewelry outside the door. As he reentered the room, his foot struck a concealed tripwire. The door slammed shut—trapping the thieves inside the chamber and sealing their stolen jewelry in the hallway.

Panic set in. The thieves were desperate to get out. There was no way they could talk their way out of this trouble. The sacks of jewelry in the hall were silent witnesses to their crime; the various rocks and pieces of dirty wood they'd packed onto the crocodile mummy would not help their case, either. They tried to break down the door but found it immovable. It could only be opened from the outside with a key. Nobody could agree on a story.

Evil and desperate to escape the truth, Ne'rah decided to slaughter his comrades to save himself. A battle broke out. He slew his comrades using his embalming knife and nearly died in the process. He planned to say that he had caught the robbers single-handed.

Morning brought the opening of the door. The jewelry sacks were found. A troop of guards appeared to arrest thieves and were shocked to behold the venerable animal embalmer Ne'rah in the room surrounded by bloody dead men. Ne'rah tried to lie and say that he had prevented a robbery from taking place. However, evidence weighed against him—especially when one guard noticed a few of the crocodile's alabaster teeth, broken, lying on the floor. The guard inspected the teeth and deduced they had been forcefully sawn with a sharp object. He compared the marks on the teeth to Ne'rah's embalming knife. Sure enough, long white scratches permanently etched onto the blade revealed the man's guilt.

Judges sentenced him to death and eternal punishment. His crime was so great that his comrades wished to stop the gods from forgiving him. Ne'rah had a long track record of successfully embalming animals who were supposed to be gods. It would be no use to allow any spiritual clients to intercede for him by giving him a decent funeral. Hell wasn't guaranteed. Making a wandering ghost out of him would be too easy—and perhaps too scary. Ne'rah had betrayed public trust and made dupes out of many respectable people. They wanted revenge. They wished to wield complete control over his eternity.

For a culture obsessed with idea of freedom in the afterlife, there was hardly any greater punishment than for a person to be deprived of afterlife and remain tormented in a state of subjugation. The ancient Egyptians were very controlling when it came to death. Funerary rituals guaranteed afterlife. Destroyed physical remains guaranteed instant hell or restless wandering. Neither option worked for horrible and complex judicial execution cases. Hell was too easy a punishment for some people, the ancients thought. Besides, who could guarantee that the goddess Ma'at, weigher of the scales of divine justice, wouldn't whimsically decide to be merciful and heap on some good deeds? The idea that certain heinous offenders could hijack eternity and float around in the green wheat fields of paradise morally outraged the Egyptian public. Thus, sometimes the ancients took godly matters into their own hands. The deeds of some criminals were horrific and so were their mortal ends. The ferocity and malice with which their peers exacted posthumous punishments upon them were arguably as bad as the original crimes themselves.

Such was the fate of Ne'rah. He was executed in public by a troop of officials wearing jackal and anteater masks. His embalming knife was the instrument of his demise. They performed purifying rituals on it to appease the spirits of any dead it had helped; then they placed a seal on it intended to trap his dishonorable ghost inside it like a bottle. The mortuary dagger squelched his life as it had those of his fellow thieves. Afterwards, his body was destroyed and cast into the desert.

The knife was buried under a doorstep outside the crocodile temple he had violated. Usually the names of criminals were scratched out to erase their life force; in Ne'rah's case, the ancients didn't bother since they wished him to go on living in torment. They imagined he would spend eternity under a doorstep getting stomped on by people visiting the Holy Crocodile temple he dared to scorn.

After a series of unfortunate events ruined the crocodile temple, the site was abandoned. The tale of Ne'rah was recorded in detail by the ancient Greek explorer and historian Herodotus, who visited Egypt and had access to records and information from lost time periods. Otherwise, apart from a few scraps of papyrus and stone confirming that a person called Ne'rah was an embalmer, no other records about him existed.

A European explorer in the late Middle Ages claimed to have found the site of the Holy Crocodile Temple. It had since been destroyed and its location lost in time. No mention was made of the doorstep or the dagger.

The historical accuracy of this tale was questionable. Modern writers theorized that the story of Ne'rah was nothing more than an old Egyptian fable meant to scare tomb robbers in ancient times. The anecdote was included in the scholarly book merely to document the alleged historical life of one of Egypt's famous animal embalmers.

The truth behind the legend remained unknown.

Von Rindl was very entertained by this diverting story. Eve's German language skills faltered slightly as she covered more complex subject matter; she lacked some of the vocabulary to describe some of the objects and situations described in the text. However, Von Rindl was able to understand the main gist of the legend of Ne'rah, the ill-fated animal embalmer.

"I believe it's possible that such a person could have existed," he announced afterwards, reflecting analytically on the story. "I have seen some of those animal mummies myself."

"Really?" Eve was surprised. "Where? Out here?"

He nodded briskly. "I've been tracking these criminals long enough to see what they've been up to," he stated. "They've been breaking into a lot of old ruins in different strange places. They usually examine the ruin first, then break through walls and stone surfaces using explosives or sometimes their jeeps. They clear out the rubble and strip everything they can. Usually, they are just interested in gold and 'attractive' sort of artifacts," he explained. "You know. Showpieces, like for museums. The other things they leave behind. Like pottery, for example. Sometimes bottles. And animal mummies. They strip the animal of funeral dressings and leave the corpse." He looked up at Eve in mild surprise. "It even just happened at the place I where I rescued you and Rusty. Did you not see it?"

"We didn't really go 'exploring,'" she replied. "At least I didn't. Maybe Frosty saw something when he went looking for supplies. But he didn't tell me. Would you describe what you saw?"

He smiled grimly. "Underneath the grounds, outside towards the back, there was a tunnel system," he said, gesturing descriptively with his hand. "Inside there were about seven carcasses of bulls—animal mummies. All of them had been torn up. I found one small piece of a stone earring. Not to mention all the junk they left behind! Cigarette packs, alcohol bottles..."

The German let the words trail off. His expression was calm. His blue eyes were full of disdain. "It's obvious what happened," he remarked. "Anyway, it's not the first time I've seen it. I have found mummies of...let me think...falcons, storks, cats," he said, counting on his fingers, "bats, 'toad beetles'..."

"'Toad beetles?'" exclaimed Eve with a laugh of disbelief.

He grinned impudently. In his irreverence, he had invented a new word for scarabs. "You know! Those big old bugs that look like toads," he said, with more emphatic hand gestures. "Who knows what to call them..."

They laughed.

He peered at her in intense curiosity. "So why, then, were you traveling with that book about animal mummies? Rusty didn't seem to care about it," he observed keenly. "But you thought it was important."

Eve was caught off guard by his incisive questions and sharp powers of observation. In some ways, he reminded her of Major Frost. However, Von Rindl had a totally different personality; he seemed like such a mellow, even-tempered person. He carried a gun but didn't give the impression of being a gunslinger. He was always calm, self-contained, and pleasant. He was as dusty and gritty as any other man who traveled in the desert. Otherwise, everything about him was neat. Somehow he managed to stay clean-shaven and neatly comb his hair. This neatness was in stark contrast to Major Frost, who had a rakishly disheveled flair. Frost was a swashbuckler; Von Rindl was a precisionist. Both were capable at their art. Also, both were extremely calculating and cunning.

Looking at Von Rindl now, Eve realized that she had underestimated his powerful intellect. He was asking questions—for an unknown purpose. She had been warned not to trust him. Nevertheless, her survival depended awkwardly on his. He had behaved decently enough; she decided to take a gamble.

"The book was part of an investigation Frosty is leading about the tomb robbers," she confessed. "They are British Army personnel gone rogue. One of them is carrying a very rare dagger..."

She ended up telling him everything about the thieves and the dagger. Hauntings, curses, plundered tombs, and murdered British soldiers flew past in a delirious blur.

Von Rindl listened sharply. Some pieces of information were new. Others were not. He finished listening with a faint, knowing smirk.

"So, you're thinking the dagger truly is haunted," he deduced. "You're wondering why the robber carries it around. That's a valid question," he pointed out. "If you know the reason why he is doing something, it could help you undo his plans."

"Exactly!" Eve fiercely agreed. "But Frosty doesn't care very much about it..."

"He just wants to get rid of the pests, that's all," Von Rindl remarked. "He, also, has a valid line of reasoning. Once they're all dead, the dagger will become irrelevant. The only question would be how to dispose of it." He glanced wryly at the book. "Are there no recipes in there for destroying evil ghosts and cursed daggers? Better take a second look!"

She flipped through the pages. There appeared to be nothing inside of any relevance to curing haunted objects or solving problems they caused. She shut it with an irritated sigh and felt tired and thirsty.

They drank stale tea in silence for awhile. Von Rindl looked at Eve with tired blue eyes. His face was sunburnt and worn from the harsh elements. He had blisters on his neck from rough sand chafing inside his shirt collar. His pale blond hair was damp and dull with dirt and grime.

"Don't ever tell anyone I said this," he muttered wearily, "but I wish the war would end tomorrow. I don't really care if we lose. I'm so tired of it all." He smirked wryly at her. "I only say that to you because you're American and you can't report me," he admitted. "If my comrades heard it, they would call me a coward. I would lose my rank and who knows what else."

"You can end your own war if you stop fighting," she suggested. "Drive to British lines and surrender."

He smirked again. Bitterly, this time. "It's not so easy," he sighed. "I would lose every tie I have to Germany because I would never outlive the public shame. Besides, it is cowardly for an able-bodied man to simply walk to the enemy with one's hands up," he explained. "I must end my fight on my own terms."

Eve listened in pensive silence. Wind rustled eerily around the vehicle.

"Listen," said Von Rindl urgently. "Since you've been so kind, I will do you a favor." He pulled out one short, worn-out map marked with red-penciled circles, dots and X marks from his overcoat pocket.

"Here is my map marked with all the places where the tomb robbers have raided recently," he said, handing it to her. "It is all there. We have charted it. I just updated it tonight."

She took it eagerly and studied it. "We?"

"Yes. Myself and some of our intelligence staff."

She looked at him with the skepticism that comes from a tried career in journalism and a track record of battling wits with people trying to manipulate information. She would have asked him a host of aggressive questions—but Von Rindl, anticipating it, had already made a plan.

"The fact is, I am a one-man-show," he deflected, before she had a chance to start interrogating. "I have proven abilities at my job, but the Army overestimates me sometimes. I simply don't have the capacity to get rid of all the robbers myself! Maybe if you leak this document to your friends in the British military, they will find it useful somehow and there will be less work for me. That is my only hope."

She stared dubiously at him. "You want me to give information to the British?"

"Yes. I have nothing against them. The war is not personal for me," he replied. "Maybe it could help us all solve a common problem."

Eve, suspicions heightened, went on the offensive. "You had this the entire time and said nothing until now. Why?" she demanded. "If you really wanted to be helpful, why didn't you give this to Frosty?"

"I didn't think of it then. I was worried he would shoot me!" retorted Von Rindl, looking honest enough. "Besides, he was not trustworthy. He would have been just as likely to tip off our German intelligence and report me as a traitor, just to be spiteful. Major Rusty is a wild and cruel man," he said, convinced of it.

"You've got him figured all wrong!"

"I most certainly have not," sassed Von Rindl, folding his arms neatly behind him. "Of course it's different for you. You're a pretty woman—of course, he would behave nicely to you!" he said with a mocking laugh. "Not so for me! I saw the way he was glaring at me. Any German who crosses his path is a sitting duck."

She started to argue, but he interrupted.

"I'm volunteering to give this map to you to be helpful," he claimed, poised and self-confident. He reached out an open hand. "If you don't want it, then give it back."

She wavered. She thought about throwing away this offer to avoid the shame of being potentially manipulated by the German army. Then she imagined the opposite. What if this were a genuine godsend? What if a gem of intelligence was floating within her grasp—with power to help the mission of her beloved Major Frost—and she threw it away like garbage? No. She couldn't accept that risk. She had to take a chance.

Von Rindl's eyes danced. His mouth curved with only the faintest hint of a smile. He had already expected this. "Just don't tell anyone I gave this to you," he insisted. "If my superiors find out that I leaked this document, I'll be in serious trouble."

The American woman knew that in German culture promises were almost sacred. Any solemn agreement she made with Von Rindl would be regarded by both of them as binding—at least if Von Rindl had any sense of personal "honor."

She looked at the German officer with mistrust. She was playing a game on Von Rindl's chessboard. His cunning mind had led to Frost's capture in the first place. He was very sly. She wasn't sure about his motivations.

Eve agreed to his terms. He offered her a handshake. A binding one, this time. She dared to accept it.

He gave his usual thin, good-humored smile and changed the subject. They talked about Germany. Places they each liked to visit. Good hiking spots. Food. He told her wistfully about his fiancée, Carla—his dearest friend, he called her, saying they planned to marry at the soonest opportunity.

Somehow, it led to a deliberate question. It seemed like a very innocent question, and this time Eve failed to suspect anything ulterior about it. Von Rindl asked Eve for her postal address.

"It's been so wonderful talking to you! I'm so glad we met. Perhaps, when this war is over, we can all visit each other as friends," he said cordially. "Please give me your address so I can write to you. Also—I will need it so that I can forward it to POW administration. They can tell you where Rusty is. It will be much easier if I inquire about him on your behalf."

In response, Eve confessed that she had no permanent address. She explained she resided in Cairo and intended to do so until further notice. She worked for *The Chicago Standard* newspaper, but couldn't expect them to reliably forward mail. Her last resort was Shepheard's Hotel.

"They have a mailbox service there," she said, desperate to get firsthand information about Major Frost. "You can send it there. Just put my name on it. You know about Shepheard's?"

"Yes. That Swiss hostel is where all the British go." The corner of his mouth twisted into a faint smile. "Of course, I've heard about it."

Eve was mildly surprised. The man spoke no English and had never been to Cairo, yet he seemed to be very well aware of the landmark Shepheard's Hotel.

Von Rindl grinned impertinently. "Confidentially," he said with understated humor, "there are probably more German guests at Shepheard's than anybody realizes." He winked at her and vanished into the night outside the truck.

She was left alone in the dark with scruples and an uneasy feeling.

CHAPTER 16: DESERT GODDESS

"There have been others before thee, Conqueror,
Who compassed more than thy ambitions hold,
Held greater worlds in fee, and grasped more
And swifter swords than thine, with surer hold."
—"To a Would-Be King" from
"Poems from the Desert" by LCpl P.A.A. Thomas

Trails of curling, pitch-black smoke rose from the empty battlefield. They spooled from the waning fires of burning tanks. Oil and fuel kept mechanical fires burning long after battles ended, and men breathed their last. A jeep with its undercarriage blasted off and its doors flung open stood in ghostly silence on the plain. A few hollow boots littered the ground nearby. The jeep had run over a mine; two men had lost their legs. The bodies and their scattered pieces had since been buried.

A shadowy figure stalked through the smoky inferno. He paced restlessly. Bloodstained sand crunched beneath his tall, black-and-tan combat moccasins as he drifted through the haze. He wandered back and forth, to and from the empty vehicles burning like death torches. He was scavenging. There were no wounded men to hassle or torture. No living soul on which to vent his malice. Only the great silence.

It left him somewhat disappointed. Despite the secretive nature of his crimes, Oliver Bryon—also known by the nicknames "Ollie" and "Flag"—craved attention. Life to him was nothing more than a show in which he starred; he constantly sought an audience.

He knew there were unexploded mines in the area. However he chose to go about his business. He enjoyed tempting death.

Suddenly, one of the shattered tanks roared to life. It was a flimsy Italian model—"flying coffins," as the British had aptly nicknamed such vehicles. A shell had burst clean through its visor, leaving a gaping hole in the front and decapitating the entire crew of four. The bodies had not been removed—some British soldiers, under orders to clean up the battlefield, had tried, but rigor mortis made the corpses immovable and the soldiers gave up in disgust. Now the rigor mortis wore off. The gunner's body loosened and collapsed forward onto the accelerator. The smoldering tank rolled forward and swooped around in circles. The dead were driving.

Ollie the tomb raider recoiled in alarm. He reached instinctively for the pistol on his hip. He watched the spooky spectacle in fright, unsure what to do.

The tank careened towards him. Ollie held still, waiting for it to turn away. It came right at him. He darted out of the way in the nick of time as the tank plowed past and crunched over a truck he had been standing next to. The ghost-driven tank rolled onward into the desert. Less than a minute later, it struck a concealed mine.

A double explosion shattered the air. The first explosion was the mine, the second was the tank's last gasoline reserve detonating. Both explosions happened almost simultaneously. Ollie, foolish enough to wander the battlefield on foot and unprotected by armor, was thrown backwards into the air. As he fell, his head struck against the broken tread of a mangled German halftrack vehicle. He was knocked unconscious.

As blackness enveloped him, he heard a man's voice mutter in a harsh, unintelligible language. The ghastly voice was accompanied by the sickening smell of ancient perfume. Ollie reached for the flint dagger on his hip as he passed out.

His mind returned to a place and time he could never forget. So much time had flown by. But that late afternoon lived on. It was an eternal day. Perhaps like some ancient Egyptian curse carved upon the walls of the hallowed tombs he plundered. That bloody, gold-dusted afternoon never faded. It stood like an immortal pillar in the shifting sands of his turbulent lifetime. It could not be undone. It could not be amended. That day changed his life forever.

He could still see the bright orange afternoon melting to starry purple as a blistering day blurred into dreamlike nightfall. He cruised across the wastes in a jeep, manning a machine gun mounted above his door. His best comrade, an unassuming Englishman called Ted Bailey, was his driver. That was in an era before they had taken aliases. Before he started calling himself "Flag." Before he lost his eye. Before robbing tombs became a fulltime business. Before Bailey adopted the alias "Harper" and ran away to Cairo. Before he murdered his former friend in cold blood at a nighttime cabaret performance.

It was certainly different back then. Back then, he was nobody special. Just Ollie, an East-End-born criminal who hitched his star to soldiering and war to turn a profit. He was born and reared in a world of vice and hatred. He genuinely disliked people. He had no real friends. However, he did have cronies. Ted was his chief admirer. They drank together, caused trouble together—killed enemies together. The isolation of the desert and the gruesomeness of their missions forged iron bonds between Special Forces commandos. It was not warm friendship. It was cold, killer understanding. Men like Ollie and his driver Ted learned to rely on each other for survival. They stalked and hunted prey together. They were wolves in a pack.

One evening they were on an assassination mission. They'd received a hazy order to wreak murder and mayhem behind a certain area of German lines. Nobody directly oversaw their actions. Superiors simply passed on general orders and turned them loose like attack beasts. Much was left to their independent judgment. Ollie, an uneducated man, was sneakier and more brutal than most of his comrades. He masterminded his own missions. He was out to kill.

He stood in the jeep as it knifed through sand clouds and nothingness. He wore a dingy khaki British uniform—and a flamboyant emerald green turban, his headgear of choice. The turban's twin tails whipped behind him in the wind.

The desert was strange that day. Mirages cropped up everywhere. The stars in the purpling horizon melted together with the fading orange of the afternoon. A jagged crescent moon appeared grinning in the sky as the dazzling sun set. It was as if day and night were suspended, blending together in a vision. As if time stood still.

They spotted a German halftrack vehicle. A rapid exchange of fire followed—machine gun blasts from Ollie, and volleys of bullets from various firearms the Germans were carrying. One German fell dead into the dunes. The others sped off, retreating.

A pursuit followed. They raced toward a canyon in the distance. Ollie wanted to "snuff" these Germans out before they had a chance to hide or call for aid. He took over driving the jeep as Bailey, gashed across the forehead by a stray bullet, struggled with blood streaming into his eyes. He drove like a fiend. They flew over a field of short, thick dunes and rattled across a chalk basin. They swept into the canyon. The Germans abandoned their vehicle and fled into the maze of red and black volcanic rock framing the canyon on either side like huge stone jaws. Ollie shot one of them. The last one disappeared.

Ollie smelled fresh blood. Leaving his wounded driver behind, he found a trail of blood leading into a gaping chasm hewn into the rock. An ancient doorway. The ghastly door into the cliff yawned like a portal into the underworld. Darkness swallowed him as he went in. The doorway led to a deep plunge. A carved granite path became a tunnel leading down into the bowels of the earth. Light faded. Hot, dry air grew colder.

Hieroglyphs and dark painted figures covered the walls in patterns. Bestial, doe-eyed faces peered out above archways. Half-naked, animal-headed people. Some had wings. They knelt, crouched, played board games, raised their bare arms towards heaven. Some had green and blue skin. Carved beetles hung like spiders above archways.

One woman appeared everywhere. A barefoot, black-haired beauty in robes of white. She wore strange horned crowns—feathers of gold sprouted from her forehead. The walls told her story. She played board games with the animal-headed monsters, bowed to jackal-faced men and danced among winged serpents. Sunrays enveloped her figure. Her beady white eyes stared from all surfaces. No corner of the underground maze was free of her strange spell.

A gunshot clapped like an echo in the dark.

Ollie recoiled as a German bullet whirred past and shot the painted face off a naked crocodile-headed woman playing a tambourine on the wall. He carelessly returned fire. A white Nazi eagle gleamed on a shadow ducking ahead of him. The air flashed red as bullets ricocheted. Modern war shattered the ancient silence.

Lamplight flickered in the darkness ahead. He saw a German silhouette and fired rapidly. The silhouette groaned aloud and staggered. The enemy was hit. The light at the end of the tunnel betrayed him. Ollie clenched his teeth and pumped more bullets into the falling figure.

A pitiful howl pierced the cold air—a gut-wrenching sound. The noise startled Ollie. His targets usually had no time to lament before dying. The German crawled across the floor with quick, jerking movements and suddenly dropped flat. The corpse's elbows froze upward like insect limbs. A freakish sight.

Ollie sauntered over and kicked the body on its side. A bright bronze knife handle stuck out from the German's chest. The blade was buried deep in the man's body. There was an empty sheath on his belt. Evidently the Afrika Korps soldier had been toting the blade. Somehow it loosened from its sheath and stabbed him as he fell. Physically, this seemed impossible—not like an accident, but like a deliberate blow. Yet the impossible had to be accepted. Nobody else was there to stab him.

He stepped over the body and boldly entered the lamp-lit chamber ahead. He found a room half-sunken in the sand, lit with kerosene lanterns. A shattered coffin lay in the center of the chamber. The stone lid had been smashed in the middle; pieces of it lay flung across the floor. Severed brown pieces of a mummified corpse were scattered in the dust. German military paraphernalia was stacked in the room—guns, ammunition, and supplies were arranged in neat German piles.

And something more. Treasure. The luster of gold gleamed in the musty darkness. There were vessels, alabaster cups, ancient mirrors, and what appeared to be a crown—a ring circlet with wings, a vulture and a double-headed rearing cobra on the front of it.

Behind it all loomed a statue of smooth red granite carved into the wall. That spooky woman again. Her figure was topless, stripped to the waist. She had large breasts and bracelets on her arms. Her face was narrow with a small forehead, pointed jaw and large amorphous lips. Ibis wings sprouted from her long headdress. She clenched symbols of power in her hands. Painted serpents coiled across the walls, wreathed with sunbeams. Vultures and falcons bowed in homage to the woman's image. A desert queen.

Once she was hailed as a divine being. Yet, death came to her as it did to all humans. Decay found bones that worshipers tried to preserve forever. Now those carefully wrapped limbs lay scattered on the floor like garbage. Thieves had stripped the gold away. Time and dust had consumed bandages and oils. Instead of bringing her eternal peace, the rich trappings heaped upon her corpse made her a target of mortal greed. The force of that greed shattered her resting place. It had ripped her body to shreds.

That same greed seized Ollie like a fever. He attacked the gold and ancient treasures stored in the chamber. He bundled as much as he could under one arm. A sense of power possessed him. It heightened his sadism. Leaving the room, he even decided to steal the knife from the dead German as a trophy. He ripped it ruthlessly from the body. Blood spurted everywhere, mixing with the dust and gold flakes on his hands.

He cleaned the blade off on the dead man's uniform. To his surprise, the curved blade was made of stone. He lightly tested the edge with his fingertip. Flint. It was finer and sharper than steel. Its handle was ancient bronze. He smiled.

Apparently the Germans had been robbing tombs, but he had bested them. He could seize their spoils—even pick up where they left off.

That was when the apparition came.

It gripped him first like an unseen dread. A presence filled the air with an almost electric energy that made the hair on his arms and neck bristle. An overpowering fragrance enveloped him. A smell like damp reeds, mixed with oil and some sickeningly sweet, musky herb odor. Perfume. A man's voice said something loudly. From nowhere. The words were unintelligible.

Ollie seized his gun and stood, baring the knife in his hand. He glanced everywhere and saw nothing. The knife trembled in his hand with unseen force, as if trying to pull away from him. He gripped it tighter. Something fell by itself with a crash. Some of the German supplies toppled over by themselves and went flying across the floor. An invisible force was knocking them over. Ollie watched the spectacle with widened eyes. It was supernatural.

"Blitherin' heck!" he hissed, backing away as a whirling sensation passed around his head. The knife moved in his hand again. He breathed rapidly in silence for a few moments as everything went still. He almost thought it was over.

Then a man's voice spoke again loudly, right behind his ear—this time saying a word he understood clearly. *"Hello."*

Ollie nearly jumped out of his skin. He spun around and saw it. The specter had unveiled itself. It was a figure like a person, composed of a tiny whirlwind of sand. It swirled behind him, then fell in a wisp to the floor.

He was stunned. Perspiration moistened his face. At first, he was afraid. Then he looked at the treasure in his arms, and at the knife he held. It continued to tremble, animated by an unseen force. His fear disappeared. He started laughing.

"Blimey! It's a genie!" he guessed, feeling pleased with this amazing discovery. He admired the knife in wonder and became determined to dominate it at all costs. "You're a genie. A genie of treasure," he said to the unseen menace. "You're the reason why I found this lot. You can bring me gold and trinkets. Can't you?"

No answer was forthcoming. The scent of perfume faded slightly.

"Fair's fair, mate. I captured you," vaunted Ollie, intoxicated by the promise of this fantasy experience. "Now you've gotta grant me wishes. That's the rule with genies, ain't it?"

A piece of stone rattled violently. Invisible footsteps rushed toward him. He bristled. He felt as though the fragrant spirit wanted to punch him. Nothing happened.

"Try and scare me all you like," announced Ollie defiantly, even as his voice trembled slightly with fear. "You'll never get away from me. I'm your master now." He laughed in triumph. "You'll be my pretty little secret."

He lived by those words ever since. From that day forward, he sought to dominate the spirit that dwelt in the ancient dagger. It never occurred to him for one moment that the spirit was not a genie.

He emerged into the fading sunlight a changed man, with bloody hands, gold and a deliriously perverse smile on his face.

His driver, Ted Bailey, noticed the change with some alarm. A native of Lancashire, he spoke with a broad, drawling accent. "What happened?" he asked, still nursing the fresh battle wound on his face. "What's wrong with you, mate?"

"Come on, Bales, wipe that scab off and get your lazy legs downstairs!" urged Ollie, stampeding towards the jeep and dumping his armload of glittering treasure in the back. "I found gold and guns and rummage to sell. What's more is there's dirty pictures on the walls! Naked people wearin' costumes. Faces like a lorries but the rest of them's all right. Come have a looksy."

"And the last Jerry?"

"Snuffed, right and proper." He giggled wickedly. "He were stuck like a pig, actually. With this!" He showed off the flint dagger. The symbols on the bronze handle glinted menacingly.

Ted peered curiously. "What's that bit of old crust, then?"

Ollie glared at the insult. "This here, twerp, is the dagger of a pharess!"

The other Englishman blinked. "A what?"

"A lady pharaoh, that's what," snapped the newly initiated tomb raider. "You ought to take a peep at her. They've got a marble of her below—a mop-headed tart with a lovely pair of torpedoes on her. Come see it, mate. We'll have us some pleasant company like that, you mark my words. Wine, women, and song—that's what's comin' our way soon." He leered victoriously. "Just imagine, Teddy boy, if you got all the money in the world, how'd you spend it?"

"I'd get meself a ticket home to Old Blighty, and leave this dry rotten hell behind forever," retorted the driver.

"Anything in the meantime, mug?"

"Only the basics," he quipped, sneering. "A seven-course meal, a mile-long bed, a swimmin' pool and clothes made out of silk." He shot his comrade a wicked look. "And a battalion of gyppo dancers to keep me company. Wearin' red lipstick."

They broke into lewd laughter.

"Hurry it up, then!" Ollie sprang from the jeep and beckoned him toward the dark portal. "I found Aladdin's treasure. Come help me bring it up."

Ted had an ominous feeling about the cave and the change that had transformed Ollie. He seemed different. Wilder and wickeder. Almost possessed. For a moment, he looked at his war comrade and thought he looked strangely disgusting. He overlooked it. Ted had always been secretly jealous and competitive with Ollie. Pride demanded he prove his mettle. If descending into the darkness was a test of manliness, he would not refuse.

It was their first haul of plunder. The first of what soon became an insatiable, lusting vice. They existed to steal. They sold the goods to whoever would buy and spent the money on pleasures. At first they enjoyed sneaking into cities and squandering their loot. Soon, however, cities repelled them. They lost enthusiasm for being among the living. The more graves they robbed, the more attracted they were to the desert and its dead.

The men became vultures who nurtured themselves by attacking corpses. Their ability to defend themselves in armed combat faded. They preyed on weak and defenseless targets. No tomb or ruin was safe from their grasp. Isolated bands of soldiers also became victims. Men too weak, tired or unsuspecting to defend themselves were brutally massacred and harvested for saleable goods. Even boots and clothing were liquidated for money.

They were never able to locate that first tomb again. It was, in fact, the tomb of an ancient Egyptian queen, according to an underworld antique dealer who bought some items from it. The robbers did not care to remember her name. They only knew that the goods were fenced to a millionaire collector in America, who paid them an outrageous sum of money they quickly spent. Their money evaporated like water in the Egyptian heat.

But there was one treasure that Ollie would never sell nor relinquish. The flint dagger, inhabited by his "lucky genie," was priceless to him.

The spirit resisted him. It turned out to be an evil companion— it hated him and fought his authority in various ways. It tried to get lost. It choked him with perfume at inopportune times and made loud noises to disturb his sleep. It was violent and occasionally broke objects. It also tried to make the knife cut him in happenstance ways, requiring him to be vigilant. He and his "genie" had an adversarial relationship.

Since owning the knife, various misfortunes had befallen him. He had lost an eye, aged prematurely, and was stricken with several parasites and diseases. He had also lost former companions. Various fellow thieves turned against him— including Ted Bailey who, lured by the dagger, stole it and fled to Cairo under the alias "Harper." No disguise had been enough to spare him from the dagger's ill fate. In the end, its jealous owner murdered him in a cabaret, and the dagger itself gored him in a last act of betrayal.

Ollie was an ignorant and greedy savage. He did not attribute any of these misfortunes to the dagger or his pillaging. He remained religiously convinced that the "genie" of the knife brought him luck and riches. He possessed it tyrannically at all costs.

He regained consciousness staring into a blood red sky filled with smoke. He was lying flat on his back.

"You are lucky that a mine did not blow up at you," said a young German voice.

Scrambling to rise, Ollie saw his fellow raider, Eislinger, looming nearby. They were no longer in the empty battlefield.

Eislinger and his team had rejoined Ollie following the Bedouin raid on Wadi Asra. Various tomb robbers traveled in groups. They regrouped at their cliffside hideout, nicknamed "Kettle Valley," to divide plunder and discuss next moves.

The groups were low on gasoline and mechanical supplies. They had been getting a steady stream of gasoline from Italian-financed black marketers in exchange for stolen antiquities; the sources were now drying up. Their stronghold at Wadi Asra, containing one of their largest supply caches, had been cleanly sacked by the Bedouins. It was a costly misfortune.

Despite this, Eislinger was popular among the men. He was polite and courteous when he wasn't killing and maiming people. He developed an orderly system of dividing plunder, organizing jeep convoys and settling disputes. He was also sadistic and prone to excess violence. He gave his cronies liberty to kill for sport rather than profit. This empowered them.

To scavenge bodies and collect more supplies, Ollie had proposed the battlefield "rummage" hunt. Various robbers had participated in it, including Eislinger and his team.

When Ollie was injured in the explosion, Eislinger ordered them to stop their supply search and bring the unconscious captain back to their Kettle Valley base. Armed jeeps were parked concealed behind sand hills; other robbers crouched and reclined in cave openings within the mountain of dry, prehistoric rock. Everyone was restless and bored.

Eislinger had used Ollie's accident as an opportunity to steal something.

Ollie reached reflexively for his dagger and realized it was gone. Its leather sheath on his belt was empty. He panicked. "Oi!" He began shouting and scrambled to his feet. "Where's my bloomin' knife? Where is it?"

Eislinger smirked coldly. It was in his possession, and he had hidden it in a secret place. He feigned innocence. "Maybe it fell off during the explosion," he suggested. "I don't know where it could be. It must be lost."

He watched with intense interest as Ollie lost his self-control and became desperate. The German spree killer's eyes narrowed thoughtfully behind his bookish glasses. He smelled panic.

"Like heck it's lost!" roared Ollie. "Which one of you filthy blighters pinched it?"

"We are all your friends here," replied Eislinger in his careful English, sounding very empathetic. "I'm sure nobody would steal it from you."

Ollie peered up at him with a baleful glare. His balance wavered. The explosion and subsequent blow to his head had affected him. His sharp criminal instincts told him Eislinger was lying. In fact, he suspected Eislinger was the guilty party.

"It were you, weren't it, Sigfried?" he accused, pointing his finger menacingly at the German. "You nicked it off me. Didn't you?"

Eislinger remained smirking in quiet defiance. Outwardly, it was a friendly smile, but the expression itself was emotionless. The German's eyes were alive with contempt. He looked like a malicious mannequin.

He chortled in disdain. "Please. That is ridiculous," he denied. "I would never steal from a comrade. That's dishonorable." He sneered. "You hit your head. Perhaps that's making you lose your temper," he scoffed, flaunting his self-control. "Relax."

A few chuckles rang out from the surrounding cliff hideouts. Ollie realized that their confrontation had an audience. The other men in the group were watching with interest. The jackals sensed conflict in the pack. Only the most vicious alpha male would command their loyalty. Who would be the leader? Tension filled the atmosphere like electricity.

Ollie's bronze face flushed. "You know what? I think I should," he said casually, and appeared calm for a moment. Then he swung violently and crashed a heavy fist straight into Eislinger's face. The blow snapped the German's glasses in half over his nose and sent him sprawling.

"I'll relax when I've bashed you to bits!" growled Ollie. He pressing his laced boot onto Eislinger's neck. "I saved your sad blinkin' little life not long ago, Hun boy. Forgot already?"

Eislinger returned a murderous stare. His mask of calm had fallen. Ollie was looking into the face of a sadist who brutally killed unarmed people for fun. It was wild and bestial. "I owe you nothing!" he snarled.

"Ungrateful scrap!" Ollie leaned down and spat in Eislinger's face. "Where's my flippin' knife?"

No answer came.

"Right. I'll take it off your sodding corpse, then," said Ollie. He coldly drew a pistol, intending to deliver a death shot.

There was a clatter as men reached for their weapons. The bandit captain looked up in alarm and realized that several of his crew—most of them former British soldiers—now pointed weapons at him in apparent support of Eislinger.

"What's all this, then?" challenged Ollie, shocked by the mutiny and struggling to maintain control. "It's this snail or me. You want to be captained by a mangy Jerry pup?"

One of the mutineers dared to speak out. "Why not?" challenged the Englishman. "We've gotten farther listening to him."

"Heck as right! He bothered the blitherin' Bedouins so they came round choppin' off heads and scarpered with our petrol," sassed Ollie. "I guess you didn't notice, did you, Susan?"

The mutineer bristled at the insult. "So what if he kills Bedouins?" he argued. "He's cleverer than you are."

"Here's somethin' clever," said Ollie, and shot the protestor in the head.

A savage shooting affray started. Ollie's brutal killing of a former crewman cost him the loyalty of other raiders who were undecided about which team to choose. They rushed to Eislinger's defense. Another group of men sided with Ollie. The cliffs echoed with gunshots and screamed insults. They ran in and out of caves to hide, picking each other off with vicious and sneaky shots. Blood poured across sand and rock. Several men were killed.

In the end, the robbers separated in two groups. Eislinger escaped with a small flock of followers in jeeps; Ollie retained the majority and remained in control of the base camp.

The ancient flint dagger remained in Eislinger's possession. He had successfully stolen it and disappeared. This plunged Ollie into torment. His life seemed to become hell whenever his "lucky genie" was gone.

He wanted above all to pursue Eislinger and reclaim his stolen treasure. However, his victory at the Kettle Valley base camp was costly. Most of the men who remained under his control had been wounded during the vicious mutiny. They needed care. Supplies, also, were low.

Ollie could not ignore these problems, otherwise the remaining men might die or desert him. As a scavenger, he could not survive well alone; as an egoist, he needed subordinates to wield power over. If he wanted to catch up with Eislinger and reclaim the dagger, he would first have to make other priorities. Emergency action was required.

He decided to make a risky move.

CHAPTER 17: RESURRECTION

"Each sunrise and each sunset at the sight
Of flaming red that puts the clouds to flight,
Still can listen to the symphony
Of the whistling wind and the restless sea."
—"Midday Swim—Mersa Matruh" from
"Poems from the Desert" by Lt. P.W.R. Russell

Major Desmond Frost stood on an outdoor portico overlooking the Mediterranean coast. He wore casual khaki trousers and a light sweater; it fit loosely over his fresh shoulder bandages and the wound dressings around his waist. After being reunited with fellow British soldiers, he was packed off on a transport to a military hospital facility in Alexandria. There he received medical treatment and made contact with Army Investigative Corps officials about his mission.

Alexandria was a beautiful old city by the sea. No longer in its prime, it had once been the jewel of several empires. Ancient Egyptians, Greeks, Romans, and Byzantines had basked in its glories. Those glories were faded now. However, the city still possessed a strange and ancient charm. It wasn't like Cairo—it was distinctly more Greek and less crowded. Its bleached coastal buildings of chalky white jarred against the dark blue of the curving ocean coastline. The climate was warm and temperate. Desert heat was balanced by cooling sea breezes. It was a nice spot to enjoy sunshine and relax in pretend peace as troop transport trucks and instruments of war rattled by.

Frost couldn't enjoy the scenery. It was meaningless without Eve. He imagined her in different grisly scenarios—all involving a desert, a German, and violence. More than anything he wanted to be out searching for her. However, he had not been given permission to leave.

The British officer's reappearance was sensational. He'd materialized like a ghost from behind enemy lines with a flock of eight Italian prisoners in his clutches. Everyone assumed he'd nabbed the whole gaggle during some mighty exploit. Frost made cynical remarks explaining the captures, but nobody listened. His reputation as a hero grew.

Tired and injured, he was triaged at a field hospital and then sent to a larger facility in Alexandria. Military doctors found him sunburnt, dehydrated, and suffering from severe blood loss. The gunshot wound to his shoulder was swollen and inflamed. The bullet nick to his side showed the early signs of a bacterial infection. He had trouble swallowing due to his smoking adventure and its effect on the old wound to his throat.

Frost hoped to be patched up quickly and sent on his way. Instead the doctors confiscated his belongings and imprisoned him in their care. He was given a blood transfusion and stitches. He was treated with penicillin, which the Army had access to in very limited supply. He also underwent a minor operation to extract debris from his gunshot wound; the bullet that struck his shoulder had splintered slightly on impact and left a small piece needing removal. The injuries were minor, and Frost recovered quickly. He was back on his feet again within a week.

He had been given a new issue of his damaged uniform. They tried to replace his dirty beret, as well. He insisted the original be washed and returned to him, which it was. Like other soldiers, Frost was superstitious when it came to "lucky" objects. Belongings that survived danger with him tended to accumulate "luck" and were sorely gotten rid of.

After being released from the hospital, he stayed temporarily in a hotel by the sea. He had briefed his military superiors, drawn some conclusions, obtained new permissions, and made a few plans. None of it mattered to him anymore. The war could drag on infinitely. The tomb robbers could rot. He didn't care. The world ended when Eve disappeared. So many days had passed. That spoiled his chances of finding her. Eve could have been swept across vast distances in any direction.

The British officer didn't know where to start. He charted his previous location on various maps and tried to work backwards to determine Eve's possible travel routes—to no avail. He stalked the halls and murdered his pencils. Duty demanded he return to Cairo. He felt lost.

A telephone call rang, forcing him to reenter his room from the balcony.

A jaunty Australian voice greeted him. Lieutenant Nye. The subordinate officer had obediently followed orders to go to a desert backwater town, Tell el-Abir, to regroup with Major Frost who planned to interview a witness to the tomb robberies. However, his mission was aborted when his commanding officer, Major Frost, failed to appear. Nye correctly assumed that something dangerous had happened to the Major and his fellow travelers in the desert. He had alerted authorities to Frost's absence. A search party poked around, but failed to locate anything. Then Frost had reappeared with fresh battle scars and a fistful of enemy prisoners. Nye had been ordered to resume their objective where it left off.

"How's the shoulder coming along, sir?"

"I'm absolutely fine. Thank you," said Frost tersely. His voice trembled slightly from emotional fatigue. "Have you interviewed Johnston?"

"Yes. I just took his statement, sir."

"Good. Write me a report and we'll review everything together in Cairo," ordered the Major. "I'm leaving in the next hour. I'll wait for you at Shepheard's. We'll need to compare notes before tomorrow. I've been given permission to launch an operation against Oliver Bryon. It'll be a bit tricky. We may have to drive out into the blue again to nab him."

"Sir?"

"It's not over. I have fresh intelligence at my disposal, and I intend to make a comeback," he stated clearly. "Commando Group Sphinx has finally choked up some information on Bryon. It'll be useful. You'll see."

"I was sorry to hear about Bob Wilmore, sir," interrupted the Australian in a sympathetic tone. "I didn't exactly get along with him, but he was a good bloke. First-rate soldier."

"No. Wilmore was a bad soldier. He failed his physicals and died bolting," Frost rebuffed icily. "Wilmore is responsible for this entire spectacle. If it hadn't been for his gross incompetence, we could've had Bryon and his posse either in custody or in coffins." He paused heavily. "There would not be a missing civilian on our conscience, either."

"What missing civilian, sir?"

He glanced down at the floor. His voice strained to repress emotion. "Eve Weathers, age 28, American citizen, Cairo resident and journalist for *The Chicago Standard* newspaper," he said hollowly. "That is, a former journalist. I just discovered," he paused to inhale, "that her employment was terminated.

Due to her absence, apparently. I tried to explain to their personnel department that she was called away on British military business, but the sods won't hear it. Those provincial Chicagoans have no worldview. They exist in an American bubble. The editor chap I dealt with was a saucy little lapdog called Milo. He's not fit to untie my bootlaces. I understand now why she hated him—"

"Actually, sir—"

"Not that her employment matters any longer," continued Frost, distracted by his own thoughts. "Miss Weathers has disappeared. She's now a missing person—"

"But, sir, she's not missing."

His eyes widened in shock. For a moment, he could not breathe. "What? What was that?"

"Eve Weathers is not a missing person," Nye replied coolly. "She was found."

He felt strength leave him. He set the telephone down on the table and sat in a nearby chair. It was an organized collapse. He leaned back and stared blindly at the ceiling. Tears filled his eyes in silence. He breathed deeply as he struggled to keep his composure. It didn't work. He staggered and grabbed the phone again. He estimated he could manage to talk normally for about two minutes before he would be forced to hang up and let despair take him.

"Did she suffer?"

Nye was plunged into confusion. "What, sir?"

"I mean...in what location was the body found?" He swallowed hard. "And in what...condition?"

"Sorry, sir. I should've been clearer," the Australian apologized, noticing the grief saturating the other end of the phone. "Miss Weathers is not dead, sir. She's very much alive. She's here in Tell el-Abir."

Frost's heart pounded. He stood quickly.

"A patrol found her out near the frontlines about a week ago. She hitched her way over here to the hospital where Johnston is. Been raising hell ever since. Demanding to interview the witness. Not sure how she figured out who our witness is or his location—to the best of my knowledge, Miss Weathers was never informed about the details. I suppose she must've eavesdropped on you or Bob Wilmore, sir, as we were leaving Khafra. It's anyone's guess how she knew to come here.

She's very sharp, sir."

"Yes, that's definitely her," said Frost anxiously. "Go on."

"She believed you were a POW, and said she intended to finish your investigation. Refused to leave the hospital. I saw her this morning and finally put a stop to it. I told her you're free as a bird. She asked lots of questions, but I didn't see the point in answering most of them. I escorted her out and got on with my assignment."

Frost hardly cared about the details. Despair had turned to hope in seconds; he was focused on only one thing. "Where is she now?"

"Likely still malingering outside. I suppose, sir, if you wanted..." Nye balked at the impropriety of what he was about to suggest. "If you wanted, I could get her on the phone here, sir."

The Major asked to speak to Eve and waited tensely for the moment to come. Seconds melted past and minutes seemed like hours. He went deaf and blind to everything except faint incoherent sounds on the other end of the phone line.

Then her voice came in a blast. Warm and alive, right into his ear. "Hello? Frosty?" The young American woman sounded very anxious. "Are you there?"

He sighed in relief. "Dear Lord in heaven..." He started to express gratitude to on high, but didn't finish. Raw feelings overcame him. The words got stuck in his throat. "My darling... you really are safe. What happened?"

"Oh, I'm so glad to hear your voice!" Her voice warmed like an approving smile, yet trembled with emotion as all her grief and worry surfaced and broke. "Are you OK? Nye said you've been in the hospital in Alexandria. Are you badly hurt?"

"No, not at all." He paused. "What about you? Were you injured in any way?"

"Nothing serious. I hit my head inside the truck and had a slight concussion. But the patrols who found me took me to a medical facility. I'm OK."

"Good," he answered. "I need to see you. Put Nye back on."

The Australian rematerialized. "I'm leaving for Cairo now, sir. Would you like me to bring Miss Weathers along?" He offered this as a favor to his commander. He pretended to be unaware of the couple's relationship for decorum's sake. "Perhaps since she's also an eyewitness to the tomb robberies, she might be able to provide useful details for the investigation."

"Yes. That's brilliant, Nye. Good man," stammered Frost. "Thank you. Please put Miss Weathers back on the line."

The phone shuffled. Her voice rematerialized. "Back to Cairo," she repeated. "I guess I'll see you tonight, then."

"Yes. Thank God!" sighed Frost, exhausted with relief. "Nye and I plan to meet at Shepheard's. I'll arrange a room for you there."

"Listen. I got some information that could help you."

He focused on his plans, oblivious to her words. "You'll have dinner with us, of course..."

She continued speaking. "Some details about the robbers."

He rushed to organize his belongings and fumbled with the phone. "I still have your suitcases stored at Giza," he said. "I'll have them sent over straightaway."

"I read Sullivan's book about the dagger. It really is haunted—" She hesitated. "Frosty, are you listening to me?"

He paused in sharp surprise. "What?"

"I think I can help with your investigation," insisted the journalist.

Frost had other things on his mind. A shadow of uncertainty crossed his face. "We'll see," he replied evasively.

CHAPTER 18: THE FRAGRANCE OF MYSTERY

"Sign and sigil well doth he know,
And can bode of weal or woe,
Of kingdoms' fall, and fate of wars,
From mystic dreams and course of stars."
—"The Bridal of Triermain, Pt. VI" by Sir Walter Scott

Later that day he stopped in a unique district outside Cairo. The area bordered the outlying suburb of Heliopolis, an ancient worship site and a portal to Egypt's desert—its Greek name meant "City of the Sun."

Near Heliopolis was a small, affluent community that was a model of Western living amid the Arabian and the ancient.

This small suburb was founded by French archaeologists who had excavated ruins near Heliopolis during Napoleon's reign. It grew from a European settlement into a bustling cosmopolitan burg with a blended majority of French, Italians, and British people as its chief residents. It was a center of academic and scholarly achievement, housing numerous institutes and libraries founded by European explorers. These institutions prospered with Egyptian cooperation. The neighborhood housed a swathe of Christian churches. Egyptians were rare to be seen here. The district, sarcastically dubbed "Little Oxford" by the British, was an island.

Major Frost was familiar with the area. No stranger to Egypt, he had perused exhibits of military interest in "Little Oxford" during a prior posting in Cairo in the 1930s. Now, the neighborhood would be rendezvous point with an old friend of his—Irish archaeologist Dr. Ben Sullivan, who unexpectedly contacted him before he left Alexandria.

Sullivan awaited him in a grand old edifice called the Osiris Institute. Founded by a French archeologist, it was a library and museum dedicated to Egyptian animal embalming research. Sullivan had picked the spot.

Frost walked through the imposing front entrance and felt the hot, dry air turn clammy as stone and shadow enveloped him. The Major looked trim in his khaki uniform. His sleeves were rolled up above his elbows. The sword on his silver CIG cap badge glinted in the dim light.

"Hey, you!" echoed a familiar Irish voice.

He turned quickly to see Sullivan rushing to greet him. The red-headed Irish archaeologist looked quite different from the last time they met. No more nomad robes or head kerchiefs. Sullivan was wearing a short-sleeved white shirt and neat gray trousers. His freckled face was tanned from the sun.

For his part, Sullivan noticed that the tough Major looked more or less the same as ever. A few minor changes came to attention. Notably, the lean and muscular Frost appeared thinner than usual. His face was etched with stress and weariness. His short brown mustache showed traces of silver.

"Glad you could make it!" said Sullivan, giving him a hearty handshake and appreciative slap on the arm. "It was lucky you got my call before you left for Cairo. Otherwise we'd have just missed each other."

"Thank you for having the presence of mind to make contact," answered Frost, tired and cynical. "You didn't have to volunteer information like this, you know. And to drive all the way over..."

"I had planned to come back to Cairo, anyway," dismissed Sullivan. "I've collected enough samples. Wife and kids need a break. And so do I." He paused sympathetically. "Anyhow, even if I didn't have information, I'd still have wanted to visit after I heard about what happened to you all out there. I heard one of your men didn't make it." He grabbed Frost's arm and escorted him to another room. "Honestly, I'm glad to see you back alive."

"Yes. Our luck was rather thin," said Frost pensively. "I largely owe my survival to Miss Weathers. She treated my injuries after I was wounded. If not for her, I might've caught gangrene before reaching a hospital."

"Quite a girl," remarked Sullivan.

"Indeed she is," admitted Frost, glancing down.

"And the lady's rejoining you this evening in Cairo, you said?"

"Yes, finally," he sighed in relief. "Thank God."

Sullivan shook grim thoughts out of his mind. "At least things worked out well in the end," he said, trying to stay optimistic. He smirked. "Now, let's cause some more trouble!"

He led Frost into the main reading room. The huge center of the library was crowned with a domed ceiling and mosaic walls. Streams of sunlight poured in through curved Arabian windowpanes. Tall ladders hung from mazes of shelves, filled with jewel-toned books, lining the room. Researchers read the books at tables and on plush couches. Combining European and Arabic architecture, the building overlooked the rest of the city and the desert beyond. The white glaring heat on rooftops and the baking orange sand bluffs in the distance produced colors richer than any painting. The cruel desert looked like a fantasy world from here.

They sat at an octagon table near a window where Sullivan had already gathered a pile of books and parchments.

"First things first," announced Sullivan, and clapped a heap of small silver pieces on the table. He pushed them towards Frost. "They're all yours, Major. Have a peek."

Frost, examining the items, discovered most were British military identity discs. Two were Italian Army dog tags.

"I traded these with some of my tribal friends," explained Sullivan with a look of dark knowledge. "They took them off the bodies of freshly killed tomb robbers. Might give you a closer perspective on who's been responsible for all this marauding." He reached into his pocket and pulled out a small, bloodstained notebook. "And then, there's this."

The Major took it and leafed through it. Scribbles in Italian, drawings of Egyptian artifacts and a few pages of badly sketched maps filled its contents halfway.

"Seems one of the Italians kept a little glossary," suggested Sullivan. "Looks like he wrote directions since he couldn't remember where he was going. Plus it seems the dirty crook had an artistic side. Lots of interesting sketches in there. See what you can make of it."

Frost smirked. He shut the notebook and put it away. "I can guess which Bedouins sold these to you," he said dryly. "I might've seen some of them running about in an old temple, carting away water cans and tinned peaches."

"That's right. I bought these from the same tribe that unknowingly came to your assistance," Sullivan admitted. "Their relatives were murdered by the robbers. It was terrible. They told me all about it." He leaned back in his wicker chair. "Which brings me to my third point. Rumor has it the robbers have split up in two factions. They were seen fighting each other on two different occasions. Last I heard, one faction was heading parallel to the Nile towards Upper Egypt. You know. In the direction of Asyut."

"Is this information reliable?" questioned Frost.

"Very," the Irishman affirmed.

"Thank you, Ben. This conversation has been indispensible." The Major offered him a grateful handshake and moved to rise. As much as he appreciated the opportunity to speak with his friend Sullivan, he was very anxious to arrive in Cairo on time to meet Eve.

"Wait just a moment, I'm not finished," chided Sullivan. He smirked in triumph. "You said on the phone that you saw the chief tomb robber carrying the stolen artifact. You know. The flint dagger!"

"Correct. Somehow he smuggled it out of Army custody."

Sullivan shuffled papyri on the table. "Well, since you're here, I'm going to clear up the dagger's history once and for all," he announced proudly. "My research has confirmed both the dagger's origin and its meaning!"

Frost snickered irreverently. "If it's anything to do with *ka's*, *ba's*, or *akh's*, no thank you," he said with an impertinent laugh. "I've already heard quite enough about that!"

"So!" exclaimed the Egyptologist in surprise. "You did read the book."

The British soldier gave a raffish grin. "In a manner of speaking."

Sullivan pulled the picture of the stolen flint dagger that Frost had given him out of a nearby book. "I finally found its origin!" he exclaimed in academic excitement. "The book I loaned you wasn't entirely correct. It's a fact that the original owner was an animal embalmer named Ne'rah. He did actually exist. He was indeed executed for desecrating a crocodile mummy. That's all true. But his dagger was absolutely not buried under a doorstep. That was just a myth circulated by Herodotus—"

"Hang on, you're going a bit too fast," interrupted Frost, unaware of the dagger's history. "What's all this about doorbells and mummies?"

"Not doorbells." The Irishman shot him a withering look. "You were bluffing, weren't you? You didn't read it!" He ruffled his curly hair in frustration and sighed to the heavens. "Well, looks like I'm going to have to educate you. Might as well run through the whole song-and-dance. Just don't try to sneak off!" He menaced. "Or I'll give you a clean thrashing, so I will."

Frost was excited at the prospect of a fight. "I'd take you up on that challenge!"

"I'd love to box you, Frosty, but remember what happened when we played a game of football," said Sullivan wryly. "We can't afford to pay repairs for destroying this place."

Both men laughed.

"Come on. I'll give you the grand tour," said Sullivan.

He led Frost through the labyrinth of the Osiris Institute and showed him a number of elaborate gold and lapis sarcophagi once used to entomb mummified animals. There was also a sizeable collection of animal mummies on display. Specimens included ibises, mice, cats, fish, monkeys, crocodiles, toads, and vultures. Some animals were adorned with amulets and jewelry. Others had coffins filled with dried food intended for them in the afterlife.

Sullivan explained that the ancient Egyptians made literally millions of animal mummies of many different species. Animals were considered more sacred than humans. It was standard practice to embalm all kinds of creatures. Other animals thought to be important deities had lavish funeral rites.

"Do you recognize her?" asked the Irish scholar, leading Sullivan into a bright adobe chamber. The room contained pedestals exhibiting some ancient statues.

In the light of a sunbeam falling from a high window stood an elegant yet freakish figure. It was a tall hooded serpent carved of red granite and inlaid with precious stones. A cobra. It was nearly human-sized. Enormous wings spread from its sides like giant pointed arms, with long blue jewel-feathers flaring towards the ceiling. The rearing snake looked ready to fly away. The most startling thing about the snake was its head. The cobra had the face of a woman. A woman with a bobbed black wig and two long purple hair ornaments framing her face. Her eyes were black as night. Her orange red lips were puffy. Her face was pitiless.

"Ah. The holy centipede!" quipped Frost blithely, just to annoy Sullivan. He shot his comrade an ornery glance. "It—I mean, she—has a name, I suppose."

"That, my ignorant friend, is the goddess Habti," the Irishman lectured, rather sternly. "Figures of her in art are very rare. She's a very obscure deity—worshiped almost exclusively by animal embalmers. She is the protectress of animals and goddess of animal mummification. That's the reason for her snake form. Cobras, you see, were viewed as fierce guardians—"

Frost strolled over to the statue. He peered into its face and irreverently nicked its nose with a flick of his finger. "Red granite, eh? Still doesn't look a bit feminine!" he pronounced. "I'm sure you're very excited by this discovery, Ben old boy, but you'll forgive me if I don't share your enthusiasm. Women with snake qualities—mythological or otherwise—are not my cup of tea." He sauntered away.

"You're missing the point!" Sullivan chased him. "This confirms that the knife was used by an animal embalmer," he said. "It's further evidence that my hypothesis is correct!"

He described the brief history of Ne'rah, the famous animal embalmer who profaned a holy crocodile. Ne'rah was executed with his flint mortuary knife in a ritual to trap his evil spirit as punishment.

The story finished differently than the tale in the book Eve read. According to a few scant papyri records Sullivan tracked down, the dagger was sunk in the Nile as an offering to appease the river's crocodile god, Sobek.

As this raised doubt about the origins of the knife stolen from Army custody, Sullivan had checked. Mortuary knives were traditionally made of flint. This particular blade, judging from its appearance and the hieroglyphs etched onto it, was made specifically for animal embalming. Its "spirit seal" was also unmistakable. Sullivan found a few other similar knives used for the same purpose. However, the biggest clue indicating Ne'rah's ownership was the hieroglyphic "water" symbol, spelling the letter 'N,' located near the blade's spirit seal. In the photograph, there also appeared to be faint white scratches on the flint surface made from white stone. This corroborated the story of Ne'rah using the knife to sever jeweled, alabaster teeth from the crocodile mummy.

The bronze handle was also part of the original knife, according to Sullivan. Research confirmed that many animal embalmers used hilted knives in order to perform mortuary procedures on animals with tough or difficult anatomy.

How did the knife surface from its watery grave in the Nile? Some daring and sneaky soul must have fished it out from the muddy black depths and repurposed it. Perhaps someone with a personal connection to the dagger's deceased master, Ne'rah? Who knew? The lawbreaker who defiantly retrieved the knife against judicial and divine orders was lost in time.

Why was this knife so important to the tomb robbers? Unclear. According to some accounts, the knife was haunted. This was backed up by what Major Frost had heard from Army associates—and his own personal experiences.

"I admit that I noticed a strong scent like perfume about the dagger, when I was near it," the British officer said with a healthy dose of skepticism. "I did hear some rather strange noises, and I did see it fall and move—apparently by itself. However," he added, "I'm not entirely ready to say that these things were supernatural. There could very well be some other explanation." He smiled sharply. "I'm a pragmatist, Ben, as you very well know."

"But you did notice the perfume!"

"It was impossible not to notice," quipped Frost wryly. "It was overpowering."

Sullivan brightened. "Can you describe it?"

Frost reflected for a few moments. "Hmm. I think I would say that it was..." He paused and pondered. "A bit like shaving cream, a bit like an old lady's handkerchief, and a bit like dirty socks. With perhaps a faint trace of soggy old tea in the background."

The Irishman blinked dubiously. "You call that a description?"

Frost grinned and glanced down, somewhat embarrassed. "Best one I can give, I'm afraid."

"Let's try something else," said Sullivan, grabbing his friend by the elbow and dragging him gruffly down a hallway. "They've got some recreated samples of ancient Egyptian perfumes here. Maybe you can identify it by memory!"

"Oh please, Ben!" protested Frost in disdain. "I don't know the least thing about perfume! Anyway, why should I waste time sniffing old jars? It would make no difference to me if the dagger smelled like roses. It's completely irrelevant—"

"Just humor me, would you?" insisted Sullivan, towing him towards a shelf with various colored bottles on it. "Identifying this fragrance will be the last piece in a puzzle I'm trying to put together. Do me at least one favor!"

Frost shot him a roguish glance. "You will take full responsibility if I sneeze and drop something."

"You'd better not!"

The Major started impatiently snatching fragrance bottles, waving them around briefly and setting them down. "No, not here. No, not that one either." He perused one delicate bottle and stared in revulsion. "What on earth is this? It's atrocious!"

"That is a certain type of red reed grown on the Nile," said Sullivan, checking the shelf label. "Frequently used as a specialized cat perfume. Also worn by court ladies..."

"Did the courtiers wear gas masks?" quipped Frost.

"Try this one!" Sullivan grabbed a violet bottle and handed it to him eagerly. "This one is blue and white lotus. Cleopatra wore it."

Frost, hearing mention of the notoriously seductive queen Cleopatra, became curious and took a hard sniff of it. "Not the least bit appetizing!" he pronounced curtly. "Mark Antony must've been desperate." He brandished the bottle at the Irishman. "Would this paltry whiff of grass make you lose your head and die like a caged rat? Tell me honestly."

Sullivan laughed.

"Ben, I have an appointment in Cairo and we are not succeeding at anything except sickening me with ungodly smells," complained Frost. He marched to the end of the shelf and glared at the remaining bottles. "I may lose my sense of taste if I keep this up!"

"Don't exaggerate."

"I don't see how any of this qualifies as perfume. It all smells like moldy hay," he grumbled. "This only further demonstrates to me that the ancient Egyptians were some of the most backward people around—" He seized several jars and whiffed them abruptly. "Here it is!"

Sullivan, ready to argue about the merits of Egyptian civilization, was dumbstruck.

"There it is. Right there," said Frost firmly, handing him the bottle and pointing at the shelf he took it from. "I can clearly say this one is a near identical match."

The Irish Egyptologist examined it in anxious wonder. "It is West Nile myrrh," he pronounced solemnly. "One of the most common and sacred perfumes used for embalming."

"'Eureka,'" rejoined Frost, arching his brows sarcastically. He paced impatiently, ducking his hands in and out of his pockets and fidgeting. "Now that I've frittered away time inhaling dandelion fumes, I'll head off to Cairo. I'm not sure what this achieved, but hopefully I repaid you for the intelligence you gave earlier." He gave a curt nod of his head and swiveled jauntily on his heels to exit. "Cheers, Ben."

"Listen, Frosty, this was no waste of time!" argued the scholar, chasing him to the front hall. "There's no way the scent of ancient myrrh would last that long on an artifact, or smell so strongly. This proves something spooky is definitely going on!"

"Which ultimately amounts to what?" contested Frost, striding briskly towards the door. "A niffy ghost won't save Oliver Bryon and his cronies from their just desserts." He paused and fixed his unflinching blue stare on Sullivan. "I'll bag the lot of them, dead or alive," he said. "Preferably dead."

"Leave that dagger in their hands, and you may get your wish without trying," Sullivan retorted sharply. "Tell me, do you have any further evidence of bad fortune associated with the dagger? Did anyone else who touched it drop dead since the last time we spoke?"

It was meant to be a facetious remark. The Irish scholar was only half-serious; he didn't expect to actually hear news of another death. However, his words jarred Frost's memory.

"Only a sergeant," said Frost after a moment of thick, frosty silence. "His name was Bob Wilmore. He had been working on the case with Major Hathaway before I took over. He had been responsible for collecting and marking evidence. It's likely he handled the dagger during the course of his duties. You met him when I visited you in Khafra."

A shadow of worry darkened Sullivan's face. "May I ask how he ended up?"

Frost's jaw tightened. He hesitated for a second. "Killed by robbers," he said tersely, "and by his own cowardice."

Sullivan paled slightly. "This is worse than I thought—"

"Don't bother citing chapter and verse from the book of rumored curses," Frost snapped back scathingly. He was annoyed and his patience had evaporated. "For all your esoteric conjecturing, you have failed to explain one thing."

"And what might that be?"

"Why is the ringleader still alive?" demanded Frost. "If the dagger really does 'zap' anybody who touches it with evil death powder, why is Ollie Bryon, the gang leader who totes it everywhere, still merrily walking about? If your theories were correct, shouldn't he have already been blasted by lightning, or swept away by a wind—"

Despite being offended, the Irishman couldn't help but smile at the Major's stinging sarcasm. "Are you going to put a timer on curses, then?" he interrupted.

Frost held back in confusion.

"Maybe Ollie's got something worse coming to him. You don't know," said Sullivan. "I don't know either. What I do know is that anybody who touches that dagger has a date with disaster. That's where all the evidence points, and three bodies in the morgue so far is nothing to sneeze at. So my advice for you still stands—stronger than ever," Sullivan intoned, gesturing emphatically with his hand. "If that dagger ever crosses your path, keep your fingers off it!" he commanded. "And boots, too," he added as an afterthought. "If I were you,

I wouldn't even kick it!"

Frost eyed the Irishman and wondered privately if the man was more of a superstitious sort than he had imagined.

"I'll make you a bet, Frosty," the scholar proposed defiantly, anxious to justify himself. "If nobody else who touched the dagger turns up dead in two weeks, call me a fool and I'll buy you a bottle of grog."

The Major grinned. "I'll take that bet."

CHAPTER 19: MOST SECRET

"White coats, coloured gowns, coloured skins,
Sandals and shoes, patch vivid, bizarre, steep shadows
On white pavements, and blue-black streets."
—"Western Oriental" from "Poems from
the Desert" by Cpl. N.A. Brown

Cairo had many faces at nighttime. Some inner-city streets bustled with sleepless human activity as the cabaret scene blazed to life. Grand old boulevards in the city's political and business sectors were secluded after dark. Riverboats floated on the Nile like glimmering torches, leaving the sounds of music and laughter trailing behind like a faint aroma. Palm trees stood like regal pillars around majestic old British colonial buildings. Egyptians silently crossed paths with Europeans along the avenues. Minarets, ancient obelisks and modern radio towers mingled under the glittering stars of a pitch-black desert sky.

Shepheard's Hotel bombarded the dry night air with bright lights and music. The place was always knee-deep in intrigue and swarming with British people. Shepheard's was the official unofficial HQ of British citizens in Cairo. The British relished the hotel for its charm, efficiency, and European atmosphere. The amenities and décor were magnificent. The long bar, parlors, and ballroom were especially inviting. Evenings were very social.

Major Frost waited outside on the front steps wearing a more formal version of his desert uniform, complete with a long-sleeved jacket and brown Army tie. Egyptian doorkeepers in long tunics and red fezzes peered suspiciously at him. It was unusual for a British gentleman to pace aimlessly in the murky lamplight and withstand hordes of Nile mosquitos for no reason. One of the doorkeepers politely suggested that Frost wait for guests inside. The Major responded with a sharp glare and a disdainful snort, ending the conversation. Frost wanted more than anything to see Eve immediately as she arrived. He was repulsed by the idea of idling around indoors waiting passively for something to happen.

She saw him first. Cruising down the boulevard in Lieutenant Nye's jeep, Eve saw the grand lights of Shepheard's and the person pacing the hotel's front sidewalk. She immediately recognized the square-shouldered, wiry figure in uniform snapping restless strides across the pavement and fidgeting with his hands in his pockets. She recognized his sharp facial features from a distance. His midnight blue Army Investigative Corps beret glowed as he stalked under a lamp. She waved her arms and yelled to him.

Frost heard the noise and looked up immediately. His piercing blue eyes widened as they saw her. He abandoned his position near the front steps and was nearly hit by a passing vehicle as he rushed to meet the jeep at the edge of the sidewalk.

Nye greeted him. He didn't hear. All he could see was Eve. The beautiful young American woman looked like a ghostly shadow of her former self. She was thin, drawn, sunburnt, and covered in white chalk dust. Her coppery red hair looked damp and tangled.

Frost leaned into the jeep. He grabbed her hand and wrung it with affection. "Thank God!" he exclaimed. His voice cracked with strong emotion.

Eve tumbled out of the jeep and embraced him with warmth. "I thought I'd never see you again," she said.

They squeezed each other tight. Nye watched the scene with skepticism as he disembarked.

She brushed her fingers gently across the shoulder of his uniform jacket, trying to gauge the status of his injury. "Are you all right?"

"Yes. Quite all right," replied Frost, his eyes glistening. "You look terrible."

The journalist smirked. "Thanks a lot," she retorted. "Being stuck in the boondocks doesn't do much for your health or appearance." She glanced at the glittering hotel doors. "I suppose we'll make a grand entrance after we hit the front door. Watch everyone stare like goldfish."

"It doesn't matter," Frost answered bluntly, showing the faint edge of a smile at her rough style of speech. He turned to Nye. "I have a table reserved. Wait for me there while I see that Miss Weathers gets settled in."

"Yes, sir," responded the Australian soldier, and disappeared.

Frost offered the woman his arm. She was surprised; it was not a gesture that she as an American was used to. She accepted the British officer's overture. They neatly linked arms and walked up the steps to the hotel's grand front doors. The Egyptian doormen, gawking curiously, almost forgot to usher them in.

Eve spoke anxiously. "Frosty, I need to tell you about—"

"Please stop calling me that," interrupted Frost in a low tone, sounding exhausted. "My name is Desmond. That is what I'd like for you to call me."

The woman reflected with quiet surprise. His first name was uncommon in her country, and she could not recall ever having said it before. Obviously she needed to get used to it.

"Do you use a nickname for it?" she asked.

"No. It's Desmond," he answered firmly, whisking her through the lobby. He summoned an elevator as onlookers goggled at his messy female companion. "I've had your suitcases brought over. You'll find them in your room—"

"Desmond," she said, trying to restart the conversation.

Frost stared intently at her as they got into the elevator. Hearing his name spoken from her lips was an enchanting experience. "How did you get here?"

She hesitated. "Von Rindl drove me near a British military outpost and let me leave. He told me what direction to walk in."

Frost's eyes flickered dangerously as suspicions crossed his mind. "Did he hurt you?"

"No," she stated emphatically. "He gave me some information about the tomb robbers." She pulled a folded map from the pocket of her dusty trousers and handed it to him. "He told me this is a map of all the places the tomb robbers have raided recently," she said. "He claimed that it was compiled by himself and German military intelligence. I'm not sure if it's fake or not," she admitted, "or if he was playing a trick on me. But I thought I'd take a chance anyway, in case it would help you..."

The Major glared at it. "In exchange for what?"

"Nothing," she replied. "I only read him some passages from Sullivan's book and told him some stories about the haunted dagger. He thanked me for being kind. He asked me for my postal address to send me information about where you were being held—"

"Address?" scoffed Frost. "I suppose you were naïve enough to admit you don't have one."

She glanced away uncomfortably. "Anyway, he offered this map to me."

Frost was almost annoyed by her actions, but was overwhelmed with love for her. He made no comment or criticism.

Eve hesitated. "He only made me promise not to tell he gave it to me—he said, if German authorities find out about the leak, he will be in danger." She smiled nervously. "He said he trusted me with it. He seemed to think you'd turn him in to Nazi authorities on purpose," she said. "Of course, that's not true—"

Frost started back with hardened apathy. "He was right," he said, crunching the map like a piece of garbage and shoving it into his pocket. "I'll see to it that the Afrika Korps discovers the map was leaked. By Captain...what's his name?" He smirked coldly. "Oh yes. Elrich von Rindl."

"What?" she asked in shock. "Why?"

"He has no business manipulating you into feeding our Army disinformation," he snapped harshly. "I won't buy anything he's selling. I'm sure it's all a pack of lies. The fact that he coerced a woman in dangerous circumstances to complete Nazi errands has lowered my shabby opinion of him to the level of vermin."

Dismay seized Eve. She considered Von Rindl a decent person. "But he treated me well!" she advocated. "He didn't turn me in as a spy. And he didn't have to drive me back to—"

"Don't bother trying to pacify me. That man dragged you out of my arms and nearly had me killed," snapped the Major. "When I was escaping, the Germans fired shells at me. I was nearly blown to bits—not to mention being shot at afterwards." He said each word coldly and watched deliberately as horror left her stunned. "I would like very much to settle accounts with Captain Von Rindl."

Strained silence fell. The elevator doors opened and they walked into the hall. Eve, upset by the Major's hardheadedness and cold fury, became angry with him.

"He expected it," she muttered. "He said you were a cruel man."

Frost cracked a cynical grin. "Well! He was fairly on the mark there, for only knowing me a few hours." He was amused and unashamed. "He should've known better than to upset me."

She glared. "I told him he was wrong about you."

"But he wasn't wrong!" The tough soldier was completely straightforward and unashamed. "I know very well that I can be ruthless. You know it too. It's quite necessary in my line of work and I make no apology for it." He steeled his jaw and put his hands in his pockets belligerently, as if bracing himself for an argument. "It's peculiar how our German opponents define 'cruel' though. Don't you think?"

He addressed Eve with renewed vehemence, growing more outraged about the accusation of cruelty by the minute.

"You are offended by the fact that I plan to get rid of the German who had me captured," he stated, staring her down with wounded defiance. "I ask you, would it have been no less cruel for me to meet my end being dismembered by a shell burst and scattered in pieces on the sands? To have bled away slowly and been dumped in a sandy hole—never to see you, touch you or hear your voice again?" His eyes burned with fury. "That, my dear girl, was the fate that Von Rindl subjected me to. Do you understand properly now?"

She grimaced and covered her eyes. Imagining the gruesome fate that could have happened to him made her hands tremble. "I'm sorry," she sighed. "I didn't mean to—"

"And he has the nerve to accuse me of cruelty!" Frost went on, his voice charged with emotion. "Of course war is a very neat bureaucratic process for little whelps like him. But not for me." His eyes flashed. "I assure you, he will understand the definition of the word 'cruelty' before his war is over. I promise you that!"

He marched past her and led her down the corridor.

"I've dreamed of the moment when I would finally see you again," she lamented, hurrying to keep up with his irritated march, "and now you're angry with me."

"No, I'm not angry with you," denied Frost, looking down with a flushed face as he walked. "We both know who I am angry with. It's not you." He felt ashamed of himself for upsetting her. "I suppose I've been very unpleasant, as usual," he muttered. "I'm sorry. You're entitled to a nice evening..."

He led her to a suite at the very end of the hall and produced a key.

"There," he announced, handing over the key. "Go in. Please wash up, rest, get a change of clothes and throw these tatters away," he said, gesturing at her dirty garments. "Take as long as you like. I'll be downstairs with Nye. You're welcome to join us for dinner. Or, if you're too tired—which would be understandable—just phone for me downstairs and I'll arrange quick room service. The restaurant can be terribly slow, but I can make sure they put a jump into it, so to speak."

He avoided eye contact. He turned on his heels and was about to efficiently disappear when she reached out and grabbed his arm insistently.

"Hey, Frosty." She corrected herself. "I mean, Desmond..."

He halted in place and felt his heart melt like candlewax in his chest. He was possessed by love for her. It made him feel weak.

"Come here!" commanded Eve, tugging his arm. "You're not just going to storm off like this. I've waited too long."

She pulled him into a tight embrace. He freely fell into it.

"Oh, it's so good to hold you again!" she sighed, closing her eyes and running her hands across his back. "I missed you like crazy."

"I missed you, too," he breathed, crushing her in his arms. "Terribly."

"Do whatever you want with the stupid map. I don't care. Burn it, throw it out the window, if you want—"

He laughed. "I might, if you tempt me."

She kept her eyes shut, savoring every ounce of him. "I just want to stay here like this forever."

He squeezed her tighter and held her in silent adoration for a few extra minutes. Eventually, he compelled himself to let go. "Listen, my darling," he said, breathless with desire, "you've had a terrible ordeal, and I'm very anxious that all your needs be taken care of. Please go in and make yourself comfortable.

I'll arrange something for you to eat—"

"Don't worry about it! I'll come downstairs for dinner," she said, feeling energetic despite the hard desert journey. "Let's have some fun together."

Frost glowed at her. He backed away hesitantly and fidgeted. "On that last note...I have something very important to discuss with you this evening," he declared suddenly. "I mean, not with Lieutenant Nye present. I mean, only with you."

They stared at each other. Eve could see his intentions plainly on his face. His expression was calm but his clear blue eyes sparkled at her, as usual.

"I suspect you can guess what I'd like to discuss," said Frost slyly. He broke into a boyish grin and glanced at the floor. "I...hope that it will turn out to be a good discussion." He shot her another melting gaze then hurried to depart. "Well! I'll leave you to it."

Watching him stride away, Eve experienced gladness and nervousness. Her speculations about the future had changed completely in the space of only a few moments. She again sensed that life would never be the same.

Half an hour later, Frost was sitting jauntily at a white-covered dining table with Lieutenant Nye seated across from him. Their place was in an upstairs corner overlooking the crowded ballroom. The two military officers were restless and on edge. They ordered stiff drinks from a fez-wearing Egyptian waiter.

"Do you think she'll come down and join us?" Nye asked.

"I'm not sure," replied Frost. "She'd like to, but surely she's exhausted. I have no idea what ordeals she's endured since I saw her last. What we experienced at the hands of Oliver Bryon and his cronies was dreadful."

The drinks arrived—large ones, fit for thirsty soldiers. Nye quaffed beer. Frost drank cognac. Silence fell for a few minutes as they guzzled alcohol and let their tense nerves fade. Then Frost got down to business. He took a folded envelope from one uniform pocket and dropped it onto the table. Nye reached for it. Inside was a typewritten memo with a violet "Most Secret" stamp imprinted on it.

Frost watched grimly as his junior opened the envelope. "Look it over carefully," he said. "This is who we're dealing with."

His story began in the gutters of East London. It had been the wrong side of town since time immemorial. Inhabitants of East London, known as cockneys, commonly distinguished themselves from other city residents through their rhythmic, nasal speech and their scorn for authority. They were a poor, working caste. To be born a cockney was a disadvantage in society. The blemish of a cockney accent was enough to guarantee an innocent East London native a lifetime of discrimination. Cockneys tended to resist outside influences and take pride in their insulation. Some were honest and lowly. Many others were criminals. Evidently that dark path was what Oliver Bryon of the British Royal Army had chosen.

Not much was known of Bryon's early life or origins. His military records contained mere data—where he was born, when, his weight, height, and other details. He had no relatives on file and no one listed as a contact in case he got killed in action.

However, his records did reveal a unique career path. Bryon did not enlist in the Army in England—rather, he joined up while serving the military as a contract laborer in Burma. Bryon was a mule driver. He had the honor of maintaining and cleaning up after pack mules used by the Army for transport and logistical purposes in the colonies. After several months of mule duty, he became a soldier. He appeared to have no education. After he enlisted, he claimed to have studied at a military training outpost in Burma, which lacked a formal cadet school. A tutor and two other officers vouched for him. Whether or not Bryon received any education and whether or not his references were dishonest merited speculation at this point. After becoming a soldier, Bryon miraculously appeared as a low-ranking officer in a respectable infantry battalion. Like a spider, he continued to climb by strange leaps and bounds into odd corners of the Army—he had a brief stint as a drill instructor, somehow served under a staff quartermaster, transferred back into the field, and bobbed up in Singapore, Ceylon, and Yemen, among other places. Bryon, currently in his mid-30s, had worn a remarkable amount of hats for someone his age.

Yemen was the scene of Bryon's meteoric ascent to Army Special Forces. The region was embroiled in armed uprisings.

Bryon was posted to a small outlying protectorate that was suddenly thrown into a regional civil war in 1938. Here Bryon distinguished himself through ruthless cunning. No acts of bravery were attributed to Bryon. His natural coldness and gifts for sneaking and sabotaging saw him promoted three times in two months, with a military decoration to boot. Bryon assassinated an enemy leader and detonated a supply cache. During this time, he came into contact with Army Intelligence Corps officers. He magically transferred across the globe again—this time, as a member of Army Special Forces.

He returned to England and underwent a rigorous secret training program in the countryside. He was spared from defending France during the German invasion in 1940. Instead, they parachuted him in a few weeks after Dunkirk. He plagued the Germans and their Vichy allies for several months. His tactics were coarse and devious. He did not content himself with blowing up railway supply lines. He made car bombs and murdered men in their sleep. He set booby traps and killed people in twisted circumstances. His targets included French citizens deemed as enemy collaborators or spies—some were women. His actions would have been crimes in peacetime, but the fact that he committed them against national wartime enemies somehow made them excusable—even praiseworthy, in the eyes of certain military superiors.

When the combined forces of Germany and Italy threatened the British presence in North Africa, Bryon was shipped there as part of the top-secret Commando Group Sphinx. His duties as a commando included deep desert scouting and "mopping up" certain enemy targets.

His official story ended there unfinished. Commando Group Sphinx redacted the names and locations of all Bryon's completed secret missions in North Africa from the file. No records existed of Bryon being wounded. His loss of an eye was unreported to his superiors.

Clearly, that was not the only thing they were blind to.

There were a few old photographs of Bryon in the file. His enlistment photo, plus a few others of him in different places and uniforms. He was a remorseless, hard-faced man. His features were ordinary yet brutish. His eyes were pale and lifeless. They brimmed with silent anger. Looking into his face was like being hit with a punch. He smiled in all his photographs. A little crooked smirk, as if he were always laughing at some inside joke. There was no joy in that smile. It was a look of emotionless mockery.

Added to all of this was the testimony that Lieutenant Nye had received from the lone witness to Bryon's crimes, currently lying mangled in a desert hospital. The Lance-Corporal called Johnston had barely survived a machine-gun massacre. He described Sphinx commando jeeps—special vehicles equipped with sand-plow tires and gun turrets. A motley assembly of men torn mostly from British ranks, with a few from other armies. And their leader—a wicked mongrel Johnston described as having dark skin, a shaved head, turban, earrings, and Chinese tattoos on his arms and hands. Despite his exotic appearance, this ringleader was definitely English. His sniping East London drawl gave him away. He also sported a Royal Army jacket and Union Jack patch in a perverse gesture of ethnic pride. Obviously, this character was Oliver Bryon.

According to the witness, Bryon admitted to stalking the soldiers for days in the wilderness before attacking them. He also expressed interest in the ancient ruins they had encamped in—he reportedly asked about "old sparkly bobs" and "dead blokes in bandages," indicating an interest in antiques and mummies. But Bryon did not limit his interests to ancient treasure. He and his crew robbed the soldiers' supplies, including clothing, weapons, and ammunition.

Johnston also revealed gruesome truths that would forever haunt him. Bryon had personally tortured him. Bryon had shot him in the arm at close range and savagely broken his wrists and knuckles. He could never forget the sound of his own bones breaking, or the feeling of Bryon's tattooed fingers gripping him like claws. The tattoo symbols were burned into his memory. Sometimes the images returned to him in his sleep. Neither could he forget his horrifying struggle with jackals after Bryon threw him outside the beasts' lair. Johnston, previously an animal lover, found himself uncontrollably convulsing with terror at the sound of the hospital chaplain's dog barking outside the building.

The stalwart British soldier tried to overcome his fears but was overpowered by feverish breakdowns. His encounter with Bryon left him physically and emotionally scarred. His interview at the hospital ended when he began shivering violently and was given a strong dose of morphine.

Nye crunched the papers back into the envelope. He shook his head in disgust and swigged the last of his beer. "I wish we would've identified Bryon sooner," he grumbled. "It would've saved us all this goose-chasing."

"Unfortunately, Miss Weathers didn't get a good look at him when he shot Harper in the nightclub," Major Frost admitted. "She only saw the outline of his turban in the dark and light reflecting off his false metal eye. She mistook him for a monster."

"She wasn't too far wrong." Nye attempted to signal a waiter for a refill of beer. His effort went unnoticed. He sighed impatiently. "I don't get why the blokes running the Sphinx Commandos never caught onto him. Are they stupid?"

"Perhaps they gave him too much freedom due to his far-reaching mission duties—that's the current excuse," replied Frost.

"The well's gone dry," said Nye, lifting his beer glass and letting it drop with an empty rattle. "Can't get a waiter to come over. I'll grab some more from the bar." He stood to leave.

"Bring me another one, would you?" asked Frost, draining the rest of his cognac.

The Australian nodded briskly and disappeared.

Frost listened to the sound of a polka playing in the nearby ballroom. It was strange being back in the glittering bustle of Cairo after his haunting plunge into the wilderness. The pomp of Shepheards' was familiar to him; he found the atmosphere British and boring. Seeing so many people frolicking during wartime disillusioned him. Society at times seemed oblivious to death and soldierly sacrifice. He closed his eyes and felt tired.

"Desmond," said a wonderful voice.

He was surprised to find Eve standing nearby. Her hair was damp from a recent shower. She wore a light coral pink dress and sandals. Frost stared. She looked beautiful in the dress. He was very glad to see her since he wasn't sure whether or not she would appear.

Eve swished her hips briefly in a belly-dancing move. "Esmeralda has entered the room!" She laughed mischievously at the bewildered expression that crossed his face and quickly seated herself next to him. "Mind if I sit here?"

"My dear, of course I don't mind—"

She interrupted him with a boisterous kiss. "Desmond, I love you!" she declared afterwards. "And I love your mustache. It's perfect. It looks spiffy and it feels wonderful. Never shave it off."

Frost, melting with affection, was speechless. Then to his horror he noticed that Lieutenant Nye was looming nearby with a pair of drinks. He fidgeted and felt embarrassed. "Don't just stand there, Nye. Come over here and sit down," he said.

Nye set the drinks on the table, smirking. "Glad to see you've recovered from your ordeals, Miss," he said dryly to Eve. "Would you like a drink?"

"Sure, but you don't have to go get it—"

"Might as well. We could all have silvery gray hair by the time the waiter comes back here. Shepheard's has a reputation for slow service," he insisted. "What'll it be?"

"Whatever he's having," she said, nudging Frost with her arm.

"Righto. Enjoy your 'cognac,' sir," he said with innuendo. He cast a parting wink at the Major before disappearing again.

The young woman wrapped her arm around him. "I'm so glad we're together again. You have no idea what I was imagining," she sighed. "I thought you had been packed off to Italy. Or sunk in the Mediterranean. Or shot. How exactly did you escape?"

Frost stared at her intensely. He was distracted by her touch and most of all by her declaration that she loved him. That was most important to him and commanded all his attention. It took him several seconds to realize she was asking something.

"Oh, it was nothing spectacular," he muttered. "I only lit someone's trousers on fire and ran off..."

She was astonished by the revelation. She found it horribly funny. Frost hadn't expected her to find his adventure comical. Mischief took hold of him. They both laughed.

"What happened to the guy?"

"I don't know. I didn't stop to turn round," said Frost. "His friends put him out, I imagine."

"He'll probably have a hard time getting over that one!" she chuckled, covering her eyes.

"Perhaps they'll give him a special wound badge," mused the Major with wry humor. "Just picture it—a solemn ceremony on a propaganda newsreel. 'The Führer decorates brave warrior who roasted his hindquarters for the Fatherland. He presents the hero with new underdrawers, embroidered with swastikas...'"

She burst into giggles.

"You can see it, too, can't you?" prodded Frost with a smile, pleased by her reaction. "Come on, spill it. You lived in Germany. You're the expert. Tell me, what reward will our hero get? What recompense does a man in Hitler's Germany receive for the holy martyrdom of his backside?"

She laughed loudly.

"Even you can't say!" continued Frost, crumbling into mischievous laughter. His eyes sparkled with mirth. "I suppose we'll have to wait and see. Next spring, I tell you. They'll come out with some horrible new marching song about it..."

She laughed so hard that tears sprung from her eyes. She leaned on his shoulder and sighed. "My gosh, you're funny..."

Frost leered. "He didn't think so!"

They laughed together. She buried her face against his shoulder. He elbowed her playfully in the arm.

"I missed you, you troublemaker," said Eve.

"I missed you, too, darling," said Frost. "More than anything."

After a moment of silence, the Major fidgeted nervously and straightened himself rigidly in the seat. "Eve!" he announced, as if making a formal speech. "I have something to say to you. I think you already know what it is." He shot her a probing glance. "You do know what it is."

Eve held her breath as he reached into one of his pockets. She half-expected him to pull out a ring. Instead it was a tightly folded piece of thin paper. He set it on the table and covered it with his hand. She waited for him to continue.

"I believe you already know the way I feel about you. In case you don't, I'll just say it plainly." He stared her into her eyes fervently. "I adore you."

His forceful manner surprised her.

"I really cannot express the deep admiration I have for you," he continued. "When I first met you, I knew you were very special. After all we've experienced together, I've seen for myself that you are an outstanding and brave person. You stood by me in the face of danger. When we were surrounded by enemies, you stood firm. You are a woman of true strength and character. Your courage merits my highest respect."

Eve felt humbled by his words. She also noticed the emphasis he placed on bravery. He sounded almost as if he were praising another soldier. "I'm not a soldier, Desmond," she said softly, self-effacing.

"Yes, you are. To me," asserted Frost. "You are magnificent. You are an exceptional woman. I've never met any person like you before in my life," he declared. He paused thoughtfully. "Don't imagine that I've lost my head over you because you're pretty," he cautioned. "That's not true!" An afterthought flustered him. "Although, of course, I do appreciate that you are pretty!" he added awkwardly. "I wouldn't change that..."

She fought back an amused smile.

Frost saw it and broke into a coltish grin. "Well! There it is," he concluded with a tense sigh. "The only thing I can do is offer you my heart and hope that you will accept it." He waited expectantly. "Do you?"

"Yes. Do you even need to ask?" Eve looked dryly at him. "I already told you the way I feel about you. I don't just go around saying 'I love you' to every guy, you know."

Frost was embarrassed. "No, of course not," he stammered and started fidgeting again. "I only meant...I wanted to make sure that you return my feelings completely. I mean..."

Eve looked questioningly at him.

"I love you with my whole heart. I won't take anything less than that in return," stated Frost firmly. He glanced down, experiencing uncertainty triggered by his past. "If you're not sure, or if you only like me just a little, then...it's not good enough."

Eve stared deeply into his eyes and perceived an unhealed wound. He had already won her heart. He was confident enough to openly express his devotion to her, yet needed a small measure of reassurance.

"I fought for you, Desmond," she reminded him. "Against the robbers and against Wilmore. He wanted to abandon you. I stopped him by crashing the jeep. I suppose you could say I killed him. I'm not sorry," she said coldly, her eyes misting with emotion. "It was choice between his life or yours. I chose you." She halted sharply. "I didn't know I would make it out alive. I could have been killed in the crash or by those men. I was willing to die for you. Did you...not notice?"

Frost balked at the accusation. "Of course, I noticed," he said somberly. "I just...Oh, blast it." He covered his face in despair. "I'm sorry. I was only trying to..."

Eve leaned on his shoulder.

"Marry me," he said bluntly, losing his eloquence. "You're the only woman I can ever love, and you're the only one I'll ever ask. You know very well I mean it."

"Yes, I do know," she agreed. "And I will."

"Good." He blushed and slid the piece of paper towards her across the table. "Then please sign this form here."

The woman was plunged into confusion. "What...is this?"

"A license. Don't read it too closely," muttered Frost. "It's complicated."

Eve snatched the paper and unfolded it. It was indeed a license for marriage. There were military stamps on it. It had already been signed, witnessed and stamped by three different civil authorities. "All that's missing is my signature," she noticed aloud. "You must have pulled some strings to do this."

"Yes, I went through a lot of trouble," admitted Frost. "You have no idea the effort it took to get a motley crew of Army staff and Egyptian officials to turn round something like this in mere hours..." He slid a pen towards her. "As you can see, I've already signed it. I've made up my mind about you, Eve," he said earnestly. "The only thing I needed to establish is how you felt about me. Now that's all settled..."

Eve snatched the pen excitedly. She was overjoyed by his proposal and thrilled to accept it. "Well, you asked for it!" she said, scribbling her signature on it with a flourish. "Once upon a time, I told you the man of my dreams wouldn't escape me once I found him. I've decided you're the man," she said boldly. "Don't say I didn't warn you."

Frost wrapped his arm around her and kissed her with gusto. He was surprised by her eagerness to accept his proposal. It made him profoundly happy. He thanked her and hurried to put the license away. He assured her he'd file the document in the morning and promised a ceremony at a future date. "In the meantime, all our worries are over!" he sighed in relief.

"What worries?" she asked sharply.

He faltered. The usually levelheaded Major tried to feign calmness and failed. "Oh, nothing terribly alarming," he conceded, looking guilty. "That is, the Egyptians wanted to deport you. But now they will no longer be able to..."

"What?" Eve's voice went shrill with disbelief.

His face flushed. "Well, to be honest, I inadvertently caused a problem when I reported your newspaper article on the stolen antiquities to the Egyptian government earlier," he confessed. "The Egyptians ransacked the Nile Delta Museum and became convinced—mistakenly—that it was a fencing operation for stolen cultural goods. They were also convinced you were some kind of criminal advertiser. My report left them unsatisfied. I managed to place you under British military jurisdiction, but nevertheless the Egyptians demanded your deportation. I found out this afternoon that their police have been looking for you everywhere. Things started to get rather sticky. Anyway, it doesn't matter anymore..."

"You forget I have certain rights as a member of the press," dismissed Eve. "They might think they can push me around. But legally they'd find it difficult to deport me without evidence when I'm working here as a reporter for *The Chicago Standard*."

Frost bit his lip. "Well, I've been meaning to talk to you about that."

She stared. "No way! Don't tell me..."

"The *Standard* let you go because you've been absent for such a long while," Frost explained. "Nobody could get hold of you and you weren't filing articles. I found out while I was recovering in Alexandria. You were still missing then. I had no idea whether I'd ever find you, but hoping you'd come back, I personally rang the newspaper and tried to—"

She covered her face and shrieked in humiliation. "You told my editors I'd been arrested?"

"I didn't say arrested!" protested Frost. "I only said you were assisting a British military inquiry..."

"Ah! It's the same thing!" she lamented in shame. "How embarrassing! They're probably gossiping and laughing at me."

"Let them laugh and stagnate in Chicago," retorted Frost. "You have triumphed."

She peered dubiously at him.

"Now nobody can deport you. You will be granted an automatic residence permit. You will no longer have need of a job if you don't want one. And most importantly, we will stay together!" He grinned jubilantly. "It's all worked out perfectly! Don't you see, darling? There's nothing really wrong, is there?"

Eve reflected on her upside-down, strangely happy life for a minute of silence. "No. Nothing's wrong," she agreed with a weary sigh, scratching her head. "It's just…getting married, almost being deported, and losing my job all at once has been….something of a shock."

"That's all right," he said, blissful and unsympathetic. "I'm here to console you."

Nye reappeared at long last with Eve's cognac. The nervous and bewildered woman quaffed half of it in almost one sip. Nye collapsed into his seat with another beer in his hand and a hazy stare.

"I propose a toast: to our American allies, and godspeed the end of the war," said Frost cordially. Their three glasses clinked.

"And to your matrimonial bliss, sir," proclaimed Nye, sounding drunk. "You've got your work cut out for you, Miss, marrying this Major. This fella's not easy to be around. He really smacks it about. He'll march you down the aisle!"

"He already did," said Eve with an approving laugh.

Meanwhile Frost was staring in disbelief above his drinking glass. "How did you know anything about it, Nye?" he demanded, his tone rising in indignation. "Were you eavesdropping?"

"Shepheard's is slow, sir, but the path from here to the bar hasn't dropped into a chasm," the Australian retorted. "It doesn't take that long to fetch a drink."

CHAPTER 20: FEVER

"As an apple tree among the trees of the woods,
so is my lover among men.
I delight to rest in his shadow,
And his fruit is sweet to my mouth.
He brings me into the banquet hall,
And his emblem over me is love."
—"The Song of Solomon"

The three of them had dinner together. Nye eventually departed to swill more alcohol at the bar with some other soldiers he recognized. The small orchestra played classical music late into the night. Frost invited Eve to dance. Under ordinary circumstances the Major was disinterested in parties and social dancing. However, he was capable of dancing. He wanted nothing more than to sway around in Eve's loving arms. She happily agreed. However, it soon became very obvious that the American could not waltz. Frost gave her an awkward lesson. He enjoyed teaching her, but also thought it was funny.

"So, you don't actually know how to dance properly," he teased, steering her clear of a collision on the crowded dance floor. "That's why you've hedged your bets on cabaret dancing. You compensate shaking for stepping."

"You're wrong. I can foxtrot!" she argued. "And don't be so quick to dismiss belly dancing. It takes talent. It's a real art form! The Egyptians call it raqs sharqi."

"Sounds exciting," remarked Frost. "I admit it—I'm an ignorant man. But I'm more than willing to be educated. You could give me a demonstration." He eyed her. "Tonight, even."

Eve read his gaze and realized that he hoped to spend the night with her.

He smiled softly. "If you're ready, that is."

The bold woman journalist was suddenly attacked by a wave of shyness. She had strong feelings for Frost and did not understand why she was nervous at the prospect of intimacy. It was probably because the atmosphere at Shepheard's was so formal. It made Eve feel self-conscious. Nevertheless, she didn't want to discourage him.

"OK," she agreed, blushing.

"All right, then," stated Frost, brisk and matter-of-fact.

Eve felt awkward. She tried to occupy herself with more dancing and conversation. But, as the hour dragged on, Frost's desire to go upstairs became increasingly obvious.

"It's getting late, don't you think?" he suggested cordially. "Would you like to turn in?"

It was indeed late. She was still inexplicably shy. She tried to pretend she wasn't. "Sure," she said, feeling nervous, and accompanied him from the dance floor to the elevators.

She continued talking to alleviate tension. "You know, Desmond, I don't know what to do anymore now that I'm not working at the *Standard*," she complained. "I have to continue being a reporter somehow. I can't quit like this."

"No, of course you don't have to quit!" rejoined Frost as they entered the elevator. "You could easily get a job writing for another publication. Perhaps a British publication."

She shot him a playful glare. "If you dare suggest I write about gardening or ladies' teas, I'll go crazy and clobber you!"

He grinned. "I'd never do that," he retorted. "I know you well enough. You're interested in fighting, just like I am. There is a war going on. No reason why you shouldn't write about that."

"That's what I've been trying to do for years," she grumbled.

"You'd be wasted on the frontlines, though. I read several of your articles—you're a good analyst and you've got a solid grasp on political reporting. What you really ought to write about is foreign policy. Government. That sort of thing," he advised. "Besides, you've got me now. I'm active military, and we'll be together from now on. As a soldier's wife, you'll pick up plenty of battlefield excitement—without actually having to go to battle."

She reflected. He had introduced new ideas to her mind that clicked together in an unusual and good way. "That all makes perfect sense."

A gloomy notion crossed the journalist's mind. She looked imploringly at him.

"Just keep one thing in mind, Desmond—I don't like being sheltered," she stated. "I understand you're a gentleman and you want to protect me. Fine. That's big of you. But don't try and cut me out of your investigation," she insisted. "We've made it this far together. I want to help track the tomb robbers down. If you go out to the desert again, I want to come with you."

Silence fell as they exited the elevator. Slowly they walked down the dimly lit, plush corridor towards her suite.

A shadow of fear fell over Frost. He looked visibly burdened. "You're asking a great deal," he said with a strain in his voice. "After everything we endured—together—I can't imagine anything worse than history repeating itself."

They paused outside the door. Eve fumbled for her keys in the dank light.

"I won't exclude you from knowing what's going on," the Major said quietly, standing next to her, "but don't ask me to take you into the desert again."

Her hand faltered on the lock.

"At least not now," he added, with gentle tact. "I really suffered when you were missing, not knowing where you were or what had happened to you. It's much too soon for me..." He let the sentence trail off and touched her arm. "Let's stop talking about it. Let's think of nothing else in the world but each other. Just for tonight."

Eve was ready to forget the world. Her mind had been tied in knots about the investigation. To let go of it suddenly was a strange relief.

The door opened. They went in and shut it behind them. It was a large modern suite blending European style and Arabic architecture. Two curved windows overlooked the Nile and a balcony faced the pyramids. There were floor-to-ceiling white curtains and a silver ceiling fan. There was also a small bar for mixing drinks. An expensive radio featured a built-in record player.

The centerpiece was the pillowy bed, freshly made, and untouched. Eve looked at the bed and was self-conscious about the night ahead. She glanced around at her tired old suitcases and scant belongings. There was Frost, the man she loved, looking very eager for attention. And there was she—a willing but awkward bundle of nerves, feeling less than confident.

Frost removed his shiny dress shoes and left them on one side of the room. He sat casually on the edge of the bed. He loosened his collar and glanced calmly at Eve.

She was fussing. She took off her sandals and unfastened her dress with self-conscious, clumsy movements. "Well! It's been a long day..."

The British officer studied her and noted nervousness. He smiled faintly. He sensed gentle reassurance was necessary. "Come over here," he beckoned lightheartedly, as if asking for some trifling favor. He gestured at his uniform jacket. "Help me get this off."

Eve glanced at him in mild surprise. The jacket seemed to have a lot of buttons and he was asking her to help undo them.

"That's right," said Frost with a smirk. "The buttons."

The young woman sat next to him and started unbuttoning his jacket. Frost made no effort to assist. He stared slyly at her and made a halfhearted attempt to shrug off one sleeve. It didn't budge. Eve pushed the jacket gently off his shoulders.

Her nervousness wore off and a spark of passion switched on. She started touching his chest. He reeled her in for more, stroked her thigh and started trying to pull her dress off. They toppled over onto the mattress and the rest was history.

Eve was pleased by how strong and assertive the man was. However, he was also gentle and romantic. It was obvious he loved her by the way he treated her. It wasn't covetous sex; it was worship. He had completely conquered her heart. She adored him. His every touch delighted her.

Frost was surprised and gladdened by how much Eve returned his feelings. She was aggressive and passionate. The soldier had lived a stale and controlled existence. He was unaccustomed to receiving any kind of passion. His intimacy with Eve marked a refreshing change in his life. He welcomed it.

It was a wonderful night for both of them. They ended up damaging part of the bed frame and neighbors complained about noise—this owed to the fact that Eve couldn't stop herself from sighing loudly and Frost inadvertently kept causing the bed's headboard to strike against the wall.

Afterwards, there was sleep and a long silence. Frost, an early riser, woke up at an ungodly hour before dawn and turned on the radio. Eve drifted awake to soft jazz and the feeling of Frost on top of her, stroking her waist and delicately kissing her face and neck. They spent the morning blissfully drowning in each other.

Daylight crept in like a glowing thief through the windowpanes. Frost was intoxicated with love. He was completely relaxed and had a feverish haze in his eyes. He looked almost drunk. "I love you—you have no idea how much. I've never felt like this before. You have me completely," he murmured, kissing her hand. "Ask me for whatever you want, darling. I'll do anything for you."

"I love you, too," she sighed, feeling lightheaded with devotion. "I'm wild about you, Desmond. You know I am..."

He kissed her.

She ran her fingers across the Hindu tattoo on his left breast. "These symbols," she said. "What do they mean?"

A look of silent mortification crossed Frost's face. He hesitated and broke eye contact. "This one's the emblem of the Wensingham Rifles," he said, indicating the griffin tattoo on his arm. "I was practically brought up in that regiment. I thought the mark should stay with me." He smirked dryly. "At least I thought so when I was 20 years younger."

She stroked his chest. "And this?"

He looked at her in helpless embarrassment. "Only promise not to laugh."

"I would never," said Eve. She regarded him with grave sobriety. It was supposed to be helpful. Instead her seriousness only made his embarrassment worse.

"Have you ever read about Hannibal Barca, the general?" he asked, in a roundabout muttering voice. "He's an idol of mine. He and his North African army brought the Roman Empire to its knees. I've always admired his military success." He paused, feeling awkward. "Hannibal's war elephants terrorized Rome, even crossing the Alps. The elephant was his symbol." He sighed and tried to conceal his discomfort. "Anyway, there was a certain 'tradition' that new recruits with my group in India needed to undergo rituals to become 'initiated'—offered a choice between several disreputable ventures, I chose the tattoo. I went to a mucky place outside Calcutta to get the job done."

He dared to look at her and cracked a sheepish half-smile. "I wanted something meaningful. I admired Hannibal and I supposed the locals would be relatively good at drawing elephants. A war elephant was what I asked for. Something fearsome! You know..." He broke down laughing in sardonic humiliation. "This is what I ended up with," he said, flexing his tattooed muscle. "Not quite what I expected. Looks more like a circus creature. Wearing a frock of paisley flowers..."

She giggled at his dry humor.

"At least there are a few swords here, somewhere," said Frost with a mortified laugh, squinting down at his chest. "Anyway there ought to be. It's a mercy my eyesight's begun to fade. Now I can no longer see..."

She melted into giggles again. He got over his embarrassment, and they both fell over laughing. They were rolling around under the covers when suddenly there was a loud knock at the door. They both looked up in alarm.

"It's probably the hotel. The room was only booked for one person. They'll want to charge me extra for spending the night." He hid under the covers and yanked a pillow over his head. "Go on, answer it. I'm not here!"

Eve grabbed her dress from the night before and pulled it on. She didn't realize she put it on backwards. She stumbled blearily to the doorway. She was annoyed by the intrusion and became more annoyed with every step. By the time she unlocked the door, she felt outraged. "Yeah, what do you want?" she challenged, yanking open the door, and recoiled in astonishment to see Lieutenant Nye.

"Good morning, sorry to disturb you, Miss," he said sharply, not seeming very sorry.

"It's Mrs. now," huffed Eve. "Anyway it will be officially in a few hours. What are you doing here?"

"Would you happen to know where Major Frost is?"

Eve glared indignantly. She looked wild with tangled red hair. "Do you have any idea what time it is?"

"I need to speak to the Major, but I can't find him," stated the officer unremorsefully. "Someone saw him go to the elevators with you last night. Nobody's seen him since." He tried to peek past her into the dim room. "Is he...here?"

She was about the slam the door in his face when Frost slammed it open. He was barefoot, wearing wrinkled trousers and a halfway-unbuttoned shirt. His brown hair was sticking up fiercely in various directions. His expression was ferocious. He pushed past Eve with flaming eyes and lunged at Nye as if to punch him. He burst into the hall and banged the door shut behind him. The force of the slam shook the wall and rattled the hinges.

Eve winced at the abusive yelling that exploded. Both men yelled, but only Frost's staccato command tone dominated the air. "How dare you!" he snapped in a crescendo. "What the blazes do you think you're doing—"

More bellowing ensued. It was Nye, trying to justify himself. The Australian had a fairly loud voice, but it withered like a squeak against the Major's well-practiced military roar. "You halfwit!" came a deafening snap. "Get out of my sight! Piss off!"

Eve considered intervening to prevent a brawl. She reached for the door handle, then jumped back as a shout burst out.

"That wasn't my order!"

Some lower tones followed. It sounded like Nye, but evidently the Major had chased him down the hall because the sound of his voice was considerably fainter. There was a brief, unintelligible conversation. It ended with an apocalyptic snarl. "Two hours, idiot!" snapped Frost. "Not a moment sooner!"

She didn't hear his footsteps returning; he was too quick and quiet. The door blew open and shut. Before she knew what happened, Frost was back again. Surprisingly, he made no effort to tidy up or leave. He flopped back onto the bed and pulled the sheets over his head.

"Desmond?" She walked over to him in confusion. "What's going on?"

"I refuse to be disturbed!" his muffled voice asserted defiantly from under the sheet. "No force on earth can make me leave this room before I'm ready. I will not be ready until... two hours from now." He poked his face out from under the sheet and saw her nowhere. "Where are you?"

"I'm getting dressed," her voice came from another room.

"No!" he called in despair. "Please don't!"

She giggled.

"Do not get dressed!" he protested. "Don't let that clod spoil everything. Eve, come back here. I command you to stop immediately and drop those clothes at once—"

She burst out laughing. The Major sounded as if he were ordering a soldier to halt and drop a weapon.

Frost was flustered. He might have joined her in laughing, too, if the situation were not so aggravating. "Eve, please! For heaven's sake—"

She emerged wearing a sloppily pulled-on sundress. Her hair was still unkempt—Frost thought it looked glorious. He smiled as she approached. The woman, however, was distracted from honeymooning by other matters. "What happened?" she questioned. "What did Nye want?"

Frost seized her by the arm and grinned as he pulled her on top of him. "Never mind that."

"Desmond, seriously," she protested. "You can't just ignore everything..."

"I most certainly can!" retorted Frost in cheerful defiance. "Just watch me."

"Did something happen with the tomb robbers?"

He touched her lips. "You're exquisite."

Eve realized he was deliberately shutting out everything except her. Reason was incapable of moving him. "Fine, then," she said dryly. "I'll just have to wring it out of you."

She kissed him softly. Frost melted. He grabbed her face with both hands and imbibed her kisses as if guzzling water. He protested when she paused. "Don't stop," he insisted with a feral haze in his eyes. "Go on forever. I want to get lost in you, darling. Let's forget the whole world..."

"What did Nye want?" asked Eve.

He looked deliriously at her. He might have objected to the question if she hadn't started stroking his face. "A group of men in military jeeps robbed an Army supply depot west of the Upper Nile this morning," he admitted. "It's believed to be the tomb robbers."

Eve was startled by the news. "Will you pursue them?"

"I don't march to their drum. I've already made a plan, and I am going to corner them...later. For now, I'm staying here." He rubbed her shoulder. "Unless I've begun to bore you and you're anxious to get rid of me..."

She glared in reproach. "No! That's not true."

Frost grinned again. He was pleased by her feisty contradiction. "Then let's make the most of the time we've got," he suggested. He touched her lips and leaned back onto the mattress with fever in his eyes again. "I'm thirsty. Give me another drink."

After two hours had passed, the Major emerged ready for action. He ordered a "wanted poster" for tomb raider Oliver Bryon to be widely disseminated through Army ranks that day.

Frost used his Army humor to author and design the pamphlet. It featured robber Oliver Bryon's photograph, embellished with age marks, a yellow pop-eye, and a bright green turban illustrated with electrifying effect.

Frost intended the flyer to create a public demand for Oliver Bryon's capture and, more importantly, demean him among British soldiers stationed in Egypt. The poster began with the catchphrase:

Have you seen Leafy?

- Wanted: Leafy the Londoner. Also known as Cockney Ollie.

- Description: Short, dark and ugly.
(Too much sun. Eye wanted.)

- Weight: Heavy, despite frequent desert
scurrying. (Ration stealer.)

- Hair color: nonexistent.

- Wears head rag. Color: leaf green. Style:
wreath/circlet. Missing some flowers.

- Interests: antiques, motoring and
jewelry. (Prefers gold earrings).

- Other distinctive features: Chinese writing
on arms, hands. Permanent sneer.

- Languages spoken: Gutter and Snipe.

- Leafy's friends in AIC miss him. Anyone giving information
will be rewarded immediate leave. (A two-month
vacation in Dearest Old Blighty or Port Said is on the
table). Contact the office of Major D. L. Frost, CIG....

The pamphlet spread rapidly through the ranks. Men loved to laugh, and the comic tone of this "wanted poster" created much mirth. At first, many soldiers took it for a joke. Curious phone calls to Major Frost's office quickly revealed that the matter was serious.

In any case, the promise of a two-month immediate vacation at home in England or in sumptuous Port Said was nothing to laugh about. Major Frost was the guarantor, and his department didn't usually guarantee anything unless it was truly warranted.

The result was that soldiers of the British Army—especially men loafing on leave or bored sentinels in Cairo, Suez, and Aswan—became hell-bent on unmasking "Leafy" and his whereabouts in a fierce competition to claim the prize.

The flyer flushed one mystery out into the open. Someone finally confessed knowledge of stealing a flint dagger from Army custody following the Forty Thieves Cabaret murder. According to one soldier hoping to collect the winnings, the mysterious "Leafy" had bribed an Army buddy to sneak the dagger out of the building.

The man had readily done so in exchange for a pure gold brick. However, he had since died—in a freak accident. The accomplice was bitten by a serpent while performing training exercises near Giza. The snake was never found. However, doctors who attempted to save him believed the venom was from an asp.

The man's Army comrade had kept silent about the theft to protect the memory of his dead chum. However, the promise of a vacation blew the lid off his loyalty. Major Frost's office rewarded him—not with the vacation, but with a reassignment out of North Africa. He took it.

Meanwhile, Oliver Bryon lost all semblance of Army prestige. His prowess as a Special Forces commando was stripped from him within 48 hours. Thanks to Frost's ridicule, he was branded with the lasting epithets of "Leafy," "Rag Man," and "Ollie Baba"—all monikers scorning his green turban, once a symbol of pride to him. In the first place, the British soldiers thought the turban looked ridiculous from a masculine point-of-view; in the second place, they scorned it because it was "oriental" and distinctly not British. They came to view Bryon as a loony Londoner darting about in the dunes with green ruffles on his head. His earrings and cockney origins heaped scorn onto scorn.

The blemish of manly disdain stamped upon him was irremovable. It was a permanent blot that could never be washed off. The Army's wolf pack of men deemed him a laughingstock. It would be very difficult, it not impossible, for a man with a silly nickname like "Leafy" to overcome the legend of his shame and prove his strength to others. Most men in such circumstances would need to quit the military to avoid a future filled with ostracism and malicious taunting.

Major Frost was pleased with the results of his "wanted poster." The results he had hoped for had been achieved.

A dragnet was closing in on the tomb raiders. There would be no escape for them once his final trap was sprung.

Hearing the story of the thief who had filched the dagger for Ollie and died from an asp bite afterwards, Frost recalled Dr. Sullivan's words of warning about the artifact's lethal power. The sudden death marked the fifth known fatality of a person who handled the dagger.

CHAPTER 21: A SHORTCUT TO CHAOS

"—'Siehst, Vater, du der Erlkönig nicht? Den Erlenkönig mit Kron' und Schweif?'
"—'Mein Sohn, es ist ein Nebelstreif.'"
—"Erlkönig" [The Elf King] by Johann Wolfgang von Goethe

A haze of pale dust hung over a wide, flat stretch of desert. The smell of salt and water hung in the air; the land was a nameless haunt in Lower Egypt not far from the Mediterranean. In the distance, a small cluster of oases towns loomed—a miniature delta of civilization fed by a system of canal tributaries from the Nile, which was not too far away.

A lone figure appeared in the emptiness, tripping past a crest of sand. Elrich von Rindl was lost, suffering from mild sunstroke and covered in white dust. His vehicle had run out of gasoline. He had been forced to abandon the vehicle and journey on foot.

The German officer looked quite haggard. He wore a long wool greatcoat over his uniform. He had discarded his brown cloth cap; instead he wore his peaked gray officer's service cap, part of his dress uniform. He had stuffed his pockets with cans of peaches. His goggles hung around his neck, and he toted his long rifle across his back, along with a rucksack and canteen. He hadn't wanted to leave these things behind. He bundled up carrying as much as he could.

A German Kubelwagen—a snail-like, military model of the "German People's Car"—was supposed to meet him a certain distance from where he'd jettisoned his old ride. At least, that's what he thought the radio operator said the last time he communicated. The signals were patchy. The German language demanded specificity. Details were important, but were sometimes confused due to human error. For example, he thought for sure the operator told him to walk in an easterly direction to meet the Kubelwagen. After an hours-long eternity of stumping through dust with no end in sight, he wondered if he had heard incorrectly and gone the wrong way.

He saw Nirvana. A large shack-like structure with a few cars outside ahead in the emptiness. A German outpost. Trucks rattled to and fro, raising dust clouds. A vehicle service station.

His weary eyes brightened. His tall black boots rushed gladly over the sand. Happy thoughts buoyed him as he raced forward with new energy. Safe and sheltered among fellow Germans. At last! He closed the distance and saw three men outside, waving friendly arms at him. He smiled.

Horror struck him as he walked closer. The men were wearing flat British helmets.

The three technicians were bored and restless. Their job was to refuel and repair passing trucks. They lived in a world of oil, heat, and gasoline. It was a tedious job that never seemed to end. They found time in between their labor to loaf and distract themselves. They had returned that morning from work at a filling station near the frontlines and still wore their battle gear, although they had never actually seen a battle—nor a German. At least not a live one up close.

Their names were Petrie, Roy Gillespie, and Luke Woolton, respectively. They would remember this day for as long as they lived because nobody would ever let them forget it.

They were smoking and joking when suddenly Gillespie, the sharp-eyed one, noticed something. "Say," he started. "Who's that person over there?"

They stared like sheep.

"There's a person," he repeated. "Walking."

"There he is. Yes. He's coming this way. Look."

They squinted.

"Good heavens! He's tramping with all his kit on," remarked Petrie. "Do you suppose he's been walking out there long?"

"Goodness, I hope not," said Woolton. "What's that coat he's got on? It's not ours."

"He must be one of those Poles," assumed Gillespie, legendary for knowing everything. "You know. The lot that Polish General What's-is-name brought over to help us. The Free Poles or whatever you call them."

"You mean like the Free French?"

"Yes, only Polish. They're stationed round here, I believe."

"Oh really?" exclaimed Woolton. "I've never met a Polish person before..."

"I have. They're quite nice fellows, actually..."

The stranger came closer into view. He grinned joyfully.

"See, look. He's quite friendly," said the all-knower Gillespie. "They're all like that."

The British soldiers grinned back and waved cheerfully, welcoming the guest. Suddenly the stranger froze in place with a startled look. They exchanged glances.

"What's the matter with him?"

"He probably has heat cramps," said Woolton sympathetically. "Perhaps he needs some help. I'll go fetch him."

Von Rindl experienced a whirl of fight-or-flight instinct. He was unmistakably a uniformed German officer. Surely, they would capture or kill him. He could run nowhere fast enough in time. There was nowhere to hide, anyway. Trucks whirred around—British trucks, he realized in despair. A gun battle seemed futile. Maybe he could launch a shootout and escape. He was debating whether or not to unleash his deadly rifle when suddenly one of the British soldiers trotted up to him, smiling.

"Hello there!" greeted the Englishman. It was Woolton. He was rather excited to meet a Polish person for the first time. "You're with the Polish brigade, aren't you?"

Von Rindl's eyes darted back and forth. He recognized the word "Polish." It sounded nearly identical to the same word in German. The cocky Afrika Korps ranger was an impudent person—who happened to be trapped in a prickly situation. He decided to bluff it.

He smiled and put on the most exaggerated Slavic accent he could muster. "*Polskana Polski!*" There was a distinct German wisp in Von Rindl's phony Polish. But it was decent enough to fool anybody who knew nothing of Poland or German accents.

"Yes, we thought so," said Woolton, falling for it. "Come over here and have some water."

Von Rindl realized that his wool overcoat hid his German uniform from view. He assumed his peaked service cap and jackboots would give him away, but apparently they didn't. Maybe because they were completely covered in powdery dust.

"Do you feel all right?" asked Woolton, leading him towards the station.

"*Polska,*" answered Von Rindl with a smile, following hesitantly.

"Yes, I know you're from Poland." He attempted to speak louder and slower to be understood. "Do you need medical assistance?"

Von Rindl got nervous. He grinned and spouted fake Polish gibberish. "*Schwinsky whisky mik nik isch!*"

The Englishman laughed in surprise. "Sorry, I didn't catch that."

The German pointed his finger at one of the oases in the distance and waved his arm insistently. He made gestures to indicate walking. He shook his arm at the oasis again.

"Oh! I see!" exclaimed Woolton happily. "You need to go over there?"

He bobbed his head frantically and smiled.

"Don't worry. We'll see that you get there. Come over and rest a moment."

Von Rindl treaded softly over to the station as British trucks whirred past him. He bowed politely to the other two Englishmen. "*Schminkie schmibinski!*" he said, inventing honorific gibberish. He looked very gracious as he walked past.

He sat down on a wooden bench next to a fuel pump. They offered him a canteen and a sandwich. He took both and smiled broadly. "*Schmeebah!*" he said, adding a slight Russian influence to his gibberish 'thank-you.' He wolfed down the sandwich in nervous silence. He hoped his charade would last.

The British trio returned to their duties as another truck came in for refueling. They bantered with the driver, joked about nylons and peered at lacy white legs in an American magazine he showed them through the window.

Petrie, in the meantime, watched the guest and noticed something suspicious. "Are you sure he's with the Polish brigade, Gilly?" he asked the omniscient Roy Gillespie. "I could swear I see a Nazi eagle on his hat."

Von Rindl noticed them peeking. They appeared to be looking at his cap. He took it off. He smiled nicely at them and hummed the "Yellow Rose of Texas" tune in between mouthfuls of food, trying to keep upbeat.

"All Polish soldiers wear eagles," uttered Gillespie in contempt. "It's their symbol."

"Oh really? How do you know?"

"Because I studied history and world affairs at St. Sullian's Academy in Bramstead," he snapped loftily. "That's how I can tell you that Poland was part of the Austro-Hungarian Empire. The eagle was their symbol first. Hitler only pilfered it later. Besides," he added, "many other countries also use the eagle as an emblem," he said. "Like the United States, for example. Therefore it is ridiculous to assume that somebody who is clearly from an Allied country is a German Nazi, just because he happens to have an eagle symbol on his cap."

"I spoke to him!" Woolton chimed in anxiously. "He's definitely Polish!"

Petrie had his doubts. "He does...I mean...he does look German though."

They peered at Von Rindl again. He was fair, blond-haired, and blue-eyed, with blunt, rugged features and a square jaw.

"That's true. But that's only because Poland is located in close proximity to Germany," said Gillespie. "The people of both countries are orthinographically related."

"You mean 'ethnographically,'" Woolton corrected sharply. "They're not blithering birds."

"That's stretching things too far, Gilly, to say Germans are related to Poles," refuted Petrie in disgust. "They've got nothing in common. Why do you think Hitler trampled over them in '39? Obviously they don't get along. That's how the whole blasted war started in the first place..."

"One doesn't always get along with one's relatives," rejoined Gillespie.

"I personally find it an offense against the dignity of the Polish people to relate them to Germans," Woolton declared with quiet indignation. "Really, Gilly, that's too much—especially given the war. It's like saying that we're related to Germans..."

"You don't know the history of Northern Europe. If you go back to Charlemagne—"

"If you dare imply that we British are in any way related to Germans—archaeologically, ethnographically or otherwise—it will be the utter end of our friendship, and I vow never to speak to you again!" threatened Woolton with outrage.

"Charlemagne? Where did he come from? He was French!"

They were so caught up in this debate that they failed to notice their "guest" sneaking around like a shadow in the background. The German darted around in a silent flurry, whisking keys from an open office and stealthily prying his way into a truck.

They looked up in confusion as an engine started and a truck careened past them in a cloud of dust. They yelled in protest. "Wait! Stop! You can't take that—"

Von Rindl grinned brilliantly and waved to them out the window. "*Tschüski!*" he shouted, combining German with fake Polish, and drove away laughing.

They grumbled and let the matter go. Thunder struck half an hour later. Radio traffic reached their ears. A German officer had been spotted driving in a British vehicle column. He got away in a high-speed chase that left several trucks wrecked, a supply line disrupted and crates of bully beef scattered across the desert. The fugitive was at large and in need of capturing.

His three unwitting accomplices looked at each other aghast. For once, they were speechless.

Von Rindl made a dangerous path wandering through the marshes of oasis moisture farms. Networks of low-lying fields and irrigation ditches allowed farmers to cultivate fruit, rice and wheat in the arid desert. He had successfully reached the small patchwork of oasis cities he had glimpsed from afar. Civilization was all around him. It was a problem. He was lost. He seemed to be far behind enemy lines. The British were alert and looking for him everywhere.

He had tried to hitch his way back to the desert by tagging along in a supply column. He was unexpectedly halted at a checkpoint and decided to make a dash for it since he was sure he would be caught. It led to quite a scramble. Von Rindl was a daring soul; he laughed afterwards at the memory of driving wildly in circles, chased by trucks and jeeps and spilling crates of beef into the road. But his situation now was no laughing matter. He had abandoned the truck and was again on foot, vulnerable. Forced to abandon his rifle for expediency, he had only his sidearm and his rucksack. He was exhausted and afraid.

He stumbled over an irrigation ditch. Losing his balance, he landed on his knees in muddy water. He braced his fall with one hand and looked up unsteadily into the pink horizon. Cairo and its sister cities glittered in the distance.

A bewildered smile crossed his face. He was the first Afrika Korps soldier to touch the waters of the Nile.

British patrols swooped everywhere in jeeps. He wandered among date palms, reeds, and the back alleys of a dirty village for hours hiding. Fortunately, he was rescued by some Egyptians. Some sharp-eyed local men noticed him and figured out what he was.

Like many Egyptians, these locals were on Germany's side of the war. They had many reasons for this allegiance. The main reason was their unhappiness with British occupiers in their country. Arrogant English foreigners had been jaunting around in Egypt for decades. British needs came first, while Egypt's sovereignty was an afterthought. A multitude of racial and moral differences contributed to the divide. British soldiers, especially, were perceived by many locals as a plague and a nuisance. They had occupied Egypt heavily for a long time, guarding the Nile and controlling shipping. Many Egyptians felt subjugated by these British intruders. They perceived the Germans as liberators and wanted them to win.

They treated Von Rindl warmly and gave him shelter in a fruit cellar. He was given food, buckets to wash with, clothing, and carpets to sleep on. Most of them only spoke Arabic. They could not communicate with him very well due to language differences.

Eventually, a young Egyptian man materialized who spoke French. Von Rindl also spoke some French, and they found common ground.

The young man introduced himself as Hassad el-Sayed. A fairly common name in Arabic—perhaps a fake one. Hassad gave nothing away. He was very resourceful and wise for someone who hardly looked a day over age 19. He knew many details about British movements in Cairo and their supply line activities. He revealed that he was part of a German network. He had many contacts and was willing to be helpful. He asked Von Rindl what his plans were.

Von Rindl asked about going back to the front. Too risky, Hassad said. The British were swarming everywhere searching for him; it was likely Von Rindl would have to live in the cellar for a long time and perhaps switch hiding places, depending on how closely the enemy searched. It would be easier to move Von Rindl to Cairo—they could disguise him, load him onto an ox cart, and haul him to the big city with a shipment of dates within a week maybe. But not now. For the time being, movement was totally impossible.

Von Rindl found himself hopelessly stranded and embedded in a nest of spies. He was certain that a trip to Cairo would inevitably end in a POW camp; there were too many British soldiers and civilians around. He wanted to go back into the desert—and finish his mission, which was now completely derailed. He needed to break out somehow.

Thankfully, he had been crafty enough to save a trump card for such an occasion.

"I must send a very urgent message," he said to his youthful Egyptian protector. "To Miss Eve Weathers. At Shepheard's Hotel."

CHAPTER 22: RAID AT DAWN

"In the name of God and Empire,
We rally to the call;
We pledge our lives and all our strength
And march—Crusaders all!"
—"We March—Crusaders All" from
"Poems from the Desert" by Lt. F.Z. Smith

Later that day, Major Frost was spirited almost a whole universe away from Cairo and its comforts. Duty demanded he take charge of a chaotic predicament in Upper Egypt.

The deserts of Upper Egypt were different from those of Nile Delta north of it. Although the region was called "Upper Egypt," it was geographically below Cairo and the belt of desert cities bordering the Mediterranean. Upper Egypt was closer to the mouth of the Nile, where the great river fed into Egypt from the Sudan. The climate in Upper Egypt was more humid and slightly more tropical. Ruins were plentiful along the riverbanks. There were considerably more mosquitos and lots of boat traffic on tributaries running parallel to the Suez Canal. As one traveled farther into Upper Egypt, the climate became distinctly more Central African. Different types of animals appeared that were not native to the Mediterranean coast.

Recognizing the difference between the two regions, the ancient Egyptians wore unique symbols representing Upper and Lower Egypt on their royal headdresses. The uraeus cobra represented Lower Egypt, with its deserts and sands. The vulture represented Upper Egypt, with its marshlands and fauna. These symbolic creatures were goddesses called "The Two Ladies," thought to protect the ancient kingdom.

There was one common factor throughout all Egypt: the whole country was dry. Nothing could grow without water and there wasn't much water west of the Nile, excepting some hidden oases. The marshlands of Upper Egypt looked perfectly green and attractive, but they were only an illusion. Taking a short drive west, a visitor would find nothing but dry sand and cliffs.

The Upper Nile boasted more military fortifications. British troops circulated around Suez and traveled to and from Aswan on the Nile—a blister of blinding heat on an otherwise humid river. Fallen obelisks and wrecked statues of half-naked gods mingled with strong outcrops of Coptic Christian churches. Hooded Eastern monks could be seen drifting around terraced courtyards and lonely haunts.

The atmosphere was hot and sleepy. There was a constant trace of anger in the air, too—the heat made people irritable. Arguments broke out at a moment's notice. That was all very typical. Nobody was prepared for the assault on the military supply station at Ras el-Ahwa, which struck like a lightning bolt from a clear desert sky in the hours before sunrise.

The supply depot was a rather small one and based near a Fellahin peasant community that could not quite be called a town. It was fairly well fortified, but not excessively guarded. Average local thieves weren't bold enough to attempt filching goods from the station. The Ras el-Ahwa facility—known among British soldiers as "RAW" or "Ras el-Awful"—was a transit point where supplies destined for the Western Desert were dropped off from Nile cruisers before being trucked off in shipments. These supplies were mostly of an industrial nature. Oil, gasoline, machinery, and ammunition were among substances filling cartons and heavy canisters at the holding station. Shipping goods using Suez Canal tributaries and the Upper Nile was ideal, because the British had complete control of these areas and would not risk their supplies being sunk in the Mediterranean—exactly the desserts they inflicted on German and Italian shipping.

A violent raid by armed men in three jeeps came as a complete shock. British soldiers guarding the depot were mowed down by machine gun bullets at close range by men they initially mistook for military comrades.

The invaders, wearing British uniforms, wore head kerchiefs and veiled their faces like Arabs. They crashed through a fence using the sand-plow tires of one jeep; another jeep drove into the gap and began circling the buildings in a dust cloud, killing everything in its path. The third jeep made it to a hold where gasoline canisters were kept.

Veiled men crashed open doors and brutally shot a sergeant seated at a desk. They knifed him multiple times while stealing his keys. The keys were then used to open several supply holds, especially the gasoline hold, which was nearly emptied of its contents. The men ran around furiously stuffing petrol canisters into their vehicles. A few attempted to steal ammunition. This angered their leader, distinguished by the glaring green scarf covering his face and head. He roared at them to leave the ammunition behind.

An argument broke out among the robbers. Someone settled it by shooting the arguer, who was left behind like a rag in the dirt. The raiders and their captain vanished like fiends into the rosy pink haze of dawn.

A savaged supply station and a pile of innocent dead were left behind. The catastrophe, however, was not finished. An old Coptic monk was misfortunate enough to walk across a dirt road in the path of the escaping robbers. The elderly man, known as Father Genesius, was a desert hermit and ascetic known for distributing food to local poor and providing free medical help to beggars. He crossed that road before dawn every morning to say his prayers on a nearby hill facing the sunrise. The old man had no time to duck out of the way when three jeeps, equipped with sand-plow tires, whirred towards him like monsters. The robbers ran straight over him. It was a deliberate act. Witnesses saw the green-veiled bandit leader swoop back and shoot the monk's body before departing.

The carnage was cleaned up by the time Major Frost arrived on the scene. Coptic mourners filled the streets grieving the loss of the generous Father Genesius, viewed as a local saint. British soldiers handled the deaths of their Army comrades in quiet suffering. Frost visited the mangled bodies left behind by the killers—the military guards onsite and the monk, whose remains had since been taken to a church.

Frost was deeply moved by the tragedy. He became silently furious. He walked out of the church with cold mist in his eyes and the firm resolve to take no prisoners. That was when they told him, at exactly the wrong time, that one robber was still alive.

The man had been shot in the breastbone. The bullet was aimed at his heart, but movement and chaos caused a miss. They had him tied down on a long wooden crate in one of the depot outbuildings. Guards kept watch to prevent angry soldiers and peasants from mauling him.

He was an English deserter. A former tank crewman, he had abandoned the British Army during its hard losing streak against the Afrika Korps in 1941. Afterwards, he ended up in the company of the robbers. He admitted these things freely to his captors. He was shamelessly self-pitying. He assumed no responsibility. He was the victim of every story. Somehow he never intended to do wrong; villains compelled him to act against his nature and bad deeds just automatically happened at his hands. His wheedling stories made no sense, accused his guards—no, they didn't, he admitted, but then he claimed nothing made sense. He was a chess pawn freefalling through a senseless and unkind world. A genuinely good person, he claimed. He just happened to be robbing and murdering for all kinds of good reasons that somehow didn't turn out so good because of things he couldn't explain.

He tried very hard to seem sympathetic towards his captors. One of them was nearly duped. The guard pitied the man's teary eyes and excuses. He moved to give him a cigarette.

That was when Major Frost entered the room. "Put those away and get out!" he ordered the guard. The cigarettes disappeared, and the robber realized that his chances of being pitied had shrunk next to nil.

The Major stared at the surviving robber. They recognized each other. The injured raider looked ready to hide under the box he was lying on.

Frost smiled icily. "Ah. You remember me, don't you? I remember you, too. I was on the ground, shot. You were standing in a jeep nearby—laughing." He strutted over and scanned the man's face with piercing cold eyes. "What's your name? Rank?"

The thief made no answer.

"Very well, it doesn't matter. No need to worry about your name," said Frost with frigid charm. "You won't be getting an obituary or a gravestone. We won't need it!"

The robber looked horrified. The prospect of actually being punished for his evils had not even remotely occurred to him. "Are you going to give me to the Egyptian police? Will they hang me?" He panicked. "You can't do that. I'm a British subject. You can't give me to the Egyptians!"

Frost did not flinch. "Where's Ollie?"

The bandit was preoccupied with his fate. "What will happen to me?"

"I didn't come here to discuss your miserable existence!" snapped Frost, losing his patience. "I want to know where Ollie is. I know very well he masterminded today's gala. I also have a pretty good idea where you lot were headed. Time to tell it all," he said with venom in his voice. "Is it Wadi Noor?"

The robber looked petrified with surprise.

"You know. That wretched old ditch you chaps call 'The Cellar,'" he prodded. "Is that Ollie's next port of call, or not?"

"How do you know about that?"

Frost's eyes flashed. "You're wasting my time."

The robber considered that he was in a position to bargain. The answer to Frost's question was obvious, but he wanted to gain an advantage by openly admitting it. "Promise I won't be hanged!" he demanded.

A look of icy calm passed over Frost. "You will not be hanged."

"The answer's yes. He is heading to Wadi Noor. Him and the whole bunch of them," answered the robber. "The group split up because of a disagreement. We got low on supplies and ran almost clean out of fuel. The other group emptied all our other caches before we could reach them. We got desperate. That's why we came all the way down here. To stock up and get some rest," he said, trying to justify their actions. "We were planning to catch the others and teach them a lesson. But we couldn't pull it off without sorting our own business out first. It's been a hard run lately. The desert is an unforgiving place, you know—"

"Yes. Filled with unforgiving people, you'll learn," the Major cut in, frosty and sardonic. "Any other scruples you'd like to clear from your conscience?"

"No one apart from Ollie and our group knows how to get into 'The Cellar,'" he asserted. "It's a secret. Not even the natives know it. You need to take me along with you," he urged. "I know all about it. I can show you the way in."

Frost scanned the man's eyeballs and saw boldfaced lies. He smirked. "That was a very decent effort at deception, mucker, but I've seen it all before," he commented. "We're done here."

He took one last hard look at the robber before turning away and marching out the door. He emerged into the sunlight and felt liberated knowing the world would be relieved of one less dangerous criminal within the next hour.

"Bring him outside and shoot him," Frost ordered the officer in charge of the group of soldiers herded around the depot grounds. "Make sure you do it properly. Rifles. Wall. A nice clean lineup. Make sure there's an audience."

The officer agreed with enthusiasm.

Frost had been vested with high powers that gave him control not only of the investigation, but the fates of the guilty robbers involved in it. He had requested death warrants for all men caught in the act of marauding, and had already received this power. He intended to make full and ruthless use of it.

The lone captured perpetrator of the Ras el-Ahwa Depot Raid was restrained, blindfolded, and executed by a neat Army firing squad approximately half an hour later. He had pillaged, raped, stolen, murdered, and destroyed. He had betrayed his country and military comrades to their deaths. Yet, he protested his innocence until the last. Like his victims, he fell to the dust in a hail of biting hot bullets. He died slowly. It took a final coup de grace shot to finish the job. His body was carted off to a wasteland and buried in an unmarked grave.

Frost did not bother to stay behind to watch the execution. He had more important matters to attend to.

Lieutenant Nye, accompanying him on the journey, dared to ask about next priorities.

"A mission briefing," Frost answered bluntly. "I'm taking the whole squad to Wadi Noor, boots and all. We're going to exterminate the dirty blackguards. Today."

The final mission briefing took place in a jungled area on the western shores of the Nile. The riverbanks were covered in long, thin reeds and packed with palm trees. Flies and mosquitos buzzed viciously in the heat. The ruins of a former cult site of an ancient Greek-Egyptian queen littered the area. Broken white pillars tumbled into the grass. Smiling, hollow-eyed female figures leered eerily from cracked pedestals between the trees.

About 50 men in a variety of military trucks and camouflaged vehicles had assembled in a gathering to receive Frost's orders. Most either belonged to the Army Investigative Corps or were affiliated with it. A handful of tough characters were from Frost's Counter-Insurgency Group; they served under him and were loyal to his leadership. Others were drawn from various Army ranks. All were seasoned combat veterans; Frost required subordinates with tested field experience.

Major Frost's announcements were very brief. He stood on top of a flat pillar base, using it as a pedestal to rally the men before they began their mission. He greeted them, then launched into a forceful and jarring address.

"The enemies facing us this time are not Hitler's soldiers," he said in sharp, loud command voice. "They are our own people. Some are members of our own Special Forces. But don't let that fool you. There's nothing remotely 'special' about these stray dogs," he continued. "They've gotten as far as they have by attacking unarmed people and ambushing sitting targets. They are cowards and they are weak by nature." A pitch of emotion roughened his voice.

"They have used brute violence and the privileges of their military status to murder, raid and steal," he went on. "They've slaughtered many of our good comrades, who fought gallantly against Nazi Germany and survived hard battles—only to be cut down at the hands of these senseless beasts."

His words stirred up emotions from the crowd of armed men surrounding him. The force of their anger was like tangible wave in the heat. Frost was psyching them up. They were almost ready to go out and kill. Just a few more sentences would make them invincible.

"These vandals are a disgrace to the uniform we wear. Their existence dishonors our country and our noble profession. They are a blight on civilization and, like all forms of pestilence, they must be cleanly wiped out." He made a clean, tight pause. "We will take no prisoners today!" he announced. "Show them no mercy. They will give none to you."

Afterwards, he detailed to the soldiers what they could expect at Wadi Noor. It was a half-sunken Nile ruin used as a supply dump by the robbers. It was not far from the river, yet hidden from view and isolated from cities. The enemy was low on ammunition. Their forces were divided. Many were injured; they would not be in position to last a siege.

Frost summed up his plan with three declarations. "We will pin them down. We will flush them out. We will exterminate them!"

The atmosphere became very solemn and electric with killer energy.

"Cash prize and film tickets for whoever splats the most rats. Two prizes, two chances," the Major added suddenly with an impudent grin. "My treat! Just don't tell any gents upstairs."

The aura of tension broke. They laughed. The dangerous mission had suddenly become a competitive hunting trip. Men liked sports and challenges; Frost did to a very high degree. Aggressive by nature, he approached battle as a contest. His optimism was infectious.

Frost hopped down from the pillar base and watched the men prepare for action under the open sky. The sun was beginning its slow descent towards the horizon. He needed to corner the nomadic robbers in their lair before they slipped through his fingers and vanished again into dust and darkness.

The clock was ticking.

CHAPTER 23: SIREN SONG

Silva: "The Duke sends us to announce your sentence."
Egmont: "Do ye also bring the headsman who is to
execute it?"
Silva: "Listen, and you will know the doom that awaits you."
—"Egmont" by Johann Wolfgang von Goethe, Act V, Scene IV

The ruin at Wadi Noor was a bizarre site. The wadi itself was a large oasis filled with thickets of date palm trees, brush and papyri reeds. At its center was what appeared to be a pile of old sandstone rocks. These were marked with hieroglyphs and Greek letters. Once the rocks had been cornerstones of a sacred shrine. Nothing of that shrine was left above ground.

The real soul of the ruin was underground. A huge fissure in the earth split the center of the oasis. The fissure was as wide as several buildings. However, it was shallow at the bottom and less than a mile deep. Geography effectively created a pocket in the earth, nicknamed "The Cellar" by the robbers.

The interior of the cavern was manmade. The ancient Egyptians, and subsequently the ancient Greeks and Romans, believed it to be a sacred site due to a natural Nile waterfall that sprang from the side of the ravine. In bygone times, an oracle had lived here. She was a priestess of Selene-Hathor—a dual deific personality combining the Greek moon goddess and the Egyptian sky goddess. Here she made her prophecies. Once the world trembled at her predictions. Now nobody remembered she existed. Ancient devotees carved steps into the earth and created stone paths. The Egyptians built sandstone arches and decorated the walls. The Greeks cut offering chambers into the cliffside. The Romans had the good sense to make the hidden cave publicly accessible. They built a paved road going straight down to the waterfall. The road, now overgrown and shattered, was wide enough for a cart to haul a sacrificial ox down and back again. It was also wide enough for a jeep. A haze of dust and mist rose from the ravine's sandstone walls.

Now a host of battle-ready soldiers crawled through the bushes. Dark rifles poked out from hiding places among the trees. Army vehicles rolled threateningly along the perimeter of the oasis. Military magic muffled the noise of the engines.

Major Frost had built a careful web around the oasis. He had used his own instincts and the intelligence he had gained from his sources to make his plan. For example, Sullivan gave him a notebook Bedouins had taken from a dead Italian robber. The drawings inside contained several maps of Wadi Noor and identified three paths leading out of the oasis. All were driving tracks. Other maps of different locations also existed in the notebook with marked driving tracks; most of these camps were located in areas near the Nile.

Based on these vehicle-specific drawings, Frost deduced that the robbers' sand-plow jeeps had difficulty driving through marshy terrain. He prepared traps.

A flare pistol launched the operation. The signal sailed into the air like a red sparrow and vanished into sparkles. A long smoke screen puffed to life and veiled a thicket of trees where concealed rifles aimed at the ravine. Then came the "hunting call."

Egyptian music blasted from a loudspeaker. A popular folk tune often heard in cabarets, on the radio and at belly dancing performances shouted from nowhere. Instruments jangled. Whining clarinets flirted with tabla drums. "Ay ya leil!" wailed a sultry female voice in Arabic with sorrowful passion. "Ay leili, ya leil! Ay ya leil..." The age-old lyrics were always the same. Oh, the night! the singer belted, moaning a lovelorn crescendo. The night!

It was a wild and weird moment. Soldiers steadied their aims, winked at each other, and touched the triggers of their firearms in anticipation of the first shot.

The siren song lured prey to the surface. Men emerged from the cavern. They were alarmed by the sound of the music. It was bizarre. However, their guard was down as they did not expect violence. They wondered many things. Who was there? Was someone playing a radio? Were Arabs frolicking in the oasis? Two robbers emerged and began blundering around the marshy turf, searching for the culprits. They did not notice the smokescreen.

A silent signal passed. Rifles cracked. Two robbers fell dead as doornails.

A brief gun battle ensued. Raiders darted back and forth out of the cave, shooting into the trees and missing the military ambushers. More robbers dropped dead. After a furious, peppery exchange of fire, two groups of thieves decided to make a breakout.

They would have escaped, if Major Frost hadn't already expected it. They sallied out of the ravine from two different directions using concealed vehicle ramps. One jeep flew east, the other west. Their machine gun turrets roared, shredding smoky trees with steel barrages.

Then, one by one, the jeeps wrecked. It was a fantastic sight. The whirring sand-plow tires stuck fast in deep reedy nets sunk in the mud. Traction stopped immediately. In fact, these humble obstructions—proposed by Frost—worked better than any roadblock. One jeep flipped over forward; the gunner shot himself dead, the driver's head was smashed under the engine, and the other passengers were cut down like grass by streams of bullets when they tried to run away. The second jeep fared no better. The driver was shot dead; the vehicle careened out of control and got stuck in a mud trap. The jeep jolted to a sideways halt and rolled over, ejecting all passengers. The gunner's hands got stuck in the turret. He hung struggling by his arms, kicked and was cut up by blasting bullets. The others fled into the oasis. They were neatly picked off by riflemen. The Egyptian romance song soared loudly in the background.

Frost ordered his men to close in after "the rats stopped coming out," as he put it. The music ceased; it had been a fine agent of confusion that was no longer needed. The men advanced in a ring around the ravine. A few more robbers emerged. All were shot.

Frost stalked across the killing grounds. His khakis were stained with sweat and grime. His sleeves were rolled lopsidedly above his elbows. His bronzed face and arms bore traces of sunburn. The silver badge on his midnight blue beret glinted like a deadly crown. He was armed and his pale blue eyes were alive with ferocity. He was very much the image of a hardened soldier forged in Britain's colonies. He reviewed the dead. All robber scum, by the looks of it. He was pleased with the outcome. No casualties on his own side so far.

Suddenly, shouts of panic burst out around him. Frost's eyes widened. He drew his pistol in a fluid motion as men started scrambling.

"Oi! It's Leafy!"

"To the right!"

"Take him!"

Shots cracked. A blurry figure melted in and out of bushes and trees. Wood splintered. Papyri burst into pieces. Thanks to Frost's "wanted poster," everyone recognized their target. Yet he was too quick. Everyone missed him. Frost aimed, training his eyes on the thickets.

"Sir!" screamed Lieutenant Nye. "Sir, he's got me!"

That was the moment when Major Frost saw the tomb robber Ollie Bryon, also dubbed Flag, for the first time since their desert standoff. It was a hideous sight. The bandit captain had camouflaged himself with mud smears all over his face and arms. The tails of his green headscarf were wrapped over his face like a veil, leaving only a muddy strip of skin and one lone murderous eye. His false metal eye was missing; it had fallen out onto the ground and lay there gleaming. Lieutenant Nye had knocked it out of his head trying to struggle against the bandit. Ollie had coiled around Nye like a snake. His arms were bent around Nye's neck in a twisted headlock. The Australian soldier was a human shield—incapable of moving. The tomb robber clutched a muddy metal rod in one fist. The makeshift weapon appeared to be some kind of truck tire lever.

Major Frost's eyes were wide with unbelief. Perspiration drenched his face as he watched Nye frozen helplessly in the grip of a monster. A disaster was imminent. Yet nothing could be done—Ollie had positioned himself in such a manner that trees shielded him from crisscrossing directions. There was no room for a sure shot. A rescue attempt at this point would doom the hostage.

Soldiers aimed rifles shakily as the bandit captain began raving at them. "How dare you lot come here! I got rights to live in peace!" the cockney marauder seethed. "I'm a soldier, I am! Commando Group Sphinx! Why is you filth here? You're abrupting me in the line of duty!"

"The proper word is 'disrupting,'" Frost called out, stepping closer into the illiterate killer's view. He tried to buy time for a perfect death shot. "And you no longer have any 'duties.' Oliver Bryon, you are not an Army commando," he declared. "You are a wanted criminal."

Silence fell.

Ollie stared in dumb amazement. He recognized the Major he'd left for dead in a desert ruin. He wondered in stupor how the man had suddenly appeared at his hideout with an armed troop. "Is that *you*, Major Muggins?"

"That's right. No sense in any more claptrap, Ollie. The jig is up," demanded Frost, keeping up the vestige of control. He seemed calm. But behind his mask, he feared for his aide's life. "We've got this whole quagmire surrounded and your lovely portrait decorating every mess from here to Cape Town. Even if you did manage to scramble out of here, you wouldn't last long." He grinned, lofty and irreverent. "A lot of greedy people are on the lookout for you! You know how that works, don't you?"

"You traitor. You did this!" accused Ollie in outrage. "A fine show of gratitude, this!" He was genuinely offended. "Treated you fair, I did. Agreed not to croak you, and even swore my hands off that bit of skirt you wanted, I did, just to be great-hearted. And now you come round here, tearin' my blinkin' roof off and clobberin' all my squaddies. Pure evil, is what you are!" shouted the sadistic killer in moral indignation. "You're a sneakin' murderer!"

Frost's eyes sparkled with ironic humor, even despite the electrifying tension in the air. His adrenaline rushed to dizzying heights. "Quit blathering and step lively in this direction," he commanded. "If you want to live, anyway."

"Like blisterin' heck I will!" the robber spat in fury. "Think you're a sight better than me, don't you, Major Muggins? Some bloomin' Lord, are you? Comin' the old posh, clickin' about this way and that. Think you're so much better! Who made you be the one to give orders, hey? Who died and made you boss?"

"In the real Army, nobody has to die for others to earn promotions. That's the difference between us," retorted Frost. "I'm bored. I'd like to watch you get shot," he stated callously, meaning every word. "Last chance to surrender."

No surrender was coming. Instead, the bandit captain dragged his Australian hostage a step back. His laced Afrika Korps moccasins sank in the mud. A papyri marsh loomed behind them. "Here's one mucker who won't have none of your orders!" he defied, baring his teeth.

"Sir, go ahead!" called Nye in a trembling voice. "Go ahead and shoot. It's fine."

The riflemen glanced around in confusion, tense out of

their minds. Their hands perspired on their guns. Their fingers hovered nervously on their triggers. They waited for an order to relieve their panic.

Frost's composure cracked faintly. Tears misted his eyes.

"Please shoot!" urged Nye. "Sir!"

The bandit roared. "Shut your filthy gob!"

Frost opened his mouth to say something. He couldn't remember what it was afterward, because he lost his breath as the world changed in slow motion. Nye sensed himself being dragged backwards; he realized the bandit intended to escape into the marsh using him as a human shield. The proud Australian soldier no longer wished to be used as a shield. In reality, the tomb robber would probably kill him when he had outlived his usefulness. With death facing him at every turn, he decided to take his fate into his own hands.

He kicked and wrestled furiously with Ollie. The robber wrestled back using the metal tire lever as a choking tool. They both fell over. Shots went off as the soldiers lost their self-control and tried to shoot the enemy. Frost screamed at them to hold their fire.

It was over and done in less than a minute. It ended when Ollie pinned Nye down and gutted him with the metal tool he was holding. It was a piercing blow straight in the stomach. A sniper bullet clipped the robber captain in the side of his arm. He dropped flat on the ground and disappeared into the reeds, scurrying on his hands and knees like a rodent.

Frost strode over to Nye, feeling numb at the sight of his assistant writhing in sopping blood with a long metal rod sticking out of him.

The instrument of death was indeed a tire lever—a large heavy one used for prying rubber tires off military trucks. The lever had been sawn in half and its edges sharpened, turning it into a crude but dangerous makeshift weapon. It had gouged a huge hole in the soldier's khaki shirt. Blood poured everywhere. The impaling wound was undoubtedly fatal.

The Major looked at the gruesome scene and desensitized his brain to another of life's casualties. It wasn't the first time he'd lost a comrade. He had learned to accept death. It came and it went. Some times were more difficult than others.

Surprisingly, the tough Australian showed no outward sign of distress or panic. "I slowed him down. He's hit in the arm," he said urgently. "Go get him!"

Frost stooped and placed his hand on the fallen man's shoulder. He meant it to be a reassuring gesture. He didn't know what to say. Tears filled his eyes and words abandoned him. He stood quickly and walked off. Behind him, others evacuated Nye for medical treatment.

Meanwhile, sniper fire crackled across the marsh. Frost's riflemen were trying to shoot Ollie by firing randomly into the thicket. No sign of movement could be seen among the reeds. Cautious ceasefire and silence, also, revealed nothing.

"We're losing him!" muttered Frost angrily through clenched teeth.

Sunset burned like a hot orange scythe across the sky. The baking air turned gold. The atmosphere glowed with creamy tangerine light as another desert day began its shift to darkness.

Major Frost took personal control of the entire oasis with iron determination. He established correctly, in a very short time, that Ollie had not escaped the dragnet. Perimeter vehicles were stationed around the edges of the oasis in such a manner that he would have been spotted immediately. He was not. A systematic search of the papyri marsh and surrounding thickets revealed nothing. The robber seemed to have vanished like mist in the heat.

Frost and his men, all battle-hardened and suspicious, were no fools for illusions. They suspected Ollie had crept back into the ruins in the sunken crater—hiding in plain sight.

"He must've slipped back into the ditch," said the Major to one of his aides. "It likely he's the last one standing, but we won't know for certain until we've broomed it out. Let's make a thorough sweep."

The perimeter tightened around the oasis. Guards lurked in the thickets and around the crevice. An assault group descended into the cavernous pit. The dirty brown waterfall from the Nile splashed out from the sandstone rock face, creating thin echoes in the dust.

Men in the assault group were somewhat surprised to see Major Frost taking the lead inside the cavern, carrying a bayoneted rifle. The sight emboldened their spirits.

"I'm trophy hunting!" said Frost, with a jocular smile and a deadly look in his blue eyes. "I want Leafy's green head rag for my mantelpiece. First dibs!"

They laughed boisterously.

Frost flashed his sharp grin. He was not joking.

CHAPTER 24: LIGHTNING STRIKE

"I am accustomed to stand amid the serried ranks of war,
and environed by the threatening forms of death,
to feel, with double zest, the energy of life."
—"Egmont" by Johann Wolfgang von Goethe, Act V, Scene IV

The ancient ruins inside the ravine had not changed much across fleeting centuries. The rushing tides of the ages cracked surfaces and peeled paint off stone reliefs. But the labyrinth of ceremonial chambers carved into the cliffsides were, in essence, unaltered. The dirty waterfall was the center of the spectacle. In former times the flowing wellspring from the Nile looked cleaner. Pollution did not mellow with age. The waterfall continued its routine performance. Muddy brown water full of reed pieces and dead insects spouted magnificently from the rock wall and poured into a deep ceremonial well. The well, shaped like a round pond, was designed to mirror the sky. It glinted orange as the water reflected the burnt gold light of sunset.

Directly behind the waterfall was the inner sanctum formerly inhabited by the oracle of the twin-faced goddess Selene-Hathor. The goddess's split face was carved into the rock above the waterfall. Her nose had broken off. She wore a round moon disc on her head with a Grecian crest shaped like a lunar crescent. The face split in half slightly, representing two different deities in one. Images of cows framed the carving on either sides. The goddess Hathor's alter ego had been a cow; strange bovine images were scattered across the cliff walls.

Splashing water echoed. Armed men darted quietly in all directions. They split into storming groups and systematically cleared several caves. Nothing but silence and still objects were to be found.

Major Frost led a small group along a broken path behind the waterfall. The incline grew steep. A false step could send a soldier toppling down into the deep ceremonial pond below. They entered the hidden chambers of the ancient oracle.

Frost led cautiously. He suspected Ollie was nearby and kept his eyes on everything, alert for the first sign of danger.

The first room was enormously wide. Once designed as an audience chamber for visiting delegations, it was large enough to hold a large gathering of people. Doors and carved stairs lined the walls.

The soldiers passed into the next room. This was the "prophecy" chamber where the oracle supposedly received divine messages. A beam of light poured down from a huge hole in the rock-hewn ceiling into a central pool. The pool appeared very deep—likely more than 12-feet deep, at first glance—and filled nearly the whole room. It was filled to the brim with brown river water that trickled in through a maze of waterfalls in the walls. An ancient irrigation system. Apparently the system still functioned. Drainage was a problem—water from the giant pool overflowed slightly over the edges of the walkways in the room. It stank like rot. Mosquitos buzzed.

Two colossi stood halfway submerged in the pool. One was an enormous statue of a cow wearing a moon disc on its head. Next to it was the giant figure of a naked Greco-Egyptian woman crowned with a lunar crescent.

The room was clear. The men branched into two groups and disappeared into two adjoining corridors, "sweeping" the area for enemies.

Frost waited behind, keeping an eye on their movements. He estimated that Ollie would not risk entrenching himself in too deep a position. The bandit captain liked being mobile. Frost predicted the robber was outside and searching the inner rooms would prove fruitless.

Echoes of the trickling waterfalls filled the air.

A dark suspicion crept up on Frost. He had a feeling that he was being watched by a murderous human presence. His muscles tensed. A sense of focused malice closed in on him.

He's here, Frost realized.

He glanced around. No hiding places existed in the ceiling. Nothing was apparent but empty air, water and the two dumbly gazing colossi in the pool. The Major stared at the deep, muddy pool. Was the water really empty?

Underwater was the only conceivable hiding place. Frost had no idea how the bandit could successfully stay submerged for so long, but he knew better than to underestimate the unnatural dark arts of Special Forces rangers. And how did he plan to attack without making a huge splash?

The loud water trickling noise would conceal a stealth ambush, Frost thought. One step in the wrong direction, and Ollie would slither out of the pool like a serpent and throttle him without making noise.

Frost considered he couldn't yell for assistance. It would be a mistake to brandish his rifle at the pool and randomly plunge bullets in. He had no idea where Ollie was actually hiding, and that lack of knowledge put him at a disadvantage. He did know the robber relied on stealth and brute strength to kill targets; poor Nye—ambushed and gored with a tire lever—was a classic example. The only logical thing for the Major to do was beat Ollie at his own game somehow.

The air bristled. Any moment now, the enemy would strike hard and fast. He couldn't see anything, but he knew it was coming. He could feel it. Like electrified spider webs tingling against his skin. He acted calm and felt suffocated by the intense silence.

Considering his options in the face of mortal danger, he remembered one of his favorite stories. His hero Hannibal versus Roman general Gaius Flaminius. Once upon a time, when Hannibal was out and about terrorizing armies across the Italian countryside, Flaminius decided to stop him. Flaminius was a brash character. He had a fairly good track record and was confident in his strength. He thought he could thrash Hannibal and stomp him out of Italy. So he followed Hannibal into a very narrow area, where Hannibal appeared poorly protected. Hannibal sat in plain sight; all Flaminius believed was necessary was to pounce. But Hannibal was a wily old soldier. Like Major Frost, he'd spent his entire life happily battling and contemplating war. Hannibal knew his foe had a reactive personality. He set a trap and waited patiently until the perfect moment to snap Flaminius right in the nose. The snap sent the whole Roman army reeling and amounted to a sheer massacre. It was called the Battle of Lake Trasimene and was one of the most horrifying defeats ever suffered by ancient Rome. Flaminius did not survive it.

In his moment of crisis, Frost recalled this uplifting story. In an instant, the dirty old pond in the oracle temple became, in his mind, a miniature Lake Trasimene. Frost decided to play Hannibal. Ollie inevitably would accept the role of Flaminius—and trip into the same coffin.

The British officer pretended cool carelessness. He deliberately turned his back towards the center of the pool. Fresh perspiration glistened on his forehead. He looked at the puddled walkway in front of him. There. He found his mark. That broken tile three steps ahead. He had three steps to pass the finish line and grip striking death by the horns.

His breath grew silent and shallow as he took the first step. He felt suffocated by the eerie silence. He experienced a raw, animal sense of being hunted. Like a man being stalked by a giant tiger. The sensible presence of a human antagonist was staggering.

He took another step. The worst thing to do would be to freeze.

There. A tiny ripple noise behind him. His ear barely caught it. A faint feeling of "Aha!" swept over him, bringing morbid relief. That was the sound of his enemy slithering out of the pond to murder him from behind. Why was it so refreshing? Because he now knew where exactly that enemy was.

In the same moment, he united his consciousness to the bayoneted rifle in his grip. He crushed his silent fear. He swore to himself that he was indeed Hannibal and this was Lake Trasimene. In an awkward position, Yes. About to be sneaked up on, Yes. Vulnerable and not expecting it? No.

He took the third step and jumped forward. No sense in pretending anymore. Water and mosquitos flew everywhere as he swung his bayoneted rifle expertly in one hand.

A bayonet, in theory, was supposed to be wielded with a series of neat thrusting and parrying movements. Nice clean little sweeps. In practice, the blade became nothing less than a spear. A combat-tested bayonet fighter knew rules meant nothing. The contraption could be used effectively pointing backwards, sideways, and upside down. All a wielder needed was strength and the visceral determination to drive a sword into a hard human body. Aim wasn't so important. Once the harpoon struck its mark not much was left unscathed.

An experienced bayonet fighter recognized, however, the importance of weak spots. Hitting the right spot caused instant death to a foe. Hitting an off spot could result in awkward and bloody wrangling. The enemy usually ended up dead, but the process of making it happen became grim and tiring.

Frost was a bayonet-fighting veteran. The first time he'd bayoneted an enemy in combat, he was mildly horrified and thought he'd done a terrible job of it. It wasn't like in the books and drills. After a few similar experiences, he learned to throw the books and drills out of his mind, and allowed his rough nature to take control. He befriended his bayonet and became something of a javelin expert. He became good enough to scare drill instructors and good enough to give enemies a run for their money. Certainly they learned to run when they saw him coming. His stint at bayoneting later led him to take an interest in ancient spear warfare. It wasn't very much different. At least not the way Frost did it.

His boots almost skidded on the wet floor as he spun to face his assassin. Frost's vision blurred. It was an experience like losing normal eyesight and awakening to see thermal radar instead. It was battle vision. A contest with death turned lucid moments to blurs and people to blobs. Time suddenly sped a million times faster. Feeling the heavy thump of his own heartbeat was the only thing that informed a man in this feral state he was still alive.

A human mass loomed ahead. A dark blob.

It took Frost less than a fraction of the second to identify where the ribs and vitals were. He launched the bayonet down like a thunderbolt with a great overhand stab of his arm. A howl pierced the air. He pushed the blade in hard, felt flesh break from bone. Frost bared his teeth and yelled savagely.

The ground slid beneath him. Human weight lurched onto the rifle. Frost could not stop himself from falling. The room turned sideways as he toppled over into the murky pool.

There was a terrific splash. Filthy, fetid water was everywhere. Frost plunged into watery darkness and slime. He felt something kicking him. Heavy legs. Boots. The bayoneted rifle stayed stuck in its target; Frost was still holding the rifle and could feel it moving. He gripped it hard and kept shoving it wildly, trying to stab.

He surfaced and spat. Even in this wild state, he knew it was dangerous to swallow the filthy water. He was slimy and disoriented. He could not feel his feet beneath him. His hand stubbornly gripped the rifle. It twisted and lost weight. Frost saw dark red liquid in the water. Lots of it, pluming everywhere. It leaked from one source—a dark blur floating just ahead of him. The blur was moving. Tattooed hands flailed in splashes. He saw a wisp of green turban. Frost fixed a rabid eye upon the enemy. He kicked forward in the water and hoisted the bayoneted rifle into the air like a javelin. He was a good swimmer; even with no footing, he managed to propel his body halfway above surface with a powerful kick and bring the spear-like blade down with a mighty crash and a barbaric scream. Another overhand strike. It struck hard and drove home like a skewer. The water turned completely red this time. He kept pushing down until the blade wouldn't go any farther. *Take that, you dirty scum!* he thought, breathing hard. *Nobody can survive this one!*

The body sank, pulling him down with it. He let go of the rifle and kicked away. It was a struggle not to swallow the water. He kept coughing and spitting. His boots were heavy and filled with water; his gun belt also pulled his hips under. He was weighed down and struggled not to sink. Looking up, he saw the face of a large cow statue looming above him. Somehow he was stranded in the center of the pool. Frost, sputtering, swam toward the poolside. He was very strong and athletic; he had a lean physique and was built of nothing but muscle. Despite being weighed down, it was easy for him to use his arm strength to stroke across.

His comrades were ready there waiting for him. They dragged him out of the water.

The soldiers had arrived on the scene moments earlier. They had witnessed the last act of Oliver Bryon's attempted ambush. They saw the bandit lurking behind Major Frost, who somehow predicted his attack and speared him with a fluid twirling motion worthy of a samurai warrior. One blinding second later, they were in the pool thrashing. Nobody could quite tell what happened. The dying Ollie appeared to attempt further violence. All they saw was Frost lurch out of the water with savage fury and smite him again with another lightning blade thrust and the roar of a lion. The entire saga lasted about two minutes and was over in the blink of an eye.

Frost sat on the floor with a flushed face, panting. He was covered in slime, mosquitos, and bloody water that stained his khakis orange-red. He was worried about catching illness from the filthy water. He wheezed.

"Cough, sir," one of his helpers said. "Force it out."

They pounded him on the back. Frost leaned over onto the floor and coughed so hard that he vomited. He was desperate not to catch a bacterial infection from the contamination.

Meanwhile, other men fished Oliver Bryon out from the pool. It was difficult to do, since the body had sunk; they ended up towing it out using the faint edge of Frost's rifle strap, which was barely floating in view. The bandit captain was indeed dead. His corpse was almost completely pale from blood loss. The bayoneted rifle was still stuck in him. The long pointed spike had bored straight through him and poked out from his back. Frost had driven it in almost beyond its limits. The bayonet was bent crooked from the force of Frost's blows. It was difficult to pry out.

The soldiers also discovered a twine of sharp metal wire around one of Ollie's fists. Seemingly he had planned to garrote Major Frost with it. Fortunately, the makeshift weapon had not been used.

The Major was exhausted and shaken. He was relieved that his enemy was dead, but it was hard to think beyond the sensation of feeling wet and disgusting. He looked at the pool and saw it had turned completely red. According to legend, the waters of Lake Trasimene had been stained scarlet red with blood after Hannibal's victory. His miniature Lake Trasimene was no less scarlet and no less victorious. Time lapsed. His battle fever faded away.

He heard the sound of cheering and felt dizzily glad. The soldiers were congratulating him. Someone handed him his midnight blue beret, which had fallen off on the poolside. He received it gratefully.

Hands pulled at him. "All right, sir. Let's head back and tell the others."

He caught his breath, still sitting on the floor. "Wait," he announced, gesturing at the body. "My trophy."

Faces peered at him in confusion.

He grinned. "Give me that blasted green head rag!"

Laughter echoed in the watery chamber as men stripped Ollie Bryon, once notorious as Flag the tomb robber, of his emerald green turban. They twirled the scarf around, tried it on and poked fun of it before tossing it into Major Frost's lap. He stood up smiling and flourished it triumphantly.

"All hail, Spartacus!" someone quipped with dry sarcasm.

There was a giant cheer, accompanied by a chorus of rough laughter and hooting. Frost joined in. They were all in high spirits. Dirty and soaking wet, the Major emerged from the cavern with a crowd of enthusiastic compatriots around him and a bright grin on his face.

It had been a successful day and their mission was accomplished.

Or at least it almost was. There was a whole other group of rival tomb robbers out there who needed to be dealt with. Frost, despite his triumph, had not forgotten.

He had also noticed something very strange about Oliver Bryon's body. The bandit's prized flint dagger was missing. That explained why Ollie had resorted to using makeshift weapons like tire levers and wire in hand-to-hand combat. His treasured dagger was seemingly lost or stolen. Searches of the area revealed nothing. It was nowhere to be found.

He rinsed off as much of his body and his filthy, blood-soaked uniform as possible using a water canister from the back of a truck. Soon afterward, he was informed by a staff officer that Lieutenant Nye's wound was beyond repair. A mobile medical unit brought along for the operation had cleaned up the Australian soldier's injury and eased his pain with morphine. However, this wouldn't last.

Difficult emotions filled Major Frost as he decided to pay a visit to his assistant for the last time. A few minutes later, he stood in the back of the mobile medical unit van and beheld a frail-looking man, ghostly pale and wrapped up in layers of bandages.

Frost smiled and pretended not to notice. "We got him!" He stepped over and wrung Nye's hand warmly. "You helped corner him. We couldn't have taken him in the marsh. But we did get him in a cave right afterwards," he said. "It was a roaring success thanks to you..."

Nye reacted with vacant gladness. The morphine dulled his senses. Also, the presence of approaching death loomed in the atmosphere. He was doubtlessly aware of his fate. He pretended not to care. "Is everybody celebrating already?" he asked. "Am I missing it?"

"No, you haven't missed a beat," said Frost, still acting cheerful. His eyes began to glisten with tears of pity. He choked them into submission. "The boys are all waiting for you."

"Do me a favor about those film tickets. Doyle is claiming my kills. You know. Sam Doyle from CIG. The fifth one was mine, not his," he rambled, thinking of the prizes promised at the beginning of their mission. "Rule in my favor this time, would you, boss? I haven't been to see a film in ages."

The tears escaped Frost this time. They swam in his eyes and started to leak out despite his rigid self-control. He remembered all the times he had been short-tempered and unnecessarily harsh towards his aide. He regretted it. He didn't know how to apologize. He stood frozen at attention, looking very composed with an optimistic half-smile and a confident demeanor. His tear-rimmed stare betrayed his mournful emotions.

Nye laughed. There was no life left in his laughter. "Don't look at me like that, Frosty," he chided. "Doesn't suit you at all. I'm fine. I'll be back up again tomorrow. Just watch."

The two men exchanged a knowing glance. Both of them knew the truth. However, Nye's denial was a classic remedy for pain in a world where death was a common blight and men were forced to face it regularly. Pretending was one way of being comforting. A man who pretended did not have to cower or admit the worst. Neither did his comrades. Pretending spared both parties from showing suffering or weakness.

Frost went along with the charade. "I'll have the tickets for you when you get back." His voice trembled slightly. "And work! Lots more work. I won't let you off easy, just because you've had a scrape."

Nye smirked in approval. He closed his eyes and felt calm. It was nice to pretend that he would see tomorrow and live as usual. "That's all right, sir," he said. "I can handle it."

The Major placed a reassuring hand on the man's arm and withdrew. "Please be assured of my prayers for your recovery," he said woodenly.

"Sure. Pray. But don't wait around here," answered Nye, sounding cynical and liberated at the same time. He attempted to seem lively. "Go on. Stir up more trouble, mate," he told Frost. "Tear 'em to pieces."

They mustered smiles. Frost performed a cavalier salute and walked away. They both knew they would never see each other again.

CHAPTER 25: VISIONS

"And o'er the hills, and far away
Beyond their utmost purple rim,
Beyond the night, across the day,
Through all the world she followed him."
—"The Day Dream" by Alfred Lord Tennyson

"Where is Major Frost?"

Eve arrived at the military depot at Ras el-Ahwa as the men returned from their mission. Sunset faded into the purple of nighttime. Stars started to sparkle in the dimming sky. Eve had received a message earlier from Frost, now officially her husband, that he expected to stay there for a few days. She refused to linger behind in Cairo alone. She hired a driver and came to join him. The small supply compound was the closest thing to a garrison in the area.

She ran across the dusty lot of the depot as the soldiers returned. Large military trucks rolled around. Dirty men carrying weapons sang and laughed. One soldier tried to halt her. "Miss, stop! You can't come through here—" She shoved her way past him.

She heard his voice. Snapping something. Sharp and lively. A curt laugh, then a command. That was her Frosty. In his element.

Following his voice, Eve came to a huge hybrid truck with giant tires. A caravan was attached to it. Heraldic British symbols were painted across the behemoth. Obviously, this was a commander's vehicle. Was it his?

Then she saw the "trophy." A stuffed burlap rice sack was mounted like a lollipop on the end of a broom handle. The stick-like dummy was fixed to the bonnet of the truck like a totem pole. Someone had drawn a comic face on it with a scratched-out eye and a bucktoothed mouth. A scribbled sign below read: "Wot? No petrol?"

Crowning the dummy's head was an emerald green turban with two long tails hanging from either side. A very familiar turban.

Eve stared at the effigy in gruesome wonder. Once she had seen that bright green cloth flying in the wind like a flag across the dune sea. It had been, at that time, an emblem of terror. Now the headscarf hung like the broken wings of a dead bat. The fear that had animated it was dead. Evidently so was its owner.

A crowd of men walked by and jeered at the turban. One of them playfully punched it; another batted the dummy head with a slap and laughed to see the turban tails swing through the air. The men frolicked with the prize like tomcats playing with the tail of a caught mouse.

"Oi, Spartacus!" someone called.

There was a boisterous giggle. Him again. Eve looked around and discerned he was near the back of the truck.

"There's a lady here to see you!" called the man again. News traveled fast.

He guffawed rowdily, thinking it a joke. "Oh, get out—"

Eve rushed around the back of the truck and saw the group of them. A motley band of British soldiers crowded around the caravan. They were bronze-skinned and covered in sweat. Their uniforms were dusty. Their caps and berets were crooked. They swaggered and toted guns. They looked like battle-hardened musketeers.

But one thing was bizarre about this soldierly scene. Each British trooper held a white china cup primly in one hand. All the men were sipping tea.

He was the spryest and jauntiest of them all. He was merrily disheveled. He looked as if he had wrestled with a tornado and won. His khaki shirt was unbuttoned past his breastbone. His sleeves were rolled up sloppily at uneven angles. He wore a pair of baggy shorts that were wrinkled beyond compare. His clothes were wet. His tan arms and legs were covered in mosquito bites. He sat on the back of the truck with one muddy boot propped up next to him, not looking very presentable. His blue beret was puffed up askew on top of his head like some tribal crown, its medal CIG pin gleaming defiantly in the sun. He swigged a cup of tea like a draught of whiskey. He was tired, sweaty, grimy, and content with himself. His short brown mustache was slightly overshadowed by stubble tingeing his face. Shadows and dust made his bronzed skin appear darker. He looked up suddenly at her with his piercingly clear blue eyes. Bright and sharp.

The young woman grinned at the sight of him. She was smitten by his dash and ruggedness. He was always handsome, but at this moment he excelled himself. This scene would live forever in her memory. He looked wild and warlike. A most attractive picture to her.

Major Frost was surprised to see his bride there. He had been raised in a world where soldiers' wives kept away from their husbands, especially on the job. Eve was a blessed change in his life, but the changes she brought would take some getting used to.

He jumped down from the truck and rushed to greet her. "Eve! What are you—"

She melted into his arms and kissed him passionately on the mouth before he could finish asking her what she was doing there. Frost enjoyed the greeting. However, the soldiers gathered around whistled and cheered. It embarrassed him. He quickly whisked her into the command caravan. Inside were stacked weapons, dust, and a narrow seating area. A dented white teapot sat on a metal shelf in the corner. The air was filled with the sweet bergamot fragrance of Earl Gray tea.

"My goodness, you know how to make an entrance!" laughed Frost, blushing. "Certainly caught me by surprise. I don't think they'll forget that one..."

"I told your office I was coming," she answered, sitting down.

"I only just got back," he replied, landing in the seat next to her. "Haven't gotten any messages all day. Field work." He flashed a lopsided smile. "I suppose you've seen it."

She looked up and saw his crisp blue eyes sparkling fiercely at her. He nudged her playfully with his elbow. "Well? Come on," he insisted, impatient for an answer.

"You mean that dummy outside?" Eve smiled. The effigy was grim but funny. "Is that really Ollie's head scarf, or is it just a joke?"

"No joke about it. My dear, it's true!" he said, his voice escalating with gusto. "Our friend Leafy has laid down the knife and fork."

The American failed to grasp his slang.

"He's dead!" announced Frost. "The blight of Ollie Bryon has been removed from the face of the earth!" He pointed to a mud-covered bayoneted rifle in the corner. "There's Excalibur," he remarked with irony. "The mighty weapon that slew the beast. Right over there."

To his surprise, Eve stepped over and peered at it. She was neither afraid nor squeamish. She inspected the weapon curiously with her eyes and noticed the dent of the bayonet blade. "He must've put up a tough fight!"

"No, not really," Frost negated quickly. "He didn't have much chance. It only looks that way because of how it went in. Sometimes the blades bend or get stuck. People have bones, you know. Not like sand bags. Most soldiers don't realize that at first. You get used to it."

He stopped, wondering if he had said too much. He trusted Eve enough to share his inmost thoughts and experiences with her, whether about matters of war or life in general. She was truly a kindred spirit, and they shared a deep understanding. But every once in awhile, his British upbringing haunted him with the notion that Eve was a "lady"—which meant, by definition, that she was too delicate to hear certain things. Now, for example, this fear bit him. One minute he was confiding in his beloved, the next he was agonizing over whether he had violated her feminine sensibilities. Blades and bones? He expected her to be horrified.

She was not. Her attitude was blasé. Approving, in fact. "Well, the rifle probably won't function anymore in battle since the blade is crooked," she said, direct and practical. "What will be done with it? Will they keep it or throw it away?"

"I'll donate it to my regiment. It's earned 'legend' value. Somebody ought to hang it up on a wall and do it some reverence. But not me," said Frost with a grim sigh.

"You mean this rifle is yours?" Eve looked at him in

confusion. "Wait a second. Who was the one who got Ollie?"

"I did!" declared Frost, slightly self-conscious.

The news astonished her. "What?" she gasped. "Why didn't you say so earlier?"

"Well, I'm saying it now," he replied with an uneasy laugh.

Eve was upset by the thought that he had been in immediate danger. "Are you all right?"

"Nothing that a bit of soap and water can't fix."

"How did it happen?"

"Well!" He sighed briskly and slapped his hands against his dusty knees. He paused and fidgeted restlessly. "We chased him into a soggy pond, ran him into a cave, and rat-trapped him in a moldy Greek swimming pool, more or less," he said lightly, trying to recount events in a facetious way. "I went in with everybody else. I ended up pretty close to where he was hiding, and, ah, ended up being the lucky one to stump him off the field," he said, using cricket slang to describe death as a batsman's dismissal.

The journalist was unsatisfied with his generalizations. "But how exactly did you get the chance to finish him off?"

Frost balked at the question. "Well, he popped out from hiding and I popped the bayonet in. That's all, really," he replied, and smiled at her. "Anyway, it's over."

Eve found his reticence surprising. Her warlike husband had an aggressive personality; he enjoyed fighting and usually enjoyed talking about it. Today was different.

She sat down next to him and wrapped her arms around him. She squeezed him tight. "I'm proud of you, Desmond," she told him gently. "I remember how awful it was when he had us trapped out there on the dunes. It seemed like nobody could catch him then. But you got him!" She pressed her face softly against his. "You did it! I'm so proud."

Her praise warmed his heart. Nevertheless, he was used deflecting compliments. He tried to joke. "Actually, you ought to be given credit."

"What?"

"Yes. I rushed the whole thing forward today just to see you again sooner." He smiled wryly. "I've been so impatient to be together again, darling. I looked at the whole mess and thought, 'I've had enough of this, Eve. Let's get it over with.' So I did. Trampled clean through!" He gave a satirical chuckle. "You motivated me. The opposition didn't quite stand a chance..."

They laughed.

"Come on. Let's go," he said, pulling her up with him.

"Where?"

"We need privacy." He held her hands. "How about a scenic drive to the Nile? I can find us someplace decent to stay." He smiled roguishly. "And hopefully someplace decent to clean up. I desperately want a shower."

Eve grinned seductively at him. "Make it a bath," she hinted in a flirtatious tone. "I'll join you."

Frost looked at her in mild astonishment. He had lived alone so long that he was unaccustomed to intimacy. Her spontaneous passion tended to surprise him.

"What's the matter?" She bit her lip suggestively. "Don't you want to?"

"Yes! I do want to." His eyes were still wide with surprise. "Of course."

They stayed in a hotel near Luxor. He drove her there. It was a long drive.

They listened to radio music and talked about all sorts of things that had nothing to do with the present circumstances.

Literature. Music. It turned out they liked works by the same authors and the same musicians—for all the same reasons they had never confided to anybody before. And then they had complimentary views on subjects of interest—she noticed things he didn't, and vice versa, in a way that pleased both of them. Like two lights meeting across the same surface. Their shared passion for military matters was refreshing to them—especially because they shared well-considered and similar opinions. She liked weapons and the gritty physical aspects of battle. So did he. Theory, of course, was a major point of mutual interest. They were familiar with much of the same war literature. He described, for example, the battle of Caesarea Philippi and his theory about how Roman commanders Brutus and Cassius, severely outnumbered, could have won it; she had already taken a similar view, but raised a few suggestions he had not considered in detail. Good ideas. They considered each other brilliant. He discussed some political headlines from Japan related to the current war situation; they ran into a crossroads there as well, as both of them were interested in Japanese military history. They somehow ended up talking about darts and throwing stars. She knew about some remarkable varieties; had a book on the subject. He had books too, but they were bit different. Wonderful stuff. And that wasn't even counting the artistic aspects. It turned out they both collected prints by the same painter. Delightful surprises. They were enchanted by each other.

Frost, despite being in good spirits, was exhausted by the time they arrived at their destination. He was also dirty and sore from fighting.

That said, Eve's plans for a romantic bath didn't quite go as she had intended. It wasn't for lack of adequate accommodations; Frost found an American-owned hotel and demanded a room with a large bathtub—"not an Egyptian wash-bin," he quipped. The tub and indeed the whole room turned out to be the largest he had ever seen, which he found very funny. The trouble was the condition he was in after his duel with the bandit captain.

He was running a slight fever due to inflamed mosquito bites. He was also quite sunburnt, which made him uncomfortable. Some other slight, but alarming afflictions, became apparent when he started to take his clothes off.

These were a few long, bloody fingernail scratches under his forearms. Apparently Ollie had clawed him while they wrestled in the pool. Frost, in the heat of the moment, did not notice it happen. Nor did he pay much attention to it, until now. The cuts weren't deep, but they were ugly. They also stung at the touch of water.

Eve spent most of the bath time rinsing dried mud out of his hair and helping him wash battle grime off. She did this lovingly, and Frost appreciated it. She asked him what exactly happened. She wanted to know the specific details of the fight. She was curious.

In response, Frost struggled in silence with words that wouldn't come out. He didn't say much of anything. However, he wished he could. He regarded Eve with conflict, like a mute who desired to speak.

"You're not upsetting me, darling," he reassured her warmly, in response to the concerned look on her face. "I'm just a bit tired, that's all."

He refused to answer further questions about the day's fight. She gave up.

Afterwards, they went to bed. Frost was amorous but felt under the weather. Eve was worried about him. She made sure he was settled in comfortably and brought him tea. They kissed and caressed each other for a long while.

"Now that we're officially married, maybe we should celebrate. I mean like a party. I know you don't like fusses," she continued, trying to lighten the atmosphere, "but maybe something small. We could invite some of your buddies. Like Nye—"

Frost stared blankly at the ceiling. A troubled frown darkened his brow. "I should have told you earlier. I meant to," he said soberly. "Lieutenant Nye died this afternoon."

"What?" she exclaimed in a loud, shrill tone. "How?"

"Ollie stabbed him with a tire lever," Frost answered bluntly. "Nothing could be done to help it. It was very unfortunate."

Tears formed in her eyes. Eve had not known Nye very well, but he was likeable enough and she deeply regretted his sudden demise.

"It wasn't so awful. I mean, he didn't die right on the spot," Frost added quickly, trying to find some bright facet to focus on in the darkness. "They patched him up a bit and gave him a pretty good dose of morphine. As far as I know, he was heavily sedated when he passed on. Didn't feel a thing. That's really not so bad, is it?"

She wept quietly.

Frost hugged her. "It's all right, my darling," he said gently, emanating calm strength. "Let it all out and then dry your eyes. It'll fade away."

Eve was surprised by his serenity of spirit. He was so composed. So imperturbable. It was incredible. There was a slight trace of pity in his blue eyes. Otherwise, he was peaceful. "You knew Nye better than I did," she observed. "Why aren't you...?"

Frost gave a cynical smile. "Oh, sniffling doesn't solve anything," he dismissed. "Anyway, if you believe in the afterlife—which I do—then we can be assured that Nye is now

swigging beer in heaven and having a blast. He loved the stuff."
He smirked with amusement, idly twirling Eve's hair. "Just think.
If Nye had been an ancient Egyptian, they'd have walled him
up with a pyramid of beer. And canopic jars of tobacco," he
imagined with dry humor. "Good gracious, that man chewed
like a locust! It was disgusting, really..."

His dry sense of humor, as always, made her laugh. But now
she felt almost guilty for laughing. At times like this, people
were supposed to grieve and lament—weren't they?

Not in Frost's book.

"They'd have chucked some gold spittoons in with him, and
some incense to cover up the tobacco fumes," he continued
deadpanning. "Good heavens, that stuff was poisonous!" He
grinned absurdly. "The sheer smell of it would've peeled the
frescos off the walls, and curled the gods' whiskers—"

She laughed with tears in her eyes. It was a strange
experience. He was the only person capable of moving her to
comical amusement at a time when she felt grief.

The British officer laughed with her. He was pleased with
the outcome of the conversation. He was no longer sad, and
she was no longer crying. He had fixed everything. He changed
the subject.

However, he was affected by Nye's death. It bothered him.
He made a comment about it a few hours later after alternate
spans of dozing and dallying with Eve.

"I will say one thing about poor Nye," he remarked grimly
out of the blue. "I find it an appalling offense against decency
that a veteran of combat against the Afrika Korps should be
snuffed out by a cockney scavenger wielding a broken tool,"
he said in cold disgust. "Don't you think it's backward? To me,
it is utterly stupid and disgraceful."

"But you got him," Eve said, thinking of the limp, green
turban hanging dismally from the totem pole. "You made the
louse pay for it."

"I did indeed." Frost closed his eyes and saw reflections of
bloodied waters in the darkness of his mind. "I can say that
Nye was avenged sevenfold."

Silence fell. A thick, heavy silence. He breathed slowly. She
felt his temperature rise. He was deliberating on something,
she knew. Thinking hard about something. Frost was a shrewd
and meticulous man. He was always thinking.

"I speared him like a fish," he suddenly announced, as if making a confession. He grabbed her hand and wrung it softly. "Gutted the sod. Plenty of times. I did a wonderful job. But it was very messy. I'd have preferred to just shoot him, but I couldn't, you see. He...tried to sneak up behind me. I heard him coming and put a quick end to it." He ran her fingers along the scratches on his arm. "That's the reason for these decorations. Don't worry," he added. "I heal quickly. They'll fade in about two weeks. They always do...I've had similar things happen before."

He said these things with no trace of shame or regret. He was callous and proud. But there was one thing he wondered about. It revealed itself in a question he asked, after a moment of self-conscious silence. "Does it...bother you?"

She folded him in her arms, touched her face to his, and thought he was perfection. She admired Frost in every way. Physically, mentally, emotionally...Only he had ever earned her total devotion and respect. She thought of telling him all those things, but in the end, she summed up all the jumbled words with a soft kiss. "I love you," she told him. "You're my fighter."

He wrapped her in his arms and melted away peacefully to her heartbeat. He drifted off to sleep with her stroking his face. She traced the lines and etches on his face with her fingers and loved him infinitely. He struggled with nightmares in the dark hours. Tension gripped him during sleep. He perspired with anxiety against invisible demons. His arm muscles tensed. She massaged his shoulders. It calmed him.

Frost was visited by a series of disturbing dreams. Bloody Greek statues in a treasure-filled swimming pool. Lieutenant Nye, swathed in hospital bandages, drinking tea outside a truck. The ghost of Ollie Bryon, pale and dripping with muddy water, asking for free film tickets. His sleep brought him little rest.

His subconscious mind knew danger was not gone. The tomb robbers were split in two groups, according to intelligence and reports. Another band of pillaging murderers remained at large.

Their second attempt at honeymooning ended somewhat abruptly the next day, although not quite as soon as that first morning at Shepheard's had.

He woke up early. Eve decided to perform a belly dancing routine she had practiced—"Esmeralda's debut," she jokingly called it. She had planned this. She put on her dancer's outfit—the one she wore when they had first met. It was a bright blue-purple bra covered with shimmering beads. The lower piece was a short, skirt-like hip wrap—a piece of vivid fuchsia linen that she tied around her hips. It barely covered her thighs. She donned a glittering ankle bracelet, too—just for fun. The young woman turned the Egyptian radio on, then shook and twirled around the room for his review. Frost's eyes grew as big as saucers, and he was delighted by what he saw. As a result, the performance came to a swift conclusion; Frost pounced on her and reeled her straight into bed. They made love. It was intense and lasted a long time. She fell sound asleep afterwards. It had been fairly recent since she had returned from her desert exile. Fatigue caught up with her.

Frost decided to prowl around for breakfast. He was an energetic man and never idle. In fact, he tended to be restless. He made himself a cup of tea and got dressed in civilian clothes. He was buttoning his shirt when the bedside phone rang. He clapped it casually to his ear, expecting to hear one of his military aides.

"Miss Eve Weathers?" said a muffled man's voice in English with a heavy French accent, giving Frost no time to utter a greeting. "I have a message for you. It's very important."

Frost spoke French fluently among a few other languages. He sensed something suspicious about the call. He decided to dare a ruse. "This is Miss Weathers' room, sir," he said in French, pretending to be hotel staff. "She stepped out for a moment. Could you give me the message?"

The caller hesitated. "Tell her this message is from Von Rindl." He repeated the name slowly. "Von Rindl. You hear?"

The Major's clear blue eyes widened in shock. "Yes, I understand," he said, after a second of electrified silence.

"He asks her to meet him at Deir el-Khadina tomorrow. The obelisk. At sunrise."

"Of course. I will tell Miss as soon as she returns," replied Frost, pouring more ooze on his French for authenticity. "Bye bye."

He hung up the phone with a rattling slam and rummaged through his uniform pockets. He ripped out the map Eve had given him in Cairo. The one that Von Rindl wanted to smuggle to the British Army. Frost had suspected it for a trap. He held firmly to that suspicion. Now armed with another fraction of Von Rindl's master plan, he intended to decipher exactly what type of trap it could be.

He decompressed the crinkled map in the sunlight on a writing table near the window. Colors, cars, and people blurred like runny ink outside; ancient and new buildings melted like wax against the awakening blue sky.

He sat at the desk and studied the map with fiendish determination. Immediately he recognized a pattern in the red circles and marks. Also, he recognized a fatal error—informing him that map, true to his suspicions, was false.

An amateur officer unfamiliar with the intricacies of Egyptian geography would have been fooled. However, Frost was more experienced. He had been stationed in Egypt previously during his career. He happened to recognize a very obscure set of map coordinates from personal experience. A certain patch of land in the middle of nowhere was the site of a Bedouin well—the British military had reluctantly gotten involved in settling a violent tribal dispute there in the 1930s. Frost had been part of the peacekeeping effort. He was not very peaceful and neither were the tribesmen. Because all negotiating parties were warlike, they understood each other, and the conflict was actually resolved. Frost would never forget the location of that stupidly important well. He and several other soldiers got lost trying to find it. They spent days sitting next to camels and feeling inclined to spit out of sullen anger. The coordinates had been burned into his brain. That pinpoint on latitude and longitude marked one of hell's many entrances, Frost had joked.

Now Von Rindl had labeled that same spot as the site of an ancient ruin. Frost knew this to be false. There was absolutely nothing in that area; no civilization, ancient or modern, whatsoever. Quite simply put, there was nothing there for robbers to raid. However, a person who had never been to that strange neck of the desert would not have noticed the lie.

He turned the map around several times, drew boxes around a few areas with a blue pen. Yes, there it was. A pattern. Von Rindl was trying to draw his attention to one particular region. It was obvious. But why? Probably to distract him from something else?

Now, he contrasted the distraction to the city of Deir el-Khadina in Lower Egypt west of the Nile. The city was in the opposite direction of where Von Rindl wanted the British to look. Why?

The Major realized it. The truth. It wasn't so hard for Frost's superior brain to figure out. He was intensely annoyed at Von Rindl. At the same time, he felt exhilarated by the prospect of netting his long-desired prey.

He clenched his teeth fiercely and growled to himself. "Now I've got you, you scab..."

He crushed the map into a wad again and rushed around the room. He tore his civilian shirt off and seized his uniform in a frenzy.

Eve was buried lazily under the sheets. She looked like a long, curvy log under the covers.

"Wake up, my pretty!" Frost, dressed in a fresh clean uniform, plopped down next to her and ruffled her red hair aggressively with his hand. "Good morning, Mrs. Frost! Look lively!" he blared at her. She was comatose. He bounced on the mattress to get her attention, then swatted her sharply on the rear end.

She shrieked and rolled over. "Desmond! What are you—"

"Up!" he barked, grinning. "Now!"

He bounced off the mattress and marched briskly around the room. Eve rolled flat on her back and stared blearily at the ceiling. She realized for the umpteenth time that her husband was an army officer.

"Come on, chop chop!" He rummaged through her belongings and hurled a pile of clothes at her. "Put these on."

She noticed his bright, ferocious grin. "You're in rare form," she remarked dryly. "What did you eat for breakfast?"

He laughed merrily. "You mean aside from honey whispers and gypsy kisses?" He sparkled with confidence. "Nothing but tea, so far." He threw his civilian clothes into a wild pile. "No civvies today! I've got a little bit of work to do. Come along!"

"What's going on?" she demanded. "What are you up to?"

Frost smiled at her, brimming with fierce focus. "You'll see!"

CHAPTER 26: THE DUEL

"Conquest, unbought by blood or harm,
That needs nor foreign aid nor arm,
A triumph all thine own."
—"The Field of Waterloo" by Sir Walter Scott

There was a small barren field of rocks with a few buildings and huts on it in the desert far west of the Lower Nile. This marvel of nothingness was called Deir el-Khadina. Its name sounded deceptively pretty. There was nothing pretty about the place. It was an eyesore—and many of the people who lived there had sores, too, due to lack of hygiene. The municipality—even if could even be called such—was slightly off the beaten path near the coastal highways connecting Cairo with Alexandria and other Western Desert cities. The majority of the residents were either relatives of desert herdsmen or transport dealers who earned a living trucking and selling things along the coastal roads.

The ruin of an ancient city lay scattered around the area. It had once been a city of craftsmen. Deir el-Khadina was located halfway between everywhere and nowhere, which once made it a convenient place for stone-cutters, weavers, cat-jewelry-makers, and tomb artists to settle. Archaeologists reveled in the shredded workmen's artifacts that frequently turned up under dust heaps and chalky gravel in the area. Nobody else cared much about the place. There were no temples in Deir el-Khadina. No mystique.

The only "attraction" it could boast of was a lonely old obelisk standing at the very border where hardly-inhabited nowhere evaporated into nowhere. Blue sky touched white earth. The obelisk was black. It caught the eye in a place where everything was blindingly pale.

A British explorer had once named it—creatively—the "Black Obelisk." The name was a winner; it stuck. The mighty Black Obelisk was supposed by the ancients to wield religious power. Its square, geometric tip—carved by human hands with myopic precision—was supposed to draw down power from heaven. What sort of power that was, nobody quite knew.

Some people guessed it was meant to inspire the ancient craftsmen. In an empty place like Deir el-Khadina, an artist likely needed inspiration.

The image of a serpent-headed god decorated the obelisk. The carved figure had the body of a man and the small, round head of a cobra. As a result, the manly character did not look very impressive. However, his bizarre appearance attracted attention. Scholars argued that the snake-man, called Thimket, was supposed to protect the ancient craftsmen from snakebites. Sometimes Thimket and his obelisk lured tourists to Deir el-Khadina. Most of them regretted the trip in the end. It was an awfully long journey, and by the time they arrived, they realized they had bitterly exhausted themselves to see a pointy black rock. Its reptilian man fresco was a poor consolation for wasted effort.

This desolate backwater had unexpectedly become the scene of a standoff. Two men from clashing armies with fiercely different goals opposed each other. Only one would win.

Major Desmond Frost and a small entourage of soldiers arrived at the outskirts of Deir el-Khadina the night before their target, German Captain Elrich Von Rindl, was supposed to appear. They slipped into the area quietly. Their small herd of jeeps and trucks adopted the disguise of as a supply transport column. Canvas tents, they were supposed to be hauling. Behind flimsy facades of canvas piled in the back of two trucks, armed men clutched rifles and prepared to go "German-hunting," as Frost dubbed it. The entire area around Deir el-Khadina had already been encircled by other British forces that Frost had already liaised with via radio.

Frost left some staff officers and his wife Eve in a larger city off the coastal highway called Terna. It was a miniature Alexandria. Placing Eve there allowed him to have her nearby and out of harm's way at the same time. The American journalist had asked curious questions all day, and had been given no answers. She was worried and frustrated.

After successfully infiltrating Deir el-Khadina, he made a phantom-like reappearance during the night to visit her. It was at that point that he decided to disclose what was going on.

"All right. I'll tell you," he announced to her over a measly dinner in a dingy Greek restaurant. He had resigned himself to eating gyros. He disliked it, but there weren't many choices, and he needed to eat. He hoped to catch a few hours rest before his planned morning strike. "This morning, I intercepted a call intended for you," he continued. "It was Von Rindl."

Eve stopped drinking her tea. She stared at him in somber surprise and set the cup down slowly. She waited for him to speak.

"Or a messenger, rather. I suppose in lieu of an address you told him to contact you at Shepheards,' and your trail got picked up by someone from there," Frost surmised coolly. "That's the only explanation. I'm not sure why they didn't mind me—surely somebody must've seen us together—but it doesn't matter. The bottom line is, some Axis agent contacted you with a message instructing you to meet Von Rindl in this neighborhood tomorrow morning." He paused and took a self-satisfied drink of bottled mineral water. "I'm here to bag him."

"How do you know the phone call wasn't a trap?" Eve demanded in apprehension. "It could've been a lie. What if Nazi spies wanted to lure you out here for some reason—"

He smirked. "No. Somebody's in for a surprise, but it's not me," he asserted. "A bit of news recently. A mysterious German soldier cascaded into one of our supply columns east of here. He passed himself off as a Pole, lifted a truck from a filling station, and made quite a show of daredevil driving trying to get away. He did get away," Frost continued. "He dodged into an oasis and hasn't been seen since." His eyes shone with amusement as he looked at her. "Who do you suppose that is?"

"I don't know why he'd contact me," Eve muttered, agitated and confused. "It's not like I'm some well-connected powerhouse. I'm an unemployed American journalist! I've got a typewriter and barely two suitcases to my name. My only priceless possessions are military books. I've left a trail of wreckage behind me wherever I go. My bosses hate me, the Egyptian government hates me..."

He flashed a crooked grin at her over his drink. "Join the club!" he interjected, and winked approvingly at her. "Did you know our life stories are exactly the same?"

She stifled a smile. "What honestly does Von Rindl expect

me to do?" she questioned, feeling indignant. "Grab a magic carpet and sail him away to Tunisia? Anyway, why would I?"

Frost grinned with appreciation at her sarcasm. "He's desperate, obviously," he retorted. "The man is stranded a foot too deep in enemy waters. Can't last very long here. Too many 'Tommies' swimming around." He took another bite of his gyro sandwich. The food suddenly tasted better.

She saw him become more animated as he ate in silence. He devoured the sandwich with fierce relish as if savoring barbecue. He looked ferocious and happy. She could guess what he was thinking.

"What are you going to do with him?"

"Depends," he said with a blazing stare.

"Nothing good, apparently."

The remark struck his funny bone. "Ha!" He laughed with gusto. "We'll see what happens tomorrow. He's had everybody running around in circles. We'll see if I have some better luck chasing him." He took her hand across the table and kissed it emphatically. "Just watch me!"

"I know you will," she answered. "Just one thing, Desmond."

"What?"

"Try to be merciful, if you can...I know we've both got every reason to be angry at him, but I still don't think he's a bad person," she said with due caution, unsure how Frost would react. "Besides, he is on an important mission. He's trying to get rid of that horrible murderer. That man called Eislinger..."

"You're very naïve. You've got a rosy view of humanity for a journalist. It's no criticism—it's a fact. Don't worry. Stay with me long enough and you'll lose your vestal innocence very quickly," he remarked, sympathetic and cynical. He twirled her hand gently in his. "For your information, the map that Von Rindl passed to you supposedly showing the locations of 'tomb robberies' was phony. It was misinformation, as I expected."

"It's not as if I didn't consider that a possibility," she argued, defending her decision. "I never trusted Von Rindl. I was just willing to take a risk, that's all.'

"No. You gambled on his good-heartedness. That's what got you," Frost corrected. His eyes narrowed with determination. "I won't make the same mistake."

A gunshot cracked, echoing through empty atmosphere.

Dawn rose over Deir el-Khadina with tangerine mist in the sky and a snap of cold air. Light breathed slowly over the barren land.

Elrich von Rindl glanced around in alarm. He heard the shot. However, nothing was visible in the immediate area. He stood a short distance from the Black Obelisk, wearing his wool overcoat, military rucksack and civilian clothes. He had little expectation that Eve Weathers would appear. It was only a gamble. He considered Eve a fellow German. He had confidence in her translating abilities and her willingness to assist him. He hoped she would be willing to ferry him back into the Western Desert to regroup with comrades and resume his mission.

"Away!" an Egyptian man's voice screamed in English.

Von Rindl instinctively reached for his pistol. Expressions of panic distorted the faces of his Egyptian helpers who suddenly appeared and disappeared from hidden places in the barrenness around him. "Away, away!"

Obviously something had gone wrong. Von Rindl knew there was only one answer. The enemy was coming.

A symphony of men, jeeps and trucks materialized everywhere with precision. Von Rindl turned and fled just as they started to arrive. The Egyptians managed to warn Von Rindl mere moments before the ambush struck, giving him a sliver of time to escape.

The German officer made a mad dash towards some crumbling stone walls scattered behind the Black Obelisk. This was a serious problem. He had little cover and no transport. Von Rindl was naturally daring. He wanted to escape. He intended not to give up.

One of the Egyptians tried to stall for him. The man rushed out of hiding, apparently from nowhere, gripping a rifle. This man had been peppering the British with shots from concealed places as they closed in to ambush. Now he emerged into the open, yelling at the British and brandishing his weapon at them.

Soldiers aimed guns at him. The civilian dropped his rifle and surrendered.

"Weapons down! Hold fire!" a loud, sharp male voice screamed suddenly. "No civilians! We don't want a riot. Hear that, boys? Hands off the Egyptians!"

Von Rindl dove behind a broken wall and flattened himself from view. He peeked through the stones and saw the person shouting. His eyes zeroed in. A familiar figure sprung out of a jeep. He stood out from all the others, with their neat and homely looks. He was shorter and tougher-looking. Lean, with jaunty mannerisms. He wore shorts, a rumpled shirt and a dark blue beret with a strange silver symbol on it. He had a hard, sharp face and a steely look. He possessed a dangerous swagger.

"Rusty?" Von Rindl wondered aloud in complete confusion and dismay. "How on earth did he get here?"

The British officer suddenly looked in his direction. Von Rindl watched as the Major snatched a loudspeaker from a soldier nearby and chanted a familiar tune across the distance.

> *"There's no Yellow Rose in Texas,*
> *That matters much to me.*
> *Only a certain Jerry,*
> *I happen now to see.*
>
> *He tried to lose me in the blue,*
> *To see how far he'd get.*
> *I do assure him now I'm back,*
> *He'll wish we'd never met!*
>
> *Von Rindl or Van Winkle,*
> *I care nothing all.*
> *Time to sweat and say some prayers!*
> *You're going to take a fall!"*

The men burst into laughter.

"He's over there," said Frost casually, pointing at a scrap of gray barely visible behind a pile of rocks. "Catch him, if you can. If not, fire away."

They advanced from all directions with lowered rifles, taunting their captive.

"Come out, pretty Polly!"

"Reach for the *Luft!*"

Von Rindl concentrated with desperate energy. He realized he was surrounded. His only option was to do something borderline insane.

An interpreter took the loudspeaker from Frost. "Surrender or die!" came a German command.

Major Frost squinted through binoculars as the renegade German soldier darted out sideways from behind the rock pile and wove a frantic zigzag path through the ruins. Someone took a shot. He ducked.

Then, to everyone's complete amazement, Von Rindl sprang up again, changed directions, and flung himself straight into a British jeep with lightning speed and suicidal abandon. The jeep was empty; the men had gotten out of it in order to capture him. It roared to life. He sped in a flash towards the open dunes.

They chased. Von Rindl found himself encircled and trapped in a steadily shrinking bubble. He was also being pursued from behind at the same time. He needed to break out.

Von Rindl, with his West African frontier expertise, deliberately drove over powdery sand piles and gravel beds to spit dust and rocks up at his pursuers. The dust fogged everything. Rock sprays hit men and cracked windscreens. He reversed the wheels back and forth, drove in circles, and fishtailed the jeep. Some of his pursuers crashed into each other. He jerked his goggles over his eyes, mastering the gears and the steering wheel. Machines bent like clay in his grip.

Clouds of chaos parted in front of him like the Biblical waters of the Red Sea. He smiled. He was barreling straight out from under their noses. Footloose and home free.

But somebody had other plans.

A ghostly figure appeared drifting toward him in dust blizzard ahead. Von Rindl hadn't seen it coming. He locked sight on a blurry figure wearing a dark cap, half-standing half-kneeling on the prow of a jeep, with tan arms braced expertly around a long rifle. Two shots cracked. They blew up each of Von Rindl's front tires.

He braked and turned. His jeep spun in circles and tipped over.

The next thing he knew, the shooter was casting a long, angular shadow over him. The dark cap was a beret and its wearer was Major Frost. He was covered in dust, looking very raffish with his rifle slung comfortably under one arm. He grinned with exhilaration.

"Hello!" He laughed wildly. "Where did you think you were going, Captain?"

Von Rindl sighed in aggravation. He shook his arms and legs, feeling for broken bones. So far he remained in one piece. He had landed unceremoniously on a large pile of dusty camel dung. The tribesman had raked it there, along with about five other piles—camel manure made good fertilizer for dry farming irrigation projects. The tall powdery pile had saved him from injury. Nevertheless, this was a humiliating capture. The German officer looked up at his vanquisher with a withering expression.

"Thank you for a very exciting morning. It was a good run. Lots of fun!" said Frost, still laughing. He stepped forward and offered his hand to the fallen German. "Come on, up with you."

Von Rindl stared at his enemy's outstretched arm with a sour expression.

Frost snickered. "Sore loser, eh?"

Von Rindl gingerly accepted the gesture. He stood and tried to compose himself. "You're making a mistake!" he intoned. "It would be more to your advantage if I escaped. Eislinger is a menace that has gotten worse. He's in your backyard right now, but you're doing nothing and I don't have the resources to continue this goose-chase..."

An interpreter appeared.

"What's he saying?" asked Frost. He listened. "Oh. Eislinger again. If you were so busy chasing after him, why waste time driving all the way out here?" He leered. "Not trying to start a rebellion on the Nile, are we?"

Von Rindl lost his temper. It rarely happened to the calm German ranger. But Major Frost had a special talent for zapping his patience. "Absolutely not!" he snapped. "I ended up here only because I got lost after I ran out of petrol—"

Frost burst into mischievous laughter before the interpreter had finished. "Egypt's greatest curse!" he quipped. "Leaky petrol."

The German's face flushed. He did not think any of it was funny. "The Panzerarmee is running out of supplies. I had to divert course from my mission to meet with reinforcements," he admitted. "I came this way by accident."

"And that little map you sent us? With your nice little scribbles on it?" Frost challenged. "What was that about?"

Von Rindl set his jaw firmly and was silent.

"You can't fool me, scrap. I've been around longer than you have, know Egypt a sight better," said Frost. He handed his rifle to an aide and paced grandly with his hands in the pockets of his shorts. "I'm sorry to break this to you, but I'm something of a barbarian," he said airily. "I've spent more than half my life in weird tropical places. I was slogging around the Sahara while you were skipping around the Alps in lederhosen." He sneered. "Granted, you have some experience in West Africa, but really..." He shook his head condescendingly. "We British soldiers are a rare breed. Especially colonial ruffians like me. That's why you'll never beat us."

"That remains to be seen!" riposted Von Rindl, brimming with nerve.

"Your map was topographically incorrect. You placed a temple on some coordinates that I am familiar with. No temples there, just an old well. Caught you out, didn't I?"

"The map was not entirely inaccurate," protested Von Rindl, objecting to accusations of dishonesty. "It did contain a record of where the tomb robberies have been occurring. I only created a few extra 'embellishments' on it for the British Army's benefit." It was a polite way of saying he had added false specks on it to augment true ones.

Frost wheeled on the German with a determined stare, scanning the depths of his eyes. "You wanted us to look south—distinctly away from the Suwan Salt Marsh area," he accused. "Why? Hiding something?"

Von Rindl was surprised by the Major's powers of calculation. He considered silence was pointless and decided to make a disclosure.

"The Suwan Salt Marsh is where the bandits have their largest base. Our intelligence service found out about it through aerial pictures a short time ago," confessed Von Rindl. "After I lost Eislinger's trail, I was sure he and the others would regroup there. But I couldn't get to it without trouble—there are British troops around that area." He crossed his arms neatly. "I hoped you would move men out of my way, so I could go in and take Eislinger. No such thing happened. Anyway, it doesn't matter anymore. Things changed. I ran out of petrol and got lost here..."

Frost regarded him in remote disgust. "If you really wanted to get rid of Eislinger so badly, why didn't your aerial 'service' drop a bomb on him and put the whole matter to rest?" he exclaimed indignantly. "You don't have any problem bombing anybody you don't like. Just ask Malta. We won't mention England. That's too obvious!"

The interpreter struggled to translate his sarcasm.

"Oh, I know. It's not your fault," dismissed Frost in casual disdain, interrupting the interpreter. "You're just a spring in a giant German mattress. You can't help but stretch when somebody in a brown uniform sits on you—"

Von Rindl shot him a seething cold stare. He was outraged by the man's disrespect. "It would serve you right if you failed to kill Eislinger," he snapped harshly. "Then Eislinger can be the one to start a 'Nile rebellion' and pitchfork you 'fine English colonials' all out of Egypt. If he wanted to redeem himself in the eyes of the Reich, that would be exactly what he would do. And, as you may have noticed," he continued, raising his nose haughtily in the air, "the peasants here would be only too willing to help him!" He turned to the interpreter with an efficient jerk. "I have nothing more to say. I'm ready to be taken away now!"

Frost arched his eyebrows. "Nope. Leave him standing here an hour," he ordered. He smiled frigidly. "You'll notice that I am in command here, Captain," he said, drawing attention to his superiority in rank.

Von Rindl heard from the interpreter what was going on. He glowered.

"That's right. You will stand here and enjoy the glory of the Black Obelisk, as my guest," the Major stated, casting a dry glance over his shoulder at a small black pillar in the distance. "I think it looks rather better from far away."

The German rolled his eyes. He sat down next to the dung heap with an irritated sigh.

"Who told you to sit?" demanded Frost. "Stand up, soldier!"

Von Rindl obeyed grudgingly. "I'm not career soldier," he grumbled. "I'm a professor of aeronautical mechanical science!" He huffed and brushed camel dung powder angrily off his uniform with swift, neat swipes. "All this trouble happened just because I grew up in Africa. I just happen to be good with cars and rifles, that's how I got into this mess. I should not have agreed to come back to Africa. I should not have volunteered for military service. I should not have passed the Army exams. I should have just pretended to be blind or deaf or—"

Frost sneered in triumph. He turned to the interpreter. "*Nicht*. I keep hearing that word," he remarked. "It's pejorative, isn't it? What does it mean?"

"No, sir. It basically means 'not,'" the interpreter quickly replied. "It can describe what can be done and what should not be done. What is and what is not."

"Oh. A word for orders and permission. Just the kind of word I like to know!" Frost swiveled to face his prisoner, looking masterful and pleased with himself. "If you think grumbling will solve your trouble, the answer, my good man, is most certainly *nicht*," he addressed Von Rindl. He turned to the interpreter. "Or *Nein*. Which is it?"

Von Rindl glared. His eyes pierced Frost like indignant beams of ice. He saw the smirk on the British officer's face and realized the man enjoyed taunting him. He decided to play another trick. "You're a ruthless guy, Major Rusty," he said, "but that's all right. I forgive you!"

Frost bristled with indignation. "You what?"

The German gave an angelic smile. "Yes. I will be merciful and regard you with forgiveness and compassion. That is the only way to bring peace into the world," he declared, with a tiny hint of understated sarcasm. "As a gesture of my goodwill, I will tell you something..."

"Oh, please—"

"The 'ghost dagger' you are after. Eislinger has it," Von Rindl announced, with a sly twinkle in his eye. "And what's more. He has been joined by Afrika Korps deserters. Now English and German bandits are working together. Isn't that so interesting?"

He studied the British man's reaction. The Major was stoic, but his eyes gleamed with interest. Obviously, he was interested in the killers' location and possible plans.

"I don't know for sure, but I bet they are hiding around the Suwan Salt Marsh," Von Rindl added with a knowing smirk.

"Maybe we just ought to carpet bomb the marsh, then," Frost remarked. "Get the whole thing shelved."

"If you like fireworks, certainly!" Von Rindl laughed in contempt, growing more confident and commanding. He grinned boyishly. "Go ahead. Blow it all up! But then you might miss Eislinger. That guy has a roach's gift for survival—can slip out of any crack." His eyes danced with clever amusement. "That's OK. Maybe you don't mind another German sneaking behind the Nile!"

Frost looked at Von Rindl and decided he was one of the craftiest individuals he had ever come across. The man looked so rugged and honest, yet had such gifts for intrigue and manipulation. Sensing another ploy, he made no reply to Von Rindl's remarks. He marched off without sparing the German another look.

"Keep him standing here an hour," he aloofly told one of the soldiers. "No chitchat and no sitting breaks. Just give him some water and a sandwich or something."

Von Rindl smiled. *Just wait, Rusty,* he thought with iron determination. *You have not gotten the best of me yet.*

CHAPTER 27: INFERNO

Adriana: "Where is thy master, Dromio? Is he well?"
Dromio of Syracuse: "No, he's in Tartar limbo, worse than hell."

—"The Comedy of Errors" by
William Shakespeare, Act II, Scene I

Death hung in the air like fog over the Suwan Salt Marsh. The area was one of the driest and bitterest stretches of the Egyptian desert. In ancient times it had been a marshland fed by a saltwater canal from the sea. The land had shifted over hundreds of years. The canal had evaporated. All moisture had dried to nothing. The only thing that remained was salt. So much salt that it poisoned the sand. No living thing could grow or live here—not even the smallest weed or the tiniest mouse. The salt caked and corroded everything it touched. It made light flash a thousand times brighter. It made the sun burn a thousand times hotter. Everything about the marsh induced the five human senses to a state of sheer agony. It was an excruciating abyss of scalding white.

Some human beings managed to survive in the marsh. These unnatural people were demons who chose to live in a burning desert hell. They hated it as much as anyone else—perhaps more than others who enjoyed normal lives. These angry wraiths chose to exile themselves from other humans. Their malice drove them to hiding places where they could conceal their dark deeds.

They had built a city of metal and sandbags. There were rooms made out of broken vehicles. There were supply dumps; troves of gasoline, oil, water, ammunition, weapons, food, clothing, and plundered treasures. There was nothing really organized about this work of dark human ingenuity. It was the creation of lazy men whose only priorities were their immediate needs. This "settlement" had been created at the instigation of the robbers' leader, Flag, once a British commando known as Ollie Bryon.

Now it was under the control of Afrika Korps exile Siegwulf Eislinger, a protégé who ruthlessly usurped Flag's authority.

The place was completely filthy. Death thickened the atmosphere. Several robbers had shot each other dead in minor arguments here. Their bleached bones rotted in the open air outside the camp. In their company was another ragged skeleton—once, she had been a civilian woman. An Italian settler living on a farm in Libya. She had been a middle-aged mother with several children. Her life ended when Ollie and his crew ransacked her home and kidnapped her. She was taken hundreds of miles away to the Suwan Salt Marsh and was forced to perform menial duties on behalf of the robbers. Ollie had used her as his personal sex slave for several days before he tired of her weeping and shot her dead. She was one of many similar victims whose stories would never be discovered.

In an ironic touch of fate, Ollie was also killed in a void of silence and his death remained unknown to his former crew. They presumed he was still alive somewhere. They guessed he would seek vengeance.

Eislinger was prepared for it. He ordered all the robber crews to remain in the salt marsh and brace themselves for a siege. The raiders were used to constant motion. Remaining in one place for a long time brought out the worst in every one of them.

The bookish young German looked different from the unassuming lad Ollie had "rescued" from a raid site. He was missing part of his ear. His skin was scorched thoroughly brown and red from constant exposure to burning sun. He continued to wear a flat British helmet with a bullet hole in it; it was now decorated with several belt buckles taken from men he killed. It was also painted with a blood-red Nazi swastika on the side. Eislinger wore a new pair of horn-rimmed glasses. He still had the face and manners of a librarian. However, the sickness that possessed him was visible in his eyes and the set of his features. His face had morbid creases. His eyes were blue, but they looked like chips of black ice.

Eislinger was no longer a popular man. His veneer of politeness and courtesy had fallen off like a paper mask. His real face showed now. It was an ugly one.

He was cruel, which his followers approved of and enjoyed. However, he was also controlling and petty. His sadism vented itself on fellow thieves in random bursts. He was bloated with conceit and had a massive sense of self-importance. He pampered himself, stealing creature comforts from others and throwing desperate fits over the slightest injuries. He was sneaky and underhanded. He took revenge on men he disagreed with by killing them in their sleep—usually using his flint dagger, formerly a prize possession of Ollie. The dagger was now a symbol of Eislinger's bloody reign of terror.

The tomb robbers had become a mixed camp. Eislinger had won over a number of German deserters from the Afrika Korps. These desperados, stranded in the dunes, were willing to rob and maim for profit; they disliked Eislinger but viewed him as "in charge" and obeyed his orders. The British raiders he had inherited from Ollie were not as easy for him to control. They spoke a different language and had a more autonomous way of thinking; Ollie had given them some degree of "voting rights," established norms for splitting plunder and allowed certain bands to hunt freely like wolves in a pack.

Eislinger, by contrast, was a total control maniac. Nothing happened without his permission. He disagreed with everyone's opinions. The only views he valued were ones he claimed to think of. He snooped on everyone; he had spies and informants. He punished and killed crewmembers for random petty acts or "disobedience," as he called it. He assigned men to menial camp "duties" and threw tantrums if these were not completed to his liking—which they never were, since he always found something to criticize. He was haughty, oversensitive and implacable.

An atmosphere of murder and malcontent sizzled the air. Everybody waited for Ollie to materialize. Nothing happened. In the meantime, supplies grew thinner. Fuel stockpiles began to grow short as Eislinger dispatched men in and out of the marsh to sell and trade their plunder. Some of the men did not return—they stole the jeeps and simply disappeared into the cities to squander money, never to reappear. Others were afraid to abscond and came back. Eislinger was a lazy and impulsive leader. He seemed to think supplies could easily be gotten anywhere. He made no attempt to conserve resources. The caches began to look leaner.

Occasionally, Eislinger took some of his crews to massacre random people. They did not have much luck finding victims. However, they did butcher some traders along the desert highway. Eislinger distinguished himself by his sheer cruelty and lack of interest in material goods. When he became bored, he victimized crewmembers. He killed several robbers to amuse himself. Many men simply watched. Some participated out of malice. Others spinelessly joined in to be part of "the pack" and save themselves from criticism.

Eislinger was feared and hated.

The Germans patiently endured Eislinger's despotism and bared their teeth behind his back. Some of them plotted. These plotters were duly ratted out by informants and killed. Other plotters carefully hid their claws and waited for the right moment to strike.

The British robbers were in a completely different situation. Many of them were all-out brutalized and decimated by Eislinger and his cronies for noncompliance with his "new procedures." The survivors unanimously decided to get rid of him. In fact, they were determined to get rid of all the Germans if they could help it, since they could not tell which ones were Eislinger's spies and which were not. They started stockpiling a secret stash of weapons, water, and money to use for their big break-away. Their top priority was to kill Eislinger; they were convinced that wiping him out would solve everything. However, killing Eislinger was a bit more complicated than they expected. He was always surrounded by guards, who would mulishly defend his life because they were too afraid of him not to. He always randomly stole others' food to eat, so poison wasn't an option. Murdering him in his sleep was an optimum idea, but unfortunately impossible—Eislinger wandered at night and nobody exactly knew where, when or if he slept at all. His bizarre habits and sadistic violence had everyone, British and German alike, terrified and on edge.

The flint dagger Eislinger carried steepened the terror. The dagger seemed to have a life of its own, such as it had never manifested before when Ollie wielded it. Gusts of sand burst around Eislinger randomly. Things flew through the air and crashed. Objects broke. All of these phenomena happened in front of many men's naked eyes. At times, the entire camp was drowned in a sickening perfume smell, like scented oil and damp reeds. An unintelligible male voice spoke sometimes out of nowhere; at times, this voice even interrupted Eislinger when he was speaking. These events, clearly supernatural, were nothing less than hair-raising. Some of the men attributed these occurrences to Eislinger; others attributed them to the dagger. In any case, the sinister ghostly presence around Eislinger discouraged rabid crewmen from attacking him.

Things went on this way for some while. It seemed like eternity in the blistering white salt marsh where the landscape remained the same and nobody bothered to tell time. Paranoia skyrocketed. Men became more and more murderously desperate.

The breaking point came when Eislinger announced a new mission. He claimed their group was now a paramilitary unit called "*Kommandotruppe Kobra*," and would serve the interests of the Third Reich. He claimed to have established contact with Nazi government agents. All the robbers thought he was delusional; he was known for having strange fantasies. Nevertheless they listened to his "official announcement." Eislinger declared the first objective of their new "military force" was to attack Cairo.

That was the last straw. All the robbers in Eislinger's group had deserted the armies of their countries. They thrived on pleasure and laziness. They murdered for fun, and robbed the dead and the defenseless. They lived for cheap gain and profit. The idea of leading a reckless charge on the Nile—heavily garrisoned by British troops—for the abstract goals of a war they cared nothing for was like asking them to sign their own death warrants. They roiled with resentment. Everyone realized the charade was over; Eislinger had taken away their reason for living, so death at his hands didn't matter so much. They had no reason to cower anymore.

Surprisingly, a seemingly loyal German instrumented Eislinger's downfall. One of his guards. A man who smiled, kowtowed and catered to all Eislinger's maniacal whims with horrible efficiency. This man waited to strike at a strange moment. Later that night, Eislinger demanded water to wash his hands—he enjoyed wasting waster and splashing it all over himself in front of everybody. His loyal servant brought him the water and waited until Eislinger got his hands wet and slippery. Then the calm man whipped a hidden metal pipe from his sleeve and went wild with rage. He tried to bludgeon Eislinger to death.

Eislinger escaped within an inch of his life. He had a hard time fighting back with slippery wet hands. He barely managed to fatally stab his attacker using his ancient flint dagger. He sustained many blunt force injuries from the beating. He fled from the camp on foot, chased by a mob of vicious, vengeful men armed with firearms and knives. The sound of gunshots echoed across the pitch-dark, salty inferno.

They looked everywhere for him. Gasoline levels plummeted dangerously low, forcing them to abandon their jeeps and search on foot. They were determined to find Eislinger and torture him for revenge—especially the British robbers, who took charge of this effort with furious gusto. They felt liberated. They planned to rejoin Ollie and live in wanton prosperity as before.

Unbeknownst to them, however, Ollie was dead. And Eislinger, mysteriously, was nowhere to be found.

CHAPTER 28: DEADLY ANGEL

"O this false soul of Egypt! This grave charm,
Whose eye beck'd forth my wars, and call'd them
home,
Whose bosom was my crownet, my chief end,
Like a right gipsy, hath...beguiled me to the very heart
of loss."

—"Antony and Cleopatra" by
William Shakespeare, Act IV, Scene XII

At a shimmering hot airfield in the desert west of the Nile sat a lone pair of American bomber planes. The airfield was under the strict control of the British Royal Air Force. However, since Britain and America had become allies in the war, some American military aircrews were permitted to land and conduct maintenance on their planes there. There were not too many American bomber crews in the region; but more increasingly, they could be seen in Mediterranean skies as they whirred to and from night raids in Europe. Occasionally, these bombers stopped in Egypt to refuel.

A bored American pilot loafed in the dusty hangar. He wore a crooked flight cap over his wavy black hair. Wearing a pale purple silk pilot's scarf, he was dressed in a disheveled jumpsuit. He was sullen and read a magazine for the 10th time. It was his first time in Egypt. He wanted to tour Cairo, see the pyramids—at eye-level, rather than from a bird's perspective—and buy souvenirs. No such luck for him. He and his crew were officially stuck at the hangar for a several-hours-long layover until they flew off to a designated location.

Suddenly, a British officer came marching towards him from nowhere. The American blinked. This guy wasn't a pilot or an air crewman. He wore a dark blue beret and a khaki army uniform, complete with fancy stripes and badges all over it. He had a neat brownish gray mustache, a swagger, and a determined glare in his eye. A ranker, this one. Definitely not a sergeant, although the American could not read British military badges. Probably a colonel, the American guessed. All British officers with hats and mustaches seemed to be colonels.

The American recoiled at his approach. He found the British to be fussy people. He didn't grasp their sense of humor or their manners. They were strange, foreign, alarmingly polite, and somehow impolite at the same time. Real oddballs. Sometimes he wasn't sure if they even spoke English. What did this lofty Colonel Whiskers want? He looked like trouble. Probably was going to yell at him for parking his plane the wrong way.

The British officer halted nearby and fixed him with a piercing blue-eyed stare. "Excuse me," he asked, sounding properly English and very serious. "Can you spare any extra bombs?"

All politeness abandoned the American in his stupefaction. He responded with a drawling, undignified question in a broad New York accent. "Whaat?"

"You know. Bombs," said Maj. Desmond Frost, brisk and unyielding. He flung a loose gesture at the plane. "Have you got any extra ones in there? Ones that you don't need, or...?"

"Why?" demanded the American. "You wanna cart them away in a wheelbarrow?"

Frost flashed a roguish smile. "No! I want to drop them."

The pilot stared in bewilderment.

"Actually, I was going to ask you to drop them for me," confessed Frost with a sheepish laugh. "On a salt marsh."

The pilot crossed his arms and squinted suspiciously at the strange British officer. This conversation was getting weirder and more interesting by the second.

"If you have any, that is," Frost demurred, fidgeting and pacing.

"I might," conceded the pilot, too intrigued to decline. "I could possibly spare a few extra fireworks. I pass them out like candy, you know."

The Major grinned in approval. He told the man an abbreviated story of his current predicament. Namely, the situation that brought him to the airfield as a last resort.

After learning that the tomb robbers were hiding in the Suwan Salt Marsh, Frost sought to conserve manpower by arranging a strategic bombing. An open-and-shut case, he presumed; there were no buildings in the marsh nor living creatures aside from marauders who needed to die.

He had contacted the British Royal Air Force to proceed with his plan. It ended badly. The RAF thwarted his ideas with an acerbic telephone conversation earlier that morning.

"Never before in history has the Royal Air Force used bomber aircraft to drop explosives on criminals!" the RAF liaison officer had exclaimed on the phone in indignation. "As a matter of fact, I can't recall any instance of explosives being dropped on criminals. To say nothing of the fact that a number of these criminals are British citizens..."

"Well, not all of them are. Some are Germans!" Frost had protested. "Besides, there's no need to worry legally about the British ones. I have already obtained their death warrants."

"I can't recall an instance of bombs being used as a form of judicial execution, either," remarked the RAF officer very dryly. "One cannot simply drop bombs wherever one likes and upon whomever one chooses."

At that point, Frost went breathless with outrage. "Are you sure you're in the right department?" he retorted, raising his voice. "What do you mean, 'one simply can't drop bombs?' Isn't that what you lot do all day?"

The RAF officer scrambled to defend his honor. "The RAF does not drop bombs on non-combatants!" he argued sourly. "The men you have described are deserters. They are not actively fighting for an organized Axis military force—for example, the armies of Germany or Italy. You would be asking an RAF bomber crew to depart from military mission objectives to drop a payload on a group of 'grave robbers.' Think about the bigger picture."

"They are most certainly combatants!" barked Frost furiously into the phone. "They kill our soldiers! My Lieutenant was gutted to death with a tire lever by one of them the other day. That's combat, isn't it?"

"There will be no bombs dropped on non-military criminals in Egypt—in a salt marsh or anywhere else!" snarled the RAF officer. "Good day!"

Frost hung up the phone and seethed. The iron-willed Major was not easily deterred. He had made up his mind to bomb the salt marsh somehow. His imagination raced across different fantastic possibilities. Then it occurred to him. The Americans. Weren't there some American airmen to be found anywhere? Maybe some enterprising Americans would "accidentally" bomb the marsh for him. They reputedly liked bombing things and would probably get away with it.

His proposal was met with even more enthusiasm than he expected. "Sure! I'll take care of it for you!" replied the bored American pilot with zest after he explained his situation. "No problem at all. We'd be glad to help. Where is the place?"

The Major beamed at the aggressive pilot. A kindred spirit. He joyfully wrung the pilot's hand and searched for words to express his sheer appreciation. "God bless America!"

The man swelled with pride. "You said it!"

Two hours later the plane went roaring off over the desert, packed with an excited crew of restless men eager to relieve boredom by dropping bombs on something. Afterwards, the bomber crew would "high-tail it" out of Egypt, as the pilot phrased it. Officially, it would be an accident. Unofficially, it would be a joke, a legend, a memorable experience worth bragging about. Frost saluted all of them with vigorous happiness. He watched the plane soar away and was filled with overflowing love for the USA. He went off grinning ecstatically.

The robbers at the Suwan Salt Marsh were still searching relentlessly for their fugitive tyrant, Eislinger, when a heavy droning noise like the hum of bees approached in the air. It was faint at first. But constant. Like a throb. It thinned, grew louder, stabilized like a motorized purr. The ear easily got used to it. That was what made it eerily fatal. The drone of a bomber was like a deadly lullaby. It rocked the senses to sleep before rocking the earth to fiery oblivion.

Old soldiers developed allergies to humming noises. They knew to run when it was early—sometimes they ran at the sound of innocent and abstract humming noises, for nothing. The rookies, the untested, the inexperienced were the ones who let their senses sleep during those first few minutes of soft, faint purring. They were usually the ones who didn't run fast enough. They usually hit the ground first and stayed there in pieces.

Most of the robbers recognized the lull of the bomber. The Germans fled like madmen. They had been bombed, strafed, and scattered for months by RAF planes in the desert war. The British robbers were slightly more spoiled. The deserters among them had little terror of German bombers; the Luftwaffe operated minimally in Africa, and not all of these British ex-soldiers had directly experienced the London Blitz. Ex-commandos were used to having bombers pass by harmlessly over their heads. Some men ignored it. Others ran for their lives.

No shelter could save them in the salty abyss. They were open targets on a flat white plain. The salt-packed earth was also hyper-reactive to heat and light.

The bomber materialized overhead. A glittering angel of death in a cloudless heaven. It moved surprisingly fast for being so large. Like a ghost.

There was a noise first. It was a horrible, whistling roar. Similar to the sound of a tornado. It was the sound of a large metal object tearing toward earth at breakneck speed, whirling end over end, and creating vortexes of wind as gravity sucked it down. The first bomb. It was followed by a symphony of identical roaring noises. More bombs. The air became a cacophony of deafening shrieks.

These were followed duly by a chorus of explosions. And the noise of material reacting to the explosions. Shattering sonic blasts, powerful enough to rip eardrums and shock a beating heart inside a person's chest. Shrieks of splintering metal. Screams and gurgles of dying men hurtling through the air. The dull growl of earth crumbling beneath feet and creating sinkholes. The jarring, squeaking slams of shattered vehicles and objects, tossed blithely into the air, striking the earth again. Amid this apocalyptic racket were the faint thuds of falling, scattered body parts. People made much less noise than machines when they died. They drowned in the affray. They usually realized it during bombings, and this sense of smallness added to their feelings of panic and hopelessness. A bombing always was a complete assault on the senses. Noise, light, heat, balance, smell, and sight turned upside down and sideways in a fiery hot maelstrom. Confusion was indescribable and injury—large or small, physical or emotional—was inescapable.

Bombings could be beautiful spectacles from a distance. Planes always swooped gloriously. Missiles, gunfire, and bombs always cut through the air very neatly. Explosions looked bright and attractive, like little splashes of color. These were followed by elegant plumes of dust and smoke that streaked across the open skies like strokes of an artist's paintbrush. That said, watching a bombing was an incomparable experience. In no other instance were appalling annihilation and aesthetic beauty so visually mingled.

The entire Suwan Salt Marsh went up in smoke and the sight of it was spectacular. The robbers were pulverized to dust. Some were incinerated. Jeeps, tins, and hoarded loot sailed frivolously through the air like scraps of flayed cardboard.

The humans who lived like demons went to hell in a salty fire. Their stolen treasures burned and sank with them. Their desire to pillage the wilderness and its dead trapped them neatly for a massive demise. From a distance, their just exit from mortal life was a marvelous display. Huge billows of sand spewed up from Egypt's sands like pale feathers. Wisps of dark smoke curled daintily among the dust clouds like genies.

The bomber wheeled, a modern bird of prey. It made a second run. More whistling and roaring. More flashes of blistering hot light. More magnificent sand billows. The earth shook like thunder.

Then, as quickly as it had come, the plane was gone. The glittering ghost hummed away serenely into light clouds and disappeared like the West Wind, never to be seen in the same stretch of wild blue heaven again.

Frost watched the aftermath of the bombing standing on a jeep a vast distance away. He regretted not being able to witness the actual moment of his enemies' destruction. The bomber plane had traveled faster to the target site than his automobile could get there. However, he rejoiced in the huge puffs of charred dust still drifting through the air when he arrived. It was a goliath of a bombing. He focused through binoculars and grinned in delight.

"How's that for a nice clean mopping, eh?" he exclaimed to the small group of officers with him. "It's beautiful!"

His comrades chuckled and cheered.

Someone interrupted the moment of exhilaration with dour efficiency. "You're wanted urgently on the wireless, sir."

Frost looked at the man and laughed hysterically at the prospect of getting barked at from upstairs. The others laughed with him. They knew he was forbidden to bomb the marsh and had resorted to unorthodox methods to get it done. They knew the situation was impossible to correct. They also knew he was totally unrepentant, which made it mortifyingly funny.

"Yes, Sahib, I'll have the Yanks take their bombs back, straightaway," he said, mimicking himself in parody.

They cackled.

"I don't care what they do to me," he said. "The scoundrels are dead, that's what matters. Timely and cost-effective, too. Tell him, Major Frost is very busy. Tell him, he's...goodness, what should I be doing? Let me think..."

He was triumphant as the messenger disappeared in frustration. Frost was a remorseless problem-solver. The robbers had been a plague in his life and a public enemy. Now he was staring at a smoking pile of their remains. Mission accomplished.

Or not.

"Sir," tried the messenger again grimly a few moments later. "I think you really ought to get on the wireless. It's that German. Von Rindl. He's escaped."

CHAPTER 29: THE CHASE

"Er in dem kampf mit ringen
kempfen, laufen und springen,
rennen und allen dingen
das best für allen tet."
—"Astilus der Kämpfer" by Hans Sachs

Major Frost learned in a series of tempestuous conversations that his prized catch, Captain Elrich von Rindl, escaped British custody disguised as woman. His current whereabouts were unknown. Miraculously, the German fugitive had also managed to take his satchel of military belongings with him.

The incredible story began with a fateful trip to the lavatory. Von Rindl was being held temporarily in an Army facility near Terna when he complained of a stomachache and showed symptoms of dysentery. He demanded to be escorted to the lavatory. His British captors were all-too familiar with the effects of dysentery—many of their Afrika Korps enemies were known to suffer from it, and it was highly contagious. Sometimes soldiers who had contact with German POWs contracted it, among other ills. The guards enthusiastically complied with Von Rindl's request. He was escorted quickly to a lavatory inside the small building.

Nobody realized that the room had a small window.

Guards patiently waited outside and heard the toilet flush about 10 times. That was arguably normal for a dysentery sufferer. However, after 20th time, they began to raise their eyebrows. After a few hollers and general confusion, they burst inside—and discovered Von Rindl gone. Nothing was left of him except a telltale open window. It was a small window; how he managed to squeeze out of it like a caterpillar was anyone's guess. The toilet flushed merrily away. Von Rindl had reworked its mechanisms; it was rigged to flush over and over again like a robot. A clever sound distraction. His engineering was so strange and effective that the guards witnessed nothing like it before or afterward.

That wasn't the end of his engineering, either. They found out the hard way when they ran to the window and tried to peer out after him. That was when they discovered Von Rindl had somehow literally unscrewed the windowpane and rigged the whole contraption, glass and all, to topple on anyone who approached it. Topple it did. Glass, screws, and pieces of metal framework fell like with a crash and din like Armageddon. The guards were smacked over the head by flying objects. Pieces flew everywhere and rolled across the floor. Soldiers hissed and tripped as they ran in pursuit. They were thwarted.

Soldiers dashed doggedly through the streets looking for the fugitive. They saw nothing. A few Fellahin peasants, of course. Nobody in the immediate area of the building—except a hunchbacked Arab peasant woman fluttering meekly down the street in long robes with a dark hood-like veil over her head. She balanced a large wicker basket of fresh pita loaves on her head, apparently fetching them from a dingy neighborhood bakery.

Nobody noticed the woman wore shiny black boots under her gown. Nor did anyone peer close enough to see the pair of startling blue eyes under her hood. They just saw a heap of flowing cloth trundling down the street. Pita bread, hunchback, basket on head–typical sights in Egypt's peasant life. Their gaze moved on.

It was Von Rindl. He pulled off quite a clever and daring escape with minimal effort. After soldiers rushed outside to find him, he had the nerve to run back inside the prison building and grab his bag of belongings. Then he ran outside again before anyone noticed. He put the backpack on, yanked dresses and veils from somebody's alleyway clothesline, and buried himself in dark sheets. He snatched the pita basket from an open bakery window. Then he pulled his best peasant woman act and hobbled away with the basket on his head. Nobody in a huge dragnet of vigilant soldiers noticed him. He slipped clean through their fingers.

After escaping, Von Rindl basked in freedom and sunshine. He decided to hike homeward. No more dirty basements and intrigues. He wanted to walk—on his own merits and by his own strength—in the fresh, clean air and on the open road. He liked hiking. "*Wandern*," the Germans called it—a concept of wandering exploration and physical sport. He was going to *wandern* his way back toward the Afrika Korps, let no man stop him. He figured out which direction west was and started trekking.

He brazenly wore his disguise for many miles. He hummed "The Yellow Rose of Texas" melody and happily munched on pita loaves. He saw palm trees and looked at interesting insects. He smiled at and petted camels. He reveled in the clean, warm wind, and vast horizon. He marveled at the magnificent sunset. Amid these wonders, he forgot to play his hunchbacked peasant act. The German walked with a clear-headed, brisk strut. He naturally stood straight and swung his arms and legs. He marched.

His merry German march drew the attention of two Sikh military couriers, resting from motorcycle errands for the British Army. They were astonished to behold a veiled Arab woman bobbing energetically down the street with spry steps like a saucy rooster, snapping one arm at her side and whistling a lively tune. They looked at each other in disorientation. This strutting peasant was the weirdest thing they had ever seen in their lives.

Von Rindl became gradually aware of two motorcycles following him from a distance. He peeked over his shoulder and saw two turbaned Sikhs in British Army uniforms coming straight for him. They craned curiously over their handlebars, trying to glimpse his face.

He waited until he turned a corner. Then he bolted.

The Sikhs sped around the corner just in time to see the weird sight get a million times weirder. The woman was running. Her wild athletic sprint rivaled that of an Olympic racer. Robes flapped like wings. Boots flashed. She sailed over hurdles with the muscle of Hercules. They gave chase. It became clear the freakish runaway was not a woman after all—it was a man. This was confirmed a few minutes into the chase, when the head veil blew off. The unveiled was a man with seemingly neon blond hair. He fled under a row of hanging carpets, scrambling to get away.

Another wild chase followed. Von Rindl led the Sikhs around a building in a circle. An enormous dust cloud bloomed. Then he jumped out of a doorway, bowled one of the Sikhs to the ground, and stole the man's motorcycle. He sped away.

He mastered the motorcycle quickly; it only took him a few seconds to grasp the soul of the gears and manipulate the machine beyond its normal power. The other Sikh chased him in vain. Equipped with gears and a motor, Von Rindl was nigh inexorable.

As his captors in the British Army were cast into distress, Von Rindl raced off into the sunset on a motorcycle wearing an Arabic woman's dress, a military knapsack on his back, and sand goggles over his face, while raising a huge plume of dust behind him.

He had unfinished work to do.

CHAPTER 30: FURY

"Avaunt! And quit my sight! Let the earth hide thee!
Thy bones are marrowless, thy blood is cold;
Thou hast no speculation in those eyes
Which thou dost glare with!"
    —"Macbeth" by William Shakespeare, Act III, Scene IV

Hello, Sigfried.
The voice shook his sleeping mind. He stirred.

No, this ain't the voice of your conscience speakin', the voice continued. You ain't got one.

That East London cockney snipe, peppered with backwardness and sarcasm. He knew exactly who it belonged to. He hoped not to see Ollie Bryon, known to him as Flag, ever again.

Yet there he was, lying tucked like a cocoon on the floor of a ruined old temple with Ollie looming over him. He dared to turn over and look over his shoulder at his unwelcome guest. Ollie looked alarmingly the same as the last time they'd met. Vividly animated, even. He had his green turban, his tall laced Afrika Korps moccasins, his jacket with that gaudy Union Jack patch sewn on it like a bloody sore. Only a few things about him were different. His eye, for example—it was no longer a gold metal ball, but a real one. His tattooed fists were bruised and scratched. His complexion was pale white. The bronze of the Egyptian sun was gone.

Ollie grinned. His stare bristled with hatred. *Havin' a nice kip?*

Eislinger struggled to keep calm. "Listen, I don't want to fight anymore. My men are all killed. They were bombed. You must have seen it," he said, trying to sound like his old practical self again. "Why don't we start over?"

Tears glowed in Ollie's eyes. He looked even more furious. *Yeah, I'd love that. Why not?*

"I see that you no longer have a false eye. Did you get surgery?" Eislinger noticed tiny drops of blood on the sandy floor near Ollie's boots. He noticed that the boots were wet and completely stained orange-red with blood. "What happened?"

he asked in confusion. "Are there soldiers outside? Did they attack you, too?"

Ollie made no answer. He sat on the floor beside Eislinger and grabbed hold of the German's arm. His grip was angrily tight. His fingers felt hot.

"Listen," said Eislinger, becoming frightened, "I understand that you're angry with me. But it's pointless now. We have to combine resources." He paused and reflected for a moment. "Actually, I came up with an idea. The Reich needs saboteurs behind British lines in Egypt. I decided to make up a German version of the Commando Group Sphinx. I called it *Kommandotruppe Kobra*. I already contacted agents of the Reich. They will pay us good money, and we can continue just as before. Only this time, we will have military status and resources." He looked hopefully at Ollie. "Since the men are killed, we need new volunteers. What do you think?"

Ollie's grip tightened. He leaned over Eislinger and glared murderously into his eyes. Eislinger tried to pull away and realized he was frozen. Some invisible force held him in place. He could not move.

"Let me go!" snapped Eislinger. He realized in disgust that Ollie's hand was wet. He saw suddenly that the bandit captain was soaking with muddy water and slime. "What happened?" asked the German in confusion. "I don't understand. What have you been doing? There is no water here..."

I thought of you, Sigfried. You're all I were thinkin' about. Right up till the last minute—you filthy little thief, Ollie snarled. He grinned and looked more ominous than before. *Now here I am. Stuck with you. It's a cruel stroke of fortune, ain't it, Siggy my lad?*

"But where did this water come from?" protested Eislinger, offended by the wet slime. "It stinks. Did you fall into a well?"

I'd give anything not to be here. Anything, said Ollie in a sorrowful, despairing growl. *Why am I still here? Let me go!*

"What are you talking about?" huffed Eislinger. He tried to flap free of Ollie's grip and remained trapped. "You are the one who is holding me here—"

Suddenly, he saw the front of the robber's jacket was ripped. There was a huge hole in it. Behind the shredded fabric was a gory, gaping laceration. Ollie's chest was slit wide open. Blood poured down in rivers, mixing with the muddy water.

Eislinger realized in terror that Ollie was dead. He screamed. He struggled to get away.

Where's my blinkin' knife? roared Ollie, wrestling violently with him. His tattooed hands were sizzling hot. *Give it back! Give it back and let me out of here!*

Eislinger thrashed. "Help!" he shrieked. "Somebody help me!"

A struggle ensued. Ollie groped for the ancient flint dagger that Eislinger wore in a leather holster. It was once his prized possession. Now he cursed it and tried fiercely to take the dagger away from his rival. Eislinger did not want to get stabbed and tried desperately to prevent him from reaching it. The angry ghost ultimately did reach it—however, Ollie could not grab it solidly. The knife quivered in his grip and flew off into the air as if by magnetic repulsion. It landed with an echoing ring somewhere nearby. Eislinger hoped that Ollie would leave afterwards. He did not.

He continued wrestling and throttling Eislinger. *I hate you!* He hissed and snarled. His hands scorched. *I'll always hate you! Rotten cur! Filthy sneakin' thief!*

Eislinger fought back with a vicious burst of energy—and cracked open his eyes.

Silence and dust motes surrounded him. He was alone, in the ruins of an old temple, just waking from a deep sleep. Nobody was there. Was it just a nightmare?

He trembled and glanced around. The place looked exactly the same as in his nightmare. The pale moonlight slipping through the pillars like white arrows. The dust motes floating through the empty desert air like little tiny lanterns. No trace of a living soul. Eislinger looked at the floor suspiciously for traces of muddy water. Nothing. He sighed and ran his fingers through his dirty dark brown hair.

That was when he felt something. A strange feverish sensation prickling his arm. He pulled up his sleeve and looked at his arm as his fear returned like a cold wind. There it was. He started trembling and rubbing his eyes, disbelieving his vision. But even in the dim moonlight, the truth was horrifically visible.

There was a set of burning red welts on his skin. They formed the outline of fingerprints.

Eislinger stared in horror. He tried to convince himself it wasn't real—that somehow his imagination had created those marks there. Deep down inside, he knew he was lying to himself. It was obvious that the burning fingerprints—and the furious soul who left them—were real.

Until now he had willfully ignored supernatural manifestations. Yes, he had always noticed some strange things about the dagger—the perfume smell, the voice, the occasional wind vortex or crash around him. Believing in his own power, he had chosen to dismiss these things. Actually they flattered him—in his egoism, he had come to believe that he somehow caused these metaphysical phenomena to happen. He flattered himself into thinking it was the strength of his "superior mind force."

But no doubt existed for him about the supernatural this time—only because he personally knew the ghost. He would never have willingly conjured the ghost of Ollie. In fact, he would have banished his ghost if he knew how. Now Eislinger realized that he had no power. Other forces were at work here over which he wielded no command or control.

The flint dagger gleamed in a patch of moonlight on the sandy floor nearby. It caught Eislinger's eye suddenly. His jaw tensed. He broke into cold sweat. How had the dagger gotten there? He remembered the violent wrestling match with Ollie's angry spirit. Clearly his "nightmare" had somehow been real.

He peered around nervously. He was alone in the temple. Carved images of insects decorated the pillars. He half-expected to glimpse Ollie's menacing figure lurking in the dusty shadows. Nothing.

Maybe it was time to leave. Yes. He wasn't far from civilization. It was still dark, but morning would come soon. He didn't want to stay here anymore—not alone with a ghost.

One last thing to bring. His treasure, his lucky charm, his trophy that symbolized his former power. He had stolen it and killed with it. He had wielded it over people and watched them cringe. Inside, Eislinger was a coward at heart—seeing people afraid made him feel strong and special. The ancient flint knife was his magic wand of oppression and intimidation. He needed it more than anything. He darted across the floor and grabbed the dagger.

A cockney voice shrieked out of nowhere. *Drop it, slime!*

Eislinger did drop the knife out of sheer shock. He glanced everywhere in confusion.

Keep your manky hands off it!

He felt a presence. An overpowering awareness of a very familiar person. It thickened the air and came at him like a rush. He hesitated, trying to convince himself until the last moment that he was imagining things.

Then he heard the faint sound of laced boots squeaking towards him across the broken tiles of floor. He lost his nerve. He took the dagger and fled.

CHAPTER 31: COBRA

"The poison of a scorpion is in his tail,
The poison of a fly is in his head,
The poison of a serpent is in his fang,
The poison of a bad man is in his whole body."

—Sanskrit Proverb

The closest thing to human civilization east of the Suwan Salt Marsh was a modest oasis town called Amara. The town infrastructure had been built by British settlers who required a stopover for military, supplies, and general travel needs near the desert highway. That said, it was more modern than other oasis towns. There were telephones, filling stations, a military hotel, a few restaurants, and some stores.

Eve was quartered in the hotel along with some other officers working with Major Frost. Frost had bolted straight to the Suwan Salt Marsh and told his entourage to follow him up. He didn't have much of an entourage left. Most of the tomb robbers had been "blotted out," Frost had announced to everyone; his task force was now being dissolved. The last thing to do was to check what remained of the raiders' former campsite at Suwan; then it would all be over.

Eve was relieved about how things had turned out. Frost's solution to destroy the robbers by bombing the salt marsh pleased her. It was an efficient decision. No more violent grapples or bayonet fights. This dark chapter in their shared life would soon end.

She admired his love of duty, but worried about the toll that the case was taking on him. He was consumed by the case. Driven to squash it with an iron fist. Beneath his icy calm surface was a secret desire for retribution. The robbers' existence morally outraged him. He was unable to rest or allow himself any personal peace until he had vanquished them. His mission left him tired. Frustrated. Preoccupied. Agitated, sometimes.

Yet he dreamed of a vacation. He promised her to take her on an idyllic Nile cruise and a "long holiday" in Port Said—one spot on Egypt's map relatively untouched by war. He had seen it before, of course. He had been most places in the world already—more than she had in her younger existence. But this was a time for new beginnings, for both of them. Port Said was a stellar place, he said, right on the sea. There were nice hotels and lovely beaches. She was energetic and active; so was he. They could swim, go yachting, visit places and see things...

"Fräulein Hecking."

She was strolling down a sun-bleached boulevard on her way back from exploring the town, thinking about their married future. A strange man's voice surprised her. Speaking German? She whirled around in confusion.

A homely young man with horn-rimmed glasses confronted her. He wore bright clean clothing but looked dark and dirty. He stared through her with deliberate, sharp purpose.

Eve was confused. She failed to recognize this person.

"What a surprise to see you again!" the man exclaimed, still in German. "I remember you well. You and your Major and your fantastic stories. It was all lies, wasn't it?" He leered with sinister arrogance. "How's life?"

The moment of recognition came when he was speaking. In an instant, Eve remembered those complacent, forgettable features. It was the lone killer. The renegade Nazi soldier. The one Von Rindl obsessively hunted. He pillaged and massacred, yet nobody noticed him. She had seen him before briefly, standing over corpses with a grin and a smoking gun. She had also seen his handiwork—a severed arm, ashes, burning tents, a camp of senselessly slain Bedouins.

Back then he wore a flat British helmet with a bullet hole in the side; some kind of sick trophy. The helmet was gone now. But it was undeniably the same man.

Eislinger smiled nicely. He was on the brink of drawing his dagger and grabbing her when everything suddenly changed.

"What a fool!" hissed Eve in perfect and indignant German. "How can you speak to me this way in public? Were you ever a soldier of the Reich?"

Her venom took him aback. Eislinger was confused. Was this woman really an agent of Nazi Germany, as she had once claimed? Or was she lying?

The axle of his actions would turn on the edge of this truth. An eye-scanning contest followed. Eislinger did his best to probe the depths of her stare with his hollow vision that was glutted with scenes of fear and torture. Eve did her best to mentally convince herself that she was the undercover Nazi "Nightingale" agent named Hannelore Hecking, a ruse she invented the last time she and Eislinger met. She steeled herself, trying to look the part.

"You have deserted our glorious army and betrayed our Fatherland by your cowardice!" she proclaimed with convincing fanaticism in her voice. She focused, doing her best to sound like a pompous German radio propaganda broadcast. "Get out of my sight, weakling!" she commanded. "Shoot yourself, if you have any honor. Go off and die!"

It was a frightening situation, but fear was not in Eve. She thought fast, dancing rapidly to a dangerous tune. Emotions were gone. Conscience was irrelevant. Determination and self-control governed her. She thought only of survival and escape.

Her ruse sufficiently fooled Eislinger. He believed her harsh snapping and her Nazi lingo—and most of all, the icy cold command in her eyes. He abandoned all thoughts of hurting her. Instead he decided to seek her help.

"You're mistaken. I'm not a deserter," he protested, suddenly sounding very meek and polite. His violent arrogance faded; he played his innocent schoolboy role again. "I am sorry if I offended you. But I'm in a difficult situation here," he explained nervously. "I am part of a special secret task force. *Kommandotruppe Kobra.*"

Eve curled her lip in disdain. "What? I have never heard of that!"

"I have to survive behind British lines to complete my mission. I must get to Cairo," insisted Eislinger. "You must help me!"

He tried to latch onto her arm. Eve pulled away.

"I need food and a safe place to stay. And a wireless—I

need to contact Germany," Eislinger demanded. "If you truly want the best for our Fatherland, you will help me pursue our common goal."

Eve looked at him with haughty disdain. "I must verify this information. I can't simply take your word for everything just because you walk up to me and say so," she sniffed, doing her best imitation of a mulish German bureaucrat. "Do you have any papers?"

Eislinger flushed with anger. "No, unfortunately, none."

"*Wie?* You expect me to believe you with no papers?" scoffed Eve, still thinking fast. "How am I supposed to know it's true? You have no proof of what you're saying—"

His hands clenched into fists as he flew into a rage. "There is no time for this!"

Eve backed away, treating him to a condescending glance. "Please control yourself, sir. There is no need for shouting," she patronized. "The fact is, I must do my job efficiently. My contacts in the OKW have rules. I must verify the identity of any German citizen who asks me for help, otherwise I cannot help them. It is the rule. I can't just go around breaking rules—otherwise I can be punished for breaching military security protocol!"

Eislinger looked at her listlessly. He appeared confused and defeated.

Eve pretended to be empathetic. Now was the moment of decision. "Look, I realize you're in a difficult position," she said with a resigned sigh. "I will try to contact someone now. There is a telephone right over there," she said, pointing at a shop across the street. "Do not move from this spot. *Ja?* I will see what I can do for you."

She turned to walk away.

Hello, Fluffy.

A chill swept over her. She recognized that voice.

She turned and looked at Eislinger in confusion, wondering if he had somehow mimicked the voice of the deceased English robber Ollie. Eislinger seemed visibly perturbed; he fidgeted and pretended to be oblivious.

Eve glared at him and waved her arm authoritatively. "Wait here!" Then she tossed her head haughtily and marched off.

Eislinger watched the woman cross the street and enter the shop. It was a small restaurant. He completely believed her and had no reason to fear. So far he'd gone about his errands in Amara unnoticed. But he intended to get to Cairo, and that would be tricky without help. How lucky, he thought, that he had stumbled into this Third Reich agent here. Fortune was definitely on his side...ghost or no ghost.

Don't try to ignore me, Sigfried. It won't do a blind bit of good.

Eislinger bristled. "You can't make me do anything," he muttered to the unseen. "You are dead. This knife belongs to me now. I will do whatever I want—"

A whip of sand blew across the pavement, hitting Eislinger's boots in a gust.

That's what you think!

Minutes dripped by like molasses. He waited. And waited. Sun scorched, sand blew, pedestrians walked blindly past. He shuffled impatiently on the cracked sidewalk and watched a pale scorpion dart past him with wandering claws. He glanced at the crooked shadow of a building. And that was when it struck him like a piece of ice in the heat. An alarming suspicion. A nameless fear that something was not right.

He ran. He moved just one second before something popped into the wall behind him and sent a shower of plaster skittering everywhere. Another pop. He ducked.

Bullets.

Eve heard the sound of gunfire outside and hoped Eislinger would get shot. A quick phone call to Major Frost's team at the military hotel settled everything quickly. A swarm of British soldiers were after Eislinger now. He was on their turf; they materialized from all directions in seconds. In the meantime, she melted out the restaurant back door and ran away as fast as she could to safety.

Her husband materialized an hour later. Last she heard, he had been out scouring the Suwan Salt Marsh. Somehow the news managed to reach him. He had a talent for fiendish driving; he promptly reappeared in her midst like a hurricane. Thorough by profession, the journalist told the British soldiers everything that happened during her brief encounter with Eislinger. Apparently that information already reached him, too. He already knew all details.

He was a sight when he blew into town. Thoroughly sun-baked. Soaked in sweat. Completely covered in crusty salt dust. His sleeves were rolled up in odd directions. He frowned.

"I'm done with the marsh. All finished. Not going back," was the first thing he said when he walked up to her in the dingy lobby of the military hotel. "We're wrapping the thing up. It'll be over by tomorrow."

He snagged a waiter and ordered iced drinks before she could say anything. Then he pulled up a wicker chair next to hers and threw his arm around her.

"Bravo!" he said with a smile, jolting her in a hug and kissing her face. "Marvelous job you did of deceiving him. Absolutely marvelous. I couldn't be more proud of you." He seized her hand and squeezed it tightly, overcome with admiration.

Eve was still rather alarmed after her encounter with the deranged Nazi spree killer. "Well, did they get him?" she asked, feeling on edge. "Nobody's told me anything. Is Eislinger dead?"

"No," he answered blithely.

She was shocked by the answer and by his blasé tone. "What? How could they miss him?"

Frost snatched a glass of iced tea from the waiter and handed her one. He took a long swig and was refreshed. "The plan is to capture him—not kill him," he announced. "I want to take Eislinger alive."

Another bolt of lightning on a clear day. Eve was temporarily speechless.

"What he told you about this supposed 'Commando Troop Cobra' is of great concern to us," Frost explained. "If there is an organized German plan to start an uprising behind our frontline, we want to know about it. If Eislinger has any information about that, it would be stupid to kill him."

"He's a liar!" protested Eve. "That's how he's managed to survive this long! He lies and cons everyone he meets. People underestimate him, they overlook him, they give him chances." Indignation swept over her at the idea of the murderer getting away with his crimes. "He knows he's running out of luck now that his buddies are dead. He's probably just making up stories to slither away like an eel. Don't believe a word he says!"

Frost tensed. He didn't appreciate her contradicting his judgment. "We will find out if he is lying after we've pumped the information out of him," he said. "Justice will come to him eventually. For now, we have bigger problems to face."

They drank in silence. She touched his chest. He relaxed.

"They've tracked Eislinger to a ruined temple just west of here," Frost said bluntly. "He's being surrounded now. I'm going there to talk him out." He looked at Eve and smiled with fierce energy. "I want to have this business all packed up by sunset." He jolted her again with his arm. "You'll like that, won't you? Just watch."

"I wish you'd just blow up the temple," she muttered.

He laughed wryly. "That'd be great fun!" he chuckled. "Don't think I could get away with it, though. Our friends in the RAF are already confused about how the Americans ended up accidentally bombing my salt marsh." He winked at her. "Anyway, I think the locals might not appreciate it if I bowled their crusty old statues to smithereens. Salt marshes are one thing, but 'cultural sites,' you know, are rather touchy..."

She couldn't help but smile at his impish humor. Yet her concerns remained. "I just don't want Eislinger to slip out. I hope the soldiers surround the whole place from every angle with machine guns, and cannons, and anti-aircraft guns, and flame-throwers—"

Frost shot her a deadpan glance, feigning confusion. "But we're not in Chicago."

That quip caught her off guard. They both laughed heartily.

"Don't worry. It's covered. The boys will shoot his glasses off if he tries anything," he said. "We'll lock him up, if we can, and let him simmer a bit. I'll arrange for somebody else from CIG to have a poke at him. Then you and I will go to Port Said..." He halted sharply. "Heavens, what's the matter?"

She was gripping her iced tea with clenched white fingers and staring into the distance.

Frost rattled her shoulder. "Eve?"

"I've been trying not to think about it, but I have to tell you," she said with difficulty, looking down at the floor. "I heard Ollie's voice. You know. That guy Ollie or Flag or whatever he called himself. Today when I was with Eislinger. I heard his voice say 'Hello, Fluffy.'"

The Major reflected on her words, troubled by them. His wife, a sensible journalist, was not the type to imagine things. "My dear, Oliver Bryon is assuredly dead," he told her after a bewildered silence. "I killed him quite effectively. He could not be any deader."

"I know. But I heard him," she said in confusion. "I tried to tell myself it was nothing, but it's been bothering me. I think Eislinger heard it, too. He looked upset when it happened." She glanced at Frost. "What do you think?"

He brooded. "Heard anything like it since?"

"No."

He fidgeted and tapped the edge of his dusty boot against the floor. "I really hate to admit this, but I'm beginning to believe Sullivan's myth gibberish," he confessed, glancing sheepishly at her. "To date, five known people who came into contact with that old flint dagger have died in grim circumstances—including Ollie." He hesitated. "The dagger is still missing. It was not located anywhere at the Suwan Salt Marsh. This seems to confirm what Von Rindl told us. He says the dagger is in Eislinger's possession."

"Maybe Eislinger still has it," said Eve.

"If so, the 'ghost' you heard is likely his problem," remarked Frost. He sighed nervously. "Not sure how we're going to cope with that when we bring him into military custody. I'm prepared to arrest a criminal, not a ghost." He turned to Eve with a smile. "Perhaps we can blow it up, too. Any ideas on how to detonate a dagger?"

She did not laugh that time. Her mind was on Eislinger, the poisonous dagger in his grasp, and the haunting. She had seen Ollie's green turban hanging dead on a dummy; yet his malicious spirit was seemingly still alive. It was a disquieting reality.

Frost sighed worriedly and looked away. It was a reality he would soon face head-on.

CHAPTER 32: MIRROR OF SAND

"Only in dreams is a ladder thrown
From the weary earth to the sapphire walls;
But the dream departs, and the vision falls,
And the sleeper wakes on his pillow of stone."
—"Gradatim" by Josiah Gilbert Holland

The most famous thing about Amara was the Palace of Four, a desert colossus stranded in the empty dunes some distance from the city. The palace was named such for its apparent connection to ancient Egyptian numerology—the vast old building and all its compounds were built in palace-structure and completely in elements of the number four. Sets of ceremonial four pillars arranged in four quads were grouped on all four sides of four great palace buildings, which were all four-cornered. The holy entities venerated at the place—gods, kings, monsters, myths, and heroes—were all depicted in statue and relief form in artistic sets of four.

The most remarkable of all the deities at the palace were the four insect gods—Khepri the scarab, Hoth the fly, Inpa the honeybee, and Tekre the praying mantis. Khepri was the guardian of the sun, Hoth a bringer of courage, Inpa a harbinger of fruitful labor, and Tekre a purveyor of wisdom. The insects were depicted on walls and pillars with human bodies and human clothing performing a wide variety of everyday activities together. Apparently, it was their palace—a large colossus of the quartet of insect-headed people inside the central chamber evidenced that the place was dedicated in their honor. The palace's architectural design and artistic depictions of obscure deities made it one of the most renowned ancient sites bordering the great Western Desert.

The palace was a hazy orange labyrinth of massive, burning pillars carved with deep, shadowy symbols. Colonnades and colonnades of sand-colored spires created mazes of shadows and lights across the hot sand. Dust played in whirling tendrils around the pillars like fairies. Eddies of sand trickled across the ground like tan snakes in the wind. Echoes clapped and rang like tabla drums in the dry air.

The wind was picking up; the makings of a summer sandstorm. A summer wind in the desert was a dry hot blast like dragon's breath; it got hotter, drier and more virulent whenever a storm brewed. Time slid by like grains in an hourglass before a sandstorm would loom suddenly like a ghastly apparition.

Major Frost had been in the desert long enough to recognize the signs of a tempest. He brought a scarf for the occasion. It was a long dark brown rag with a round, knotted black cord the Army issued him years ago to use as a kerchief on desert travel duty. He had worn it badly during a 1930s peacekeeping errand to a tribal well in the middle of nowhere; a Bedouin elder took pity on his absurd appearance and taught him how to put it on properly. He knew how to roll a fairly decent turban and wrap a decent veil across his nose and mouth. His flair wasn't quite on par with Sinbad, but Frost cared nothing about how he looked. He despised wearing head kerchiefs; it was only protection from wind and sand.

His interpreter was a novice. The lad was lost blissfully in his 20s and in Egypt on his first tour of duty. He came from a rosy green area of England where sheep grazed and the closest thing to a sandstorm was a strong wet squall from the Scottish border. He could speak German with the fire of Schiller and the brimstone of Wagner, having studied German language and literature at a fine university. Somehow, he landed in the staff of the Royal Army Investigative Corps and was the only creature capable of interpreting for Frost that day. He, too, wore a head kerchief to ward off sand—it looked like a cross between a beekeeper's mask and something the Pharaoh Ramses II might have worn on a bad hair day.

Frost gave him a withering glare above his veil and gestured to signal the young man was wearing his headgear wrong. The interpreter smiled with his eyes and remained oblivious. Frost, disdainful, decided to let blind youth reap its own bitter harvest; the Major was not the mothering type.

Gusts of sand picked up as the two walked amid the baking hot courtyards of the Palace of Four. They planned to talk the fugitive Siegwulf Eislinger into a peaceful surrender. It should have been neat. They were in control. He was all surrounded. A shot had wounded him, last time he'd been sighted—in the leg, allegedly. It was in Eislinger's interest to cooperate. Familiar with Eislinger's rodent-like lust for survival, Major Frost had no doubt he would quickly capitulate.

"Tell him that he is surrounded, and that it would be to his advantage if—"

Frost never got the chance to finish that sentence. A violent gust of wind billowed from nowhere and knocked the loudspeaker clean out of the interpreter's hand.

Confusion. More sand. The loudspeaker rolled away in the grip of a whirlwind. Frost yelled at the interpreter to cut his losses, but the young man chased the tool anyway. Now they were separated. Frost drew his side arm reflexively. He barked orders to rein the interpreter back in.

Sand encores came in flying curtains now. The interpreter was beyond hearing. The wind was too loud. He reclaimed the loudspeaker and returned in triumph. Except Frost was gone. The Major was not at the spot where they had last stood. Or where was that spot, exactly? The interpreter was wondering this when another blast of rabid wind lunged and carried his mangled headscarf clear off. In an instant, he lost his ability to see or speak. He floundered and panicked.

Frost lingered vainly for the interpreter's return. He hissed in anger. The stupid fool had probably gotten lost. Was his mission really ruined? Would he really have to withdraw and risk Eislinger escaping during the sandstorm, or...?

A gunshot in the wind decided the issue. A bullet whizzed past Frost and bit a pillar behind him with a puff of broken stone.

He took cover.

Time's up, Sigfried.

Concealed in a long dusty archway sat Eislinger, nursing a grazed thigh. He was a tiny, ragged brown speck in a tunnel of shadows and orange sunlight stripes. The German spree killer had been struck by a ricocheting bullet during his narrow escape. He was also sore and covered with bruises from his violent struggle with his former crew earlier. His comrades were dead, but the marks of their blows survived upon him. Ghostly fingers still burned through the handprint welt on his arm. Somewhere outside the palace complex, he sensed the approach of armed men prepared to end his life.

He had never been more vulnerable. That made him more dangerous.

A spray of sand kicked itself at him, driven by an unseen foot. A wicked London laugh rang in the dust. *How'd you like to join me?*

"I don't care about your threats. I will do what I like. The knife is mine," Eislinger said to the seething emptiness. "Eventually you will be forced to accept it and go away."

Except I can't flippin' 'go away,' clever clogs, sassed the voice. *Ain't you understood that yet?* Invisible laced boots shuffled across broken tiles. *I'd love to leave you, peaches, but you got my knife. Lose it, lose me.*

"No. I refuse!" Eislinger drew the flint knife and stared covetously at it. The bronze serpentine hilt gleamed in the dusty orange light. The cobra's human face looked vividly alive in the dry heat. "I am going to surrender to the English," he announced smugly. "They'll give me a chance. You'll see. This knife is coming with me—there is not a thing you can do to change it."

An unintelligible whisper sounded near his ear. He smelled reed perfume—and a faint trace of musty water. Then Ollie's furious voice again. *We won't come quietly.*

Eislinger was puzzled. "We?"

The knife rattled. Sand blew outside the portico. Enormous gusts. A withering storm had come. But was it a natural storm? Eislinger could not tell. The flying grains bit and stung him. Sheets of sand bounced off the pillars. Flying grains lashed him in bursts like tiny shotgun pellets.

Voices echoed in the emptiness. Eislinger peered from his hiding place. He saw human figures approaching. Two men in khaki uniforms. Englishmen.

Once his enemies. Now his rescuers. So many times his luck had almost run out, yet somehow his deceit always managed to save him. It gave him confidence. Hubris, even. Today he'd get yet another chance at life.

"See? Here they come to capture me," he told his phantom follower, whose furious presence he felt strongly in the chaotic winds. "This nonsense ends today."

A disembodied voice laughed.

Eislinger reacted angrily to the sound. It startled him and he hated to feel frightened. He sheathed the dagger, dragged himself to his feet and hobbled towards the British soldiers. "Laugh all you like. You're dead," he muttered. "There's nothing you can do."

I ain't even started yet.

The voice disappeared into a gust of wind. Eislinger ignored it. He had learned to live with the annoying phantom; it wasn't relevant to him. His own needs and survival were his top priorities. He limped in the direction of the approaching soldiers, raising his arms over his head in surrender. Sand blew. Visibility decreased. He despised the grating wind.

Yes, it was time to surrender. Time to leave the hardship of the desert behind for the comforts of prisoner life. Attention, status, free food, clean clothes...They'd keep all his personal effects in a box, of course, and return them to him when the war was over. Including his dagger. Naturally, he expected Germany to win; he would be a hero and return home with a wreath of laurels on his head and a sparkling array of sinister medals decorating him...

A horrible sight ended the fantasy. It came like a minotaur from the darkness of the whirling sands. The air was dim with wind and flying brown muck. A blurry figure materialized in the haze ahead of him. It should have been a British officer—at least that's what Eislinger thought it was based on his first peek from hiding. True enough, the monster was wearing a British uniform—khakis, sloppy rolled sleeves, heraldic badges in the usual places. Unmistakable.

But the wraith's crown was what made it ghastly and hideous. A turban. The figure wore a long turban with two tails whipping around like flags in the wind. A veil obscured the obscure face. The turban had no color—sheets of sand reduced everything to shadowy shapes. But the sight was instantly recognizable to Eislinger. He knew only one person who wore a turban like that—Ollie.

This was no man. It was the ghost. Coming to get him.

Panic swept in. He was no longer sure of anything. Eislinger thought he saw two English soldiers coming; now there was only this horrible specter. What terrifying magic was this?

Here I come, Siggy boy!

He scrambled back into hiding and swooped up a pistol he had scavenged. He fired a shot. The phantom disappeared. Sand continued to gust through the ruins. The atmosphere turned into an orange-brown haze.

An invisible force puffed a flowering burst of sand right next to him. He saw a gauzy human shape, with the cold bronze glint of a bandolier and a distinct wisp of green. Another shot. Losing his self-control, he fired it straight through the figure with a trembling grip and watched the bullet charge recklessly into a wall.

An echo. The shot returned to him—a bullet struck the wall over his head.

Complete panic filled Eislinger. The ghost was fighting back. It was rebounding bullets back at him. It was inexorable, invincible, everywhere. No wall could hold the spirit back. Nothing could kill it—it was already dead and out of reach.

But apparently he was within the ghost's grasp. Now the threats made sense. Yes. Just like Ollie. Toying with him before closing in for the kill. Sands flashed, wind howled. He saw the turban again—a dim ring of fire, whipping around in the darkness. It loomed, then melted away in the haze.

Eislinger totally lost his composure and fled. He cast aside his gun—guns were useless against ghosts, and he was convinced every shot he fired would return to strike him. Meanwhile, the phantom chased him. He saw it in flashes between the arches and alcoves. Green. Brown murk. Flashes of flying fabric. Nothing more than a shadow. The only thing clear about it was that British khaki uniform, so infernally recognizable even in the dusty gloom. The phantom seemed to chase from two different directions.

Go on, try to scarper. Bein' dead makes me faster than you. Ain't it?

The voice was everywhere. Teasing, heckling, threatening. It was loud and clear above the racing wind. Immortal. Vindictive. Doomed.

He fled into a courtyard. Once it had been a desert garden. Mirrored wells and pools of colored sand had adorned it. Wall art remained, telling stories of gods and heroes. Kneeling figures of half-animal, half-human characters wearing robes and headdresses paid homage to the rays of the sun and frolicked with insect divinities.

He tripped over a fragment of stone and fell flat on his face. His glasses shattered. Blood stained the cracked granite tile below him. He lifted his face in agony.

The dagger had left him. Somehow it flew a fair distance in front of him and sat on the ground ahead—defiant and out of his reach. He glared at it. This was one battle he wasn't losing. Ollie could chase him, shoot at him, torment him—maybe even kill him—but the ghost would never take the knife away if he could prevent it. Eislinger viewed the dagger as his trophy. His prize. A symbol of his former power.

Lethal footsteps approached. Eislinger barely heard them. Instead of running away, he crawled across the tile to reclaim the dagger. The marvelous flint knife of Ne'rah the embalmer. The "royal scepter" of Ollie Bryon. The blade had once been their mortal glory—now it was their eternal prison. Eislinger didn't realize the significance; he was short-sighted when it came to things he wanted.

He picked the knife up. It rattled in his grip, then went quiet. No voice was heard. No threats. All calm and orderly, just like it used to be. He sat up and looked at the knife, its craftsmanship, the winged cobra woman glaring dumbly at him with beady white eyes—he saw it all in just a few seconds, admiring its morbid beauty one last time.

There was a puff and Eislinger's head exploded. His motion to sit up lined his head straight up with a long rifle barrel pointing at him from behind. A nice, clean, smooth shot—from a short distance. He didn't know what hit him; the bullet cut clean through his skull and he dropped dead instantly. There was a huge gory plume of blood like a miniature fountain. It splattered into the air and continued to drip into a large morass as he fell over on the ground with a heavy thud. The dagger sliced his wrist as he fell, as if biting him for his impertinence.

A pair of tall black leather boots strolled over across the courtyard as the wind died down. Winds quieted. The violent orange haze in the air began to fade. The boots were light and graceful. They halted sharply next to Eislinger and turned his body over with a swift, unceremonious kick.

Dead?

Certainly. The shot left the target bereft of brains and missing an eye—eerily, the same eye that Ollie Bryon had once been deprived of. Could it have been the workings of an evil supernatural power?

Maybe. But Captain Elrich von Rindl didn't care to notice. He was focused on his own priorities. The man he had hunted across crazed wildernesses for what seemed like eternity was now, at last, vanquished. Or was he? Von Rindl watched intently for any sign of breathing to make sure his target was really destroyed.

To be extra sure, he stepped back and took one more shot.

"Well, well! If it isn't our runaway Princess Scheherazade," exclaimed a clear, commanding British voice. "I almost didn't recognize you without your petticoats."

Von Rindl was unpleasantly surprised to see Major Desmond Frost standing across from him in a courtyard archway. The

Major was a fierce-looking wreck of sand powder. He had removed his head kerchief, leaving a shock of wind-blasted brown hair and white stripes across his face where dust hadn't coated him. The stripes brightened his piercing sky-blue eyes. He toted a handgun. Above him loomed an impressive wall carving of the lion-headed Sekhmet, goddess of war, roaring and spearing a frog demon.

The British Major was just as unpleasantly surprised to see Von Rindl. The last he heard, the wily German had escaped in an Arab woman's disguise on a hijacked motorcycle. Now he was here. Looking so calm in his ant-like sand goggles, crooked cap and long gray overcoat. He carried his rifle. His knapsack was slung over his shoulder. Dust powder covered him, but somehow he did not look a bit windblown. Von Rindl's gift for appearing neat was a great mystery. It made him a hundred times more annoying to Frost, who was irritated by his caprices. Von Rindl stood framed against a wall fresco showing a laughing, jackal-headed man playing a board game with a sun spirit.

Neither man aimed their weapon at the other. Von Rindl lowered his rifle; Frost slung his pistol into its holster and ventured further into the courtyard. Eislinger lay sprawled on the sandy granite between them.

It was a mystery to both men how Eislinger abandoned reason and plunged to his death. Nobody would never know the mirror effect in the blurry sands that Eislinger experienced in his fleeting last moments; the illusions of two figures of British khaki uniforms, turbaned and veiled, advancing from all directions as physical and spiritual worlds collided. The last memory Eislinger left behind was one of madness; he died, as he had lived, a crazy man.

Both onlookers witnessed the calculating spree killer lose his sanity at the end. Von Rindl saw him in the very act of surrendering to Frost before suddenly changing course and shooting at the Major. Frost hadn't seen Eislinger coming; he only experienced getting shot at. He had no choice but to shoot back. Logically a gun battle might have ensued. Instead Eislinger tossed away his firearm and fled helter-skelter through the ruins in a path that made no sense. He changed directions frequently, as if reacting to something that wasn't there. The sight of Frost terrified him; a mere glimpse of the British officer was enough to send Eislinger running in a new direction. Frost chased him relentlessly—he was angry, tired and eager for a vacation, all of which made him 10 times more ferocious than usual.

Von Rindl was in position to act as sniper, but flying sand ruined his plan. He descended from a hidden perch and stalked Eislinger at ground level. Ultimately Eislinger barreled past him into a courtyard. Here Von Rindl expected no instant success; Eislinger had sharp senses and was notorious for escaping wildly at the last second. It had happened so many times before. Also it was not an easy to fire a long-range rifle quickly at such a short distance. Von Rindl braced himself for an awkward shooting contest and prayed to heaven he could zap Eislinger and have time to run away before the British notched two German marks to their death tally. Opposite to his prediction, Eislinger hovered in the open like a sitting duck and literally lifted his head into the jaws of death. The jaws snapped and Eislinger was finished.

But the present business wasn't.

"Congratulations. You pegged him," remarked Frost, eyeing the bloody mess on the ground. The British officer was devoid of regret or emotion. He had wanted to capture Eislinger alive, but the man's death did not upset him. One less enemy soldier was nothing to regret. He was confident he could get the information he needed elsewhere.

Von Rindl was pleased at his success. Everything had gone according to his far-fetched yet effective plotting. Tipping off Frost about the robbers' lair at the Suwan Salt Marsh flushed Eislinger out, as Von Rindl had hoped. He escaped British custody in time to start tracking the fugitive again; the commotion caused by the shootout in Amara and ensuing manhunt to the ruined palace created a trail easy enough to follow.

"Not bad marksmanship for a civvy draft-in," Frost gibed, peeking dangerously at Von Rindl. "What was your occupation again? A professor of flying whirligigs?"

Von Rindl stared intently at his rival. "It's better this way," he said suddenly in clear English. "Eislinger was a problem for everyone. Nobody loses."

"So! You do speak English!" exclaimed Frost, laughing in outrage and delight. "I thought so! You sly weasel..."

"Not really," retorted Von Rindl. "My English is terrible."

"Indeed," replied Frost dryly.

Von Rindl grinned and flicked his hand in a slapdash salute. "You're a tough opponent, Major," he remarked. "But you have still not gotten the best of me."

Frost smiled in calm defiance. "I haven't really given it a hard try."

The conversation was brought to an abrupt close. A billowing gust of wind swept through the ruins—a giant dust cloud that looked like a large round creature flailing a thousand wispy arms and legs in all directions. Sand buoyed from the earth. Streams of dust trickled. The loud echo of a shouting man clapped against the walls—Frost's interpreter.

"Sir! Where are you? Can you hear me? Good Lord, where has he gone?"

The Major turned away for a moment, stepping back as a curtain of sand flew past his eyes and scourged Eislinger's corpse. Footsteps darted towards him.

When Frost looked back again, Von Rindl had vanished without a trace.

It was startling. But Frost was sure the wily German couldn't have gone too far. The Major could sound the alarm, convene a hunt and scramble around the ruin for another few hours searching for Von Rindl—all for the mere pleasure of tackling him and packing him off to a POW camp. Frost sighed. Maybe back in the days when he didn't have a home life, he might have found it an exciting game to play. But it seemed a dull prospect now. He had Eve on his mind. Ankle bracelets, bathtubs, tea, and pillows. A long seaside vacation...

Would Von Rindl try to start an uprising behind the Nile? Not likely. The fact that he ruthlessly gunned down Eislinger, a fellow German who claimed to be acting in Nazi interests, demonstrated that Von Rindl was coldly focused on his duties as a desert ranger. Instead of using his escape as an opportunity to ignite turmoil behind British lines, Von Rindl risked his life to stubbornly follow Eislinger into the ruin and execute him amid a sandstorm and a nest of British soldiers. He completed his original army orders—cut and dried. Was Von Rindl daring, stupid or narrow-minded? Frost couldn't tell. Maybe a strange combination of the three, he supposed. Anyway, Von Rindl, for all his wit, had proven he had no genius for espionage or sabotage. Frost decided that catching him now was not a priority—he was confident he'd get an opportunity to beat Von Rindl in a contest of skill later.

"Sir!" The interpreter tumbled into the courtyard with relief and optimism on his sloppily veiled face, a walking testimony to the blunders of youth. He almost tripped over the bloody body of Eislinger. The sight horrified him. "Good gracious..."

"You're just in time to pronounce his last rites," Frost said dryly. "Although at this point I don't think he'll care if they're in German or English."

The Major reached over and ripped the interpreter's head kerchief off with a rough swipe. The young man flinched. Frost threw the cloth over Eislinger's mauled face, covering the hideous spectacle. "Get out of here!" he ordered the interpreter icily, and watched the young soldier flee.

He looked at the corpse again. The bronze-hilted dagger gleamed brilliantly above a pool of blood. Frost felt apprehensive.

His duty was not over. One last thing remained to be disposed of.

CHAPTER 33: RIDDLES

"Choking dust, and blinding sand,
In a pitiless, barren, land."

—"M.E. Medley" from "Poems from
the Desert" by Pvt. J. Broome

A full-blown sandstorm struck like a smothering brown hurricane right after Frost and his aide regrouped with their men outside the ruin. Sheets of billowing dust grated like claws on all surfaces. Men rasped for breath and were reduced to choking fits. Pieces of pumice rock, stones, kangaroo rats, uprooted camel weeds, and scorpions whirled like dancing puppets through the air.

Vehicles driving at full-speed slowed to a crawl. Eventually the raging abyss thinned enough to allow the soldiers to leave—the storm left them no other choice but to go.

Frost found his way to a small military outbuilding with Arabic-graffitied walls and broken windows. Trickles of sand leaked in. He commandeered a phone from a reasonably offended staff officer and sat at the man's desk, dripping in dust.

He impatiently dialed a number. "I must speak immediately with Dr. Sullivan," he ordered at the person who answered. The person did not speak English well and was outdoors, which prompted the Major to repeat himself with a yell. Men in the office winced.

"Ben? Hello, is that you? Oh, for heaven's...Ben!"

A familiar Irish voice garbled something friendly and sarcastic at him.

"At last! What does it take to get hold of you these days?" He plucked pieces of dead snakeskin off his socks and wondered how they got there. Probably the same way a dry weed found its way under his shirt collar. It itched. He threw it on the floor.

"Listen. I am at Amara not far from the Palace of Four ruin. I found the dagger...No, I didn't touch it! I left it where I found it. But that's exactly the problem. You see, there is a terrific storm here, and it is—"

A chorus of squealing male voices rocked the room. Frost glanced up in alarm. A camel spider was prowling in the room. Apparently the monstrous creature had been tossed up by the sandstorm and took a ride into the office on Frost's boot. For some reason, the crawling horror had not bitten Frost. It leapt across the office floor and lunged at a passing staff officer. Men ran screaming from the room at the sight. The would-be victim jumped a mile high in the air and went dancing away—"like a ballerina," his chums later said, to his eternal embarrassment. Someone grabbed a chair and wielded it like a bullfighting toreador against the darting beast. A spooked crowd chased the monstrosity into the hall and tried to kill it.

Frost got up with a blasé expression and shut the door. He resumed his phone call and tried to ignore the din of shrieking and crashing that thundered from the hallway.

"Hello, Ben? Still there? Sorry—"

"What's all that racket?" the Irish scholar demanded in apprehension. "Is it a battle? Are the Germans invading?"

"Hardly. Just a camel spider, that's all. Now listen—"

"Now I understand the screaming," said Sullivan dryly. "My advice: drop the phone and hide in the nearest closet."

"Your advice about the 'haunted dagger' is what I'm after," Frost replied, not losing focus. "It may interest you that there have been six deaths so far. The last chap who had it lost his mind before he died."

A tense silence. "He went mad?"

"Completely off his trolley, so far as I could tell. He wasn't one of ours and very much not in need of mourning, so don't spare him a second thought. I'm only concerned about how to properly dispose of the thing," insisted Frost. "I am not superstitious but six deaths is nothing to sneeze at. Have you got any recommendations for how to get rid of the dagger without actually touching it?" He laughed at his own question, thinking it absurd.

"Where is it now?"

"Outside getting buried in sand, I assume," replied Frost. "Unless it's flown away to Tunis. Which is entirely possible. We've had a terrific storm here. The winds are still pretty strong."

"You left it out in a sandstorm?" squalled Sullivan in disbelief and indignation. "For heaven's sake, man, you should've weighted it down by throwing some rocks over it or something instead of leaving it out there to freely plague humanity..."

"It just so happened I left all my spare rocks at home," answered Frost with arid, biting sarcasm. "If I do see it again, what method of extermination would you prescribe? Do you think a grenade would do the trick?"

"The answer to this problem, my friend, is not a grenade," the Irishman intoned disapprovingly. "Nor any other kind of violence. We don't know what that might cause. We do know the Egyptians intended for the dagger to be sunk in the waters of the Nile. That could be the best option—to leave it according to the original intention of its makers."

"Can't very well fling it in the Nile if I can't touch it," sassed Frost. "What's more, Ben, I won't touch it. I properly refuse. You can't make me—nor could you make any of the other lads around here. Everybody believes that dagger to be a force of evil, and I've come to agree with them." He paused solemnly. "My wife, for example, can attest to the fact that a man's voice spoke from that dagger. It was the voice of a robber we recently killed. You've met Eve. You know she's a very sensible person. There isn't—"

"She heard it come from the dagger?" Sullivan sounded worried. "In that case, it might explain why the last owner went crazy. It's possible the dagger is haunted by more than one ghost. Maybe due to the spirit seal. Remember, that little symbol on the blade is supposed to 'trap' a spirit like a bottle? I'm not sure how or why it happened, but it could be another ghost has become attached to it. That's quite unsettling." There was a pause, then a shrill exclamation. "Wait a minute! You got married?"

"A double haunting is all the more reason in my opinion to destroy the dagger rather than cart it to the Nile," countered Frost. "And yes, I am a married man now," he disclosed after an awkward pause. "I suppose I should've mentioned that, but I haven't been able to come up for air at all while putting this case to rest. The dagger is the last thing to deal with."

The Irishman laughed. "Congratulations to you and the new Mrs. Major then. You don't waste any time, do you?" Noises of shuffling papers, wind and muttering Arabic voices bustled in the background. "I have some ideas for how to 'neutralize' the dagger, so to speak. I'll come over and address the problem myself."

Frost would have argued with him, but a boisterous cheer interrupted. He jerked around in the chair. The men had slain the camel spider at long last. It was a long siege, but in the end the creature was surrounded and pulverized with a broken mop. The victory cries were deafening. He did not get the chance to protest Sullivan's visit. During the ruckus, the Irish Egyptologist hung up the phone.

Sullivan arrived the next morning in an atmosphere of anticipation. The Irish explorer came with several Egyptian scholars who wished to partake in the adventure, since the artifact was of interest to them. They were confident they could "reverse" the dagger's dark spirituality.

They found Major Frost waiting for them at the ruin, drinking tea from a canteen. Frost was glad to chat with Sullivan, but not thrilled about the prospect of revisiting the ruin. He was not confident they'd achieve anything. Nevertheless, he escorted the group to the spot where he had last seen the dagger.

They found the body of the deceased German war criminal Siegwulf Eislinger across the courtyard from where Frost had left it. Sandstorm winds had evidently tossed the body over the ground and rolled it up against a broken wall.

The dagger was not discovered anywhere on the body or around it. Searches of the courtyard and probes into various sand hills proved fruitless. The cursed embalmer's knife had seemingly disappeared.

The group—especially Dr. Sullivan—reacted to this discovery with alarm.

In Frost's opinion, the phenomenon owed to the sandstorm. Much of the landscape looked different after the desert maelstrom. Also, a full night of driving wind had passed over the place. Like currents of water, these strong winds dragged along with them anything they could carry. They had raged for hours.

The stubborn Irishman was reluctant to admit defeat. In mounting desperation, he and his associates searched adjoining courtyards and temple enclosures. After hours of sifting dust and wandering back and forth hectically, no trace of the dagger could be found.

Frost was more than ready to give up the search. Quoting his long career of tropical military service, the Major cited instances of British soldiers vanishing into thin air during sandstorms and corpses on desert battlefields seemingly evaporating after strong wind passed by. Sand had an eerie way of devouring things in its cloak. No object was safe from it. Sandstorms were known to carry odd items through the air for miles. A German helmet landed near Giza, once, complete with a shrapnel hole in it. And then there was the time a lady's silk negligee got wrapped around a flagpole at an Army outpost in Sinai. That was unforgettably funny...

He recommended a withdrawal and eventually Sullivan was forced to agree. Everybody was worn to a dripping crisp by noontime. There was no point in continuing.

The ancient dagger of ghastly menace was gone.

"The desert has reclaimed its own," said Frost buoyantly as they departed.

Sullivan frowned with uncertainty. "Let's hope so."

Frost and Sullivan talked for a while afterwards as they walked along the neatly paved and busy streets of Amara. The Major informed his archaeologist friend about some of the recent events that had occurred—about the destruction of the tomb robbers and the successful conclusion of his investigation.

Frost especially thanked him for providing much-needed intelligence about the tomb robbers' location and passing along items captured by the Bedouins. This had ultimately resulted in the manhunt that killed Ollie and led to the takedown of the criminal organization.

The Major disclosed that there was some worry about the existence of a German "Cobra" commando group associated with the last man who carried the dagger. British intelligence had checked available resources and was on the lookout. Fortunately, as yet there was no evidence whatsoever that such an organization existed.

Sullivan was glad to hear the good news. He made some conversation with Frost about the latter's unexpected marriage, about which the Irishman was very encouraging and congratulatory. Above all else, however, the Irish scholar was disturbed that the unearthly dagger whose evil presence had poisoned so many human destinies was still unaccounted for.

"It seems the wicked thing truly was swept away in the sand, then," commented Sullivan as they walked. "Perhaps its energy even whipped up the sandstorm in the first place—the ghosts could've wished to get rid of their handler and planned an exit. Who knows. I just hope it never shows up again. May nobody find it!"

"That reminds me," said Frost thoughtfully, "you made me a bet once about the dagger. Said I would owe you a 'bottle of grog' if your hypothesis about its deadly charm proved correct. All right, I admit it—I lost. So, what do you drink, Ben?" His eyes glimmered with humor. "Aside from homebrewed date wine, I mean."

"Forget it. It seemed fun back then, but toasting a bottle of good stuff over a pile of tombstones doesn't seem sporting now," declined Sullivan, halfway sarcastic and mostly foreboding. "How about we write this one off?"

"No. I never renege on a bet, lost or won," stated Frost with iron in his will. "If you really don't want the stuff, I'll pick out something I like and then you could just give it back to me, if you insisted. If you want to, you can simply wave adieu to a bottle of imported Hearth's Irish Whiskey. That's what I would buy."

Sullivan arched an eyebrow, tempted. "Well—"

Frost hid a triumphant smile. He took Sullivan to a small British commissary in Amara. Officers went there sometimes in search of fare from their home countries. He found the prize whiskey, paid for it and presented it to Sullivan on the sunny sidewalk outside the doorway.

"Well, you didn't have to, but thanks all the same," said the scholar, pretending not to be delighted. He admired the bottle of hearty Celtic brew. Suddenly ancient Egyptian date wine didn't seem so tasty anymore.

"It's all right," said Frost, cracking a wry grin. "You buy me one next time."

"Hopefully there won't be a next time when it comes to that dagger!" chided Sullivan, recalling what had given rise to the bet. He checked his watch and realized he was late to catch his transportation back to Cairo. He rushed off. "Take care, Frosty. I'll see you around."

Frost basked in the sunshine and felt relief for the first time in what seemed an eternity. Unlike his scholarly comrade, he rejoiced at the dagger's disappearance. He thought it was an appropriate end for such an evil object.

The desert had yielded the dark artifact, and now it seemed the desert had taken it back. As far as Frost was concerned, the desert could keep it forever.

CHAPTER 34: NEW JOURNEY

"Until, by hopeless hope no more distressed,
I kiss thine eyes awake again, and rest
In the sweet compass of thine arms, dear Heart,
And with new eyes that thy dear lips have pressed
I watch the dawn."

—"Poems of Exile" from
"Poems from the Desert" by LCpl P.A.A. Thomas.

The sky over the sea was a soothing shade of pale cerulean blue. Cloud drifts and trails of planes formed creamy patterns in the endless blue. The seas were calm and the weather was sunny yet cool. A mild breeze swept across the harbor from the western Mediterranean. It was an exceptionally beautiful midmorning to sail.

The noise from the harbor faded into the distance as the clean white cruiser departed the Nile Delta area for Port Said. It was a large British passenger vessel. Major Frost and Eve had reserved a private cabin in one of the upper decks for what would be their first resolute attempt at honeymooning—and the first holiday leave the workaholic he had taken in more than three years.

Frost stared at the sky through dark sunglasses and felt peace. He lay stretched on his back across a large rattan sofa on a top outdoor deck. He wore a loose white shirt and tan shorts. Eve lay nestled next to him with one arm around him and her head resting on his chest. She wore a flowing blue sundress. They soaked up the sun and each other's company, and didn't say anything for a long while.

Eventually, she asked him a question. "Do you think we've left the Nile behind yet?"

"I hope so," answered Frost lazily. "I don't want to check. I just want to open my eyes and be somewhere else."

Silence fell. She traced the outline of his tattoo under the fabric of his partially unbuttoned shirt. There was a ring on her finger now. It was a silver wedding ring with a large diamond in the center.

"There is one last thing I'd like to do before we take leave of the Nile," Frost said suddenly after a moment of deliberation.

Eve glanced questioningly at him.

"I want to watch the pyramids disappear," he declared, ironic but earnest. "I want to watch them shrink into tiny dots and vanish like puffs of smoke." He lifted himself slightly and rattled her shoulder. "Come on, let's have a look. It'll be fun to see them evaporate."

She giggled at the fiery mischief in his voice. "Can we even see them from this distance?"

"Of course, we can see them!" answered Frost, tugging her off the sofa with him. "They're only as big as monsters. They're visible for leagues across the water on a clear day. Who needs lighthouses when you have the pyramids..."

She laughed.

"That's why I want to watch them vanish—because I've seen far too much of them," said Frost. "I reckon you have, too. It's time to bid them an enthusiastic farewell."

They moved to a spot across the deck where the view of the Nile Delta coastline was straight and clear. Mosque domes and pinnacles, radio towers, jungles of buildings, and Middle Eastern urban density crushed the coast between fringes of devastating wide stretches of golden-brown sand. Eventually the pyramids drifted into view—three great stone giants, shadowy, orange and impassive in the sun. They looked colossal even from far off, dominating the horizon past boats and glittering crests of seawater.

A pair of British bomber planes cut across the vista like vicious metal hawks, soaring through the scenery right in front of the pyramids. These wings of war ascended rapidly into the skies above the Mediterranean, heading the opposite direction from Major Frost and Eve as they traveled to bomb German supply ships embarking across the water from Sicily. Trailing clouds of smoke left by the planes obscured the pyramids from view before distance gave the ancient monuments a chance to fade away.

Eve, although briefly excited by the sight of the bombers, was somewhat disappointed at the sudden smoking-out of the pyramids. The memorable scene had evaporated too quickly.

Frost grinned. He could not have been happier. He squeezed her and cheered. "At last, they're gone! I told you it'd be fun to watch," he exclaimed. He glanced at the young woman and noticed her squinting at the smoke clouds in the distance with a look of faint disapproval. "What's the matter? The pyramids went by too fast?"

"A little," answered Eve. "Don't you think so?"

"Well, it's not our last chance to see them from this view." Frost glanced at the bomber trails in the sky and had a cynical thought. "Hopefully they'll still be here when we get back."

He hadn't intended the comment to be funny; he was only thinking out loud. Yet his flair for dry irony always surprised and amused Eve. Frost looked at her and was disarmed by her smile. Her mirth was contagious. He held her tightly in his arms and they shared a passionate kiss as they began their new journey.

THE END

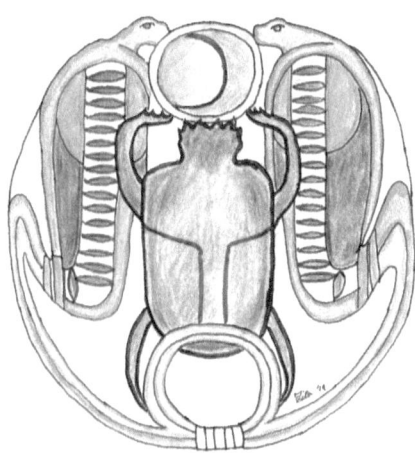

ABOUT

Zita Ballinger Fletcher

Zita Ballinger Fletcher (whose pen name is Zita Steele) is a journalist, author and military history writer. She writes fiction and nonfiction books, and has published more than 10 works. With a background in art, she designs and illustrates her published work. She also produces videos and creates multimedia content.

Zita is the author of the first published collection of Field Marshal Erwin Rommel's wartime photography. She has written military history articles for *World War II History* magazine in addition to her ground-breaking series on Rommel.

Zita is a member of the British Military Historical Society and the National Society of the Washington Family Descendants. Her articles on history and genealogy have been published by the Max Kade Institute for German-American Studies, in the